THUNDER OF THE
MOUNTAIN MAN

THUNDER OF THE
MOUNTAIN MAN

WILLIAM W.
JOHNSTONE

AND J.A. JOHNSTONE

PINNACLE BOOKS
Kensington Publishing Corp.
kensingtonbooks.com

PINNACLE BOOKS are published by

Kensington Publishing Corp.
900 Third Avenue
New York, NY 10022

PUBLISHER'S NOTE: Following the death of William W. Johnstone, the Johnstone family is working with a carefully selected writer to organize and complete Mr. Johnstone's outlines and many unfinished manuscripts to create additional novels in all of his series, like The Last Gunfighter, Mountain Man, and Eagles, among others. This novel was inspired by Mr. Johnstone's superb storytelling.

All Kensington titles, imprints, and distributed lines are available at special quantity discounts for bulk purchases for sales promotion, premiums, fundraising, and educational or institutional use.

Special book excerpts or customized printings can also be created to fit specific needs. For details, write or phone the office of the Kensington Sales Manager: Kensington Publishing Corp., 900 Third Avenue, New York, NY 10022. Attn. Sales Department. Phone: 1-800-221-2647.

PINNACLE BOOKS, the Pinnacle logo, and the WWJ steer head logo Reg. U.S. Pat. & TM Off.

First Printing: December 2025
ISBN-13: 978-0-7860-5077-2
ISBN-13: 978-0-7860-5078-9 (eBook)

10 9 8 7 6 5 4 3 2 1

The authorized representative in the EU for product safety and compliance is eucomply OU, Parnu mnt 139b-14, Apt 123
Tallinn, Berlin 11317, hello@eucompliancepartner.com.

CHAPTER 1

"I don't have any interest in killing you today, son," Smoke Jensen said. "I'd just as soon you didn't make me do it."

A sneer twisted the lips of the young man facing Smoke in Longmont's, Big Rock's finest saloon and gambling house that also happened to be one of the best restaurants between Kansas City and San Francisco.

"What you mean is that you want to weasel outta drawin' against me, Jensen," the youngster said. He was a lanky, rawboned redhead with a craggy, sunburned face made even uglier by the arrogant expression it wore. "I've heard all about you, and I never believed a blasted word of it. Fastest gun in the West, my hind foot! Just because you got fellas writin' those yellow-back novels about you, that don't mean a dadgum thing. I figure them drunken bums'll write anything for money."

The cowboy had come into Longmont's accompanied by four somewhat older men, all of them dressed in range clothes. Smoke, who lived west of town on the Sugarloaf Ranch and knew just about everybody in this lush Colorado valley, didn't recognize any of them.

But the redhead had recognized him somehow and stalked over to the table where Smoke was sitting peacefully having coffee with his old friend Louis Longmont, the gambler and gunman who owned this establishment. The youngster had hooked his thumbs in his gunbelt, grinned unpleasantly at Smoke, and started prodding him, asking him in an overly polite, offensive drawl if he wasn't the notorious gunslinger Smoke Jensen.

"The hero of American youth, ain't that what them scribblers call you?" he had added.

Smoke had tried to brush him off, but the young fella was too full of himself to brush. After a minute, Smoke had stood up and said, "All right, I'm Smoke Jensen. What of it?"

"I'm faster than you, Jensen. And I'm willin' to prove it, once and for all, right here and now."

That was when Smoke had sighed and told the redhead he didn't want to kill him. Smoke meant it, too. He had never been the sort of man to carve notches in his gun butts, which was a good thing because by now he'd have just about whittled them down to nothing. He didn't keep track of the number of men he'd killed, and he didn't lose any sleep over them, either. Every man he'd pulled the trigger on hadn't given him any choice.

But this kid's overbearing self-confidence wasn't any reason for him to die. If he'd just shut his trap and go on about his business, he might grow up and amount to something someday.

Unfortunately, the chances of that happening didn't look too good.

"How about it, Jensen?" the redheaded cowboy went on. "You willin' to test your speed against a real fast draw?"

The four men who had come into Longmont's with him had ambled over to the bar and ordered beers. They nursed the mugs while watching their partner confront Smoke. They didn't show any signs of wanting to take a hand in whatever play the redhead made, but Smoke knew better than to ignore them.

Fortunately, Smoke also knew he could count on Louis to keep an eye on the men. Johnny McVey behind the bar had a sawed-off Greener handy on a shelf under the hardwood, too. Between the two of them, those four strangers wouldn't stand a chance if they tried to horn in.

Smoke still hoped he could head off trouble. He shook his head and said, "I'm not going to draw on you."

"Then I'll just have to shoot you down like the dirty yellow dog you—"

One of the men set down his half-empty beer mug and stepped away from the bar. His voice cracked through the now-quiet room.

"That's enough, Fletch."

The redhead stiffened. With a grimace, he looked over his shoulder toward the bar and said, "You stay outta this, Coolidge. It ain't any of your business."

"The boss told me to keep an eye on you boys," the man called Coolidge replied. "That makes it my business."

"But I been waitin' for a chance like this. A chance to prove how fast I really am!"

"A chance to die, you mean. You're not in the same league as Jensen."

"I killed Hank Wilton in Tascosa—"

"Hank Wilton was done as a fast gun three years ago," Coolidge said, scorn plainly audible in his voice. "My eighty-year-old grandma could've beaten him to the draw that day you faced him."

"That—that's a blasted lie!" Fletch sputtered. "Wilton was still quick on the shoot—"

"Not quick enough." Coolidge's voice took on a more persuasive tone. "Come on over and have a drink with the rest of us, then we'll head back to the herd."

The man's words held a note of authority. He was somewhat older than the others, Smoke noted now, in his late twenties, maybe, a dark-haired man with a lean, hard-planed face and dark, observant eyes. He was a tad below medium height, and his body was wiry. If Smoke had had to pick out the most dangerous one in the bunch, it would be Coolidge. Fletch was all bluster— although bluster could be dangerous, too, if it was reckless enough. Fletch just might fit that bill.

The mention of a herd caught Smoke's attention, too. He wasn't aware that any of the ranchers in the valley were putting together a herd to drive to market. It was the wrong time of year for that. It stood to reason that the cattle these newcomers handled were freshly arrived in the area, as well.

Fletch said, "There'll be time for a drink once I've shown the world that I'm quicker on the draw than the famous Smoke Jensen. Then folks'll be talkin' about me when the subject of fast guns comes up. Gib Fletcher, he's the fastest one of all, they'll say. Maybe they'll even write some o' them dime novels about m—"

Smoke's patience for the youngster's yammering ran out. He wore crossed gunbelts with a Colt .45 holstered on each hip. He flicked his right hand toward the gun butt on that side.

Fletch saw that and his eyes widened. He'd been standing tensely ready to make his move, shoulders hunched, head forward a little, eyes peeled for even the smallest motion Smoke might make. When Smoke's right hand jerked, Fletch's right hand dived for his gun and a look of mingled fear and excitement lit up his sun-burned face.

Before Fletch could clear leather, Smoke took a quick half-step forward and smashed his left fist into the middle of his face, flattening his nose and pulping his lips. Smoke wasn't overly tall, but his shoulders were about as broad as an ax handle, and he packed an incredible amount of strength in his body. The punch hit Fletch like a piledriver.

Fletch flew backward. Coolidge let out a surprised yelp and caught him, probably out of instinct and self-preservation. If he hadn't, Fletch would have crashed to the floor.

The young cowboy's gun had slipped back into its holster when Smoke hit him. Smoke nodded toward the weapon and told Coolidge, "You'd best take that Colt away from him while you've got the chance."

The other three strangers had stepped away from the bar and were watching with intense interest, but none of them had made a move to pull iron. More than likely, they had seen the smooth, unhurried way Louis Longmont had stood up and moved the tail of his coat aside so that his gun was clear. Menace seemed to crackle in the air around the gambler.

Coolidge kept his left arm around Fletch's waist. Fletch's head swung slowly, ponderously, from side to side, as if he were only half-aware of what was going on around him. With his right hand, Coolidge motioned to his other three companions, tamping down the air to tell them not to start anything.

"That's probably a good idea, Mr. Jensen," he said, then used the same hand to pluck the undrawn and un-fired revolver from Fletch's holster. He shoved it into the waistband of his trousers and added, "I'm obliged to you for not killin' this young jackass."

"Too many young men have died from being jack-asses." A faint smile curved Smoke's lips for a second. "Came close to it myself a time or two. But it's not a very good reason for dying."

"No, sir, it ain't." Coolidge turned the groggy Fletch and gave him a shove that sent him stumbling toward the other three cowboys, who grabbed him and kept him from tripping and falling. Coolidge turned back to Smoke and extended his hand. "Matt Coolidge."

"Smoke Jensen," Smoke said as he returned the other man's firm handclasp. "But I reckon you probably figured that out."

Coolidge chuckled. "Fletch is the one who recognized you, but I've heard of you, sure enough."

Smoke wondered what had brought Coolidge and the other men to Big Rock, but out here on the frontier, that wasn't the sort of thing a man asked another man.

Coolidge satisfied Smoke's curiosity anyway by continuing, "I'm the ramrod of the Triangle B outfit. We just threw our herd onto a bedground north of town, and we've been on the trail long enough I figured the boys deserved some time off. They'll be takin' turns comin' into town, four or five at a time so there won't be enough of 'em at one time to get too rambunctious."

"That's not a bad idea," Smoke said with a nod. "You might want to check in with our local sheriff, Monte Carson, though, and let him know what you're doing."

"The sheriff's office was gonna be my next stop."

"No need for that," Louis said as he nodded toward the entrance. "Here's Monte now."

The lawman wasn't running as he came into the room, but he wasn't wasting any time, either, and he had a double-barreled shotgun held firmly in his capable hands. He slowed as he saw that no trouble was going on at the moment.

By way of explanation, Louis added to Smoke, "I gave the high sign to one of the girls to slip out and fetch Monte when it appeared as if that young firebrand wasn't going to be dissuaded from drawing on you."

Monte came up and nodded to Smoke and Louis. All three men were old friends and had been part of the violent ruckus when Big Rock was founded to replace the outlaw town of Fontana a few years earlier. Smoke and Monte had been on opposite sides in that fight at first, but that hadn't lasted long once Monte realized he'd backed the wrong play.

"Heard there was about to be a shootout," Monte drawled, "so I figured you'd be right in the big middle of it, Smoke."

"I didn't think you knew I was even in town today," Smoke said.

Monte shook his head. "Doesn't matter. Guns start going off, I figure Smoke Jensen has to be around somewhere close by. But it looks like the trouble is all over."

"There wasn't much trouble," Louis said. "Nobody even died."

"Well, that's a welcome change."

Coolidge had been taking in the conversation. He said, "You fellas are joshing with each other, right?"

"Oh, mostly," Monte admitted. "I don't believe we've met. Monte Carson, sheriff of Big Rock."

"I'm Matt Coolidge, the foreman of the Triangle B crew."

The two men shook hands, and then Louis said, "We weren't formally introduced. I'm Louis Longmont. This is my establishment."

"Glad to meet you, Mr. Longmont," Coolidge said as they shook hands. "Mighty nice place you've got here."

"Triangle B, Triangle B," Monte mused. "I don't think I've heard of that spread."

"We just pulled in today," Coolidge explained. "Drove eight hundred head up here from the Panhandle, down in Texas."

"Eight hundred head?" Monte repeated. "Where do you plan on putting them?"

"Right now, they're grazing just north of town. Reckon we should've asked you first if that was all right, Sheriff. My apologies."

Monte waved that off. "That's fine, shouldn't cause a problem. But you can't leave them there."

"Never planned to. First thing in the morning, we'll drive 'em on out to the spread the boss bought. I wasn't sure exactly how long it'd take to get there, so I thought we'd play it safe and lay over one more night before finishin' the drive."

Smoke said, "You're talking about the old Hunsacker place."

Coolidge nodded. "It does seem like I've heard that name. That's what's gonna be known as the Triangle B from now on."

Smoke looked at Monte and Louis and said, "I'd heard rumors that Linus Hunsacker's widow sold out to somebody from back east. Never bothered checking it out with the county clerk because I knew we'd find out sooner or later."

"That'd be my boss," Coolidge said. "Mr. Thaddeus Bolton. He bought the ranch from the old lady and the eight hundred head from one of those big outfits in the Panhandle to stock it with. From what I understand, there wasn't much left of the herd that had been on the place."

"No," Smoke said, "Linus let it dwindle down more and more the worse his health got. He had a good crew, but he was one of those fellas who couldn't stand for anybody else to be out working on his spread if he wasn't right there with them, doing his part. He probably didn't have more than seventy or eighty head left when he passed." He recalled something else his wife, Sally, had told him. "I think Mrs. Hunsacker was moving back to Kansas City to live with her sister."

Coolidge said, "You sound like you know the place well, Mr. Jensen."

"I ought to. Linus Hunsacker was my neighbor for several years. Part of his range adjoined mine."

"Is that so?" Coolidge glanced toward the bar, where Fletch was hunched over the hardwood with a shot of whiskey in front of him. The other cowboys were standing around him, almost like they were trying to make sure he didn't start any more trouble.

Coolidge went on, "I reckon we'll be neighbors, then, which makes me even happier that you didn't put a bullet through ol' Fletch there. That wouldn't have been a very good foot to start out on."

"I take it that's the near gunfight I heard about," Monte said.

Louis chuckled. "Yes, another young, would-be pistoleer full of himself and flushed with self-confidence because he hadn't managed to get himself killed yet."

"The same sort you've had to deal with over and over again," Monte said to Smoke.

"Unfortunately, yes," Smoke agreed. "But I was able to bust him in the snoot instead of drilling him."

"I appreciate that. Less paperwork for me. The undertaker might not be too happy about it if this peaceful trend keeps up, though."

"That's one thing I don't believe we'll have to worry about," Louis said dryly. "As you pointed out, Monte, things never stay peaceful around Smoke for very long."

Smoke frowned—but he couldn't exactly argue with the sentiment his old friend had just expressed, either.

CHAPTER 2

Gib Fletcher's nose was swollen almost twice its normal size already. His lips were bruised and bloody, and every time he took a sip of whiskey it stung so much he winced. By morning, both eyes probably would be so blackened that he'd look like a raccoon.

Fletch still believed he could hold his own with Jensen when it came to gun-handling, but he had to admit the fella hit like the kick of a mule.

"You're lucky Jensen just hauled off and walloped you one, Fletch," stocky, dark-haired Bart Hudson said quietly as he stood to Fletch's right at the bar. "More than likely he'd have killed you if he drew on you, just like he said."

Hudson was one of Fletch's best friends, but he liked to pick at a man and rile him up. Thought it was funny. Fletch didn't see anything funny about what had happened here.

"Findin' out who's faster will just have to wait," Fletch said. His voice sounded funny in his own ears as it came painfully through his thick lips. "But that day's gonna come. You can bet a hat on that, Bart."

"No thanks." Bart grinned. "If I'm gonna buy a new hat, I'd just as soon it was for myself, not you." He chuckled. "But I don't figure I'd have to worry about that. And since you'd be dead, you couldn't buy me a new hat to pay off the bet. No, sir, that sounds like a losin' proposition all the way around to me."

"You think you're so blasted hilarious," Fletch muttered.

He threw back the whiskey that was left in his glass and thumped the empty down on the bar. A glance over his shoulder showed him that Matt Coolidge was still talking to Jensen and those other two fellas.

"Matt's supposed to be on our side," he went on. "We ride for the same brand. Just look at him over there, suckin' up to Jensen like that. It's plumb disgustin', that's what it is."

Phil Armentrout leaned in on Fletch's left and said, "You'd best watch what you're sayin', kid. You don't want to get Coolidge mad at you. He's got a mean streak. He don't show it very often, but when he does— well, it's devil take the hindmost then."

"I ain't scared of Coolidge, neither."

"I'm not sayin' to be scared of him. Just be careful, that's all."

Hudson asked, "You want another shot o' whiskey?"

Fletch could have used one, but to tell the truth, it hurt like blazes the way the stuff burned his split lips. He was starting to have trouble breathing through his nose. It made funny sounds when he did. The thing was broken, he was sure of it.

"Let's just go back out to the herd," he said disgustedly. "Some of the other boys will be wantin' to come into town. They oughta have their turn."

Nate Kyle, standing on the other side of Armentrout, protested, "We've only had one drink! Haven't played any cards nor found any gals willin' to have a good time with us. What kind of visit to town is that?"

"That ranch where we're goin' ain't so far away we can't ride into town once a week or so," Hudson pointed out. "It ain't like this will be our only chance to cut loose our wolves." He inclined his head toward the door. "Fletch is right. Come on, let's go."

Kyle continued to grumble about it, but the four young cowboys turned away from the bar. Coolidge saw what they were doing and called, "Headed back to the herd?"

"That's right, Matt," Hudson said.

Coolidge nodded. "Send the next bunch in when you get there."

Hudson smiled and said, "Sure will."

Fletch watched the little group from the corner of his eye as he shuffled out with the others. Jensen was just standing there, smiling a little, acting like nothing had happened. Like he had already forgotten all about Fletch.

But Fletch hadn't forgotten. No, sir, he hadn't, and he never would. Jensen might think he was the big skookum he-wolf of these parts, but it wouldn't always be that way.

One of these days there would be a reckoning, Fletch promised himself, and he would kill Smoke Jensen.

* * *

"That young fella still looks pretty resentful," Smoke commented as he watched the four cowboys leave Longmont's.

"Don't worry about him," Coolidge said. "He's a hothead, but I'll keep a tight rein on him until he cools down a mite."

"I'd be obliged," Smoke said. He smiled at Monte and Louis. "Despite what these two make it sound like, I'm a peaceable man. And I like to stay on good terms with my neighbors."

Monte said to Coolidge, "This fella Bolton you ride for, did you say he comes from Texas?"

Coolidge shook his head. "I said he bought that eight hundred head in Texas. Mr. Bolton is from Nashville, Tennessee. He had himself a handful of successful businesses back there. He owned a hotel, a bank, a freight company, several mercantile stores, and a plantation where he and his family lived. But he sold 'em all to move out here, once he found a spread he wanted and some cattle to stock it with."

"Why in the world would he do that?" Monte asked with a frown. "It sounds to me like he had a mighty good life back there in Tennessee."

"I can't argue with that. But you see, Mr. Bolton always had it in his head he wanted to be a rancher, ever since he was a little boy. Once he had enough money, he made that dream come true." Coolidge smiled. "I reckon if you have enough money, you can make just about anything come true."

That wasn't right, Smoke mused. Years earlier, he and the old mountain man Preacher had found gold on what eventually became the Sugarloaf Ranch. They could have been rich men—but all the gold in the world wouldn't have been enough to bring back his wife, Nicole, murdered by hired killers working for some of Smoke's enemies, nor their son Arthur, slain by the same men. Smoke had evened that score, at least the way most folks would see it, but it wasn't really even at all. Nicole and Arthur were still dead.

But while he was avenging his wife and son, he had met Sally Reynolds and she had taught him how to love again and move ahead in life, and because of that he considered himself the luckiest man in the world. Bad memories faded and good memories lingered, and Smoke really was, as he said, a peaceable man.

When people would allow him to be.

Matt Coolidge had continued the story. "Mr. Bolton came down to the Panhandle to settle the deal for the cows, and while he was there, he put together a crew to bring the critters up here to Colorado."

"Then you haven't been working for him for a long time?" Monte asked.

"Nope. Just a couple of months. It took us a little while to road-brand all that stock, and then when we had the Triangle B iron on 'em, we headed 'em north, through Injun Territory, and then west."

"An easier route than cutting through New Mexico Territory and over Raton Pass," Smoke commented. "You can take cattle through there, but it's quite a climb."

"Yes, sir," Coolidge agreed.

"Is your employer with you?" Louis asked.

"Yeah, Mr. Bolton went back to Tennessee from the Panhandle to fetch his wife and daughter, then they took the train to Cheyenne and traveled on from there by wagon. As a matter of fact, they caught up to us just yesterday. They were comin' into town this afternoon, too." Coolidge chuckled. "Miz Bolton, she's got a hankerin' to spend the night in a soft bed under a roof, I think. You've got a hotel here in Big Rock, don't you?"

Monte said, "We have a couple of good ones. The Big Rock Hotel is probably the best."

"That's what she'd want," Coolidge said with a nod. "Nothin' but the best for Miz Bolton."

Smoke thought a faint hint of coolness had come into the foreman's voice as if he didn't fully approve of Mrs. Bolton's fondness for the finest. That was none of Smoke's business, though, so he put it aside and didn't worry about it.

"I hope they enjoy living here," Louis said. "As new arrivals to the area, I'd be happy to welcome them with a meal here, on the house."

Coolidge glanced around and said, "In a, uh, saloon?"

"Don't let that fool you," Monte said. "Louis has the best cook you'll find in these parts. Folks in Big Rock and the rest of the valley know this is where you get the best eats."

"Well, I'll pass that along. Don't be offended, though, if Miz Bolton decides she wants to dine somewhere a mite fancier."

"No offense," Louis assured him, "and the offer stands." He took a silver dollar from his pocket and extended it. "If you'd be so kind as to pay your men back for those beers they bought, I'd like to buy a round for all the Triangle B men the first time they come in here."

"Mighty nice of you." Coolidge shrugged and took the coin with his left hand. "The boys'll appreciate that. I'll let the rest of the crew know." He slipped the dollar in his pocket and then reached up with the same hand to pinch the brim of his hat. "I'd best be movin' on. I wouldn't say the camp can't get along without me, but I like to keep an eye on things. It was a pleasure to meet you fellas."

"Same here," Smoke said.

"And again, I'm sorry Fletch had to go on the prod like that."

Smoke shrugged. "It happens with young men. To be honest, when a man rides for me, I like for him to have a little vinegar in him."

"It comes in handy in times of trouble," Coolidge agreed. "So long."

Smoke, Monte, and Louis watched him leave. Monte said, "Seems like a nice enough fella."

"He's a killer," Smoke said.

Monte frowned. "What are you talking about?"

"You've lived in town too long," Louis said. "You've lost a little of your edge."

"We've lived in Big Rock the same amount of time," Monte pointed out.

"Yes, but you didn't notice that Coolidge's right hand never strayed very far from his gun."

"He shook hands with all of us," Monte objected. Then he said, "Which, come to think of it, means that our right hands were occupied, too. I guess he was ready for trouble if any cropped up, but I'm not sure that makes him a killer."

Smoke said, "That was in his eyes. But I have to agree, he was perfectly pleasant to talk to. I don't think he'd ever go hunting a showdown like that kid did, but he wouldn't back away from one, either."

"You're right, dang it. Both of you. I *have* lost my edge. That's a dangerous thing for a lawman to have happen. Maybe I ought to turn in my badge."

"Now, don't be hasty," Louis urged. "You've done a fine job as sheriff, Monte, and I'm sure you'll continue to do so. I'd rather have you siding me in a fight than anybody else I can think of."

Monte grunted. "Well, almost anybody else, if you're telling the truth." He glanced at Smoke. "We all know who's the best hombre to have beside you when the bullets start to fly."

"Oh, I don't know about that," Louis replied with a sly smile. "Remember, Smoke attracts more of that hot lead than anyone else."

"That's true," Monte agreed solemnly.

"There you two go again," Smoke said. He picked up the cup of coffee he had been working on when the four cowboys from the Triangle B had come in. There was a little of the strong black brew left in the cup. Smoke drank it and went on, "I'd better head back to the ranch."

"You never did say what brought you into town today," Louis commented.

"Nothing in particular. I just felt like getting out and taking a ride. Pearlie has things running so smoothly on the ranch that it doesn't really matter if I'm around all the time."

"Pearlie's made you a good foreman," Monte said.

"That he has."

Like Monte, Pearlie Fontaine had been a hired gun at one point in his life. Both men had worked for Tilden Franklin when Franklin tried to take over the valley some years earlier. Also, like Monte, he had changed sides when he realized what a no-good skunk Franklin really was.

Since then, he had been a good friend to Smoke and the most valued member of his ranch crew.

"I'll walk outside with you, Smoke," Monte said. "I ought to take this Greener back to the office. Wasn't sure if I'd need it or not."

The two men said their goodbyes to Louis and stepped out onto the boardwalk. Monte had the shotgun tucked under his arm now. His face wore a worried frown as he paused and said, "Seriously now, Smoke, do you reckon it's time I hung up my gun and resigned as sheriff? I mean, since I never pegged that fella Coolidge as a gunman—"

"Don't be loco," Smoke interrupted him. "There's nobody better suited to be sheriff of Big Rock than you, Monte."

"Yeah, but if I can't spot trouble coming before it starts, I may not be able to do the job."

"Coolidge was pretty good at covering it up. Anyway, I have a hunch he actually is a pretty likable, reasonable fella. He was doing his best to head off trouble and keep any gunplay from breaking out. Just because he's a bad man to cross doesn't mean he's going to go out of his way hunting trouble."

Monte cocked an eyebrow. "Sort of like you, eh?"

"I reckon you could say that."

"All right, I can live with that—" Monte began. He broke off what he was saying as he glanced along the street. "Look there."

"I see it," Smoke said as he gazed at the fancy buggy pulling up in front of the Big Rock Hotel. In the late afternoon light, Smoke could tell that a well-dressed man in a dark suit was handling the reins of the impressive-looking matched pair of black horses hitched to the buggy.

A woman sat beside the man on the front seat. Smoke thought someone was riding in back, too, but he couldn't make out any details at this distance.

"You don't suppose that's that fella Bolton Coolidge was talking about, do you?" Monte said. "I don't recognize that buggy or the driver."

"Coolidge said they came down from Cheyenne in a wagon. More than likely they didn't come alone, though. I can't see a rich man from back east doing that. Chances are they hired men to ride along with them, and they could have bought a buggy in Cheyenne as well as a wagon."

"I'm still the sheriff and they're strangers in town, so I reckon I have a right to go and welcome them to Big Rock—and make sure who they really are."

Smoke was curious, too, so he sauntered along the street with Monte as the man at the reins brought the buggy to a neat stop next to the hitch rail in front of the hotel. The man stepped down from the vehicle with easy grace and agility and tied the reins around the rail.

Then he turned back to the buggy and lifted his arms to help the woman disembark.

Smoke and Monte were close enough now that Smoke could make out the man's handsome features. He had a deep enough tan that the white hair under his dark gray hat stood out in sharp contrast.

It wasn't the white hair of an old man, though, Smoke realized. The newcomer might be middle-aged, but he was still vital and full of life.

So was the woman who took the hands he extended to her as she stepped down from the buggy. She wore a dark blue traveling outfit and matching hat with a short, colorful feather attached to it. Blond hair curved closely around her very attractive face. Gemstones glittered on the rings she wore. She gave off an air of sleek, well-bred beauty.

So did the younger woman who stepped down from the buggy's rear seat. Smoke remembered Matt Coolidge saying that Thaddeus Bolton had returned to Nashville to fetch his wife and daughter. Smoke had a strong hunch that was who he was looking at now.

The man and the two women went up the steps onto the hotel porch. As Smoke and Monte neared those steps, the lawman called, "Mr. Bolton?"

The stranger paused. The women flanked him, the older one to his right, the younger to his left. He had his hands lightly on their arms, guiding them toward the hotel's double-doored entrance. He stopped and let go of them so that he could turn to face Smoke and Monte.

Now that they were closer, Smoke's estimate of the man's age was confirmed. Despite the snow-white hair, he was in his forties, no more than that.

"Yes?" he said, confirming as well that he was Thaddeus Bolton. "What can I do for you?"

Before Monte could introduce himself, the swift rataplan of hoofbeats made everyone turn and look along the street. Smoke spotted a rider galloping toward the center of Big Rock and recognized Matt Coolidge.

At the same time from the other direction, someone yelled, "Jensen! Damn your hide, Jensen, you ain't gonna run away from me this time! Go for your gun, you—"

Obscenities spewed from the challenger's mouth as Smoke swung around. He had already recognized Gib Fletcher's voice. Fletch stood about fifty feet away, shoulders hunched, right hand hovering claw-like over his Colt. The slur in his voice and the way he swayed a little told Smoke that he'd been drinking more since leaving Longmont's.

But drunk or not, he was still a threat, as he proved when his hand jerked down, closed around the butt of his gun, and yanked the revolver out of its holster.

CHAPTER 3

"Fletch, no!" Matt Coolidge yelled as he charged along the street on the galloping horse. He was still a block away, though, and Fletch ignored him.

Smoke couldn't ignore the young cowboy's threat anymore or turn it aside with only limited violence. Fletch's gun had cleared leather, and the barrel was starting to tip up—

Smoke's right hand was a blur as he drew the Colt on that side. Fletch's gun was still rising when Smoke's was leveled and spouting flame and smoke. The blast echoed from the buildings on both sides of the street.

Fletch's right arm jerked back. The gun flew out of his now-useless fingers and thudded to the dirt of the street. He staggered a couple of steps to the side, instinctively clutching his wounded right arm with his left hand as he did so. The shock of being shot caused his knees to buckle. He dropped to them and, unable to hold himself up, pitched forward, twisting to land on his uninjured left side.

Coolidge swept past Smoke on horseback and swung down in a running dismount while the animal was still moving. He stumbled, caught his balance, and knelt beside Fletch.

"You damn loco kid," he said. "How bad are you hit?"

Smoke and Monte walked up on Fletch's other side. Smoke hadn't pouched his iron yet, but he held it down alongside his leg and didn't point it at the wounded man. Monte bent to scoop up the gun Fletch had dropped in the dirt. Smoke relaxed then, thumbed a fresh round from one of the loops on his shell belt into the Colt's cylinder to replace the one he'd fired, and slid the gun back into leather.

Fletch moaned but didn't answer Coolidge's question. The foreman expertly probed the wounded arm, which caused the young cowboy to cry out in pain.

"The bone's busted about halfway between the shoulder and the elbow," Coolidge announced. "He won't be goin' around tryin' to prove he's a fast draw for a long time, if ever."

"We have a good doctor here in Big Rock," Monte said. "He can set that broken bone, and once it's healed up, the kid ought to be able to still do his job on the ranch."

"Yeah, in six weeks or a couple of months," Coolidge said with a note of bitterness in his voice. "And that arm may not ever be quite the same. I've seen plenty of hombres who got busted bones from bein' tossed off broncs, and that's the way it was for them. A bullet's even worse."

"He shouldn't have drawn on Smoke. You know, the boy started it. I could throw him behind bars once the doc's finished with him and charge him with disturbing the peace and endangering the citizens."

"I'd be obliged to you if you didn't do that," Coolidge said as he looked up at the lawman.

Smoke said, "As far as I'm concerned, there's no need for that. The boy will heal up better in a bunkhouse than he would in a jail cell."

Monte nodded. "Since you're the one he was set on killing, I reckon I can go along with that."

Fletch hadn't passed out. He lay there quietly whimpering as Coolidge came to his feet. Coolidge looked at Smoke and nodded.

"I'm obliged to you, too, Mr. Jensen," he said. "You could have killed him, couldn't you?"

"He wasn't as fast as he thought he was," Smoke said. "I couldn't have him spraying bullets all around the street, though. Making it so that he couldn't do that seemed like a strong enough response."

Coolidge glanced down at Fletch, and now there was a slight note of fondness in his voice as he said, "Young idiot." He looked at Smoke and Monte again and went on, "I didn't realize until I was back at the camp that he'd slipped off from the others. When they told me they didn't know where he was, I figured he must've stayed in town to get liquored up more—and to stir up more trouble. I rattled my hocks back here as fast as I could. Sorry I didn't make it in time to stop him."

The shooting had attracted plenty of attention, not to mention Coolidge riding into town hellbent-for-leather like that had created a commotion, too. Monte called to one of the curious bystanders to fetch the doctor. The townsman hurried off to comply.

"Sheriff, a word, please."

The brisk, business-like voice caused Smoke and Monte to turn around. Thaddeus Bolton had left the hotel porch and walked up the street to join the small group gathered around the wounded cowboy. Smoke glanced past the newcomer and saw that the two women were still on the porch, watching intently.

As soon as Smoke and Monte were facing him, Bolton went on, "This young man works for me." He gestured toward Fletch. "Are you going to arrest the man who shot him?"

"Arrest Smoke, you mean?" Monte asked with a puzzled frown.

Bolton nodded toward Smoke. "This man, whoever he is. The one who shot Mr. Fletcher."

"Well, I don't know how close you were watching," Monte said, "but this puncher of yours drew first. Smoke would've been within his legal rights to kill him instead of just wounding him. That's what most fellas would have done."

"I see," Bolton said, although he looked like he didn't understand—or agree with—what Monte had just said. "Did this man provoke the fight?"

"This man's got a name," Smoke said, trying to keep a tight rein on his temper. "It's Smoke Jensen. As a matter of fact, we're going to be neighbors, Mr. Bolton. I own the Sugarloaf Ranch."

"Is that so?" Bolton's attitude changed immediately. "I apologize for jumping to hasty conclusions, sir.

I know that disputes are often settled at gunpoint out here, and I wanted to be certain that my man was treated fairly." He held out his hand. "Thaddeus Bolton, at your service."

"Pleased to meet you, Mr. Bolton," Smoke said as he shook hands with the man, although that was stretching the truth more than a mite.

"If what the sheriff says is true and my rider drew his weapon first—"

"Oh, it's true, all right," Monte broke in, starting to sound a little annoyed himself now.

"What prompted him to do so?" Bolton continued as if Monte hadn't said anything.

"He figured he was a fast gun and wanted to make a reputation for himself," Smoke explained.

Bolton seemed genuinely interested as he asked, "And he could accomplish that by killing you?"

Monte said, "Smoke's one of the fastest guns out here on the frontier, or anywhere else, for that matter. More than likely *the* fastest."

"Then it was rather foolish for Fletcher to challenge you," Bolton said.

"Most young men don't lack for self-confidence," Smoke said, smiling a little. "Fletch, here, certainly doesn't."

The circle of men parted as the doctor bustled through to kneel beside Fletch and begin examining his wounded arm. After a moment, he looked up and announced, "I need to get this man back to my surgery so I can set his arm properly and prepare a cast for it."

Fletch was still coherent enough to groan and ask, "I'm gonna have to wear a cast?"

"If you want to ever use that arm again properly, you will," the sawbones told him.

Monte waved over several of the townsmen to help. The doctor sent one of them running back to the house where he both lived and conducted his medical practice to fetch a stretcher on which they would carefully transport Fletch.

While that was going on, Smoke, Monte, Bolton, and Coolidge moved off to one side, well out of the way. Coolidge said, "I'm sorry for lettin' things get out of hand, Mr. Bolton. I never figured Fletch would get such a burr under his saddle that he'd try to draw on Mr. Jensen here."

"Just see to it that he receives proper medical attention and then gets back out to our camp all right. Will he be able to travel out to the ranch tomorrow?"

"You'd have to ask the doc to be sure, but I've got a hunch it'd be better for him to recuperate here in town for a few days before we try to move him."

"So we'll be short-handed, is that what you're saying?" Bolton asked with a frown.

"Only for a while until Fletch heals up."

Smoke said, "If you find yourself in a tight spot, Mr. Bolton, I could send one or two of my hands over to your place to help you out."

"That's generous of you, Jensen. Mighty generous." Bolton paused to slide a cigar out of his vest pocket. Putting it in his mouth without lighting it, he said around it, "Of course, considering that you're the one who broke his arm with a bullet . . ."

"It was either that or kill him," Smoke said.

"Certainly. You did the only thing you could, and I appreciate your restraint." Bolton smiled around the cigar. "Now, if you'll come with me, I'd like to introduce you to my wife and daughter. Seeing as we're going to be neighbors, after all."

Smoke didn't particularly like Thaddeus Bolton even though the man was trying to be pleasant now, but he couldn't see any polite way of refusing the request. He fell in step beside Bolton as they headed for the Big Rock Hotel. Monte came along, too, with the shotgun still tucked under his arm.

The two women watched them approaching. The older one, Bolton's wife, looked intently at Smoke, regarding him with such open interest that it made him feel a little on edge. Bolton didn't seem to notice, though.

The younger woman just looked bored, as if she wished she were somewhere else.

The three men went up the steps to the porch. Bolton said, "My dear, allow me to introduce Mr. Smoke Jensen and—I'm sorry, Sheriff, I don't think I got your name."

"Monte Carson," Monte supplied.

"Sheriff Monte Carson," Bolton went on. "Sheriff Carson is the local law, of course, and Mr. Jensen is going to be our neighbor. He owns the—what was it? The Sugarloaf Ranch?"

Smoke took off his hat and nodded. "That's right."

"Gentlemen, my wife, Emmaline, and our daughter Susannah."

Emmaline Bolton moved closer to Smoke and extended a slim, expensively gloved hand.

"Mr. Jensen, it's such a pleasure to meet you," she said, smiling up at him. She wasn't a tall woman, but the body in the blue traveling outfit was well-curved and she had very blue eyes. She was a looker, all right, Smoke thought, just the kind of wife a rich man like Thaddeus Bolton would have.

Smoke took her hand; it would have been impolite not to. "It's my pleasure, ma'am," he told her.

"How could you do that?" Susannah Bolton burst out. She looked annoyed now, not bored. "You shot poor Fletch. You could have killed him!"

Smoke took the opportunity to let go of Emmaline's hand. She'd been clinging to his hand a mite longer than he was comfortable with. He turned to the younger woman and said, "I'm sorry, miss, but the fella was trying to kill me, so shooting him seemed like the thing to do at the time."

"He wouldn't have been able to hit you. He was drunk."

"With my life on the line—not to mention the lives of other folks on the street, including you, who might've got in the way of a stray slug—I couldn't exactly count on that, could I?"

"Mr. Jensen is right, Susannah," Bolton said. He scratched a lucifer to life on the porch railing and lit the cigar he had clamped between his teeth. Once he had it going, he continued, "I realized that once I stopped and thought about it. We actually owe Mr. Jensen our thanks. He prevented Fletcher from hurting anyone and did so without killing the young fool."

"Don't call him a fool, Father," Susannah said.

Judging by her chilly tone, she might be sweet on Fletch, Smoke thought. That didn't really make sense, given the differences in their stations. Susannah was a rich man's daughter and Fletch was a forty-a-month-and-found cowhand, and not a particularly handsome one, at that.

But if there was one thing love didn't have to do, it was make sense. Smoke wasn't all that old, but he was old enough to have figured that out.

Mrs. Bolton somehow got in front of Smoke again. "I was so frightened there for a moment when it looked like there was going to be a killing right in front of our eyes," she said. "Is it always like that out here in the West?"

She addressed the question to Smoke, but her husband was the one who answered it. "Certainly not," Bolton said. "The West is civilized now. Isn't it, Sheriff?"

"Well," Monte said, looking uncomfortable, "that sort of depends on what you call civilized. It *can* be, most of the time. But I'd say it's a long way from being completely tame."

"You see, we shouldn't have come out here," Susannah said. "It's a wilderness full of savage men."

She glared at Smoke as if to emphasize who she was talking about.

That didn't bother him; the opinion of some spoiled rich girl from back east didn't matter a hill of beans, as the old saying went. He wanted to stay on good terms with these folks if possible, though, so he didn't argue with her.

Emmaline came at him again with single-minded determination. "I believe my husband said you own a ranch, Mr. Jensen?"

"That's right. It's called the Sugarloaf. In fact, this whole valley is known as the Sugarloaf Valley because of one of the mountains that flanks it."

"Your ranch doesn't include the whole valley, though, does it? I mean, I was under the impression that the ranch Thaddeus bought is located here, too."

"No, my ranch is just part of it," Smoke said, smiling. "The whole valley would be a little too big for one man to keep up with."

"But do you run your ranch all by yourself? Out there all alone?"

He knew what information she was angling for. Everybody on the hotel porch had to know. And yet, Bolton's face was serene now, as if he didn't mind at all that his wife was showing so much interest in another man.

Maybe they were both just being polite, Smoke told himself.

"No, ma'am," he said. "I have the best crew of cowboys any man could ever ask for. And more than that, I have my wife, Sally."

"Sally?" Emmaline repeated. "Your wife?"

"That's right. I'm sure the two of you will get along just fine. In fact, when I tell her that you folks have taken over the old Hudsacker place, I'm sure she's going to want to have you come over for a visit and a big dinner."

"That sounds wonderful," Emmaline said without the least note of sincerity in her voice. "I'll look forward to it."

Susannah spoke up again, asking, "Is Fletch going to be all right?"

"Don't worry yourself about that young hothead," Bolton said.

"From the way the doctor talked, he'll recover," Smoke told the young woman. "If he's lucky, his arm will work as well as it did before. If he's smart, though, he won't go around trying any more fast draws." Smoke shook his head. "He's just not fast enough to be doing that."

Bolton puffed on the cigar, took it out of his mouth, and put his other hand on his wife's arm.

"We'd best be going in now," he said. "It's been a long day, and we all need some rest. And we don't need to keep you any longer, Mr. Jensen. I'm sure you want to get home."

"Yes," Emmaline said, "home to your wife. Sally."

Smoke put his hat on, nodded, and said, "Welcome to Big Rock."

Susannah sniffed and walked through the door into the hotel lobby. Her mother followed her, and Bolton went last, pausing in the doorway to look back over his shoulder and say to Smoke, "I'm sure we'll be seeing a lot of each other."

He went inside and closed the door behind him.

Smoke and Monte stood there for a moment in silence, and then Monte said, "You know, I may be loco, but something about the way he said that—it almost sounded like a threat."

"Yeah," Smoke said. "It did, didn't it?"

CHAPTER 4

Sally reacted the way Smoke figured she would when she found out they were getting new neighbors.

"We'll have them over for dinner Saturday afternoon," she said. "We can make it a party for the hands and invite their whole crew, too."

"I'm sure they'd appreciate that," Smoke said. "They've been on the trail for a while, and they'd probably enjoy a meal that wasn't fixed by a chuckwagon cook."

"What are they like? The Boltons?"

The two of them were sitting on the ranch house porch, enjoying the evening air after supper. Smoke had a cup of coffee he was sipping. Sally had brought some needlework out with her to work on in the light that spilled through the window behind her, but she hadn't actually done so yet. She probably wouldn't because now she was occupied with making plans for the weekend festivities.

"Well, they're Easterners," Smoke said.

"Like my family."

"Not exactly. The Boltons are from Tennessee, not

from up in New England like the Reynoldses. Tennessee's not exactly the frontier anymore, but it was not too many decades ago. In this century, anyway."

"So they're rugged?" Sally asked.

"The Boltons? No, I wouldn't say that. They're town folks, no doubt about that. I'd guess that living has always been pretty comfortable for them. I don't know anything about Thaddeus Bolton's background, though. He's been very successful in business, but I don't know if he built it all from the ground up or inherited it."

"Even when you inherit something, it takes some effort to keep it going."

"It sure does," Smoke allowed. "And Bolton struck me as a man who's not afraid to work. He's pretty brisk and business-like."

"What about his wife and daughter?"

"They're very attractive women," Smoke answered honestly. He noticed that Sally cocked an eyebrow but didn't seem overly bothered by his assessment of Emmaline and Susannah Bolton. She wouldn't be—she was a very beautiful woman and had complete faith in Smoke's fidelity. He had never given her the faintest reason to feel otherwise.

He went on, "Mrs. Bolton looks some younger than her husband, but she's still, ah, a mature lady. Miss Bolton is probably around twenty years old, I'd say. Both of them are blondes. Well-dressed, and they know how to wear good clothes."

"So they're ornaments intended to make Mr. Bolton

look good," Sally said with a hint of crispness in her voice.

"I don't know that I'd go so far as to say that. Both of them struck me as being a mite strong-willed. They're not the types to just stand around and look pretty, I don't think."

Sally nodded and said, "Good. Perhaps I can be friends with them, then."

"I hope you will be. Oh, one other thing: Mrs. Bolton has a little bit of a southern drawl. It wouldn't surprise me if she grew up on a plantation or something like that."

"I'm looking forward to getting to know her." Sally's expression grew more serious as she added, "Smoke, do you think they're going to fit in, here in the valley?"

Smoke considered the question and then said, "It's too soon to say. I don't know if they're really aware of what it's like to live on a ranch. But they're about to find out, and I hope they like it here."

"I'll send someone over to the—what did you say the spread is going to be called? The Triangle B?"

"That's right."

"I'll send someone over there tomorrow morning to invite everybody to the fiesta."

Smoke grinned. "So it's a fiesta now, is it?"

"Why not? Maybe I'll invite all the other ranching families in the valley, too. That way the Boltons could get acquainted with everyone at once. And it's been a long time since everyone in these parts got together."

"That's true. All right, it sounds like a good idea. But you might want to give them at least a day to get settled in before you spring this on them. They're still in Big Rock tonight and won't even be on the ranch until sometime tomorrow."

"Let's see." Sally's forehead creased prettily in thought. "This is Monday. I suppose if I waited until Wednesday to send word, that would still allow enough time for all the preparations. In fact, I could go ahead and start getting ready tomorrow, even though it wouldn't be official until the next day."

"Yeah, you go ahead and do that," Smoke said, nodding.

"I wonder if I should go myself or if I should send someone," she mused. "It might be better if I send someone. Then I can meet them for the first time here at home where everything will be familiar and comfortable. Who do you think I should send?"

"Sounds to me like that would be a good job for Cal."

"Do you think so? I was considering Pearlie."

Smoke shook his head. "I need Pearlie out on the range. Cal's a good hand, too, don't get me wrong. He'll be a top hand one of these days. He's close to it now. But there's a reason Pearlie's the foreman. He keeps things running smooth around here."

Sally laughed softly and said, "You're right about that. As long as I keep him well-supplied with bear sign, there's no one better than Pearlie!"

That brought a laugh from Smoke, too. Pearlie's fondness for the doughnuts Sally fried up—called "bear sign" by cowboys because their round shape gave them a resemblance to bear tracks—was legendary, although in truth, Cal and the rest of the crew loved the sweet treats, too. So did Smoke, for that matter.

"Cal can handle it," he said. "As long as he takes a good horse, he can make the rounds of the valley in a day and deliver all the invitations."

"It's settled, then," Sally said with a decisive nod of her head. "Fiesta this Saturday! It'll be a fine day."

Smoke hoped she was right.

Calvin Woods' time on the Sugarloaf had gotten off to a bad start, to say the least.

A youngster on his own, fourteen years old and trying to make his way in the world, Cal had been spectacularly unsuccessful at everything he tried. Flat broke and so hungry it seemed to his belly like his mouth must have forgotten how to work, he was so desperate that he had no choice except to do something he had sworn he would never do.

He turned outlaw.

Or at least he tried to. Trudging along a road in Colorado, he had decided he would hold up the next person to come along. He hated the idea, but he had to have money for food. He had an old gun he could threaten them with. All he had to do was get the drop on his intended victim.

Of course, he didn't have any bullets for the gun, and it probably wouldn't work even if he did, but whoever he robbed didn't have to know that.

When he heard horses coming along the trail, he retreated into the brush and waited. A minute later a buckboard came into view, being driven by a woman. In a way, Cal hated that fate had presented him with a female victim. He would have rather robbed a man. On the other hand, a man was more likely to fight back, and Cal knew he stood no chance of winning a battle like that, not as weak from hunger as he was.

When he judged the woman in the buckboard was close enough, he stepped out of hiding and pointed the old hogleg at her, calling out for her to stop and give him all the money she had. A part of his brain realized she was fairly young and really, really pretty, but he didn't care about that right now. The only thing that mattered was filling his empty belly.

He expected her to cower and beg him not to shoot her, but that wasn't what happened at all. Instead, she had looked amused and angry at the same time, and when she told him to put the gun away and stop acting so foolish, it was in the scolding tone of a mother disciplining a wayward child.

Cal's determination to be a badman crumbled in response to that unflinching attitude. Even worse, when he tried to cock the gun to show her he meant business, the blasted thing fell apart on him. As he watched pieces of it fall into the dust of the trail, he felt like crying.

As it turned out, though, his lack of resolve and his gun falling apart were good things, as he realized very clearly a moment later when the beautiful woman produced a gun of her own—a working gun—and proceeded to shoot a branch off a nearby tree with unerring aim.

She could have put that bullet right through his head, Cal realized, and she would have if he'd forced her to.

But then she did something even more unexpected. She explained that her name was Sally Jensen, that she was on her way home to the Sugarloaf Ranch from the nearby town of Big Rock—and she asked him to come with her, have a good meal, and maybe even talk about a job for him with the ranch crew. Her husband Smoke would have to go along with that, but she figured there was a good chance he would.

Cal had often thought of that day as his real birthday. Before that, he had been alive, but he hadn't really been living. Not until he met Smoke and Sally and Pearlie and everybody else on the Sugarloaf, because that was where his true destiny lay. From that day forward, Cal had found his real family, and in the years that had passed, those bonds had become even stronger.

He couldn't help but think about those things every time he rode along the trail to Big Rock and passed the spot where his meeting with Sally had taken place. He loped past it on a rangy dun saddle mount today and shortly came to another road that angled back to the northwest.

This route led to the old Hunsacker spread, which he would have to get used to thinking of as the Triangle B since Thaddeus Bolton had bought the place. He could have ridden across open country and gotten there a little faster, but since a new crew rode the range there now and they didn't know him, he figured it might be a better idea to approach the ranch on the road.

Some fellas got a mite proddy if they found a

stranger riding across their boss's range. Until he got to know the cowboys on the Triangle B, it would be a good idea to do things by the book. Pearlie would be proud of him for thinking of that instead of acting impulsively, Cal reasoned.

He followed the trail at a brisk pace. He had a considerable amount of riding to do today in order to carry out the chore Sally had given him, delivering invitations to all the ranches in the area. The Triangle B was just his first stop on a trip that would take him around the valley. He knew from previous visits that it would take him a while to reach the ranch headquarters, so he didn't want to waste any time.

After a while, he knew he had to be on Triangle B range. The rolling, grassy landscape on both sides of the trail now belonged to Thaddeus Bolton. He spotted a few small groups of cattle grazing here and there but no riders.

Bolton's crew had brought the cattle from Texas, Smoke had explained. Cal was curious to see what kind of critters they were, but a closer examination of them would have to wait. If he started poking around somebody else's livestock, he might get shot for a rustler or strung up from the nearest tree branch.

The sound of hoofbeats drifted to Cal's ears and made him rein in. They were pounding the ground in a swift beat as they came closer to him. Somebody was in a real hurry, but as he looked around, he couldn't locate the rider.

Then a man on horseback burst out of some trees about a hundred yards to Cal's right. As fast as the horse was running, the hombre on its back was lucky he hadn't dashed his brains out on a low-hanging branch. Cal tried to watch the rider and the trees at the same time, figuring that somebody else on horseback would emerge at any time. The fella up ahead was sure covering ground like somebody was chasing him.

But no other riders appeared. The man crossed the road some twenty yards ahead of Cal without ever glancing in his direction. The wind generated by such high speed finally plucked the rider's hat off, although the chin strap caught it behind his neck and kept it from flying away.

With the hat no longer crammed down on the rider's head, thick, fair hair streamed out in the wind.

Cal's eyes widened when he saw that. Some men wore their hair long, of course. He'd seen photographs of the late Wild Bill Hickok in illustrated newspapers and knew the famous pistoleer had sported long curls.

But even though he had only gotten a glimpse of this rider's body in profile as the galloping mount lunged across the road, that had been enough to make Cal realize his mistake in thinking of the person on the horse's back as "he."

Men didn't have curves like the ones on display in that tight shirt.

That was a girl, Cal thought, and the frantic screams he now heard over the pounding hoofbeats told him that she was trapped on a runaway.

She was across the road now and headed at a breakneck pace through a broad, open stretch of grassland toward another line of trees several hundred yards in the distance. Cal knew those trees marked the course of a creek that meandered across the Sugarloaf and then through what was now the Triangle B. He had fished that creek farther up in its headwaters just below the spring where it originated in a rugged canyon. He had pulled some fine trout out of it, too.

That didn't matter now. What was important was that over here in this stretch, the stream flowed between steep banks about twenty feet high. Chances were the runaway horse would stop when it reached the trees, but if it didn't—if it plunged between a couple of them and kept going full speed—it would run over the edge of that bank and plummet to the creek below. That was a high enough fall it might prove fatal to both horse and rider.

That potential disaster flashed through Cal's mind in a shaved whisker of a second. Without hesitation, he jerked the dun's head over and dug his boot heels into the horse's flanks. The dun leaped into a gallop and went after the other horse. Cal reached up with his left hand and pushed his hat down tighter on his head as the wind tugged at it.

The girl had a lead on him, and she was mounted on a good horse, but the dun was speedy, too, and Cal urged all he could get out of it. The girl leaned back in the saddle and still grasped the reins, so even though it probably wasn't intentional, she was holding her horse back slightly. Cal angled after her, trying to cut every foot off her lead that he could.

If he could come up alongside her, he could reach over and grab her horse's reins. Then he could bring the animal to a stop. He would need time and space to do that, however, and he didn't know if he would have enough of either before they reached the creek.

He had to try, though. He couldn't sit by and watch while she killed herself.

She wasn't screaming anymore as he closed in on her. In fact, the way she swayed back and forth in the saddle told him she might have passed out or at least was coming close to fainting. He leaned forward more and prodded the dun to pour on the speed. If the girl toppled off the horse as fast as it was going, she'd be badly hurt, for sure. An even worse possibility was that her foot might hang in the stirrup and she would be dragged across the rough ground.

Ten yards away . . . five . . . She was still in the saddle, although she leaned over so far a couple of times that Cal's breath caught in his throat in fear for her. The trees and the creek bank just beyond them were only twenty yards away now. Cal was just about out of time.

The dun stretched out a little more in its racing stride. Cal came alongside the girl. Her eyes were open, but she didn't seem to be seeing anything. He couldn't afford to try to stop her horse. Instead, he leaned over in the saddle himself, reached out with his right arm, and looped it around her waist.

He hauled back on the dun's reins with his left hand as he closed his right arm around the girl. The dun threw on the brakes and Cal hung on to the girl for dear life. His strong grip pulled her off her galloping mount. Thankfully, her small, booted feet came cleanly out of the stirrups and the reins slipped from her hands. The horse charged ahead without her as Cal swung her onto the dun's back in front of him.

The dun came to a stop. Without a rider in the saddle anymore, the girl's mount slowed and wheeled away from the trees, no longer in danger of charging off the bank into the creek. Cal kicked his feet free of the stirrups and slid to the ground, bringing the girl with him.

She was limp, and although he tried, he couldn't keep his balance and hold both of them up at the same time. He fell but managed to keep his grip on her so that she sprawled on top of him. That way, he was able to break her fall. His head bounced off the ground hard enough that he was slightly stunned, though, and couldn't do anything for a moment except lie there with his arms around her.

When his senses returned to him, he saw that she was blinking her eyes and shaking her head groggily, as if she were starting to come around, too. Those eyes were a startling shade of blue that reminded him of high mountain lakes and vaulting skies. Wings of thick, fair hair fell around her face and brushed his cheeks because only inches separated them. It was sort of like being in a cave, he thought crazily, a cave where there were only the two of them and everybody else in the world was shut out.

That wasn't the case at all, of course, and a flurry of hoofbeats that pounded the ground nearby and made it shiver slightly under him reminded him of that fact.

And so did the harsh, angry voice that yelled, "What the hell! It's the boss's daughter! Get that no-good son of a buck who's attackin' her!"

CHAPTER 5

Cal wanted to yell that he wasn't attacking anybody. He had saved the girl from almost certain injury and possible death. Couldn't those fools, whoever they were, see that?

But stunned as he still was, he couldn't find the breath, especially with the girl lying on top of him like that. He heard rapid footsteps rush up, and then strong hands grabbed hold of the girl, jerked her away from him, and lifted her to her feet.

Cal didn't get much of a chance to catch his breath before other men seized him and roughly hauled him upright, too.

With them crowded around him, he couldn't be sure how many there were. Eight or ten, he guessed, and a couple of them were helping the girl stay on her feet and fussing over her.

But that left at least half a dozen to start shoving him around as they yelled at him. Some of them cursed while others shouted questions, demanding to know who he was and why he had attacked Miss Bolton.

He'd already heard them call her the boss's daughter,

so the fact that she was Susannah Bolton came as no surprise. Smoke had mentioned her name when he told Cal and Pearlie about Thaddeus Bolton buying the old Hunsacker spread.

Smoke hadn't said anything about how good-looking she was, or how blue her eyes were, but Cal wouldn't have expected Smoke to go into detail about that. Shoot, Smoke was a married man; he'd probably never even noticed how attractive Susannah was.

Cal was getting tired of being thrown back and forth like a rag doll. He tried to brace himself so they couldn't do that. Anger boiled up inside him. He shouted, "Damn it, stop that! I didn't do anything—"

One of the men hauled off and punched him in the jaw.

Cal had been hit harder in his life, but the blow packed enough power to drive him backward. He might have fallen again if two of his tormentors hadn't caught him.

The man who had punched him was stocky, dark-haired, and florid-faced. Like the others, he wore range clothes and looked like a cowboy. He glared at Cal and said, "Hold on to him, boys, and we'll teach him a lesson he'll never forget!"

Cal tasted blood in his mouth. One of his teeth must have cut the inside of his cheek when the man hit him. That just added to the outrage he felt at this injustice they were carrying out.

"Too yellow to take me on by yourself?" he yelled.

The stocky man's eyes widened. His face flushed even darker as angry blood flooded it. He roared, "Let him go!" and planted his feet as he raised his fists.

Cal didn't try to trade punches with the man. Instead,

as soon as the others released him, he charged forward and launched into a diving tackle. His opponent wasn't able to get out of the way in time. Cal crashed into him, wrapped his arms around the man's midsection, and drove him off his feet. A couple of the other cowboys had to leap aside to get out of the way. The stocky man slammed down on his back.

Cal scrambled up on hands and knees. He had caught his breath now, and the anger he felt allowed him to ignore being shaken up by what had happened already. He lunged forward and planted one knee in the stocky man's belly to pin him to the ground. He heaved his body upward and braced himself on his left hand while he used his right fist to hammer punches into the stocky man's face.

He landed only a couple of punches before a boot toe caught him in the ribs in a vicious kick. That knocked Cal off his opponent and rolled him on the ground. He saw another boot coming at his face and flung his hands up in time to grab it before it crashed into him. Heaving as hard as he could, he sent the would-be stomper reeling backward.

None of them tried to stop Cal as he rolled again, came up on one knee, and forced himself to his feet. He hadn't straightened all the way before they were on him again, slamming punches into his body that jolted him back and forth. They didn't try to hit him in the head now. They must have decided that might end the fight too soon, before he had been punished enough.

Cal tried to fight back. He managed to land a few blows, and he felt some slight satisfaction as those impacts shivered up his arms and he saw blood spurt from noses or mouths.

But the odds against him were overwhelming, and it wasn't long before he was practically out on his feet. They battered him back and forth, and finally, as he swung a wild punch that didn't hit anything, he pitched forward on his face. The cowboys stepped back to give him room to fall.

He lay there, face in the dirt, breathing hard, unable to move. A voice he thought belonged to the stocky man said, "Gimme my quirt. Get him back on his feet and rip the shirt off him."

"What are you gonna do, Bart?" another man asked.

"What do you think I'm gonna do? I'm gonna give this varmint such a hiding that he'll never try to molest Miss Susannah or any other decent woman again!"

Cal was powerless to fight back as hands clamped onto his arms and lifted him to his feet. He felt his shirt being ripped from him. He was stripped to the waist.

"Two of you hang on to him," the man called Bart ordered. "And the rest of you, step back and give me room to swing this quirt."

Cal knew the agony that was coming. His lips drew back from his teeth as he clenched his jaw to keep from crying out when the vicious strokes landed. He wasn't going to give them the satisfaction of hearing him yell.

Before the quirt could fall the first time, a gunshot sounded thunderously, shockingly loud in the warm air.

"Stop it! Let go of him!"

The voice that cried out and cut through the echoes of the shot was female. Cal's head drooped forward, and his eyes were closed, but he forced them open and compelled his muscles to work well enough to raise his head. He looked over his shoulder and saw the blond girl standing there with a Remington revolver gripped in both hands. Smoke curled from the gun's muzzle as she moved it back and forth shakily.

The cowboy called Hudson took a step toward her. He clutched the wooden handle of a braided rawhide quirt in his right hand, but he held out his empty left hand toward the girl and said, "Now, Miss Susannah, you need to put that gun down. It's liable to go off again and hurt somebody."

One of the men who had been holding Susannah said, "I'm sorry, Bart. She grabbed that hogleg right out o' my holster before I knew what she was doin'."

Hudson ignored that and made calming motions. "I know you don't want to shoot anybody," he told Susannah. "At least point that thing at the ground."

She let the Remington's barrel sag slightly, but she didn't point it at the ground. "I'm not going to give the gun back," she said, "until you promise me you won't whip that man."

Hudson's frustration came through in his voice as he said, "Miss Susannah, I just don't see why you're stickin' up for this saddle tramp. When we rode up, he was takin' improper liberties with you. If your pa was here, he'd probably have us do more than whip him. He'd probably tell us to string him up!"

"Then he'd be wrong, too. That young man didn't attack me. He saved my life."

Cal started to breathe a little easier, even though he

knew he wasn't out of trouble yet. There were enough of these punchers that they could do whatever they decided to do, even with the girl waving a gun around. He knew they wouldn't have a problem taking that Remington away from her. Already, one of the men was sidling over behind her, getting ready to reach around and jerk the gun out of her hands. If he grabbed it so the cylinder couldn't turn, she couldn't cock and fire.

She should have eared the hammer back as soon as she squeezed off that shot, but clearly, she didn't know that. This might be the first time she'd ever fired a gun, Cal told himself.

"No offense," Hudson said, "but what are you talkin' about? He had you on the ground—"

"Where we fell after dismounting, which we did after he saved me from that runaway horse."

Susannah sounded like she was thinking straight again and had recovered from the shock of being stuck on a horse that bolted with her in the saddle. Cal was thankful for that. If she hadn't regained her senses, there was no telling what these hotheaded cowboys might do to him.

"What runaway horse?" Hudson demanded.

Susannah finally allowed the gun to drop to her side as she held it with her right hand. She used her left to point at the mount she'd been on, which had ended its panic-stricken flight by stopping to graze a couple of hundred yards away.

"That one. I don't understand what happened. It's always been gentle when I rode it before, while we were still on our way out here to Colorado. And it was fine when we started this morning, but then I heard some buzzing sound, and it just seemed to go mad."

Cal didn't know how his captors would react if he talked to her, but he decided to risk it. He called, "That explains it, Miss. The horse heard a rattlesnake and spooked. When you weren't able to get it back under control, it just kept running."

Hudson drove a fist into the small of Cal's back, causing him to gasp and arch his body in the grip of the men holding his arms.

"Shut up," Hudson grated. "Nobody told you you could speak to the young lady, saddle tramp."

At the same time, the puncher who had slipped up behind Susannah made a lunging grab for the Remington. It was easier now since she had lowered the gun. She cried out as he ripped it from her hand.

Fury boiled up Cal's throat. "I'm not a saddle tramp!" he yelled. "I ride for Smoke Jensen and the Sugarloaf Ranch!"

Several of the men leaned back as their eyes widened in surprise. "Smoke Jensen!" one of them muttered. The name meant something to them, no doubt about that.

"Will you just listen to me, Bart?" Susannah said as she rubbed her hand. It must have hurt when the Remington was snatched away from her. "My horse ran away with me. I was so frightened I almost passed out. I was too scared to even try to stop it. All I could do was hang on. But this man came along, saw what was happening, and helped me. He lifted me off the runaway horse, and then when he dismounted, that was when we fell. That's what you saw when you rode up."

Hudson still looked unhappy about the situation. He said, "All that may be true, Miss Susannah, but it still doesn't explain what this fella is doin' here. This is Triangle B range, and he's a stranger. He doesn't have any right to be here."

"I was on the road to your ranch headquarters when I saw that runaway horse," Cal explained. He was having a hard time keeping a tight rein on his temper, but he managed. Susannah Bolton seemed to be reasonable, even if the cowboys who rode for her father weren't, and for some reason he wanted to be sure she understood he had meant no harm or disrespect to her.

He went on, "Most folks in these parts are more understanding when it comes to visitors. I can see escorting a stranger to headquarters to make sure he's up to no good, but taking a quirt to him—"

"There was no reason for that," Susannah broke in. "And why are you men still holding him like he's a prisoner? Let him go."

Hudson said, "All due respect, ma'am, but we ride for your pa, not you. He or Matt Coolidge usually give the orders."

Susannah looked like she was going to argue, but then something else caught her attention. She looked back toward the road. Cal followed the direction of her gaze and saw two men riding toward the group near the creek.

"Now we'll find out what both Father and Mr. Coolidge think about this," Susannah said. "Here they come."

Hudson made a face and then gestured sharply

toward his companions. "Let him go," he ordered, adding, "But keep a close eye on him in case he tries anything."

Cal wasn't interested in trying anything except getting his shirt back on. Being stripped to the waist like that in front of Susannah Bolton made him uncomfortable. When the men released him, he bent and picked up the shirt. Some of the buttons had torn loose when they ripped it off him, but he managed to get it back on and fastened well enough to be respectable.

By the time he'd done that, the two newcomers were nearly there. The men rode up the rest of the way and reined in.

The older man, who had white hair under a broad-brimmed tan hat even though he seemed too young for that, had to be Thaddeus Bolton. He wore range clothes, but they were much newer and more expensive than the other men's outfits. From the looks of those clothes, nobody had ever done any actual work while wearing them.

The man with him was younger, lean and wiry and much more at home in the saddle. That would be Matt Coolidge. Smoke had mentioned him, too, Cal recalled. He ramrodded the Triangle B crew.

"What's going on here?" Bolton asked in a sharp voice that showed he was accustomed to being in charge. Without giving anyone a chance to answer, he went on, "Susannah, are you all right?"

"I'm fine, Father, thanks to this young man," she replied with a nod toward Cal.

Bolton looked at him. "Who are you?"

"My name is Calvin Woods, sir," Cal said in a respectful tone. "I ride for the Sugarloaf Ranch."

Bolton's slightly bushy white eyebrows rose. "The Sugarloaf. That's Smoke Jensen's ranch, isn't it?"

"Yes, sir, it sure is."

"And why are you here?"

"Miss Sally—that is, Mrs. Jensen—asked me to ride over here and deliver an invitation to you and your family. She and Smoke would like for you to join them on the Sugarloaf for dinner and some festivities Saturday afternoon." Cal smiled, even though he was starting to ache like the devil from the knocking around he had gotten. "All the other ranching families are going to be invited, too. Miss Sally called it a fiesta to welcome you folks to the valley."

"Why, that's . . ." Bolton seemed a little flustered, and Cal got the feeling that wasn't a common reaction where this man was concerned. "That's very nice. I'm quite pleased. But you look like you've been fighting."

"There was a little misunderstanding—" Cal began.

"A lot more than a little," Susannah interrupted him. She proceeded to recount what had happened, interspersed with a number of angry glares she directed toward Bart Hudson and the other Triangle B riders. They looked so uncomfortable that Cal almost felt sorry for them.

Almost—but he couldn't forget the thrashing they had given him, or the fact that Hudson had been about to rawhide him with that quirt.

When Susannah was finished, Bolton said, "I believe there's a creek just on the other side of those trees with a steep drop-off to the bank."

"Yes, sir, there sure is," Coolidge drawled. "I took a good look at it yesterday."

"So this young man may well have saved your life, Susannah," Bolton said. "And the thanks he got for it was to be beaten and nearly whipped."

Hudson looked like he would have rather been just about anywhere else in the world right about now, but he summoned up the gumption to say, "It wasn't our fault, boss. When we rode up, that fella was rollin' around on the ground with Miss Susannah like he was tryin' to—well, like he was—I mean, it didn't look good, sir!"

Coolidge leaned forward in the saddle and said, "I can see how it might've been easy for Bart and the other boys to get the wrong idea, Mr. Bolton. They probably went a mite too far in how they handled it, especially after Miss Susannah tried to set 'em straight, but I think they believed they were just lookin' out for her."

Bolton considered that for a moment and then nodded. "I suppose I can see that." He looked at the cowboys. "But in the future, Hudson, before you go around whipping anyone, you wait for me to give the order, you understand?"

Hudson swallowed and said, "Yes, sir, I sure do."

That was an odd thing for Bolton to say, Cal thought. He'd almost made it sound like he was in the habit of ordering that folks be whipped. That didn't seem very likely.

Bolton looked at Cal again. "You say your name is Calvin Woods?"

"Yes, sir, but my friends call me Cal."

"Where's your hat, Woods?"

Cal didn't miss how Bolton referred to him, but he didn't figure it was worth worrying about. Bolton didn't seem like the sort of fellow who would consider any young range rider his friend.

In answer to Bolton's question, he looked around and said, "It must've fallen off during the ruckus, but it ought to be around here somewhere—"

One of the punchers picked up the hat and held it out to him. "Here you go."

Cal took it and brushed the dust off then raked the hair back from his forehead and put the hat on.

"Straighten yourself up a little more and then ride on to the ranch headquarters," Bolton said. "I want you to extend Mrs. Jensen's gracious invitation to my wife in person."

"Sure, I reckon I can do that," Cal said. "I'll be happy to, sir."

"Matt, you ride with young Mr. Woods to make sure there aren't any more incidents."

Coolidge nodded.

Susannah spoke up, saying, "I thought I might do that—"

Bolton cut her off. "You're coming with me. I think you've had enough adventures for one day, especially our first full day here. One of you men catch Miss Bolton's horse and bring it over here."

Again, Susannah looked like she wanted to argue, but she didn't say anything else. When one of the cowboys fetched her horse, she mounted up and moved the animal alongside her father's mount.

"The rest of you men get back to work," Bolton ordered. "Come along, Susannah. I'm taking a look around the ranch, and you should be familiar with it, too."

"That's what I was doing when my horse ran away with me," she answered in a slightly sullen tone.

"Well, that's not going to happen again. Let's go."

They headed off, and Hudson and the other cowboys departed in a different direction, leaving Cal and Matt Coolidge alone.

"I'm sorry about what happened," the foreman said. "They're a good crew, but they're young and they can be hotheaded. I expect you know something about that, since you ain't exactly an old-timer yourself."

"I never took it in my head to whip anybody with a quirt," Cal muttered.

"Yeah, that was a pretty raw thing for Bart to do. Heat of the moment, as they say. And he probably got carried away because he's a mite sweet on Miss Susannah." Coolidge chuckled. "Just about all those boys are, if I'm bein' honest. Can't really blame 'em."

If Coolidge was trying to get him to say something about how pretty Susannah was, Cal didn't take the bait. He just swung up into the saddle and nudged his horse into motion as he and the foreman headed for the road. He didn't want to risk stirring up more trouble by admitting that he found the young woman very attractive, too.

But he knew, deep down, that it was going to be a long time before he forgot how good it had felt to have Susannah Bolton in his arms with her face so close to his and that blond hair of hers brushing his cheeks.

CHAPTER 6

Cal's misadventure on the Triangle B threw him behind schedule, so it was after dark by the time he returned to the Sugarloaf that evening. He tended to his horse, unsaddling it and giving it some grain, then walked over to the ranch house where several lamps still burned.

He found Smoke and Pearlie on the porch, Smoke sitting in one of the rocking chairs with his feet propped up while Pearlie perched a lean hip on the railing. The Sugarloaf foreman had his pipe going, and clouds of aromatic smoke wreathed his head, blurring the rugged lines of his face.

Pearlie took the pipe out of his mouth and said, "We were startin' to wonder if we were gonna have to send out a search party for you, kid."

"It took time to ride around to all the ranches in the valley," Cal said. "And everywhere I went, they offered me coffee or lemonade or some such. I ate dinner with the McKinnons, up at the Cloverleaf spread. Before that, though, I got delayed on the Triangle B."

"What happened?" Smoke asked.

"A misunderstanding."

Pearlie said, "I noticed when you walked up that you was movin' a mite stiff. Step over here in the light so we can get a better look at you."

"That's not necessary."

"Move over in the light, Cal," Smoke said, and this time the young cowboy did as he was told. He wasn't going to disobey a direct order from Smoke.

At the sight of Cal's bruised, swollen face, Pearlie straightened quickly from his casual pose and set the pipe on the top rail.

"What in blazes happened to you, boy? You look like you got jumped by a whole gang."

"I guess you could call it that," Cal said. "There were eight or ten of them."

Smoke stood up, too. "Bolton's men?"

"Yeah." Smoke could tell that the young man was reluctant to go into detail, but Cal added, "The ringleader seemed to be a fella called Hudson. Bart Hudson."

Smoke shook his head. "I don't know which one that is. The youngster I had to wing the other day was called Fletch. But it doesn't matter. What caused them to attack you?"

"Well, there was this girl—"

"I should've knowed," Pearlie broke in. "I suppose she was pretty, wasn't she?"

"As a matter of fact," Cal said, "she sure was."

Pearlie snorted. "This ain't the first time you've got yourself in a scrape over a gal. I swear, boy, you got to learn to behave yourself around proper young ladies. She *was* a proper young lady, I reckon?"

"Absolutely. Miss Susannah Bolton."

"Bolton's daughter," Smoke said. "I think you'd better tell us the whole story."

Cal did so, and as he talked, Pearlie's attitude changed. The Sugarloaf foreman went from being annoyed with Cal to being mad at Hudson and the other Triangle B cowboys.

"Dadblast it," Pearlie burst out when Cal was finished, "we can't let those varmints get away with that. They can't jump a Sugarloaf rider."

"Take it easy," Smoke told him, even though he shared some of Pearlie's anger. Out here, a man rode for the brand and stuck up for anyone else who did the same. "From the sound of it, it actually was a misunderstanding like Cal said—although those boys definitely got too carried away."

"I'm sorry I wasn't able to put up a better fight, Smoke," Cal said. "I tried, but there were just too many of them. If I'd been packing iron—"

"I'm glad you weren't," Smoke said. "That might've gotten somebody killed, and there was no need for that."

Since he hadn't been expecting trouble when he set out that morning, Cal hadn't strapped on a Colt. He'd had a Winchester in the saddle boot because out on the range a fella never knew when he might need to shoot a rattlesnake or a mountain lion, but once he and Susannah had dismounted, he'd had no chance to reach the saddle gun.

Smoke was genuinely glad it had played out that way. He wanted to remain on good terms with all his neighbors, and a shooting scrape so soon after the Boltons arrived in the valley definitely would have soured things with them.

Sally would have been upset about that. She was looking forward to making a new friend in Emmaline Bolton.

Although, remembering the way the blond woman had looked at him and been so friendly, Smoke wasn't sure if a friendship between her and Sally was in the cards.

Emmaline might act less provocatively toward him under other circumstances, Smoke told himself. He could only hope so.

"Were you able to deliver the invitation to Mrs. Bolton in person?" he went on.

"Yes, sir. That fella Coolidge took me to the ranch house, like Mr. Bolton told him to, and I talked to the lady. She said she was plumb happy to accept and that they would be here on Saturday. Well, she didn't say 'plumb happy,' but that's what it amounted to."

"You told Coolidge that he and the rest of the crew are invited, too?"

Cal made a face. "Yeah. That was a mite harder after the way they jumped me like that, but I did what you said, Smoke. Coolidge said he and some of the others would be here, but he'd have to leave a few hands on the ranch to look after things." Cal paused. "I think maybe he intends for Hudson to be one of those left behind, and if I'm being honest, that's all right with me."

Smoke chuckled and nodded. "Probably for the

best. Were you able to visit all the other ranches in the valley?"

"Yeah, I sure did. And just about everybody said they'd be here. Miss Sally's going to have a good turnout for her fiesta."

"She'll be glad to hear it. We'll keep any mention of this trouble you had with that bunch to ourselves. There's no need for Sally to worry about it."

"That means you'd best keep yourself to the bunkhouse for the next couple of days," Pearlie told Cal. "If she sees you lookin' like somebody walloped you a few times with an ax handle, she'll know somethin' happened."

"I don't know if these bruises will go away even by the weekend," Cal said.

"They'll fade enough. Just lie low like I told you."

Cal nodded his agreement and then said, "You don't think there'll be any more trouble at the party, do you?"

"There'd durned well better not be," Pearlie said ominously.

Smoke said, "I'm sure Bolton will tell his men to be on their best behavior, and you'll see to it that the same holds true for our men, Pearlie."

The foreman gave a curt nod. "They can be a salty bunch, but I'll ride herd on 'em."

"We'll put all this behind us and just have a good time," Smoke said. "It won't be long at all before the whole thing is forgotten."

* * *

Sally had already thrown herself into preparations for the party, even before the invitations were issued, and now that the other ladies in the valley knew about it, several of them drove over to the Sugarloaf in buggies and buckboards to help her during the next few days.

That meant the house was so full of delicious cooking aromas that it seemed like Smoke's mouth watered twenty-four hours a day. Pearlie was just about in heaven smelling the pies and cakes and fresh loaves of bread.

On Friday, Pearlie and some of the crew butchered and dressed out a steer, caching the meat in the root cellar. They were up early on Saturday morning to get it cooking in a big pit full of glowing red coals, and that just added to the appetizing atmosphere that hung over the ranch headquarters.

Several members of the crew set up tables and chairs in the shade of some towering cottonwoods. Before the day was over, those tables would be practically groaning under the weight of platters filled with delicious food.

The guests began to arrive around mid-morning. Families were crowded onto wagons. Some of the older kids rode horseback, as did the cowboys who had come along. A couple of cowboys from the Sugarloaf crew had been designated as hostlers for the day. They took charge of the horses, unsaddling them and leading them into corrals. Other punchers unhitched wagon teams and tended to them.

The place was bustling, sure enough, Smoke thought as he looked around, satisfied with how things were going so far.

The Boltons hadn't put in an appearance yet, which wasn't surprising. Being easterners, they probably wouldn't show up until after most of the other guests had arrived. They were more likely to stand on ceremony than these unpretentious, informal westerners.

Sally came up to Smoke as he stood on the porch. She wore a white apron tied around her waist over a dark blue skirt. A lighter blue shirt and a blue ribbon of the same shade in her lustrous dark hair completed the appealing outfit. Her face was a little flushed because she had been so busy all morning, but as far as Smoke was concerned that just made her prettier, if such a thing was even possible.

"Smoke, I just spoke to Cal," she said. "What in the world happened to him? He said he had a little accident a few days ago, but it looked worse than that to me."

Cal had done an even better job of staying out of Sally's sight for the past several days than Smoke had expected. Smoke had seen him earlier that morning, and although most of the bruises on the young cowboy's face had faded considerably, some of them were still visible.

"It's nothing for you to worry about," Smoke assured Sally. "He had a little run-in with some fellas, but it's all settled now."

"A little accident, he called it. A little run-in, according to you. He got in a fight, didn't he? With some of our men?"

Smoke knew better than to try to keep something from Sally once she got wind of it. He said, "When he delivered the invitation for today to the Bolton ranch, he had some trouble with a few of the Triangle B cowboys."

"Oh, my goodness. There's not going to be a fight here today, is there? Should we not have had this party?"

"No, it didn't amount to that much," Smoke said— but at the same time, he knew that was a matter of luck. If Cal had come home with his back bloody and shredded from a whipping, there would have been trouble. The rest of the Sugarloaf crew would have stampeded over to the Triangle B looking for a fight, and Smoke wasn't sure he could have stopped them. He wasn't sure he would have wanted to.

But that wasn't the way it had played out, so he went on, "Cal's not carrying any grudge, and Matt Coolidge, the Triangle B foreman, said he'd keep a few of his hands on the ranch to look after things there, including the main one Cal had trouble with. I'll tell you all about it later, but for now, don't let it bother you."

"All right. I suppose I can't do anything except go along with what you suggest. But I feel like you've been keeping things from me, and I don't like it. Now I understand why I haven't seen Cal for several days, though." She shook her head. "He must have looked quite a sight after it happened. Can I at least hope the other fellow looked worse?"

"He would have if it had been a fair fight, I'm sure," Smoke said. "We can talk about it once everybody's gone home."

She nodded, and he was certain that they would, indeed, talk about it. But for now, Sally had too much else on her mind to dwell on the matter.

A short time later, Smoke was standing with Pearlie and Cal near the pit where slabs of beef were roasting slowly over hot coals, when Cal nodded toward the road and said, "Here come the Boltons."

Smoke looked in that direction and saw the same buggy in which the newcomers had arrived in Big Rock five days earlier. As before, Thaddeus Bolton was handling the reins. He wore the same sort of outfit he'd had on while riding around his ranch, so that he looked like a westerner but wasn't likely to fool anyone into believing he actually was one.

Beside him, his wife Emmaline wore a yellow dress with a bright red sash around her waist. She wasn't wearing a hat today, and her fair hair shone in the sunlight.

Susannah wasn't riding in the buggy's back seat this time. In fact, she was on horseback, moving along briskly beside the vehicle in which her parents traveled. Smoke leaned over to Cal and said, "That's not the same horse that spooked and ran away with her, is it?"

"No, that's a different one," Cal said. "She looks like she's doing a good job of handling it today."

Pearlie commented, "I'm a mite surprised her ma lets her go out dressed like a boy."

"Maybe," Cal said, "but it looks good."

That was true. Susannah wore boots and denim trousers and rode astride. She had on a buckskin shirt with fringe on the sleeves, and a brown hat was pushed back on her blond hair. She looked like she wanted to be a genuine western ranch girl, but whether she could manage that, only time would tell.

Cal was studying her with frank admiration in his gaze, Smoke noted, and he hoped that wouldn't lead to any friction with the Triangle B crew.

A dozen men on horseback rode behind the buggy. Smoke didn't know how many punchers Bolton had working for him, but given the size of the ranch, it seemed possible there could be that many more again on his payroll. But Matt Coolidge had said from the start that he was going to leave some of them behind, Smoke reminded himself.

Thinking of that made him look for Coolidge, who had planned to attend today's festivities. Smoke didn't see the foreman. Maybe Coolidge was coming later, or not at all. Something could have come up that demanded his presence on the ranch.

"I'd better go greet our guests of honor," Smoke said.

"Do you see the hombre who tried to take a quirt to you?" Pearlie asked Cal.

The young cowboy shook his head. "No, he's not part of that bunch. Coolidge promised he'd leave him behind."

"What about the others who were with him that day?"

"I don't know. None of those fellas with the Boltons look familiar, but everything was so wild that day it's hard to be sure."

"The two of you stay here," Smoke told them. He started forward to meet the buggy as it rolled up to the ranch yard. He saw that Sally had emerged from the house and was on a similar course from a different angle.

He increased his pace so he could intercept her and

linked his arm with hers as he came alongside her. A few yards away, Thaddeus Bolton brought the buggy to a stop and Susannah reined in her mount, a chestnut mare.

"Mr. and Mrs. Bolton, welcome to the Sugarloaf!" Sally called to them. "I'm Sally Jensen. I know you've already met my husband Smoke. I'm so glad you could come over today so we can all get to know you."

Bolton stepped down from the buggy and took his hat off. He smiled as he said, "Thank you, Mrs. Jensen. It's an honor to be invited to your ranch and our pleasure to be here." He put his hat on and turned back to the buggy. "Let me give you a hand, my dear."

He took Emmaline's hand. Climbing out of a buggy wasn't a very graceful thing to do, but she made it look easy. She turned to Sally and clasped both of her hands.

"It's wonderful to meet you," she said. "Please, call me Emmaline."

"And I'm Sally."

Bolton shook hands with Smoke and said, "Jensen, how are you?"

"Fine," Smoke said.

"Listen, about that trouble between our men the other day—"

Smoke waved off whatever Bolton was about to say. "Already forgotten," he assured the man, even though he was certain it hadn't been, not by Cal. But he also knew that Cal was going to be on his best behavior today. "Why don't we walk around, and I'll introduce you to the other ranchers who have spreads here in the valley?"

"I'd like that," Bolton said.

"And I'll introduce you to the other ladies," Sally said to Emmaline, who linked arms with her as if they were already old friends.

Smoke noticed that Susannah Bolton was still mounted. Pearlie had ambled up, so Smoke said to him, "Pearlie, take Miss Bolton's horse and put it in the corral with the others, if you don't mind."

"Be happy to," Pearlie agreed, but as he reached for the reins, Susannah pulled back a little.

"Where's that young man I met the other day?" she asked. "Mr. Woods?"

"Cal's around somewhere," Smoke said, "but Pearlie can take care of you, Miss Bolton. Pearlie Fontaine, my foreman," he added by way of introduction.

Pearlie and Bolton shook, and then once again Pearlie tried to get the mare's reins from Susannah. She turned them over with obvious reluctance and swung down from the saddle.

"I was hoping to see Mr. Woods again so I can make sure he's all right after what happened."

"Oh, the boy's fine," Pearlie told her. "He hobbled a mite for a day or two, but he's gettin' around without any problem now."

"I'm going to go look for him."

Bolton said, "Susannah, you promised me you'd behave today."

She gave her father a resentful look and said, "I'm not going to cause any problems."

She walked away muttering something under her breath.

Bolton shook his head as he turned to Smoke. "Do you and your wife have any children, Jensen?"

"Not yet," Smoke answered honestly. "We're figuring on starting a family any time now, though."

"It can be a real challenge. Rewarding, of course— but still a challenge."

Smoke let that pass, put a hand lightly on Bolton's arm, and steered him toward the group of men gathered around the cooking pit.

Bolton was friendly enough when Smoke introduced him to the other ranchers, but he maintained a certain reserve that Smoke decided was just his natural personality. He might not ever be close friends with these other men, but he didn't have to be in order to get along in the valley. As long as he kept his crew in line and didn't encroach on anyone else's range, he would be fine.

Smoke kept his eye on Sally and Emmaline, as well, as they circulated among the other women. The smile on Emmaline's face never budged as Sally performed numerous introductions. She seemed to be having a good time.

She hadn't eyed him boldly, either, or even paid that much attention to him. Smoke was grateful for that. He didn't need any complications in his life.

At one point, however, as if she sensed that he was looking at her, Emmaline shot a glance toward Smoke and their eyes met. The contact lasted only a second, but that was long enough for Smoke to see the flash of interest in her gaze. He kept a polite smile on his face, but he was glad when she looked away and didn't prolong the connection between them.

That was enough to make him wary. It would be a good idea, he told himself sternly, if he saw to it that he was never alone anywhere with Emmaline Bolton. Not even for a few moments.

Shortly after that, Sally stepped up on the porch and announced that dinner was ready. Everyone moved over to the tables, and the ranch hands who had been dragooned into serving the meal began filling plates and passing them out. The happy sounds of talk and laughter filled the air.

Sally and Emmaline rejoined Smoke and Bolton. The couples sat across from each other at one of the tables. Emmaline was back to being friendly but distant with Smoke now. Clearly, she didn't mind indulging in bolder behavior in front of her husband but wasn't going to do that in front of her new friend Sally.

The food was delicious, especially the biscuits, Smoke thought. Sally had a great touch with them, and they were always light and fluffy. He enjoyed the food and washed it down with lemonade that had just the right blend of tartness and sweetness. Everything was so good that he had to be careful not to eat too much. He wanted to leave plenty of room for a bowl of deep-dish apple pie.

As they ate, Smoke said to Bolton, "I thought your foreman was going to come along with you today."

"Matt got worried about leaving the ranch, so he decided to stay behind." Bolton smiled. "I think he just hasn't quite settled in yet. He's a very good man. I was lucky to hire him."

"Seems like it. I know I'm mighty lucky to have Pearlie riding for the Sugarloaf. Having a good foreman makes all the difference in the world in how a spread operates."

"I imagine so," Bolton agreed. He speared another bite of beef with his fork and popped it in his mouth. While he was chewing, he lifted his head and peered past the crowd toward the road. A frown creased his forehead. Curious as to what had caught Bolton's sudden interest, Smoke half turned on his chair to look in that direction himself.

He saw a rider coming fast toward the ranch house and the adjoining yard. Smoke didn't recognize him, but Bolton evidently did.

"Is that one of your men?" Smoke asked.

"That's right. He's one of the group that stayed behind. I don't know what he's doing here or why he's riding so fast."

Anybody pushing a horse hellbent-for-leather like that usually had only one reason, Smoke thought—trouble. He pushed himself to his feet and so did Bolton.

"Thaddeus, what is it?" Emmaline asked. "Is something wrong?"

"I don't know, but I intend to find out."

Bolton dropped his napkin on the table and walked around it to start toward the approaching rider. Smoke fell in with him. The talking and laughter under the trees hadn't stopped, but it diminished in volume as more and more of the guests realized that something unexpected might be happening.

"That's my man Hudson," Bolton said. "I thought it might be, but now I'm certain."

Hudson's name was familiar. After a second, Smoke placed it. Hudson was the Triangle B hand who had wanted to whip Cal with a quirt. Above all the others, he was one who wasn't supposed to be here today.

But he was, and obviously bent on some urgent errand to judge the way he was riding. Hudson hauled back on the reins and brought his lathered mount to a sliding stop in front of Smoke and Bolton, who had paused at the edge of the ranch yard to meet him.

"Mr. Bolton!" he called. "Mr. Bolton, they hit that bunch of cattle we pastured along the creek! Rustlers!"

CHAPTER 7

Cal had seen the Boltons drive up in their buggy, but most of his attention was focused on the rider who trotted along smoothly beside the vehicle. Susannah had been dressed for riding the day he had rescued her from the runaway, but today she looked even more like a Westerner. Most of the ranch girls in the valley had donned their fanciest dresses and put ribbons and bows in their hair for the festivities, but Susannah had taken the opposite tack: she looked like she was ready to get out and ride the range with the Triangle B crew.

Somehow, that made her even prettier, Cal thought, although that shouldn't have been possible.

"You'd best put your eyes back in your head, boy," Pearlie said as he stood beside Cal. "Moonin' over the Bolton gal ain't gonna get you anywhere."

"I'm not mooning over her. You've got to admit, though, Pearlie, she's mighty pretty."

"Cute as a speckled pup, no doubt about it. And her ma and pa probably think so, too, which is why they ain't gonna let a young brushpopper like you get anywhere near her. No, a gal like that is destined for one thing and one thing only—to marry the son of some other rich man and have babies that'll grow up to inherit a heap of dinero."

Cal frowned. "Don't talk about her like that. She's not some broodmare."

"I'm just sayin', son, don't get your hopes up. Because if you do, they'll get kicked right out from under you, sure as shootin'."

Cal didn't want to believe that, but he was enough of a realist to know that Pearlie was probably correct. Susannah's parents would find a good match for her, and it sure wouldn't be some forty-a-month-and-found cowpoke. The best thing he could do was forget about Susannah Bolton.

Besides, he'd had romances before, some of them serious, and none of them had ended particularly well. One or two had been downright tragic. He didn't need that sort of thing again. He had sworn off females a while back. It was better for a fella to just concentrate on his work.

He had known that resolve probably wouldn't last—but he hadn't figured on it starting to weaken quite so soon.

"There's nothing wrong with me welcoming her to the Sugarloaf," he said. "That's the polite thing to do."

"Blast it, Cal—" Pearlie began in a warning tone.

Cal ignored him and started toward the spot where the Boltons were talking to Smoke and Sally. Pearlie muttered something under his breath and clamped a hand on Cal's shoulder.

"Let me go," Cal protested as Pearlie stopped him.

Pearlie maintained his firm grip and said, "Go to the barn and check on all those wagon and buggy teams that've been put up."

"They're fine and you know it. You're just trying to get me out of the way."

"I'm tryin' to keep you from landin' in hot water. Now go on like I told you. That's an order."

Cal glared at the foreman. He knew good and well why Pearlie was sending him off to the barn. But he also knew he wasn't going to refuse a direct order from the older man. The chain of command in a ranch crew wasn't as strict as it was in the military, but Pearlie was the boss around here. The only ones higher up on the Sugarloaf were Smoke and Sally.

"All right," Cal said with ill grace. "But are you planning on mother henning me all day?"

"I will if I have to," Pearlie declared. "Or maybe I'll just tell you to saddle a horse and go check on the stock in the northwest pasture."

"That's the farthest place away on the whole spread!"

"Yeah, I know."

"And I haven't even eaten yet."

"Then maybe you'd best do as you're told."

Scowling, Cal headed for the barn, his steps slow and reluctant. He looked back over his shoulder, and his glare deepened as he saw Pearlie taking Susannah's horse from her. The old son of a gun was just trying to beat his time!

That was a loco thought and Cal knew it. There were

several gals at Longmont's and the Brown Dirt Cowboy Saloon who were sweet on Pearlie, and he returned the feeling. He wouldn't have any interest in a girl like Susannah, who was twenty years old at most, if that. He was just being polite by tending to her horse, and more than likely, Smoke had told him to do it.

Cal sighed and went on into the barn.

All the wagon and buggy teams that had been brought in, fed, and watered were fine, just as he had known they would be. Pearlie had just wanted to get him out of the way for a while. But as he had told the foreman, Pearlie couldn't keep an eye on him all day, not with so many folks on hand and moving around so much. Cal walked out of the barn, figuring on taking a look around for Susannah Bolton.

He hadn't figured on running right into her—literally.

She bumped into his shoulder and said, "Oh!" before stepping back. Even in that split-second collision, Cal had been aware of the intriguing softness filling out the buckskin shirt Susannah wore. He told himself not to think about that and snatched his hat off his head.

Holding the Stetson in front of his chest, he said, "I'm sorry, Miss Bolton. Are you all right?"

"You shouldn't be apologizing to me, Mr. Woods," she said. "I'm the one who ran into you. And I'm fine. No harm done."

"I'm mighty glad to hear that. Ah . . . are you having a good time so far?"

He wanted to cuss himself for feeling and sounding

so awkward, but Susannah didn't seem to notice, thank goodness.

"Do you mean today, or since we arrived in the valley?" she asked.

"Well, I meant today, but I reckon you could look at it either way."

She smiled. "We haven't been here very long today, but it's quite a party."

"Miss Sally called it a *fiesta*."

"She seems very nice."

"She is." Cal didn't mention the history he had with Sally, which included attempted robbery and her demonstrating that she could put a bullet through his head if she'd been of a mind to. "She's just about the nicest lady you'd ever want to be around." He added hastily, "But I'm sure your ma is just as nice."

Susannah smiled at that but didn't respond one way or the other to his comment about her mother.

"How are you feeling?" she asked. "Your friend said you had trouble getting around for a few days. I'm still very sorry about what happened."

"Oh, I'm fine," Cal said, waving a hand dismissively at the thought he might have been stiff and sore for days after the beating he had suffered—which, of course, he had. But Susannah didn't need to know that. "I hope you didn't spend a lot of time worrying about me."

"I wouldn't call it a lot of time, but I did want to make sure you were all right. That's one of the main reasons I came along today. I still feel like what happened was my fault."

"Not a bit," Cal said. "It sure wasn't your fault that your horse spooked when it nearly stepped on a rattlesnake, and after that there wasn't anything you could do."

"I didn't have to get so scared that I practically fainted."

"Have you ever been stuck on a runaway horse before?"

"Well, no, I haven't."

Cal nodded. "There you go, then. You did good just to hang on and not fall off. You could have been hurt bad if that had happened."

As they talked, they strolled under the trees, not far from the tables where food was being brought out. People were all around them, and that was a good thing, Cal thought. Despite knowing that getting involved with Susannah Bolton would be a mistake, if they had been alone, he might have been tempted to try to kiss her. The way she looked, he knew there was a good chance he would give in to that temptation.

In a crowd such as this, though, nothing improper was going to happen. Maybe someday, he mused, it would be just the two of them alone somewhere. There was no telling what might happen in a case like that—

He shook his head to force those thoughts out of his brain. Pearlie was right; they didn't have any place there.

He showed her around the ranch headquarters. Maybe she was just being polite, but she seemed interested. Anytime they got near either of her parents, though, Susannah quickly steered them away, as if she knew what their reaction would be if they caught her spending time with Cal. That was all right with him. He wanted to enjoy today without any trouble, and so far, despite what the older people had said, that was what was happening.

When Sally announced that dinner was ready, Cal and Susannah found a place to eat at the opposite end of the tables from where Smoke and Sally were sitting across from Mr. and Mrs. Bolton. Cal was enjoying both the meal and the company when a hand fell heavily on his shoulder.

"Is this boy behavin' himself, Miss Bolton?" Pearlie asked as he stood behind Cal.

She gave the foreman a brilliant smile. "He's been a charming host and a perfect gentleman, Mr. Fontaine. You don't have anything to worry about."

Pearlie grunted. "I ain't sure Cal's ever been a perfect anything, let alone a gentleman. But I reckon I'll have to take your word for it, miss—" He stopped and squinted toward the road for a moment before saying, "Somebody's in a big hurry. That usually means something's wrong."

Cal stood up to look, too, and beside him, Susannah rose to her feet, as well. Clearly startled, she said, "That looks like Bart Hudson."

Cal stiffened as he recognized the rider. This morning when he'd looked into the mirror to shave, he'd had stubborn reminders of what Hudson had done in the form of fading bruises on his face that were still visible if a fella knew where to look. Every twinge of a still-sore muscle joined in the chorus of remembered dislike.

He might forgive Hudson and the other Triangle B

hands who had jumped him because that was what Smoke wanted. But he darned sure wasn't going to forget.

Pearlie must have seen the look on Cal's face. He asked, "Who's that?"

"The hombre who wanted to take a quirt after me," Cal said.

Pearlie's jaw tightened enough that a little muscle jumped in it. "Is that so?" he said. "I didn't think he was comin' today."

"He wasn't supposed to," Susannah said. "Father told me he gave strict orders for Bart and the other men who were involved in that incident to stay on the ranch today."

"He didn't do what he was supposed to, then," Pearlie said as they watched the newcomer rein in and speak to Smoke and Thaddeus Bolton, who had walked away from the tables to meet him. Hudson looked excited and his voice rose so that Cal and Pearlie didn't have any trouble making out the most important word he uttered.

"Rustlers!"

Cal and Pearlie glanced at each other. Out here, rustlers were in the same loathsome league as wildfires, cyclones, and blizzards. They could wipe out a ranch just as easily as those other disasters, although it usually took longer. They were a scourge on the range, that was for sure.

"You two youngsters stay here," Pearlie told Cal and Susannah. "I'll find out what's goin' on."

"I'm coming with you," Cal declared. "If rustlers have struck anywhere in the valley, it's my business, too."

"It's even more my business," Susannah said. "It's one of our hands who brought the news, so that must mean some of the Triangle B stock has been stolen!"

She had a good point there, and the two men knew it. Neither of them looked happy about it, but they didn't object to Susannah accompanying them as they began weaving through the crowd toward the spot where Smoke and Thaddeus Bolton talked to Bart Hudson.

Others among the guests had heard the dreaded word *rustlers*, too, and after a momentary shocked hush, a renewed hubbub filled the air.

Folks weren't trading pleasantries and laughing now, though. Instead, they were voicing their worries over the news Hudson was delivering.

Cal, Susannah, and Pearlie came up just as Bolton asked, "Was anyone hurt?"

"Joe Archibald was killed," Hudson replied. His voice and face were grim. "He was out there with Shotwell, Kermit, and Claybourne when they happened on the rustlers pushing fifty or sixty head toward those hills to the west. Our boys opened fire, of course, and the rustlers fought back. They knocked Archibald out of the saddle, and the others stopped to tend to him. The rustlers got away with the stock while they were doing that." Hudson shook his head. "It was too late to do anything for poor Joe, though."

Cal looked over at Susannah as she lifted a hand and pressed it to her mouth in horror.

"You know the fella who got killed?" he asked.

"Of course," she said. "I got to know all of the cowboys on the way here, even though we were only part of the drive for a few days at the end. Mr. Archibald was always laughing and joking about things. I—I can't believe he's dead."

His face mottled with anger, Bolton turned to Smoke and said, "We've been here less than a week and already we've had a man killed and stock stolen! Is that the kind of outrage we can expect to happen regularly in this valley, Jensen?"

Cal could tell that the accusatory tone of Bolton's voice put a burr under Smoke's saddle, but as always, Smoke had his temper well under control.

"It's been quite a while since we've had any problems with rustlers around here," he said. "I think it's just a coincidence that this happened so soon after you moved in."

Bolton snorted as if he didn't believe that.

Smoke acted like he hadn't heard the man's reaction. "And I can tell you something else," he went on, "we're not going to stand for it. Stolen stock leaves tracks just like any other kind." Smoke looked around and his gaze lit on the Sugarloaf foreman. "Pearlie, have a dozen men saddle their horses and get ready to ride."

"We're goin' after those dang wideloopers?"

"Of course we are." Smoke turned back to Bolton. "Any of your men who want to come along are welcome. I'll need someone to show us where this happened."

"I can do that," Hudson spoke up.

"Very well," Bolton said. He still scowled as he added, "I wouldn't be much good to you. I'd probably just hold you back and slow you down."

"It would be a good idea for you to stay here," Smoke agreed. "We'll run those rustlers down if we can."

Susannah made all the men turn sharply toward her in surprise as she spoke up. "Can I come along?"

"Good Lord, no!" her father burst out. "What in the world possessed you to ask such a thing, Susannah?"

"I'm a good rider," she said. "*I* won't slow anybody down."

The way she phrased that made her father's face flush even more with anger, but he didn't say anything.

Smoke said, "When we catch up to those killers, Miss Bolton, there's liable to be a lot of lead flying. You don't need to be around that."

"I'm not afraid," Susannah insisted.

"It's not a matter of fear," Cal told her. "Smoke doesn't want to be looking out for you when he ought to be concentrating on rounding up those rustlers."

As soon as the words left his mouth, Cal knew he had been too blunt and plain-spoken in expressing himself. Susannah glared at him and said, "Are you going along?"

"I figured I would, if Smoke will let me."

"Well, don't get your head shot off!"

With that, she turned and stalked away. Cal started to call after her but then thought better of it.

With a barely suppressed grin, Pearlie said, "Shoot,

son, I'm just an ol' bachelor, but even I know better than to talk down to a gal like that."

"I just don't want her to get hurt—"

"Nobody does," Smoke said. "Come on. We've got some rustlers to catch."

CHAPTER 8

More than two dozen men were in the group that rode away from the Sugarloaf headquarters a short time later. Smoke, Pearlie, Cal, and nine more members of their crew made up the largest part of the assemblage.

Bart Hudson and six Triangle B punchers who had been at the fiesta were among the others, and the rest were ranchers who owned spreads in the valley, along with some of their men. Rustlers were a threat to all the cattlemen in these parts, even though it was the newest among them whose herd had been hit today, so the others were more than willing to take part in tracking down the thieves.

Smoke's mouth was set in a tight line as he rode. It seemed likely that the thieves had picked today to strike because they knew the celebration at the Sugarloaf would be going on and the Triangle B wouldn't have a full crew on hand. Smoke couldn't be sure of that, but it was a strong hunch.

Thaddeus Bolton hadn't come right out and said that

he blamed Smoke and Sally for what had happened, but Smoke figured that was in the back of the man's mind.

He couldn't bring back the unfortunate cowboy who had been killed in the raid, but he would do his best to recover the stolen cattle and bring the rustlers to justice, as he had done many times in the past.

The riders didn't take the long way around to the Triangle B as Cal had done the day he delivered the invitation and ran into so much trouble. Instead, they cut across the range. Smoke was familiar with every inch of this valley. Years earlier, as a youngster, he had been one of the first white men to set foot in it and knew the shortest route to any destination.

Smoke turned in the saddle and motioned for Bart Hudson to join him and Pearlie at the front of the group. He knew this was the man who had been largely responsible for the beating Cal had gotten, and Hudson would have done even worse if Susannah Bolton hadn't stopped him. Because of that, Smoke didn't like him—but he didn't have to like Hudson to pay attention to what the cowboy had to say.

"What part of the creek were those cattle near when they were stolen?" Smoke asked when the man had pulled alongside him.

"Not far from the spot where Miss Susannah had that horse run away with her on the other side." Hudson paused and then added, "Listen, Mr. Jensen, I'm sure sorry—"

"You're talking to the wrong man," Smoke broke in

and told him. "If you've got something you feel like you need to say, you'd best tell it to Cal."

"Yes, sir, I reckon I ought to do that, all right. I just don't want to be the cause of bad blood between the two spreads."

"That's an admirable attitude. I reckon we can probably get over any friction you caused." Despite the seriousness of the situation, Smoke smiled. "After all, a Triangle B hand tried to shoot me a few days ago, and I'm not holding any grudges about that. By the way, how is Fletch?"

"Healing up. He sure doesn't like layin' around and not doin' anything, but I reckon he'll have to stand it for a while longer. The doctor came out from town yesterday to check on him. Said the bone's knittin' up just like it's supposed to."

"I'm glad to hear it. Tell Fletch I asked about him and that there aren't any hard feelings. He just needs to be smart and not go around thinking he's faster on the draw than he actually is."

"Yes, sir. I don't know how well that'll go over, but I'll tell him."

For the next few minutes, they discussed where they were going, with Pearlie listening in, too. The Sugarloaf foreman knew the valley just about as well as Smoke did.

It wasn't long before they were on Triangle B range. Smoke led the way, setting a fast pace around hills, over ridges, and through draws. When they came to the tree-lined creek, they were on the opposite side of it from where Cal had rescued Susannah Bolton from the runaway and Hudson and the other cowboys had jumped him. There was plenty of good graze on this side of the stream, too. The grass was thick and reasonably high in the pastures.

Hudson had just pointed out the spot where the encounter with the rustlers had taken place, several hundred yards ahead, when Smoke noticed a rider emerging from the shade of the trees along that part of the creek. Something about the way the man sat the saddle struck him as familiar. Over the long, dangerous years, Smoke had made a habit of noticing things like that, and it had helped save his life more than once.

"Looks like your foreman's headed this way," Smoke said to Hudson.

The Triangle B cowboy leaned forward and squinted. "Yeah, that's Matt," he agreed after a moment. "You've got good eyes, Mr. Jensen."

Smoke turned his horse slightly so it would be easier for the group's path to intersect that of Matt Coolidge. As they met, Coolidge reined in and raised his left hand in greeting.

"Howdy, Mr. Jensen," he called. "I wish we were meetin' again under more pleasant circumstances, like at that big party you and your missus are throwin' today."

"That would have been better, all right," Smoke said. "I reckon you rode out to take a look at where the shooting happened."

"Yes, sir, that's right. Some of the boys brought a

wagon out so they could take poor Joe back to the ranch house. I came along with 'em and stayed to see if I could pick up the trail of that stolen stock." Coolidge pointed to the foothills along the northwestern edge of the valley where mountains began to rear their rocky heights. "That's the direction they headed. What's the country like up that way?"

"Pretty rugged," Smoke said. "I don't know of any trail over the mountains in that area. They'd reach a point where they'd have to turn either north or south."

With a musing tone in his voice, Pearlie said, "If they headed north, they could make it to Wyoming in a week or so. Quicker if they were willin' to run a little fat off them beeves. Then it wouldn't be too hard to cut over to Rock Springs. With the railroad runnin' through there, they probably wouldn't have much trouble findin' some cattle buyer willin' to take the stock off their hands and ship it back east. Some of those fellas don't worry overmuch about bills o' sale and such as long as they can make a big enough profit out of the deal."

"That sounds like a real possibility to me," Coolidge said. "We ought to be moving, though. They're gainin' on us with every minute that goes by."

Smoke nodded and said, "Let's go."

The men nudged their horses into motion again. The trail left by the stolen cattle was easy enough to follow. The animals would have been spread out while they were grazing, but once they were rounded up and pushed into a group, their hooves beat down the grass and churned up the dirt. Smoke could follow that trail as if it had been a plainly printed map.

Although the determined set of his features didn't reveal it, Smoke was concerned that they wouldn't be able to catch up to the stolen stock before nightfall. Once darkness settled over the landscape, the rustlers would have to stop. They couldn't drive cattle over this terrain without being able to see.

But the pursuers would have to call a halt, as well, or risk losing the trail, which might end the chase right then and there. They hadn't brought along supplies for a chase that might last several days, although there was plenty of water to be found in the streams and they probably could survive on game they shot. Even so, it would be best to end this today if at all possible.

Because of that, he set a brisk pace that covered a lot of ground without wearing out the horses. The landscape became more rugged as a number of hogback ridges cropped up, but nothing so tall or steep that the stolen cattle would have had any trouble crossing them.

Smoke, with Pearlie riding to his right and Coolidge to his left, had just crested the top of one of those ridges when he felt as much as heard the flat *whap!* of a bullet passing close by his right ear. It was an unmistakable sound because he had heard it many times before.

A fraction of a second later, the crack of a rifle reached his ears, as well. That meant the shot had come from long range since the bullet had reached him first, if only by a hair.

Smoke's instincts took over instantly. "Back!" he

shouted as he hauled his horse around. With his other arm, he waved at the men with him, signaling for them to retreat, which kept them below the ridge top. At the angle from where the bushwhacker was located, he wouldn't be able to draw a bead on them.

There wasn't just one hidden rifleman, Smoke realized a moment later. More shots blasted. Pearlie yelled in pain. Smoke threw a glance at him, felt a surge of alarm as he spotted blood on his old friend's face.

"It ain't nothin'!" Pearlie said before Smoke could even ask him how badly he was hit. "Just a little nick!"

Smoke heard more slugs whining through the air as he, Pearlie, and Coolidge leaped their mounts back over the crest. They reached safety without the ambushers scoring any more hits.

"Everybody all right?" Smoke called to the rest of the group. The men all nodded or spoke up to let him know they were unhurt.

"That was mighty close," Coolidge said as they calmed their horses. The sudden burst of action had made some of the mounts skittish.

Smoke saw that Pearlie had taken off his bandana and was using the cloth to dab at the blood on his cheek.

"That looks too close for comfort," Smoke commented.

Pearlie snorted. "This little scratch? I've cut myself worse shavin', plenty o' times."

Although the wound had bled enough to appear fairly serious, it was, in fact, pretty small, just a nick as Pearlie had said. Half an inch closer and it might have been a different story.

Smoke motioned for the men to pull back farther down the ridge and then swung down from his saddle. Pearlie, Cal, and Coolidge joined him in dismounting. Smoke went up the slope on foot, and when he was close enough to the top, he took off his hat and stretched out on his belly so he could edge his head up and take a look. The other three men did likewise.

The bushwhackers' rifles had fallen silent, leaving behind a hush that seemed to echo over the landscape.

Coolidge asked, "How many of 'em do you reckon there are, Mr. Jensen?"

"By the sound of the rifles I heard, I'd say three," Smoke replied. "They were shooting so much all the reports sort of ran together, though, so I guess there could have been one or two more."

Pearlie said, "They have to be down yonder in those trees. That's the only real cover close enough for them to try an ambush like that."

The clump of trees Pearlie mentioned stood about five hundred yards away at the base of the next ridge.

"That's mighty long range for a Winchester," Coolidge said. "I reckon those rustlers couldn't find any place closer to set their trap, though."

"You think the men we're after left somebody behind to discourage pursuit?" Smoke said.

"That's the only explanation that makes any sense, ain't it? Unless you think somebody took those shots at us for no good reason."

"No, they had a good reason, all right," Smoke said. "You're right, it must be the bunch that stole those cattle. The question now is, are they still there, or did they light a shuck when they didn't manage to down any of us on the first try?"

"Only one way I can think of to find out," Coolidge said. He started to push himself up onto hands and knees.

"Hold on," Pearlie said. "What in blazes do you think you're doin'?"

"I figured I'd stand up and see if they take any more potshots at me."

"That's a good way to get your head blowed off!"

Coolidge grinned. "No, they ain't likely to hit anything at that range."

Pearlie pointed at the smear of blood drying on his leathery cheek and said, "They came mighty blamed close! If they can get that close to a target, there's no guarantee they won't hit it the next time."

Coolidge eased down on his belly again. "I don't guess I can argue with that," he admitted. "But we can't let them pin us down here, either. That rustled stock's gettin' away."

Smoke considered the problem for a moment and then said, "A couple of us can go the long way around this ridge and then come up on their flank if they're still there."

"That's liable to take an hour!"

Smoke nodded in agreement with Coolidge's objection and said, "I know, but I can't think of any other way to tackle the job." Now that the decision had been made, he didn't waste any time. "Pearlie, you're in charge. I'll take Cal with me. The rest of you wait here until we've found out whether those bushwhackers are still there. If you hear a bunch of shooting in those trees, it'll mean that Cal and I ran into those varmints and have our hands full with them. In that case, you'll need to charge down there as fast as you can and pitch in."

"You'll get yourselves killed is what you'll do," Pearlie groused. "But I don't see no other way to do it, neither."

Coolidge said, "I'm comin' with you two fellas."

Smoke shook his head. "No, you stick here with the others. Two men are enough for a scouting job like this. Any more would be too easy to spot."

Coolidge looked like he didn't agree with the decision, but Smoke's firm tone left no room for argument. And none of the men here doubted for an instant that Smoke was in charge. His calm demeanor didn't take anything away from the air of command that surrounded him.

"We'll keep an eye on the trees," Pearlie promised. "And we'll come a-runnin' if you need us."

Smoke and Cal slipped back down the ridge to where they'd left their horses. Smoke quickly explained the plan to the rest of the group and then he and the young cowboy mounted up.

"We're closer to the northern end of this ridge," Smoke said. "That's the way we'll go."

They headed in that direction, moving at a rapid pace

because Smoke was all too aware of how quickly time was slipping away from them.

Something else had started to worry him, too. He cast several glances at dark clouds building up over the mountains. There might be rain in those clouds, and a downpour would make it even more difficult to follow the trail of the stolen cattle.

Luck seemed to be breaking in favor of the rustlers. They might have been smart enough to strike on a day when the Triangle B would have a reduced crew on hand, but they couldn't have foreseen and planned on a possible rainstorm. That would be pure good fortune for them if it happened—and a bad break for Smoke and his companions.

When they had gone far enough to be well out of sight if the ambushers were still holed up in those trees, Smoke led the way up the ridge again. It was steeper and rougher here, which slowed them down, but eventually, they topped the rugged spine of land and started down the other side.

When they came to a shallow dry wash that also ran north and south, Smoke said, "This will take us down to where those bushwhackers were hiding. We'll come in right behind them if they're still there."

By now, the clouds boiling up in the west had swallowed the sun. It was late afternoon but looked more like dusk, and the clouds continued to thicken.

"A cloudburst is headed this way, Smoke," Cal said. "If it's already raining up in the mountains, this wash may not stay dry for long."

"I know, but it's the quickest way for us to travel.

I think we've got enough time to get where we're going before any water starts running in it. We can get out in a hurry, too, if we need to. The banks aren't steep enough that our horses can't climb them."

Cal nodded. Smoke knew the youngster wasn't going to argue with him. Cal would charge hell with a bucket of water if Smoke told him to. Knowing that just added to the responsibility Smoke felt for keeping him safe if he could.

At the same time, they both wanted to catch up to those rustlers, and Smoke knew Cal was willing to run any risk necessary, just as Smoke himself was.

They put their horses down the slope to the sandy bottom of the wash and turned south.

Off to their right, in the clouds gathering over the mountains, talons of brilliant lightning suddenly clawed the darkening heavens, and a rumble of thunder rolled down the rocky slopes.

Before this suddenly gloomy day was over, it might be the roar of gun-thunder washing over them.

CHAPTER 9

An ominous stillness hung in the air as Smoke and Cal followed the wash south. They hadn't gone very far when a sudden gust of wind buffeted them from the west. It was chilly for the time of year and carried the scent of rain.

"Here it comes," Cal said.

No sooner were the words out of his mouth than the storm struck. Rain sluiced down from the sky in heavy drops that pounded the riders like millions of tiny fists. Wind whipped it around and blew it under their hat brims into their faces.

Smoke and Cal hadn't brought along slickers, and it was doubtful that the garments would have done much good if they had, the way the wind was blowing. Within moments, they were soaked to the skin.

"Come on," Smoke yelled over the downpour's racket. "No point in trying to sneak up on them now! If they're still there, they'll never hear us coming!"

Both men urged their mounts into a hard run along the wash. A flash flood, if one was going to sweep through here, would come from behind them, so the farther south they moved, the better. As they rode, more lightning flashed overhead. Thunder boomed so loudly it seemed to shake the earth.

With this chaos surrounding them, it was difficult to tell how much time had passed or how far they had gone. Between the thickening clouds and the sheets of rain, Smoke and Cal couldn't see more than a few yards in front of them. But as they charged around a bend in the wash, they both spotted four men on horseback ahead of them.

In the flickering glare of frequent lightning bolts, Smoke saw one of the men look back over his shoulder. He must have spotted the two pursuers, because he poured on the speed. The others urged their mounts into hard gallops, as well.

The fact that they were trying to get away wasn't concrete evidence these men were the bushwhackers, but a moment later, they twisted around in their saddles as they fled and opened fire on Smoke and Cal. Spurts of orange muzzle flame blended with the nightmarish glare of lightning.

That was plenty of proof as far as Smoke was concerned.

The hurricane deck of a galloping horse was no place for accurate shooting, especially in the middle of a fierce thunderstorm. Smoke and Cal returned the fire anyway. Just as Smoke had mused earlier, gun-thunder played a grim harmony with the real thing.

One of the men up ahead threw his arms in the air and pitched out of the saddle. When he landed, he rolled over a couple of times and came to a stop in a motionless heap. As Smoke and Cal pounded closer, Smoke told the young cowboy, "Stay here and keep him covered just in case he's not hit as bad as it looked!"

"One of us got him! He's dead, Smoke!"

"Probably, but if he's not, I don't want him coming up behind us!"

That must have made sense to Cal. He reined in and stayed in his saddle as he pointed his Colt at the man lying face down in the wash's sandy bottom, which had turned to mud in the downpour.

At a slower pace, Smoke rode on after the other three men who had vanished around a bend. He had slowed down because he knew that if he charged blindly around that same bend, they might be waiting to blast him full of holes.

Instead of doing that, he angled his horse toward the wash's right-hand bank and urged the animal to climb it.

The horse's hooves slipped in the mud as it made a valiant effort to ascend the slope. For a second, Smoke thought it was going to lose its footing and fall out from under him, but the horse managed to stay up and struggled on to the top.

As they reached level ground, Smoke pulled his Winchester from its scabbard and dropped out of the saddle. He worked the rifle's loading lever and threw a round into the chamber as he ran ahead to the edge of the wash where it ran around the bend.

Sure enough, the other three bushwhackers were there below him, still mounted, with their guns aimed back the way they had come from. They were ready to spring another ambush, but they didn't know that their intended target had already slipped out of the trap.

Smoke brought the Winchester to his shoulder and shouted over the storm's racket, "Throw down your guns!"

He was willing to take the men prisoner if they were willing to surrender, but he didn't expect that to happen. He wasn't surprised when they yelled startled curses and twisted in their saddles to jerk their guns up and blaze away at him.

The Winchester cracked and bucked against Smoke's shoulder. One of the men went off his horse in a backflip, driven out of the saddle by the slug punching into his chest.

Smoke heard bullets singing around him as he worked the rifle's lever and shifted his aim. The Winchester blasted again, and one of the remaining ambushers slewed around, dropped his gun, and hung on to the saddle horn to keep from toppling off his horse. The animal took off at a wild run, still heading south.

The fourth and final man stopped shooting and banged his bootheels against his horse's flanks instead. The horse charged after the other one. Smoke fired again and saw the fleeing rustler's hat fly in the air. The man stayed glued to the saddle, though, as he leaned forward over the mount's neck to make himself a smaller target.

Smoke fired again, but the horse never broke stride. A few bounds took it beyond the thick curtains of falling rain. Smoke saw horse and rider only vaguely.

The man he had wounded was completely out of sight by now and the fourth man soon disappeared, as well.

Smoke's face was grim as he lowered the Winchester. He had hoped to take at least one of the bushwhackers alive so the man could be questioned. It looked like that wasn't going to work out.

Very little about today had worked out, he thought. Sally's fiesta had been interrupted by news of the rustling and killing, and now the thieves were going to get away with the stolen cattle. After a storm like this, tracking them was going to be impossible, particularly because the light was fading quickly, and any further pursuit would have to wait until morning.

But maybe he could learn something from the men he had shot, he told himself, even if neither of them had survived their wounds.

He went back to his horse and slid the Winchester into the saddle boot. Leading the horse, he carefully descended the bank into the wash. The slope was even more slippery now, but they managed to reach the bottom without any mishaps. Once they were there, Smoke mounted up and rode around the bend to check on the man he had blown out of the saddle.

The hombre was lying on his back with his arms flung out to the sides. His right leg was drawn up slightly. His eyes were open and stared sightlessly into the rain that had washed the mud from his face, which was lantern-jawed and stubbled with a sandy beard. His hair was long and tangled.

Smoke had never seen him before.

The dead man's horse was gone. It had followed the

other mounts into the storm. Smoke turned and rode back along the wash until he approached the spot where he'd left Cal and the first fallen bushwhacker.

"It's me, Cal," Smoke called. "Hold your fire."

Cal was level-headed and not likely to be trigger-happy, but it wouldn't hurt to let him know who was riding up to him. After being ambushed, he had to be a little tense.

"I'm here, Smoke," the young cowboy replied. "This fella hasn't moved."

There had been a chance the rustler was just wounded, but Smoke was pretty sure now that wasn't the case. Nobody would have stayed face down in the mud like that for so long unless they were dead. He reined in and dismounted, then hunkered on his heels next to the corpse. Gripping the man's shoulder, Smoke rolled him over onto his back.

His face was covered with mud, but the pelting rain washed that off in a hurry, not that it did any good. This man was a stranger, too. He had a round face and curly red hair, with piggish little eyes that were glassy in death.

"I never saw him before," Cal said. He pouched his iron now that he no longer needed to cover the man.

Smoke straightened. "Same thing was true with the other one I downed," he said. "There were two more, but they got away."

"You don't reckon they'd double back, do you?" Cal asked with a worried frown.

"It's possible, but not very likely. One of them was

hit, and they both looked like all they wanted to do was put as much distance behind them as they could."

The rain had slacked off slightly but still fell in a steady, pounding rhythm accentuated by peals of thunder. As the echoes of one particularly long rumble faded, Smoke and Cal heard a voice calling their names.

"That's Pearlie," Cal said.

Smoke lifted his voice. "Pearlie! Over here in this wash! Pearlie!"

Within minutes, Pearlie and the rest of the group that had pursued the rustlers appeared on the wash's bank. "Are you boys all right?" the Sugarloaf foreman asked. "We heard some shootin', but it didn't come from the trees where those bushwhackers were holed up. Wasn't nobody there when we checked it out."

"That's because they were over here in this wash trying to get away," Smoke said. "A couple of them managed to escape, but the other two didn't."

"Yeah, I can see that." Pearlie leaned over in the saddle and craned his neck to get a look at the dead man. "It's hard to tell in this rain, but I don't reckon I've ever seen that gent before."

"Neither have Cal or I."

"Let me take a look at the varmint," Matt Coolidge said. He dismounted and came down the slope, slipping and sliding a little. He joined Smoke and Cal and studied the dead man's face for a moment before shaking his head. "Nope. He's a stranger to me, too."

"That's probably to be expected," Smoke said. "After all, you haven't been in the valley very long."

"No, but I thought maybe the bunch that stole those

cattle might've followed us while we were drivin' 'em here. Maybe somebody we ran into back up the trail."

That explanation made sense. Smoke nodded and said, "This was probably the work of some drifting hard-cases who heard about the party at the Sugarloaf and figured it would be a good time to raid the Triangle B."

"If that's the case, we won't ever catch 'em, more than likely," Coolidge said as he shook his head ruefully. "This rain will wash out their trail." He shrugged and went on, "But the good thing is they might move on and not bother anybody else in these parts, just take whatever they make off those stolen cows and head for somewhere else."

"Could happen," Smoke agreed. "For now, we might as well load up the bodies of the two who got killed and head back to the Sugarloaf."

Cal said, "I don't imagine there'll be much of a party going on by the time we get there."

"If this frog-strangler makes it all the way to the Sugarloaf," Pearlie said, "that fandango will be plumb washed out!"

CHAPTER 10

The horse that had belonged to the first dead man was still hanging around. One of the Sugarloaf hands caught it and held the reins while the two bodies were draped over its back and lashed in place.

While they were doing that, Smoke searched the rustlers' pockets, as well as the saddlebags on the horse. He didn't find anything except the usual odds and ends a man carried around with him—cigarette makings, a few greenbacks, some gold and silver coins, folding knives, chewing tobacco, and strips of jerky. There was nothing to identify either man.

The cash didn't add up to much, which reinforced Coolidge's theory that these were drifters who had tried their hands at rustling, only to lose their lives in the bargain.

Darkness had settled down over the valley by the time the group returned to the Sugarloaf. The rain was no longer a downpour but fell now in a steady drizzle. Thunder rumbled and lightning flickered in the distance, well to the southeast. All the men were soaked and miserable.

The ranch house was ablaze with light. The big double doors on the main barn were open and light spilled from inside there, too. Smoke saw that quite a few people were in the barn, as well as the tables that had been outside in the middle of the day. They had been moved in out of the rain, along with the food, and more food had been brought from the house so that people could eat supper. A large crowd was still on hand, but the festive mood had disappeared.

"We don't want to carry those bodies in there where folks are eating," Smoke told Pearlie. "Take them to the blacksmith shop and leave them there. Better get some blankets to spread over them, too. There shouldn't be any women or children going in there, but just in case they do, there's no need to upset them with such a sight."

Pearlie nodded. "Sure thing, Smoke. Me and the boys will take care of it."

One of the other ranchers said, "I'm gathering up my family and heading home, Smoke. I want to get out of these wet clothes."

Several others in the group echoed that sentiment.

Sally must have been watching and waiting for Smoke's return. She came out of the house and stood on the covered porch, out of the rain, as she called to him. He rode over along with Cal and Coolidge, who had accompanied them here instead of going back to the Triangle B.

"Smoke, are you all right?" she asked as they reined to a halt in front of the porch.

"Soaked to the bone, but other than that, fine," he told her with a weary smile. He swung down from the saddle and handed his reins to Cal, who would tend to the horses.

Even wet and tired, Coolidge was polite. He lifted a hand to his hat brim and said, "Ma'am, do you happen to know whether my boss is still here, or has he gone back to the Triangle B?"

Sally didn't have to answer that question because Thaddeus Bolton emerged from the house at that moment and said sharply, "Matt, is that you?"

"Yes, sir."

"Did you find those da—" Bolton stopped short, glanced at Sally, and amended what he'd been about to say. "Did you find those rustlers and our cattle?"

"We got a couple of the rustlers, but the rest of 'em got away and took our stock with 'em."

"Where are the prisoners?" Bolton demanded, mis-understanding what Coolidge meant. "We'll make them tell us where the others took those cows."

Smoke shook his head as he stepped up onto the porch. "There aren't any prisoners," he said. "We had to kill those two. They're strangers in these parts and didn't have anything in their belongings to identify them, so we aren't going to learn anything from them."

"Blast it. Now what do we do?"

"Figured I'd head back to the ranch," Coolidge said. "Me and some of the boys can ride out there tomorrow to see if we can pick up the trail, but I'll tell you right now, sir, it ain't too likely that'll be possible after all this rain. It really came a gullywasher this evenin'."

Bolton waved a hand and nodded impatiently. "Yes, yes, whatever you think is best, Coolidge. Mrs. Bolton and I are going to spend the night here rather than returning home in this miserable weather. Mrs. Jensen was kind enough to offer her hospitality." He looked at Smoke. "I assume that invitation meets with your approval, Jensen?"

"Just about anything Sally wants to do meets with my approval," Smoke said. "But as far as I'm concerned, you're welcome to stay."

He noticed that Cal was still sitting there on horseback, holding the reins to Smoke's mount. Smoke figured that the young cowboy was waiting to see if Susannah Bolton was going to make an appearance out here on the porch. Her father was in a bad enough mood already without having Cal annoy him by paying too much attention to Susannah.

"Take those horses and tend to them, Cal," Smoke told him. "They're wet and tired, too."

Cal looked disappointed, but he said, "Sure, Smoke. Good night."

Cal turned away from the house. Coolidge had already ridden out of the ranch yard, heading back to the Triangle B. That left Smoke, Sally, and Bolton standing on the porch. Bolton took a cigar from his vest, put it in his mouth, and went back into the house without lighting up the cheroot.

Sally put a hand on Smoke's arm and said, "Come on inside and warm up. There's hot food and coffee ready for you, but you'll want to dry off and change clothes first."

"That sounds mighty good," Smoke admitted. It

seemed as if days had gone by since he'd ridden away from the Sugarloaf in pursuit of those rustlers.

And despite their best efforts, they had almost nothing to show for it.

Up in the bedroom he shared with Sally, Smoke stripped off the wet clothes and used the thick towel she had brought him to dry himself, rubbing vigorously to get the blood flowing better while Sally went back downstairs. Even though the weather was still fairly warm, hours of being soaked like that had put a chill in Smoke's bones. It felt good to be dry.

He had pulled on the bottoms from a pair of long underwear and a clean pair of denim trousers when the bedroom door opened. He finished buttoning the trousers as he looked up, expecting to see his wife in the doorway.

Instead, Emmaline Bolton stood there with a smile on her face, looking pleased with herself and not the least bit embarrassed.

"I'm sorry, Mr. Jensen," she said. "I didn't mean to barge in on you like this. I'm afraid I've gotten turned around. Your lovely wife said I could come up here and lie down for a few minutes, and I thought this was the room she told me to use."

"Are you not feeling well, Mrs. Bolton?" Smoke asked. He didn't believe what she had just told him about her reason for being here, but he was too much of a gentleman to call her a liar or even imply such a thing.

"I'm just a bit weary. It's been a very long day, you

know." She laughed. "Of course you know. It's been even longer for you, I suppose, chasing after those dreadful rustlers that way and getting into a gunfight with them." A frown creased her forehead. "You *are* all right, aren't you? I heard that two of the thieves were killed, but I didn't think any of the men who went after them were hurt."

"That's right, mostly," Smoke said. "My foreman Pearlie Fontaine got a little nick from a bullet, but it doesn't amount to much. Other than that, we're all fine, just wet and chilled and tired."

"Oh, but you're all dried off now, aren't you?"

Most women—especially respectable married women—would have babbled mortified apologies and beaten a hasty retreat by now if they'd walked in on a half-dressed man who wasn't their husband.

Not Emmaline Bolton, though. She stood there with one hand resting gracefully on the door jamb and looked as if she didn't intend to budge until Smoke finished putting on his clothes.

Smoke wasn't the sort of man to get flustered easily. He didn't do so now. Instead, he ignored the question she'd asked and said coolly, "There's a guest room a couple of doors down on this side of the hall. I expect that's the room Sally meant for you to use. I can show you if you'd like."

"That's not necessary, and I'm in no hurry. I'm feeling better now, anyway. I'm not sure that I still need to lie down—although the idea does have a certain appeal."

The smile on her face and the light in her eyes made it clear what she was talking about. Smoke didn't rise to the bait. He turned to the bed and picked up the clean blue shirt he had tossed there earlier. As he shrugged into the garment, he said, "I'm going down to get something to eat. It's been a long time since that dinner in the middle of the day."

Emmaline left the doorway and came into the room with an unmistakable sway to her hips. She didn't stop until she was close enough he could have reached out and touched her. For a moment, he thought that was what she was about to do. She half-raised a hand, and the way she was looking at his bare chest as he began buttoning up the shirt, he wouldn't have been surprised if she'd pressed her palm against his skin.

She lowered her hand, as if not quite ready to make such a daring approach, and said as he finished buttoning the shirt, "I'll go back down with you. I'm not tired at all now. In fact, I feel absolutely revitalized."

"If you'll excuse me, ma'am, I need to put my boots on—"

"Go ahead. It won't bother me. And you certainly don't have to call me ma'am, or Mrs. Bolton, either. My name is Emmaline . . . Smoke."

"Seems like a mighty informal way for a married man to talk to another man's wife."

She was even closer now. "Some formalities are highly overrated."

Blast it, she was going to kiss him! He could see that in her eyes. She was going to come up on her toes and put her arms around his neck and press her mouth to his, and he couldn't see any way to stop her from doing it other than putting his hands on her shoulders and physically holding her off. He didn't want to do that, didn't want to touch her at all, in fact, but it looked like he was going to have to—

"Oh, dear," Sally said from the doorway. "I must have gotten mixed up and told you the wrong room to use, Emmaline. This is my bedroom. Mine and Smoke's."

Smoke tried to keep his face expressionless and not show how relieved he was that Sally had shown up when she did. Sally's voice was polite enough, even friendly, but he heard a cool edge in it and Emmaline probably did, too.

Emmaline didn't react in any sort of guilty fashion, however. Moving very casually, as if she weren't the least bit startled, she stepped back and turned toward the door.

"I'm sorry, Sally," she said. "It's not your fault at all. I simply got turned around and opened the wrong door. And then when I saw Smoke, I wanted to ask him about what happened today. I was worried that he or some of the other men might have been hurt while they were out chasing those rustlers."

"I assured Mrs. Bolton that we were all fine except for that little scratch Pearlie got." Smoke saw the annoyed glance she shot at him when he called her Mrs. Bolton, but he ignored the reaction. "And then I told her you must have meant for her to use the guest room a little farther along this hall."

"That's right," Sally said. She held out a hand. "I'll show you, Emmaline."

"That's not necessary," Emmaline replied with a curt

shake of her head. "I'm feeling much better now. I believe I'll go back downstairs."

"That's a good idea." Sally's voice was all sweetness, but Smoke saw sparks flashing in her eyes.

Emmaline looked back at Smoke. "I hope you'll visit me at our ranch sometime, Smoke. I keep hearing gossip about what an adventurous life you've led, and I'd love to hear some of those stories firsthand."

"I'm afraid all those yarns are mighty exaggerated."

"If even half of them are true, you're quite a man."

Sally cleared her throat.

Emmaline threw a smile in her direction and then swept past her into the second-floor corridor. Sally watched her go and then came into the room, closing the door behind her.

"I'm going to scratch that brazen witch's eyes out," she said.

"Hold on," Smoke said. "You know you don't mean that."

"Don't be so sure." She shrugged and then admitted, "But probably not. Not yet, anyway. Just how much did she try to get away with?"

"I reckon it looked considerably worse than it was," Smoke said, stretching the truth a little. It had probably looked like Emmaline was about to kiss him, and he was convinced that had been her intention.

Sally crossed her arms over her bosom, blew out a breath, and said, "Well, at least I know that whatever she might have done, you wouldn't have reciprocated. You'd never throw me over for the likes of her. A married woman, and a shameless hussy, to boot!"

"I'd never throw you over for the likes of anybody," Smoke said. "It wouldn't matter who she was."

"I know. It's still nice to hear it, of course." She shook her head. "I never should have told them they could spend the night. Mr. Bolton was complaining about having to go all the way back to the Triangle B headquarters in the rain, so I just thought it would be the hospitable thing to do to offer them a room."

"Did their daughter stay, too?"

Sally nodded. "Yes, she's here in another of the guest rooms. She seems like a nice girl. Strong-willed and definitely with her own opinions, but I think she's all right."

"Strong-willed and opinionated." Smoke grinned. "Reminds me of somebody else."

"Put your boots on and come downstairs before the food and coffee gets completely cold," she said firmly. She turned and went to the door, where she paused and looked back at Smoke. "But if Emmaline Bolton ever tries anything else funny with you, there'll be hell to pay."

Smoke didn't doubt that for a second.

CHAPTER 11

Smoke ate in the kitchen rather than the dining room. He didn't see Emmaline Bolton after he came downstairs, and he was grateful for that. Sally had a nice thick slab of roast beef waiting for him, along with potatoes and biscuits and hot coffee to wash down the food.

She sat at the table to keep him company while he ate and explained that the other men who had gone along on the chase were having their late supper out in the barn with the cowboys from the other spreads who were staying overnight on the Sugarloaf.

"The hayloft's going to be full tonight," she said. "Several of the other ranchers and their families are staying here in the house, too."

"But there was still a guest room empty for Mrs. Bolton to use," Smoke commented. He knew why that was true, too. As he had expanded the original ranch house, he'd built it so there would be plenty of room for the large family he and Sally intended to have, one of these days. No children had come along yet, but it was only a matter of time.

Sally sniffed. "She never had any intention of using

that room. That was just an excuse for her to get upstairs where she hoped to sink her claws into you."

Footsteps in the hallway leading to the kitchen made Sally stop talking. She and Smoke both looked around as Thaddeus Bolton came into the room. Neither of them knew if he had overheard what they'd just been saying about his wife.

If he had, he gave no sign of it. Bolton had taken off his jacket but still wore his vest and tie and looked almost as stiff and formal as he had earlier in the day. He had a lit cigar in his mouth, but he took it out and said, "I hope you don't mind me smoking, Mrs. Jensen."

"No, that's fine," she assured him. "Would you like a cup of coffee?"

"No, thank you. I was hoping to talk to your husband."

Smoke took a sip of his coffee and said, "Go ahead."

Bolton glanced at Sally.

"Anything you want to say to me, you can say in front of my wife," Smoke said.

"This is about the cattle business," Bolton said as if that explained his reticence.

"Sally and I are equal partners in this ranch. Go ahead," Smoke told him again.

"Very well." Bolton cleared his throat. "What are we going to do about those rustlers?"

"We've already done all we can do right now," Smoke said as he leaned back in his chair. "With all that rain, it'll be impossible to follow them. We could send a search party in the same direction they were going and hope to pick up the trail eventually, but it would just be guesswork and pure luck if we found anything."

Bolton frowned. "So we do nothing? I just have to accept the loss of those cattle?"

"And the puncher who was killed shooting it out with the rustlers."

Bolton waved the hand that held the cigar between two fingers. "Of course, of course. A tragic thing. I intend to find out if the man had any relatives who should be notified. If he does, I can send his things and the wages he was owed to them."

"That would be a good thing to do. As for the stock, you took a solid hit, but your herd's big enough to absorb it."

"I know, but the principle of the thing bothers me."

"Me, too," Smoke said. "It's always bad when rustlers are prowling around. It's happened around here before, and more than likely it'll happen again."

"You mean those men will be back to steal more?" Bolton asked sharply.

Smoke's shoulders rose and fell. "It's impossible to say. The fact that the two we downed were strangers means the bunch might've been passing through. They could be in Wyoming in a few days, and we may never see them again."

"You think they're driving the stolen stock to Wyoming?"

"That's the mostly likely place," Smoke said, "but really, there's no telling. I thought I'd ride into Big Rock in the morning and talk to Monte Carson. He can send telegrams to all the lawmen in the southern part of Wyoming and ask them to be on the lookout for any suspicious cattle deals in their towns. The chances of that doing any good are pretty slim, but at least it's something."

Bolton puffed a couple of times on the cigar and then frowned in thought as he rubbed his chin. After a moment, he said, "*Something* isn't good enough. I was thinking it might be wise for us to put together some sort of armed force devoted to protecting the interests of the ranchers in the area."

"Like a cattleman's association? We have one. There's a local organization along with a larger one that covers the Western states, and most of us belong to it, as well."

"But neither of them patrols the valley, do they?"

"Well, no. The big organization has some mighty good range detectives who work for it, though. Two of them are old friends of mine."

"Detectives like that arrive on the scene after a crime has been committed. What we need are men who will not only track down outlaws but also put a stop to further outrages by determining who's responsible for such things—and dealing with them."

Sally said, "You're talking about vigilantes."

Bolton inclined his head toward her. "Call them what you will, but I've heard that such groups have been very effective out here in the West."

"That depends on what you mean by effective," Smoke said. "It's true that in places where there isn't any law, folks have to step up and take care of things themselves. But that can get out of hand mighty easily, too. Innocent men have been strung up for crimes they didn't commit. The organizers of such groups have used them to settle personal scores. Sometimes you wind up with more lawbreaking instead of less. It's just a different bunch doing it."

"That's not what I'm talking about," Bolton insisted. "Any such group that operated around here would have to be both well-organized and highly disciplined. How many deputies does Sheriff Carson have?"

The quick change in subject surprised Smoke a little but didn't throw him. He replied, "There are three regular deputies and a couple of men who help out when necessary."

"So half a dozen men, including the sheriff, are responsible for maintaining law and order in this entire valley."

"You can look at it that way," Smoke said.

"That doesn't seem like nearly enough. If the local ranchers have already formed a cattleman's association, it would be simple for them to hire armed men to patrol all the ranches and prevent rustling in the future."

Smoke could tell that Bolton was going to cling stubbornly to the idea. He said, "You could bring that up at the next meeting and see what the fellas think of it. That is, assuming you plan on joining."

"Absolutely, I do. When will this meeting take place?"

"There's one next week, as a matter of fact," Smoke said. "Wednesday evening, in the town hall in Big Rock."

Bolton put the cigar in his mouth, clamped his teeth on it, and gave a curt nod.

"I'll be there," he declared. "Thanks, Jensen. You'll see I'm right."

Smoke shrugged, not wanting to continue this discussion any longer.

Bolton turned to leave the kitchen, but he paused and said over his shoulder, "I'm curious. What would you call the group that went after those rustlers today, if not vigilantes?"

Smoke didn't have an answer for that.

The rain fell steadily most of the night, but along toward morning it finally stopped. By the time dawn crept in, the clouds were breaking up and the glow of approaching sunrise poked through in slanting reddish-gold rays.

Sally invited everyone who was still at the ranch to come into the house for breakfast. She had been up most of the night cooking and getting ready for the meal.

Smoke told her she shouldn't wear herself out like that, but she dismissed his concerns. Things hadn't gone the way she planned the day before, she told him, and she wanted to at least send her guests home having enjoyed a good hot breakfast.

The Sugarloaf crew ate in the house, as well, which meant the place was crowded. Cal hoped to see Susannah Bolton again. This might be his last chance to talk to her for a while.

Pearlie, who had a bandage on his cheek where the

bullet had nicked him, saw Cal looking around the dining room as they came in.

"If you're hopin' to spy that gal, you'd better forget it," he told the young cowboy. "You're lucky you didn't get in trouble for bein' alone in the barn with her yesterday. Best not to push that luck."

"I swear, you act like you think I'm going to do something loco, Pearlie. It's not like Susannah and I are going to run off and get married or anything like that."

"You'd better hope not. Her pa would have the marriage thrown out in court and see to it that you were sent to prison for kidnappin'."

Cal's outrage was genuine. "I'd never kidnap Susannah!"

"Yeah, I know that, but that's what some fancy lawyer would call it, and judges tend to side with fancy lawyers over scruffy young cowpokes."

"I just want to say good morning to her and, uh, ask her if I could come calling on her sometime at the Triangle B."

"You try ridin' over there and Bolton'll have his cowboys give you a good wallopin' again. I'll bet that hombre Hudson would still like to take a whip to you if he got the chance."

Cal knew his friend probably was right. He wouldn't get a friendly reception at the Bolton spread, especially if they knew he'd come courting.

Seeing Sally carrying in a platter heaped high with biscuits, Cal hurried over to take it from her and said, "Let me help you with that, Miss Sally."

"Thank you, Cal. I could have gotten it, but I appreciate you giving me a hand."

"I was wondering, uh, if you'd seen Miss Bolton this morning."

The smile she gave him held a trace of regret that echoed in her voice. "I'm sorry, Cal. Susannah left for home with her parents about half an hour ago. They didn't stay to have breakfast." With a cooler tone, she added, "I don't think Mr. Bolton could get out of here fast enough to suit himself."

"Oh," Cal said, sounding as crestfallen as he looked.

"But Susannah asked me to tell you something."

That made Cal's interest perk up immediately. "She did?"

"That's right. She said for me to tell you that she hopes to see you again sometime."

Cal felt a grin stretch across his face. "That's mighty nice of her," he said. "I hope I see her again sometime, too. Pearlie warned me against it, though. He acts like he thinks Susannah's father might dust my britches with buckshot."

"Pearlie is the best foreman anyone could ever hope for. But it could be that he's starting to forget what it's like to be young."

"Yes, ma'am. But I wouldn't let him hear you say that."

Sally laughed and said, "I certainly won't."

Two days passed with nothing unusual happening. On the morning of the third day, which was Tuesday,

Smoke and Sally headed into Big Rock, Smoke riding horseback while Sally skillfully handled the reins of the ranch buckboard. She was going to pick up supplies at Goldstein's Mercantile. He figured on passing the time of day with Louis Longmont at the gambler's saloon and restaurant.

Smoke also wanted to see if Monte Carson had had any response to the wires he had sent to lawmen in Wyoming, warning that a herd of stolen cattle might be headed their way. Smoke knew that was unlikely. A certain amount of rustling went on in many places, nearly all the time. Pinning down one particular bunch of wideloopers was difficult.

They were still about a mile from town when Smoke heard rapid hoofbeats drumming behind them. He reined in and told Sally, "Hold up a minute. Somebody's coming after us in a hurry."

Sally hauled back on the lines and brought the two horses hitched to the buckboard to a halt.

"Or someone's headed to Big Rock in a hurry," she said. "They don't necessarily have to be looking for us."

Logically, Smoke knew she was right. However, his instincts told him that the approaching rider was trying to catch up to them.

As usual, his gut wasn't lying to him. When the man on horseback came into view, Smoke recognized him as Cal Woods.

Cal drew up alongside them and stopped. Smoke asked, "Something wrong at the ranch?"

"Not our ranch," Cal replied, "but a rider from the

SB Connected showed up a while ago looking for you. He had news from Mr. Brant."

The SB Connected was a ranch in the northern part of the valley owned by a cattleman named Sam Brant. He had been in the valley for a couple of years and had been a good neighbor. A widower, he didn't socialize much, but he had been at the fiesta a few days earlier.

"Sam doesn't have trouble, does he?" Smoke asked.

Cal's face was grim as he nodded. "Yes, sir, he does. Rustlers hit his place last night."

"Oh, no," Sally said. "Was anyone hurt?"

"Nobody killed," Cal reported, "but after what happened last weekend, Mr. Brant put men on nighthawk duty to watch over his herd. One of them caught a bullet when the shooting started. He's expected to recover, though."

"That's good," Smoke said. "How many cattle did the rustlers make off with?"

"At least eighty head."

Smoke knew that Sam Brant ran only about four hundred head on his ranch, which was one of the smaller spreads in the valley, so losing that many of them would be quite a blow.

"Any of Sam's men get a good look at the thieves?"

"No, it was too dark. Mr. Brant sent riders out to all the other ranches first thing this morning to let them know what had happened. After his man showed up at the Sugarloaf, Pearlie figured you ought to be told right away instead of waiting until you and Miss Sally got back from town. What are you going to do, Smoke?"

Instead of answering the young cowboy directly,

Smoke turned to Sally and asked, "Do you mind going on into Big Rock without me?"

"Of course not. You're going to see Mr. Brant?"

"I think it would be a good idea. I'll find out as much as I can about what happened."

"You go ahead and do that," Sally told him. "Don't worry about me. I'll be fine."

"I know you will," Smoke said, "because Cal will go on into Big Rock with you and then accompany you back to the ranch."

The youngster looked dismayed. "Aw, Smoke, I thought maybe I'd go with you and maybe get a chance to chase some rustlers again."

"Not much chance of that. Those thieves will be long gone. But I wouldn't mind taking a look at the place where it happened. You never know what you might notice that could come in handy."

Cal sighed and nodded. "Sure. I'll look after Miss Sally."

Crisply, Sally said, "I'm right here, you know, and I don't need that much looking after. Or have you forgotten the first time we met, Cal?"

"Uh, no, ma'am. Not hardly. And I'm not likely to."

"Good." She smiled to take the sting out of the rebuke. "But I'll be happy to have your company."

She lifted the reins and flapped them against the horses' rumps, starting them toward Big Rock again. Cal lifted a hand to Smoke in farewell and rode after her.

Smoke turned his horse north and heeled it into a lope. Again, he didn't need a trail or a road to get where he was going. Once he had ridden over a piece of ground, he knew it well and would for all time.

As he rode, he mulled over the unpleasant news Cal had delivered. The idea that this was a second group of rustlers striking so soon after the first couldn't be ruled out, but that possibility seemed too farfetched for Smoke to take it seriously.

No, he told himself, this was the same bunch. And if that was true, it gave rise to another question. Was the gang large enough that some of them had driven the stock stolen from the Triangle B on out of the country while others returned to hit the SB Connected?

Or did this latest outrage mean they were holding Bolton's stock somewhere while they tried to steal more cattle and put together a larger herd?

That was possible, too, and if the gang had a hideout in the area, that gave Smoke something else to look for. He started thinking about places where outlaws could hold a stolen herd and keep it hidden.

With that occupying his mind, he almost didn't see the morning sun glinting off metal in time, but when he did, his reactions were lightning fast. He dived out of the saddle just before a rifle cracked and a slug ripped through the air where he'd been less than an eyeblink earlier.

CHAPTER 12

Smoke hit the ground hard, rolled over, and came up on one knee with a gun in each hand. The twin Colts roared and bucked as he poured a storm of lead toward a clump of rocks and brush fifty yards away.

Even while he was in mid-air, his keen eyes had spotted the muzzle flash of a second shot coming from that cover. He didn't know where that bullet had gone, but so far, he wasn't hit.

The shots he fired made the brush jerk and jump. Some of the slugs ricocheted off the rocks with high-pitched whines. When he had triggered three rounds from each gun, he leaped to his feet and dashed toward a nearby grassy hummock. He hoped the withering fire he had laid down was enough to make the bushwhackers duck for cover. With luck, it would take them a few seconds to recover and start shooting at him again.

High-heeled cowboy boots weren't made for running, but Smoke covered the ground pretty quickly. He was running so hard his hat flew off. Just as a shot cracked behind him and he felt as much as heard the wind-rip of a bullet past his head, he left his feet in a diving somersault that carried him over the hummock. Another chunk of ambusher's lead kicked up dirt that sprayed against his cheek as he rolled into cover.

Smoke heard a couple of bullets strike the hummock as he lay behind it on his back. Moving with the swift efficiency of a task he had performed thousands of times, he holstered one gun, plucked four fresh cartridges from the loops on his shell belt, and fed them into the other Colt's cylinder. Normally he carried his guns with one chamber empty so the hammer could rest on it, but that precaution went out the window during a fight.

When he had a full wheel in that gun, he repeated the process with the other revolver. The rifle had fallen silent. Smoke thought there was only one ambusher, but he could be wrong about that. Either way, whoever wanted him dead had decided not to waste any more bullets shooting at the hummock.

That didn't mean the varmint was gone, though.

Smoke lay there quietly, breathing easily, listening. A part of his brain wondered who had been lying in wait for him this morning. *Had* the bushwhacker been waiting for him? That conclusion seemed unavoidable.

However, the rifleman's identity was a problem that could be pondered later. Right now, living through this ambush was Smoke's top priority. To increase his odds of doing that, he rolled over onto his belly and lifted his head enough to take a good look at his surroundings.

Before the shooting started, he'd been riding downhill at a slight angle. A hundred yards away at the slope's base was a cluster of boulders with some hardy brush growing between them. It was a larger version of the rocks and brush where the bushwhacker was hidden. That would have been a better spot for the rifleman to hole up and wait, but for some reason he hadn't chosen it.

Smoke glanced back the way he had come from. He had just ridden out of some trees when he caught the reflection from the would-be killer's weapon. More than likely, the bushwhacker hadn't taken cover behind the larger rocks because they were twice as far away from where Smoke had ridden out into the open. The unavoidable conclusion was that he'd wanted to increase the chances of downing Smoke with the first shot.

That thought reminded Smoke of the other recent attempt on his life. In that case, the bushwhackers had opened fire too soon, when their target was still too far away. This was the opposite setup.

Did that mean they had learned their lesson and this rifleman was one of the same bunch of rustlers?

How was that possible? Smoke hadn't even known the gang had struck again until he was on his way into town with Sally. There was no way the rustlers could have predicted he would ride through here this morning.

Again, Smoke had to force his thoughts back to the problem at hand. The trees through which he had been riding curved back around in a wide sweep to his left and backed up to the rocks where the ambusher was hidden. If the man had left his horse in those trees, it was possible he could back away without being seen, get into cover, mount up, and work his way around until he was *behind* Smoke . . .

The instant that thought occurred to Smoke, he rolled over again, pushed up on his knees, and flung himself to the side. As he did that, a shot slammed out from the trees and the bullet kicked up dirt where Smoke had been lying.

On his belly now, propped up on his elbows and gripping both Colts, he opened fire on the spot where he caught a glimpse of movement in the shadows under the trees. Gun-thunder rolled across the landscape as flame belched from the muzzles of both guns.

The rifle cracked again, but judging by the sound of the bullet, it sailed well above Smoke. He triggered another pair of shots as the ambusher tried to shift position from one tree to another. Smoke thought the man stumbled as if he might be hit, but he couldn't be sure about that.

With the Colts still roaring and bucking in his fists, Smoke heaved himself to his feet and backed up the slope. When he was on the far side of the hummock, he dropped to the ground again. The little swell of earth wasn't very big, but it was enough to protect him as long as he kept his head down. He began reloading again.

The rifle had fallen silent. A moment later, a swift rataplan of hoofbeats replaced the gunfire. Smoke had a hunch that meant the bushwhacker was fleeing, but he couldn't be certain. It could be a trick intended to lure him out into the open again.

He stayed where he was with both guns loaded again. If that rifleman was trying to fool him, he would discover that Smoke could be as patient as he needed to be.

Only a few minutes had gone by, however, when Smoke heard more hoofbeats, these coming from the direction he'd been heading. The riders coming toward him could be more of the rustlers, in which case he'd be caught between a rock and a hard place.

Half a dozen men on horseback came into sight. Smoke thought he recognized the stocky figure leading the group, and as they drew nearer, he was sure of it. That was Sam Brant, owner of the SB Connected. Smoke was pretty sure the other men were some of Brant's ranch hands. He didn't have anything to fear from them.

Smoke got to his feet as the men reined in. He cast a glance toward the trees. If the bushwhacker wasn't gone, he might try one final shot at his intended target.

That didn't happen. Instead, Sam Brant leaned forward in his saddle and said, "It sounded like a small-scale war going on over here! Are you all right, Smoke?"

Smoke holstered both Colts and nodded.

"I'm fine," he said. "Somebody tried to bushwhack me. They came closer than I like to think about but never connected."

"I'm mighty glad to hear that. There's been enough bad news for a while." Brant sighed. "But I've got a hunch we haven't seen the end of it."

He was a man in late middle age with a square face and red hair that had gone mostly gray. Smoke had heard him talk about being a Texas Ranger when he was a young man, before he'd gotten married and settled down to become a cattleman. He had come to Colorado from the Brazos country of Texas after his wife died, wanting to leave those memories behind and make a fresh start.

"I heard about the trouble you had, Sam," Smoke said. "I'm sorry about the stock you lost but glad none of your men were killed."

"So am I. If I could get my hands on the sidewinders who stole those cattle, though—" Brant broke off with a shake of his head. "We were out looking around to see if we might be able to pick up their trail," he went on. "But then we heard all that shooting and figured we'd better come take a look. What happened to the men who bushwhacked you, Smoke?"

"I think there was just one," Smoke replied. "He took off for the tall and uncut a few minutes before you got here. I might have winged him, but I'm not sure about that. Even if he wasn't wounded, he probably spotted you fellas in the distance, coming this way, and decided it was about to get too hot around here for his liking."

"Well, if we helped run him off, I'm glad," Brant said with a nod. "Were you on your way to the SB Connected?"

"That's right. I got word that the rustlers hit you last night, and I wanted to see if there's anything I can do to help."

"Come with us and take a look around where it happened," Brant invited. "We didn't find anything, but I know that old mountain man friend of yours taught you how to track. You might see something we didn't."

"It's too bad Preacher's not here," Smoke said as he

picked up his hat. "He can track a single snowflake through a blizzard."

Brant told one of his men to catch Smoke's mount and bring it back. The horse had wandered off a couple of hundred yards before stopping to graze. Within minutes, Smoke was back in the saddle, and the group was headed toward the pasture where Brant's stock had been rustled.

As they rode, Brant said, "I've heard talk about how that new fella Bolton wants the local branch of the CPA to hire some range detectives."

"It's more than that," Smoke said. "He thinks we ought to fund an armed force to patrol the valley all the time."

"Like the cavalry, you mean?"

"Something like that. But it would be more like a group of vigilantes."

Brant frowned. "I'm not sure I care for that idea. When folks take the law into their own hands, things can get out of control. On the other hand, sometimes you don't have much choice except to do that. Let's face it, Smoke. Monte Carson spends most of his time keeping the peace in Big Rock. That's really all he and a handful of deputies can manage. The county sheriff over in Red Cliff is always short-handed when it comes to deputies, too. They can't be expected to break up a big gang of rustlers."

"You think it's a big gang?"

"At least half a dozen men raided my herd. Probably

more than that, but it's hard to tell when the ground's all churned to mush by hooves."

"You had men riding nighthawk?"

"Yeah," Brant said. "One of them, Chuck Stanley, caught a bullet when the shooting started. The fella who was riding with him, Walker Reeves, picked him up and had to get out of there before they both wound up filled with lead. Neither man got a real close look at the rustlers."

That sounded like about what Smoke had expected. The rustlers were still shadowy figures, striking out of the darkness, not hesitating to gun down anybody who got in their way.

With the SB Connected being a fairly small spread, it didn't take long for the riders to reach the spot where the shooting and rustling had taken place. Smoke spent more than an hour combing over the scene with Brant. He didn't find any tracks that he could identify as belonging to the rustlers' horses, nor had any of the gang left behind anything that would point to who they were or where they had gone.

"They're canny devils," Brant said after letting out a resigned sigh.

"You tried tracking the herd?" Smoke asked. There hadn't been any convenient rainstorm to wipe out the trail this time.

"We followed them a couple of miles before we lost them in a really rocky stretch of the foothills. Rough going for cattle but effective at hiding their trail."

Smoke nodded slowly. He tugged on his right earlobe as he frowned in thought.

"Were they anywhere close to the creek that runs across the western part of the Sugarloaf and the Triangle B?" he asked.

"The Triangle B . . . ? Wait, that's what Bolton calls the spread he bought, isn't it?"

"That's right."

"I'd say where we lost the trail was a mile or two on the other side of that creek," Brant said. "Why?"

"The rustlers drove the stock they stole from Bolton through the same general area," Smoke replied.

"Then I'm not surprised they used it for a getaway with my stuff. If something works one time, it's liable to work again."

"That's true," Smoke allowed. "Are you going to be at the association meeting tomorrow night, Sam?"

"I figured I'd go. I usually do. Why?"

"I've got a hunch Bolton is going to join the association and then ask for a chance to speak. He wants to see if he can convince the rest of us to go along with his idea for putting a stop to the rustling."

"You mean the vigilantes?" Brant rubbed his chin. "I've got to tell you, Smoke, as much as I don't cotton to the whole idea, I'm not sure but what it's the best way to put a stop to this. And we've got to put a stop to it, one way or another. If it comes to a vote, I might have a hard time voting against it."

Smoke said, "I expect some of the others will agree with you. Men will want those rustlers corralled before their herds get hit, and you can't blame them for feeling that way."

"How about you, Smoke?" Brant asked. "How are you going to vote?"

"I reckon I'll have to wait and see what Bolton has to say first," Smoke said.

CHAPTER 13

The regular meeting of the Sugarloaf Valley branch of the Cattlemen's Protective Association was scheduled to begin at seven o'clock in the Big Rock Town Hall, but most of the ranch owners began to arrive well before that time. Some brought their wives and children with them, and the families had supper together in various of the settlement's restaurants before the men headed for the meeting.

Sally had come with Smoke, and Pearlie and Cal had ridden into town with them. Smoke was glad to have Pearlie along; as the Sugarloaf's foreman, he was intimately involved with all the decisions when it came to running the ranch.

Cal was just hoping to catch a glimpse of Susannah Bolton again, Smoke knew, but there was no guarantee Thaddeus Bolton would bring his wife and daughter to town with him. In fact, it seemed more likely to Smoke that he wouldn't. Bolton didn't strike him as the sort of man who gave much weight to his wife's opinions, and he certainly wasn't the kind to listen to advice from his daughter.

When they got to Big Rock, Cal tended to the buckboard team and the saddle mounts he and Pearlie had ridden. Smoke and Sally headed for Longmont's while Pearlie and Cal planned to eat at Lambert's Restaurant. Pearlie had declared that he was in the mood for some of the "throwed rolls" Lambert's was known for. They were the best rolls in this part of the country, the foreman had said—other than the ones Sally baked, of course.

As they strolled through the late afternoon light toward Longmont's, Sally commented, "I'm not sure I've ever understood the appeal of having people throw rolls at you."

Smoke chuckled. "That's just how they do it, and you've got to admit, the rolls are good. So's the other food they serve there."

"Well, yes, but what if you try to catch one of them and miss?"

"Somebody else'll probably snag it for you. It's always entertaining to eat there, but I prefer the table Louis sets."

"So do I," Sally agreed.

The gambler welcomed them and ushered them to his private table. A couple of other ranchers were eating in Longmont's. Smoke nodded a greeting to them as he and Sally walked through the room.

"Big Rock is busy this evening," Louis said as they sat down to their meals. "And there's an air of tension I don't normally feel when the association has its meetings."

"Everybody's on edge because of the rustling," Smoke said. "So far that gang has run off more than a hundred head of cattle, killed one man, and wounded another. Wounded two, counting the nick Pearlie got when we were chasing them. I reckon most folks feel like it's only a matter of time before the situation gets even worse."

"You believe the same outlaw gang is behind both raids so far?"

Smoke nodded. "I don't have any proof of that, but I do believe it. I have a hunch it's a big, well-organized bunch, and we know they're ruthless."

"How can you stop something like that?" Louis asked.

"That's what we're going to be talking about tonight. I think Thaddeus Bolton has some idea."

Sally said, "I know that wife of his has ideas."

Louis cocked an eyebrow inquisitively.

"That's nothing we need to get into," Smoke said. "Anyway, it doesn't have anything to do with the rustling, and that's why we're here in town tonight."

"I'm told that Mrs. Bolton is a beautiful woman," Louis murmured.

"Very beautiful," Sally said. "If you like that type."

"And what is that?"

"The type that can't be trusted—especially around other women's husbands."

"I thought we weren't going to talk about this," Smoke said.

"I've said all I have to say," Sally replied serenely.

Smoke didn't believe she was actually jealous—well, not too much, anyway—but he was just as glad when the conversation moved on to other subjects. Smoke told Louis what they had found out about the rustlers so far, which didn't amount to much of anything, and then said, "I've got a few ideas stirring around in the back of my head, but it's too soon to say anything."

"You're among friends," Louis pointed out.

"Yeah, but I don't like to accuse anybody of anything until I'm pretty sure I'm right."

They went on eating and finished off the meal with a dish of apple pie and cream. Smoke drank the last of a second cup of Longmont's finest coffee and then asked Sally, "Are you coming along to the meeting?"

She toyed with the stem of her wineglass. "Do you think Mrs. Bolton will be there?"

"I don't have any earthly idea," Smoke said. "I kind of doubt it, though. She didn't strike me as the sort of woman who'd enjoy sitting around at a meeting and watching a bunch of men argue."

"And neither am I," Sally said. "Besides, you'll tell me everything that's decided."

"Of course, I will."

"In that case, I believe I'll have another glass of this excellent wine while I sit here and visit with Louis."

The gambler sat forward and smiled. "Why don't I have Johnny fetch us the bottle?"

"I think that's a superb idea," Sally said.

Smoke hid a grin. If the tables were turned, he could have exhibited some jealousy over Sally's decision to spend the evening here in a saloon with a suave, sleekly handsome gambler. But he knew he didn't have anything to worry about, just as, deep down, Sally knew she didn't have to worry about him and Emmaline Bolton.

"I'll be back," he said as he got to his feet.

"We'll be here," Sally told him with a smile.

Smoke chuckled again as he left the saloon to head for the town hall. As he approached the building, he saw a number of men going inside.

And rolling along the street toward him, with its fancy trim shining even in the fading dusk, was the buggy belonging to Thaddeus Bolton. The man from Tennessee was at the reins. His foreman, Matt Coolidge, rode alongside.

However, Smoke didn't see any sign of Emmaline, and he wasn't too proud to admit to himself that he felt a mite relieved about that.

Smoke reached the building's porch as Bolton brought the buggy to a halt in front of the town hall. Coolidge reined his horse to a stop beside the buggy and nodded to Smoke.

"Evenin', Mr. Jensen," the Triangle B foreman said. "Good to see you again."

"You, too," Smoke replied. "Any more trouble out there on your spread?"

"Not so far. But that don't mean it ain't lurkin' right around the corner."

Bolton said, "If it is, we're going to put a stop to it before those villains have a chance to carry out any more crimes."

"I hope you're right," Smoke said.

Bolton stepped down lithely from the buggy and looped the team's reins around the hitch rail. Coolidge swung down from the saddle at the same time. They joined Smoke on the porch.

"Did your foreman come in with you?" Coolidge asked.

Smoke nodded. "Pearlie will be along soon, I expect. He and Cal stopped at Lambert's for supper."

"Calvin Woods?" Bolton asked with a frown. "He's here tonight?"

"He is."

Bolton grunted. "Then it's a good thing I left Susannah at home. She wanted to come into town with us, but I told her in no uncertain terms that she wasn't going to."

"Cal's a fine young man," Smoke said. "You don't have to worry about him."

"I especially don't have to worry about him if I never allow him to get anywhere near my daughter ever again." Bolton turned toward the door and gestured sharply at Coolidge. "Come on, Matt."

Coolidge gave Smoke a friendly nod as he followed his employer into the town hall. Smoke went in behind them.

The meeting hadn't come to order yet. Conversation filled the air in the big room as the association members talked among themselves. There was a little laughter, but for the most part, the discussion was solemn. The men were justifiably worried about the violence that had taken place and the stock that had been stolen.

This evening the room was set up for a meeting with numerous rows of chairs facing a table in front. Town socials were held in here, too, and on those occasions, the floor would be cleared for dancing, and the musicians would stand on a small platform at the front of the room. Nobody was in a celebratory mood tonight, though.

Smoke lingered in the back of the room near the door,

waiting for Pearlie and Cal. They showed up a few minutes later. Cal craned his neck and looked around the room.

"You're out of luck," Smoke told him. "Susannah's not here. She wanted to come but her pa wouldn't let her."

"That's a shame," Cal said. "Susannah seems like a mighty smart girl. I'm sure she'd be interested in what goes on in a meeting like this."

"A lot o' wranglin', that's what usually goes on," Pearlie said. "I don't expect tonight to be any different."

Neither did Smoke, but he would reserve judgment and wait to see what happened.

After a few more minutes, Jackson Crowe, the current president of the local association, walked to the front of the room and went behind the table. He was an older man with thinning gray hair who looked more like a teacher or minister than a rancher, but his spread was one of the best in the valley and he was widely respected, which was responsible for his position as president.

Crowe didn't wield a gavel like a judge, but when he raised his voice and said in clear tones, "All right, fellows, settle down so the meeting can come to order," everyone in the room did what he requested with no hesitation. The place quieted down within moments.

Crowe waited a few seconds longer and then said, "All right, this meeting of the Sugarloaf Valley branch of the Cattlemen's Protective Association is officially underway, Jackson Crowe, presiding. I'll ask our secretary, Walt Hendryx, to read the minutes of the last meeting. Go ahead, Walt."

For the next few minutes, Crowe dealt with the details necessary to follow parliamentary procedure. When the minutes had been read and approved and a couple of items of old business dealt with, the gray-haired cattleman cleared his throat and said, "Now, we'll move on to new business—"

Before he could finish, Thaddeus Bolton was on his feet.

"I have some new business," Bolton said. "I'd like to join your organization."

Crowe frowned. "Mr. Bolton—yes, I know who you are—you need to speak to our secretary about that. Until then, you have no voice in this room."

"So you're going to try to shut me up?" Bolton said defiantly. "I believe this is the Cattlemen's Protective Association. I'm a cattleman, and my interests need protecting!"

"There's a way to do this according to the rules—"

"All right, all right. Let's get this out of the way." Bolton turned to Walt Hendryx. "How much are the dues?"

"They're, uh, twenty dollars a year," Hendryx replied.

Bolton must have known that already because he was prepared. He took a gold double eagle from his pocket, walked over to where Hendryx was sitting, and handed the coin to him.

"There are my dues. My name is Thaddeus Bolton. I own the Triangle B Ranch. What else do you need to know to make my membership official?"

Hendryx shook his head. "I reckon that's all."

"Very well, then." Bolton looked challengingly at Jackson Crowe.

The older man sighed. "All right. Write his name down in the book, Walt. Mr. Bolton, I reckon you've got the floor."

"Thank you." Bolton turned to face the assembled men. His attitude changed in front of their eyes. "First of all, allow me to apologize. I know it looks like I've bulled my way in here and been disrespectful to your president." He turned toward the table. "Mr. Crowe, my sincere apologies. I'm just so upset about what's happened. One of my men was killed, you know, a loyal man who lost his life trying to protect my cattle from those unprincipled thieves."

Watching and listening, Smoke knew exactly what Bolton was doing. He had looked out at the men assembled in this room and realized that he was on the verge of getting off on the wrong foot with them. They didn't like his abrasive and condescending manner. Unless he changed the way they perceived him, he wouldn't be able to persuade them to go along with what he wanted.

And getting what he wanted was always going to be the most important thing to Thaddeus Bolton, Smoke realized, no matter what he had to do to get it.

Mentioning the cowboy who had been gunned down instead of the stock he'd lost was a good move by Bolton, as well, making it easier for these cattlemen to sympathize with him. Cowboys were known for "riding for the brand," but the brands for which they rode had to stand up for them, too.

Crowe nodded in acceptance of Bolton's apology

and waved a hand for him to proceed, saying, "Go on, Mr. Bolton."

Bolton turned toward the association's members and said, "You all know that I've lost some of my herd to rustlers. Ruthless outlaws who didn't hesitate to gun down my rider Joe Archibald. Since then, they've also struck at one of the other ranches, the SB Connected, which I believe is owned by Sam Brant. Mr. Brant, are you here?"

Sam Brant stood up and said, "Yeah, I sure am."

"I understand one of your men was wounded, Mr. Brant?"

"That's right. When those rustlers hit my herd, they shot Chuck Stanley." Brant looked around. "A lot of you fellas know Chuck. He's a fine hombre. He didn't deserve to get ventilated by some widelooping skunks!"

Several men in the crowd called out their support for that statement.

"We're kindred spirits, Mr. Brant," Bolton said, "both victims of these lawbreakers." His voice rose a little and took on a dramatic tone. "It's only a matter of time until they attack the rest of you! They'll steal your cattle and gun down your riders unless we put a stop to their reign of terror and lawlessness!"

In a few minutes of skillful speaking, the ranchers had gone from disliking Bolton to agreeing with what he said. His emphatic statements drew enthusiastic responses of support.

Jackson Crowe said, "You sound like you've got something in mind, Mr. Bolton. What is it?"

Bolton paced back and forth a couple of times before

he answered. He was a showman, Smoke thought, and knew how to keep an audience's attention on him.

"First of all, let me say that I mean no disrespect to Sheriff Carson," he began as he stopped pacing. "I've met the man only once, but I could tell that he's an honest, forthright lawman. But he's only one man. Even with the help of his deputies, there's only so much he can do. He can't be everywhere at once."

"Neither can anybody else," Smoke said.

For a second, irritation flashed in Bolton's eyes. After everything he had done earlier, though, he couldn't very well complain about being interrupted.

Instead, he smiled and said, "You're absolutely right, Mr. Jensen. No one lawman can cover this entire valley. That's why, in addition to Sheriff Carson and his deputies, we need a group of men of our own, men who work for the CPA, riding the range night and day, protecting our herds and the loyal ranch hands who work for us."

That wasn't exactly what Smoke had said, but before he could point that out, one of the other men said, "The organization's regional office down in Texas has range detectives working out of there. We can request help from them any time we need it."

"And they'll do what?" Bolton asked. "Send a couple of men who won't get here until long after the thieves and murderers have struck again?" He shook his head. "No, the only strategy that stands a chance of working is to have men—armed men, capable men—ready to meet the attacks when they come. Ready to fight off the rustlers and make them pay the price for their ruthless audacity!"

Another rancher stood up, scratched his head, and said, "So we ought to hire armed guards, is that what you're sayin', Mr. Bolton?"

"Not simple guards. Fighting men!"

"But you can't hire enough men to cover the whole valley. Not without callin' in the army or something like that."

Bolton nodded. "I understand. It's not an iron-clad solution, by any means. Practically speaking, no, we can't have men everywhere at once. But if we have an armed force patrolling the valley on a regular basis, the chances of them being close enough to either fight off a raid or go after the rustlers immediately will be greatly improved. You all know that the sooner the pursuit starts, the better the odds of catching the rustlers."

What Bolton was saying made perfect sense. No one could argue with the logic of it. Yet Smoke was convinced that, in practical terms, the idea would not work.

And every idea, he thought, could also have unintended consequences.

That led him to stand up and say, "What you're talking about is bringing in hired guns. That's even worse than vigilantes."

"It takes men who are good with their guns to fight such a threat effectively," Bolton countered. "And I believe our local sheriff was once considered a hired gun, Mr. Jensen—as was your own foreman."

Pearlie was on his feet instantly, saying, "That was a whole heap different—"

"Was it?" Bolton cut him off. "Didn't you take money to come into this valley and fight other men hired by your employer's enemies?" He smiled. "Perhaps you're right. This situation *is* different. What I'm suggesting is that we hire men to protect our homes, our families, our livelihoods. That's not nearly as mercenary a goal, is it, Mr. Fontaine?"

Smoke wasn't sure how Bolton had found out about Pearlie's and Monte's backgrounds, but it didn't matter. Not every man in the room was nodding in agreement with the newcomer, but enough of them were.

Pearlie just looked mad, but Smoke caught his eye and gave a tiny shake of his head. It wouldn't help anything for Pearlie to fly off the handle, even though such a reaction might be justified.

Smoke said, "What you're saying sounds reasonable, but these things have a way of getting out of hand. I've seen it happen before."

Bolton chuckled, but it wasn't a pleasant sound. "Why, Jensen, you sound almost timid. I wouldn't have expected that from a man of your reputation. I'm told that you've taken the law into your own hands many times over the years, such as when you went into a town taken over by outlaws and wiped them out to avenge the murder of your wife and child."

Smoke stiffened. Bolton hadn't needed to bring Nicole and little Arthur into this.

Bolton wasn't finished. "In fact, I believe you've been known to say that you never killed a man who didn't need killing. But you decided that, Jensen, not the law. Isn't that true?" Without giving Smoke a chance to answer, Bolton turned to the other men again. "Surely all of you can see that what I'm suggesting is for a noble cause, the cause of protecting everything we've worked for. There's no personal vengeance involved in the plan I'm suggesting, only a practical matter of self-defense. We have to put a stop to this rustling before it ruins the whole valley!"

Several men, caught up in the emotions of Bolton's words, let out excited whoops. Jackson Crowe waved his arms and shouted, "Settle down, settle down!"

Gradually, the hubbub in the town hall subsided. Once it had, Crowe said, "You've done some pretty speechifying, Mr. Bolton, but do you have a motion to make, now that you're a member of this organization?"

"I do, Mr. Crowe. I move that we organize a protective force to patrol the valley and protect the ranches from rustlers, as much as is practically possible, and in the event that the thieves do manage to strike again, our men will track them down and bring them to justice."

"I'll second that motion," one of the other ranchers called out.

"All right," Crowe said. "Those in favor, say aye."

The ayes weren't unanimous, by any means, but the question drew a rousing response.

"And those opposed?"

The nays were numerous but clearly not as many as those in favor.

"The motion passes," Crowe said. "Mr. Bolton, since this was your idea, I'll get together with you and a couple of the other fellows, and we'll work out the practical details of putting your plan into action."

"Any time, Mr. Crowe," Bolton said with a satisfied smile on his face. "I'm at your service."

Quietly, Pearlie said to Smoke, "You didn't vote with the fella, Smoke. What are you gonna do about this?"

"There's nothing I can do," Smoke replied. "Bolton won the day fair and square."

"Maybe so, but I hope this don't blow up in everybody's face!"

"So do I," Smoke said, nodding slowly. "So do I."

CHAPTER 14

Not surprisingly, Smoke wasn't asked to be part of the group that handled hiring and organizing the force of regulators, as folks soon began referring to them. It was a common name often used when a group of professional gunmen were called in, although such tactics were usually employed during range wars. This trouble was much different from that. The valley's ranch owners were all united instead of battling among themselves.

Bolton acted with the swift efficiency of the successful businessman he had been back in Tennessee. Since Sam Brant had also suffered losses to the rustlers, he was invited to join Bolton, Jackson Crowe, and a couple of other men in putting together the group of regulators. Smoke knew and trusted all the men, other than Bolton, and hoped they would keep things from getting out of control.

He went into Big Rock a week later with Pearlie to pick up some fencing supplies. While Pearlie was seeing to it that the supplies were loaded into the wagon they had brought into town, Smoke walked over to the sheriff's office to say hello to Monte Carson and visit with him for a few minutes.

Monte glanced up from the paperwork spread out on his desk when Smoke came into the office. Without waiting for a greeting from the visitor, he said, "Are you sure you want to associate with a worthless varmint like me, Smoke? I never caught an outlaw in my life, to hear some fellas tell it."

Smoke grinned and hung his hat on one of the hooks on the wall just inside the door. He took hold of a ladder-back chair in front of the desk, turned it around, and straddled it so he could rest his arms on the back.

"I don't think that's exactly what Thaddeus Bolton said about you, Monte," he told the sheriff. "He just said you're stretched too thin. You can't keep up with everything that happens in the valley. I've heard you make the same complaint yourself, so there's some truth to it."

Monte snorted. "Yeah, but when I complain about it, I'm trying to get money from the county to hire more deputies, not bringing in a bunch of hardcases to replace me."

"We don't know who they're going to bring in yet."

Monte made a face and said, "We know the type they're going to be, though. In fact, Pearlie and I were right there with them in a lot of fights, even though I'm kind of ashamed to say it now."

"Nothing to be ashamed about," Smoke told him. "Both of you tried to make sure you were fighting on the right side. Any time you found out you weren't, including in that business with Tilden Franklin, you got out of those messes in a hurry."

"Let's change the subject," Monte said. "I'd just as soon not remember all that. How's Sally?"

"Fine as can be."

They chatted idly for a few more minutes until the office door opened again and Pearlie came in this time. He seemed to be in a hurry, and his craggy face wore a worried expression.

"Smoke, you ain't gonna guess who I just saw ride into town." Pearlie glanced at the sheriff and added, "Howdy, Monte."

"Howdy to you, too," Monte said. "Do I get a guess?"

"You might as well. You're acquainted with the hombre, too. Better than Smoke is, come to think of it."

"Why don't you just go ahead and tell us?" Smoke suggested.

"All right, I will. It's Deke Stratten."

Monte sat up straighter. "Stratten!"

"I know the name," Smoke said. "I don't recall ever crossing his trail, though."

"You'd remember it if you had," Monte said. "He's an ugly son of a gun, and just about the coldest-eyed gent I ever ran into." He put his hands on the desk and pushed himself to his feet. "Are you sure it's Stratten? I heard rumors that he'd been killed in some big dust-up in Montana."

"Like you said, you don't forget somebody that ugly. Anyway," Pearlie went on, "he talked to me. He remembered when we rode for the same outfit down in Texas. It was him, all right."

"He's a hired gun, isn't he?" Smoke said. "Got a reputation for being fast and ruthless."

"That's him, and he deserves ever' bit of that rep." Pearlie took a breath. "What's more, he's the one Bolton's bringin' in to head up that bunch of regulators."

Monte shook his head. "I hate to hear that. Stratten's a cold-blooded snake. There's no telling how many men he's killed after claiming they were rustlers, but I've heard that not all of them were actually guilty."

"After I'd drifted on from that job down in Texas, Stratten and a bunch of hombres ridin' with him strung up half a dozen men at once. Another time, they burned out a fella they claimed was hidin' some outlaws, but all they really managed to do was kill some women and kids." Pearlie's face was set in bleak lines as he continued, "Of course, the men Stratten was workin' for were rich enough they had the law in their pockets. The whole thing got swept under the rug."

Monte clenched a fist and thumped it on the desk. "That's not gonna happen here, by grab! I'll see to that."

"See to what?" a man's gravelly voice drawled from the doorway.

Pearlie had left the office door open when he came in. None of them had seen the man who'd walked up outside and now lounged in the doorway with his left shoulder propped against the jamb.

Smoke stood up smoothly from the chair where he'd been sitting. Every instinct in his body was on full alert. All it took to prompt that reaction was looking at the newcomer and realizing what sort of man he was.

He was tall and lean almost to the point of gauntness, and that showed up the most in his lantern-jawed face. The skin seemed so tight it resembled a skull. The deep-set eyes burned with life, though. It was a cold fire, but still a fire.

His black hat was thumbed back on a bald pate, adding to the illusion that the men in the office were looking at a walking cadaver. His eyebrows were startlingly black, though, and his cheeks were shadowed with equally black stubble.

That aura of darkness continued with the black shirt, trousers, and boots he wore. The gunbelt strapped around his waist was black, as well. The gun butt sticking up from the attached holster sported walnut grips. A knife with a staghorn handle was sheathed on his left hip. The weapons were the only things about him that weren't either black or pale, unhealthy-looking skin.

"Hello, Deke," Monte said, although the greeting held no friendliness or warmth.

Deke Stratten nodded. "Monte. Fontaine told me you were here in town." The gunman straightened from his casual pose and ambled into the room, coming closer to the desk as he went on, "And wearing a tin star. I'll be honest with you, Monte, I never thought I'd see the day."

"Yeah, well, I reckon everything changes sooner or later."

Stratten shook his head. "Maybe so, but when I heard rumors that Monte Carson had become a lawman, I didn't believe them. Any time somebody told me that, I said there had to be some sort of mistake. Now I see it with my own eyes."

"What do you want, Deke?"

Stratten's bony shoulders rose and fell. "Can't a fella stop by to say hello to an old friend?"

"I don't recall us being what you'd call amigos."

"Suit yourself, but we fought on the same side most of the time and I was always fond of you, Monte." Stratten hooked his thumbs in his gunbelt and went on, "Call this visit a matter of professional courtesy, then. When I'm going to be working somewhere, I like to let the local law know about it just to make sure there aren't any mis-understandings farther along the trail."

"Just what sort of work are you fixin' to do?"

Monte already knew the answer to that question, Smoke mused, but he supposed the lawman wanted it to be a matter of record.

"Some friends of mine and I have been hired by the local cattlemen's association to serve as guards for their ranches. So I reckon we're in the same line of work— enforcing the law."

"You can't do that, not officially."

"Sure we can," Stratten said. "A man's got a right to protect his property, doesn't he?"

Monte jerked his head in a nod.

"And that includes hiring somebody to help him protect it," Stratten continued. "You know that falls well within the bounds of the law, Monte. You've been in the same situation yourself."

"Not from this side of the badge, I haven't," Monte snapped. He drew in a breath. "But I reckon you've got a point, legally speaking. There are lines you can't cross, though."

"Sure. We understand that."

"See that you do understand—and that you don't cross them."

Stratten turned toward Smoke and gave him a cool smile. "You've been standing there all along, stranger, without saying anything. Monte, introduce me to your friend."

Smoke saved Monte from having to do that. He said, "My name's Jensen. Smoke Jensen."

Stratten raised one of those unnaturally black eyebrows. "Smoke Jensen," he repeated. "I kind of thought that might be you. Pearlie mentioned that he's riding for your ranch these days. The Sugarloaf, is that right?"

"Pearlie does more than just ride for the Sugarloaf. He's the foreman and one of the top hands in the valley."

"Ol' Pearlie always was good at whatever he set his mind to doing." Stratten paused for a moment and then added, "I suppose you're a member of the local cattlemen's association, Mr. Jensen?"

"I certainly am."

"Then you're entitled to protection provided by me and my men, too." The boss of the regulators smiled. "If you have any trouble with rustlers, you just let us know. We'll get right on that for you."

A big part of Smoke wanted to knock that smirk down Deke Stratten's throat. Stratten must have sensed that. Smoke saw the anticipation dancing in the gunman's eyes.

More than likely, Stratten hadn't come in here to force a showdown with Smoke or anyone else, but the man's natural arrogance goaded him on and wouldn't allow him to back down.

A man who made his living with a gun couldn't afford to show any weakness. Word of that always got around, and it emboldened other men to push their luck against him.

These days, Smoke didn't live by the gun. It was a tool he used when he needed to, that was all. He was a rancher, a husband, a friend and neighbor. He knew he had a reputation as a fast gun, but he had earned it through his actions, not his words, and certainly not by preening.

So in response to the unspoken challenge on Stratten's face, he just nodded and said coolly and calmly, "I'll remember that."

Let the hired gun interpret *that* however he wanted to.

Clearly, Stratten was a little surprised that Smoke didn't rise to the bait. After a moment, he jerked his head in a nod and bit off, "Fine." He turned back to Monte. "Be seeing you around, Sheriff."

"I expect to be notified if you come across any illegal activity," Monte said.

Straten smiled, and as thin as his lips were, that made the expression little more than a slash across his face.

"A man can expect just about anything he wants to," he said. "Doesn't mean he'll always get it."

With that, he turned and stalked back out through the still-open door.

Monte glared after him and said to Pearlie, "Shut that door, would you? I don't want any more snakes crawlin' in here."

"So that's Deke Stratten," Smoke said once Pearlie had closed the office door. "I reckon he lives up to what I've heard about him."

"Or down to it," Monte said. "What are we gonna do about this, Smoke?"

"I'm not sure there's anything we can do about it. Like Stratten says, a man's got a right to hire somebody to protect his property. As long as Stratten and those other regulators don't break any actual laws, I don't see how you can arrest them or even justify running them out of the valley."

Pearlie said, "I reckon it's possible they might catch those rustlers, or at least force 'em to move on."

"If they catch anybody stealing cattle, you can bet they won't bring them into town for the law to deal with," Monte said. "They'll just hang them, right then and there."

"That's always been considered an acceptable way to deal with that problem," Smoke pointed out. "There have been times when the three of us in this room haven't waited for a trial, let alone for a judge to pass sentence."

"I know, I know," Monte said, shaking his head. "I just can't bring myself to trust that fella, and if the rest of the bunch are cut from the same cloth—"

"I'd bet a hat they are," Pearlie put in.

"Then I don't trust them, either. They're gonna shoot somebody, or string somebody up, and it'll turn out the folks they killed weren't guilty of anything except being in the wrong place at the wrong time."

Smoke said, "Maybe we can keep that from happening."

"How are we going to do that?"

"Somebody needs to keep an eye on them as much of the time as possible. We won't be able to do that all day, every day, but once we find out where their headquarters are going to be located, we can keep an eye on the place and follow them around on their patrols."

Monte nodded and said, "Somebody to regulate the regulators. That's not a bad idea. But it's liable to be a dangerous job. If Stratten's gonna cross the line and do something illegal, he won't want any witnesses."

"That's why we won't use anybody but volunteers," Smoke said. "And I figure on taking the first turn myself."

CHAPTER 15

Over the next week, the situation grew clearer. Deke Stratten and the fifteen men in his crew of regulators made their headquarters at Thaddeus Bolton's Triangle B ranch. Bolton was the one who had pushed for them to be hired, so it made sense for him to provide their quarters.

Logistically, it was a sound move, as well. Other than the Sugarloaf, the Triangle B was the central-most ranch in the valley. From there, the regulators could reach any of the other spreads in a reasonably short amount of time.

Stratten divided his force into four-man patrols. Two of those patrols were out riding the range at all times, one in the western half of the valley, the other in the east. The other eight men remained at the Triangle B as a reserve force that could be called upon as reinforcements.

During the first week of patrols, however, the regulators weren't needed. The rustlers were nowhere to be found. None of the ranches lost any cattle. Some people might assume that peace had descended once again upon the valley.

Smoke didn't believe that. He thought it was more likely the rustlers were just biding their time, spying on everything that was going on in the valley, and figuring out just when it would be safe for them to strike again.

Smoke was tireless, but not even he could keep going around the clock, nor could he be in two places at once.

Because of that, he had to recruit help from among the Sugarloaf's ranch hands. All of them were eager to volunteer, of course. Not only were they loyal to Smoke, but they felt a natural rivalry with the Triangle B, as well, and the regulators, by extension, worked for Bolton the same as the ranch crew. That was how it seemed to Smoke's cowboys, anyway.

Next to Pearlie, Smoke trusted Cal the most of all the hands, and Smoke knew the young cowboy could take care of himself. Cal was a good hand and Smoke hated to lose him from ranch work, but right now it seemed more important to keep tabs on Deke Stratten and the other hired gunmen roaming over the valley, so when Cal volunteered to help keep an eye on the regulators, Smoke agreed without hesitation.

That was how it came to be that on a particularly dark night a week and a half after the regulators instituted their patrols, Cal found himself trailing one of them across the range.

Smoke's orders had been clear: Don't follow the gunmen too closely. Cal was hanging back far enough that he had to trail them by the sounds of their horses' hooves. The moon was just a thin orange crescent hanging low in the sky tonight. He would have had to be practically on top of the men in order to see them.

Cal had been dogging these patrols for several nights now, and so far nothing had happened. He wouldn't wish trouble on any of the ranchers in the valley, but he was torn between being glad the rustlers hadn't struck again and being bored.

At the moment, the patrol was crossing the spread known as the Mirror 3, owned by a man named Warren Dunlap. Dunlap was a likable sort, a family man with a nice wife and three little girls all under the age of ten. Cal didn't want him to lose any stock to wideloopers.

From time to time, Cal paused to listen so that he wouldn't run up on the regulators from behind. They wouldn't know who he was, and there was a good chance they would start shooting if a stranger blundered into their midst in the dark.

During one of those brief halts, he realized he couldn't hear their horses anymore. They must have stopped for some reason, too. He was prepared to wait until he heard them moving again before he heeled his horse into motion once more.

Only a few minutes had passed, though, before he heard something more than hoofbeats.

Gunfire shattered the night's stillness, erupting in several ragged waves.

Cal launched his horse into a run toward the shooting. It came from ahead of him, maybe half a mile away. The guns continued roaring and the reports became louder as he drew closer.

He came out on top of a shallow ridge with a good view of a wide, open stretch in front of him. The light from the sliver of moon and a canopy of stars wasn't bright enough for him to make out any details at first.

He saw plenty of muzzle flashes, though, blooming like crimson flowers in the dark. He could tell there were two groups shooting at each other. Had to be rustlers and regulators.

Squinting, Cal made out a dark, moving mass beyond the second group of riders. That would be a herd of stolen cattle, he guessed. The regulators had come on a bunch of rustlers at work and were trying to stop them.

Cal held a tight rein on his horse and on his own burgeoning emotions, as well. He had a cowboy's natural hostility toward rustlers. He wanted to charge down there and plunge into the middle of that fight.

If he did that, though, he would be in danger from both sides as they would each take him for one of the enemy. No matter how difficult it was to hold back, he had to do the job Smoke had given him. He would sit here and watch to see what happened.

The fight moved away from him. He couldn't see as many muzzle flashes, and the peals of gun-thunder receded. Were the rustlers getting away with the stolen stock? Cal leaned forward in the saddle as he realized that was what it looked like. The regulators had slowed their pursuit. He wondered if some of them had been wounded in the fierce exchange of bullets and that was why they weren't pressing the rustlers as closely as they had been.

Within moments, the shooting stopped completely. Cal watched in amazement as the men he'd been following earlier in the evening turned around and rode back toward him instead of pursuing the cattle thieves.

Cal didn't want to be caught here watching them. He moved his horse into the trees and stopped in the thickest shadows he could find. The regulators rode up the slope and onto the little bench at the top of the ridge. They didn't appear to be in any hurry now. Cal made out four riders. None of them were slumped over, as he would have expected if they were wounded.

What in blazes was going on here? They hadn't let the rustlers get away deliberately—the gun battle had been a hot and heavy affair, with plenty of lead flying on both sides—but Cal had expected the regulators to go after the rustlers.

Maybe they had felt that they were too outnumbered. Maybe they were heading back to the Triangle B to get some help and then pick up the trail again.

But whatever the regulators were doing, Cal figured it would be a good idea for him to follow the rustlers and find out where they were going. Smoke suspected that the gang might have a hideout in the area where they were holding the stock they had stolen. If Cal could find that hideout, Smoke and Monte Carson could put together a posse and smash the rustlers once and for all. If the regulators wanted to be part of that effort, it would be up to them to cooperate.

With that thought in mind, Cal waited until the four members of the regulator patrol were out of sight and he could no longer hear their horses.

Then he eased his mount out of the shadows where they had taken cover and started down the slope. It was too dark to follow the tracks left by the stolen herd, but he could head in the direction they had been going and hope to catch up to them.

The eastern skies were turning gray with the approach of dawn, but it was still more than an hour until sunrise when Cal reined in and stared at the cliffs rising in front of him, several hundred yards away. They loomed dark and featureless, ominous and foreboding in the gloom.

For hours, Cal had been following the rustlers and the stolen cattle, tracking them by the smell of dust that lingered in the air after it was churned up by hooves, as well as the occasional clash of horns and the thudding rumble of the herd as it moved along. He had come up on them fairly quickly and had had to be careful not to get too close.

Somewhat to Cal's surprise, the trail had taken him south instead of north. After the rustlers had struck for the first time on the Triangle B, the thinking was that they would drive the stolen stock north to Wyoming and dispose of it there.

Then, when no sign of those cattle had turned up there, according to Monte Carson's contacts among the Wyoming lawmen, and the same was true of the animals stolen from Sam Brant's SB Connected spread, Smoke had come up with the idea that the stolen stock was hidden somewhere around here. He had discussed that possibility with Pearlie and Cal several times.

It was looking as if Smoke had been on to something there, Cal mused as he sat staring at the distant cliffs, but he was still puzzled. The cliffs blocked off this end of the valley and stretched for miles. There was no good way around them, not without swinging north or south for a day's drive, if not more. If the rustlers wanted to have those cows tucked away out of sight by the time the sun came up, they couldn't do it this way.

Cal nudged his horse into motion again. The answer to the mystery had to be up there ahead of him somewhere, and he wouldn't find it by sitting here.

As he rode, he sniffed the air. He could still smell the dust from the herd's passage. It was faint but definitely still there. He was lucky it hadn't rained in these parts since that big storm a couple of weeks earlier, and it had been a fairly dry season overall. If not for that, the stolen cattle might not have raised as much dust.

He heard the *clack-clack* of horns bumping together, as well, and then he was surprised to hear a low-voiced call as one of the rustlers either spoke to another outlaw or sang out to the cattle. He was closer to the herd than he had thought he was, Cal realized.

He reined in sharply. He needed to let them get farther ahead of him again, he told himself. The rustlers must have slowed the herd's pace. He shouldn't have been this close to the cattle.

Cal stiffened as a couple of dark figures on horseback loomed up on his right, maybe twenty yards away. They must have seen him at the same time as he spotted them.

As the two men reined in abruptly, one of them exclaimed, "Hey, who's that?"

The other man shouted, "Stay where you are!"

Cal whirled his mount. If they caught him and struck a match, they could tell by its light that he wasn't one of them. More than likely, that wouldn't get him anything except a quick bullet. He jabbed his heels into his horse's flanks and sent it leaping into a gallop back the way he had come from.

The two riders yelled curses and jerked their mounts toward him. Tongues of flame licked out from their guns as they opened fire on him. They couldn't know who he was, but they must have figured him running like that meant he wasn't friendly.

That was an accurate assumption. He wasn't friendly at all to a bunch of no-good rustlers.

As the horse stretched out in a ground-eating gallop beneath him, Cal leaned forward in the saddle to make himself a smaller target. He held the reins in his left hand and drew his Colt with his right. Twisting in the saddle, he threw a couple of wild shots in the general direction of the men chasing him. He didn't expect to hit either of them, but lucky shots happened sometimes. If nothing else, he wanted to discourage them a little.

Bullets whined overhead, but none of them found their target. Cal's horse was fast, and he thought there was at least a chance he could outrun his pursuers.

Of course, even if he got away, that would mean he had failed to find out where the rustlers were taking all those stolen cattle. Tracking them to their hideout would have to wait for another dark night when they raided one of the ranches in the valley—

That thought had just gone through Cal's mind when his horse went down with no warning as if its hooves had been jerked out from under it. Pure instinct made the young cowboy kick his feet free of the stirrups as soon as he felt the animal falter.

That swift reaction was all that saved him. If he hadn't done it, he probably would have been crushed under the horse as it fell and rolled.

As it was, he was flung out of the saddle and over the horse's head to go sailing out of control through the air. His hat flew off his head, but he managed to hang on to the gun in his hand.

The ground came up and slammed into him like a giant fist. Stunned by the impact, Cal was only vaguely aware that momentum was carrying him over and over.

His stop was abrupt and painful as he crashed into a rock. He lay there on his belly, half senseless. In the tiny fragment of his brain that was still working, he thought that his mount must have stepped in a hole. He hadn't felt any kind of jerk or shudder before the collapse, as he would have if one of the pursuers' bullets had struck the animal.

No, this mishap was pure luck—all of it bad.

The swift rataplan of approaching hoofbeats forced its way through the cobwebs cloaking his mind. Two of the rustlers had been chasing him, he recalled. And shooting at him. That had to be them pounding toward him now. He needed to get behind cover and prepare to put up a fight.

He was already outnumbered two-to-one, and more rustlers might hurry to help their friends if they'd heard the shooting, but those odds didn't mean Cal could give up. Smoke never gave up, no matter how badly the deck was stacked against him, and Smoke was the person Cal admired more than anyone else, even Pearlie. Smoke would keep fighting, and so would Cal.

He heaved himself up on hands and knees then pushed to one knee as he rested his hands on the rock slab into which he had crashed.

"There he is!" a man yelled not far away.

Cal forced his muscles to work. He levered himself forward and rolled across the rock to drop to the ground on the other side. Guns roared in the darkness. Bullets thudded into the rock and sprayed dust and chips of stone into the air.

Cal thrust the Colt over the slab and triggered it twice, then ducked down again as more lead stormed back at him.

He kept his head down and thumbed fresh rounds from his shell belt into the revolver's cylinder. The gun-fire from the rustlers continued, but after a few seconds, Cal realized something was different about it.

Only one gun was blasting at him now. One of the men was keeping him pinned down, distracted, while the other rustler—

A shot roared to Cal's left. He felt the slug's hot breath against his cheek as it barely missed him and splattered against the rock slab. Tiny pieces of stone stung his cheek. He rolled onto his belly and spotted the would-be killer charging toward him. The man had circled around to launch this flank attack.

Cal squeezed off a shot at the same time as a bullet struck the ground in front of him and kicked dirt and gravel into his eyes, effectively blinding him for a moment. He pulled the trigger again anyway, not knowing where the slug went.

He pawed at his eyes, trying to get his vision cleared in time to fight off the attacker who had to be coming at him from the front. He was half-deaf from the thunderous gunfire, but he heard boots pounding the ground nearby and twisted toward the sound as he pushed himself up.

From the corner of his eye, he spotted a dark, crumpled shape lying on the ground a few yards away and knew at least one of his bullets had found the man who'd charged from his left. That hombre looked like he was out of the fight. But the other man, the one who'd kept Cal pinned down, was almost right on top of him now.

The muzzle flash as the rustler's gun went off was blinding. Cal felt the bullet strike his left side like a terrific punch. The impact slewed him halfway around.

But he'd pulled the trigger at the same instant as the rustler. His Colt roared and bucked in his hand, the jets of flame from the two weapons crossing in the night. The rustler stumbled and pitched forward, falling across the rock to crash into Cal and drive him off his feet.

The man's weight pinned Cal to the ground. He had a hunch it was literally dead weight. The rustler hadn't moved since they'd fallen. Cal struggled to move the body aside, but weakness was spreading hotly through him from the wound in his side.

More riders were coming! He heard the hoofbeats and knew it had to be some of the other rustlers checking to see what all the shooting was about. He had to get out of here and couldn't afford to waste any time.

Desperation gave him strength. He shoved the dead man off him and reached out to grab hold of the rock slab. Bracing himself on it, he pulled and pushed until he was on his feet. Then he turned to look for his horse, remembering that it had fallen. Depending on how badly it was injured, he might have to try to catch one of the rustlers' mounts.

He didn't have a chance to do any of that. He had barely taken a step when he was surrounded, the men on horseback towering over him in dark, grotesque shapes against the night sky. Angry shouts filled the air. Cal expected them to start shooting and riddle him with bullets. But he'd take one or two of the varmints with him, he vowed fuzzily as he started to lift his gun.

A boot came out of the darkness and slammed into his head. He was on the ground without really realizing he had fallen. He must have dropped his gun because his hands were empty.

"Becker and Simmons are dead!" a man shouted.

Curses rained down on Cal. A couple of men yelled for the others to shoot him.

Then another voice cut through all the hubbub. "Get him on a horse," it ordered. "We'll take him with us, find out who he is and how much he knows."

Strong, brutal hands gripped Cal, jerked him to his

feet. He felt himself lifted and forced into a saddle. The pain in his side had receded and been replaced by a numbness that threatened to engulf him. He knew he was on the verge of passing out.

But even at that moment, a tiny something in the back of his head insisted that he had heard that last voice, the one that gave orders, somewhere before. Something was familiar about it, but no matter how hard he tried, he couldn't dredge up the identity of the man it belonged to.

That was his final thought as he slumped forward into oblivion.

CHAPTER 16

Years of living on the edge of danger had made Smoke a light sleeper. One of the windows in the bedroom he shared with Sally was open to let in fresh air. This morning, an hour or so before dawn, it also let in the sound of hoofbeats approaching the ranch in a hurry.

Smoke was completely awake in an instant when his ears picked up that sound. He sat up and swung his legs out of bed, stood and moved quickly to the window. Pushing the curtain back, he peered out into the gray, pre-dawn gloom.

"What is it?" Sally asked from the bed. The hoofbeats, and his reaction to them, had roused her from slumber, as well.

"Don't know," Smoke replied without looking around. "Somebody headed this way, moving fast."

"That means trouble, doesn't it?"

"Usually," Smoke agreed.

He wasn't the only one who had heard the approaching rider. The bunkhouse door swung open and Pearlie stepped out, barefooted and wearing a pair of hastily donned denim trousers over long underwear.

The Sugarloaf foreman held a lantern in his left hand, raised above his head so that it spilled a circle of light around him. His right hand gripped a Winchester, ready to fire.

Pearlie stood there peering toward the trail leading to the ranch yard, tensely awaiting trouble if that was what the unknown rider was bringing with him.

A few moments later, a man on horseback appeared and reined his mount to a halt not far from Pearlie, who tipped the rifle muzzle up toward him. The man called, "Hold your fire, Fontaine. It's Carl Hodges."

Pearlie lowered the Winchester and responded, "So it is. Howdy, Hodges. What brings you ridin' in hellbent for leather at this hour of the mornin'?"

"What do you think?" Hodges said. "We've been hit. Those damned rustlers!"

Watching and listening from the second-floor bedroom window, Smoke recalled that the puncher named Carl Hodges rode for Warren Dunlap's Mirror 3 spread. Dunlap was a likable young man with an equally likable family, and Smoke hated to hear that he had fallen victim to the wideloopers.

Pearlie turned his head to look up at the window. Smoke raised the pane the rest of the way and leaned out.

"I heard," he called. "I'll be right down."

As Smoke turned away from the window, Sally asked, "Which ranch did they hit this time?"

"Warren Dunlap's."

"Oh, no! He and his wife Janie have the most precious little girls."

"I'm sure she and the kids are fine," Smoke said as he pulled on trousers and a shirt. "Rustlers just want the cattle. They don't bother families."

"Generally speaking."

Smoke shrugged. "That's true, I suppose. We've seen that this bunch doesn't hesitate to start shooting any time somebody interferes with them. I'll go down and find out for sure what happened."

Out of habit, he buckled on one of his gunbelts. He hadn't taken the time to put on his boots, but he would have felt naked without a Colt.

By the time Smoke walked out of the house, Hodges had dismounted and stood beside his winded horse, holding the reins. Smoke walked over to him and Pearlie, nodded to the Mirror 3 cowboy, and said, "Tell me what happened."

"Those rustlers who have been raising hell in the valley raided our herd tonight. The Mirror 3's not a very big spread, you know that, Mr. Jensen. Warren only hires three hands, which means there was just one of us watching over the cattle at a time. Rob Ballinger had the shift when the rustlers struck." The words threatened to catch in Hodges' throat as he went on, "They killed him, Mr. Jensen. Shot him right off his horse."

"I'm sorry, Carl," Smoke said. "I didn't know Ballinger well, but he seemed like a good hombre."

"He was. But that didn't stop those no-good snakes—" Hodges choked up again and had to stop this time. After a moment, he cleared his throat and went on, "As it happened, one of those regulator patrols wasn't far off. They heard the shooting, came to check it out, found Rob's body, and took off after the rustlers. They sent a man to the ranch house to tell Warren about it. We rode out to get on the trail, too, but we ran into the other regulators coming back. They had swapped lead with the rustlers, but the varmints got away. Warren sent me to spread the word to the other ranches."

"How'd they get away?" Pearlie asked. "Seems like them regulators should'a been able to follow 'em, anyway."

"We heard the shooting in the distance. It sounded like a war. The regulators said the rustlers had an ambush set up to drive them back while the rest of the bunch hustled those stolen cows away somewhere. They're a well-organized bunch."

Smoke said, "We'll put together a search party. It'll be light enough to trail them by the time a group can gather at the Mirror 3."

Hodges nodded. "That's what Warren said we should do. There won't be any shortage of volunteers to look for them, Mr. Jensen. We have to do something to put a stop to this before the whole valley's ruined."

The valley was a long way from ruined, Smoke thought, although the rustlers had done significant damage to the spreads they had raided so far. If that continued, there was no telling how extensive the losses might be.

Smoke turned to Pearlie and said, "Pick out half a dozen of the men and tell them to get ready to ride. We'll head over to the Dunlap spread as quickly as we can."

"Smoke, Cal ain't here." Pearlie started to say something else but stopped abruptly. The other ranchers weren't aware that Smoke had men keeping an eye on the regulators, and Pearlie had realized in time that he probably shouldn't spill that fact in front of Hodges.

"I know," Smoke said. He was well aware that Cal had been assigned to that watchdog duty the previous night. In fact, he was counting on that—and counting on Cal to provide valuable information for them.

When consciousness seeped back into Cal's brain, the first thing he was aware of was that he was lying on something hard. Immediately after that, he felt pain washing through him, originating from the wound in his side.

He didn't know how badly he was hurt, but he had hopes that it wasn't a mortal wound. He was still alive, after all. Pain was the ultimate proof of that. The dead didn't hurt this much. At least, he hoped they didn't . . .

Cal forced his eyes open. That didn't help because darkness still surrounded him. But as seconds dragged past, his vision adjusted and he realized the blackness around him wasn't as complete as he had thought at first. Streaks of light showed here and there.

After a while, he figured out that those streaks were rays of sunlight slanting in through the cracks in a log wall. He was inside a building, and from the angle of the wall above him, he could tell that he was lying on the floor. On the ground, rather, because when he moved his fingers slightly, they rasped over hard-packed dirt.

He closed his eyes, lay still, and concentrated on breathing in and out. Gradually, the cobwebs receded from his brain and he was able to push the pain in his side away until it was just a dull ache that could be ignored.

Taking inventory of his condition, he found that his arms and legs weren't tied, but he was too weak to move them much, probably from loss of blood because of that wound. His head throbbed from being kicked, but he figured that wasn't serious.

Pearlie had always said he was too hard-headed for his noggin to be dented easily.

When Cal had taken stock of the shape he was in, he summoned up his strength and rolled onto his right side to get a better look around.

He was in a small cabin with log walls. He saw the underside of a thatched roof above him. It was a crude shelter with a couple of cots, some bedrolls, and a few empty crates that might serve as seats. No fireplace or stove. Whoever had thrown this place up in a hurry didn't intend to spend the winter here. It wouldn't be livable without any source of heat.

The door was closed. More light came in around it. Cal was looking in that direction when something blocked the light. A heavy footstep sounded outside.

The door swung open on its leather hinges. A bulky figure was silhouetted against orange-gold light outside. The sun was up, but it was still very early in the morning.

If he had still been lying on his back, Cal might have pretended to be unconscious. Over on his uninjured side, staring at the door, he couldn't do that and get away with it. He didn't even try.

The newcomer grunted and came a step into the

cabin. "You're awake, are you?" he said. "That's good. I never cottoned much to killin' a man in his sleep. I'd rather him see it comin'."

If he was trying to frighten Cal, the young cowboy wasn't going to let it work. He stared coldly at the man, unable to make out many details about him because the light was behind the varmint.

"What do you want?" he asked in a flat, hard voice. It sounded a little strange to him because so much of his strength had been drained, but he made his tone as resolute as he could.

"What I want is to blast a few holes through you, sonny boy," the stranger rasped. "You killed a couple of good men."

"I killed a couple of outlaws. They weren't good men."

The stranger ignored that and went on as if Cal hadn't spoken.

"What I'm gonna do," the man said, "is try to see that you don't die from that bullet hole in your side. The boss wants you alive, and I don't question what the boss tells me to do."

He came on into the cabin, moving to one side so that the morning light wasn't directly behind him anymore. The backwash of illumination revealed a roly-poly figure with an ample belly putting a strain on the buttons of his dirty gray shirt. The man had a black hat shoved back on thinning black hair. A dark mustache hung over his lips. He looked more like somebody's jovial uncle than a ruthless owlhoot.

The malice in his piggish eyes ruined that illusion. He hunkered awkwardly next to Cal and probed at the dressing on the young cowboy's side. Cal hadn't realized until that moment that somebody had tended to the bullet wound he'd suffered.

The fat man grunted and said, "Bandage hasn't soaked through. That's good, I reckon. Maybe you won't bleed to death." He straightened. "Now that you're awake, I'll bring you some coffee and something to eat." He chuckled, but the sound was more ominous than amused. "Got to keep you in good shape for whatever the boss has in mind for you."

A memory flashed into Cal's brain. After he'd been shot and the rustlers had surrounded him, he remembered there had been something familiar about the voice of the man giving orders. He said, "Who is this boss of yours?"

"I don't reckon that's any of your business. You didn't really expect me to answer that, did you?"

Cal ignored that response and asked, "Where are we?"

"The last place you're ever gonna see, more than likely."

Anger and frustration bubbled up inside Cal. "You could at least tell me your name!"

The fat man laughed again. "Sure, since it's not gonna do you any good. You can call me Charley. That's enough of a handle. You don't need to know anything else."

"How long are you going to keep me here, Charley?"

"Until the boss is done with you. Best not get in a hurry, though, because once he's finished, you don't have anything waitin' for you except a hole in the ground. That's if we don't decide to just throw your body in a ravine somewhere and leave it for the buzzards and coyotes. I wouldn't be surprised if that's where you wind up, kid."

Cal might have pestered the fat man with more questions, but a wave of weakness rolled over him at that moment. His eyelids seemed incredibly heavy. He didn't want to pass out again, but it would feel so good to close his eyes and shut out all his troubles for a few moments . . .

He was gone again, just like that, and he didn't even have time to hope that his luck would have changed by the time he woke up again.

Assuming he *did* wake up again.

CHAPTER 17

Riders from several of the ranches in the valley assembled at the Mirror 3 that morning. Smoke and Pearlie led the group from the Sugarloaf. A contingent of Triangle B hands showed up with Matt Coolidge at their head. The members of the unofficial posse drank coffee and enjoyed biscuits and bacon provided by Janie Dunlap, whose three blond little girls helped with distributing the food and drink.

Then Deke Stratten rode up with a dozen of the regulators and glared at the ranchers and cowboys as he reined in. The hired guns following him looked equally unfriendly.

The valley men set cups and plates aside in response to the obvious hostility from the new arrivals.

"Looks like you boys are having a picnic," Stratten drawled. His voice dripped with contempt.

Smoke started to step forward and respond, but he stopped when he saw Warren Dunlap striding toward Stratten. This was Dunlap's spread; it was his right to speak up if he wanted to.

"My friends and I are getting ready to ride after those

rustlers," Dunlap said. "You're welcome to come along with us if you'd like."

Stratten leaned forward in the saddle and said, "It's our job to track down those thieves. That's what you're paying us to do. You need to leave it to us."

"I know what we're paying you to do, Mr. Stratten. But those are my cows they stole, and one of my hands they murdered. I've got too big a stake in this to just sit back and do nothing."

Smoke figured it was time for him to say something. "Everybody in this valley feels that way," he declared as he stepped up beside Dunlap.

Stratten sneered at him. "Last I heard, you hadn't lost any cattle, Jensen."

"Warren is one of us. Around here, we stick up for our friends."

Stratten looked around at the determined faces of the cattlemen and the cowboys who rode for them. With an abrupt shrug of his shoulders, he snapped, "Fine. Just don't get in our way if it comes to a fight. We'll be busy killing rustlers, not looking out for a bunch of amateurs."

Pearlie said, "Reckon you must not know who you're talkin' to, mister. When it comes to trouble, Smoke Jensen ain't no amateur."

"Oh, I know who I'm talking to, all right. A man with a big reputation. But I haven't seen any proof of it so far."

Pearlie's craggy face darkened with anger as he moved forward, but Smoke lifted a hand to stop him from continuing the tense exchange with Stratten.

"Let's just mount up and get started after those rustlers,"

he said. "They've already had more than enough time to get a good lead on us."

"That's right," Dunlap said. "But we'll be able to pick up their trail and follow them to wherever they took those cows."

That seemed like a pretty optimistic stance to Smoke, but pointing that out wouldn't do any good. He just nodded in agreement with the young rancher's suggestion.

A few minutes later, they rode out, nearly forty strong. If they did manage to locate the rustlers, they ought to be more than a match for any outlaw gang.

Since the rustling and killing had taken place on Warren Dunlap's range, he rode in the forefront of the group with Smoke to his right and Deke Stratten to his left. It didn't take long for him to lead them to the scene of the raid.

When they got there, Dunlap pointed to a spot near where the ground was churned up by hooves and said, "That's where we found Rob Ballinger's body. He'd been shot half a dozen times. He never had a chance."

"I'm sorry," Smoke said. "It's cold comfort, but he rode for the brand. I reckon he knew the risks he was running by guarding your herd like that."

"Ever'body's takin' a chance when rustlers are runnin' loose like they have been," Pearlie put in from behind them. "That's why we've got to put a stop to it."

Stratten spoke up, repeating what Carl Hodges had told Smoke and Pearlie early that morning about a regulator patrol being nearby when the shooting started.

"They sent one man to the ranch house to spread the

word and the others started on the rustlers' trail right away," Stratten went on. "I've spoken to all four of those men. They caught up and made a good running fight of it until they ran into an ambush. The rustlers had riflemen hidden to drive back any pursuers."

Stratten's bony shoulders went up and down as he continued, "It worked. Those bushwhackers threw up a blasted wall of lead, and my men couldn't get through it. They didn't have any choice but to turn back."

"That's too bad," Smoke said.

"I trust my men's judgment," Stratten snapped. "If you're implying they shouldn't have given up the chase—"

"I'm not implying anything, just saying it's a shame they couldn't follow the gang any farther than they did. But we'll pick up the trail if we can."

Dunlap said, "They've had a long time to get away with those cows. If they pushed the critters all night, they could be a dozen or more miles away by now."

"Yes, that's possible," Smoke agreed. "But they had to go somewhere, and it's up to us to find out where."

Unfortunately, as the day went on it became obvious that wasn't going to be easy. The trail led into the foothills, and once in that rugged country, the terrain was stony and the tracks were harder to spot.

"Where in blazes were they goin'?" Pearlie mused during a halt to rest the horses and allow the men to brew up a quick pot of coffee to wash down biscuits and jerky. "They sure didn't head for Wyoming like we thought that first time, and there ain't no place in this direction they could get rid of those cattle without takin' 'em over the mountains."

"That could be done," Smoke said. "It wouldn't be an easy chore, but it's not impossible."

"No, I know that." Pearlie glanced around them. Nobody was very close to him and Smoke at the moment, so he dropped his voice even more and said, "I've been expectin' to come across some sign of Cal, but I ain't seen hide nor hair of him."

Smoke gave a tiny shake of his head. "Neither have I. If he'd been following the herd like us, he would have blazed a trail to let us know we're going the right way. Instead, it's like he dropped off the face of the earth."

"At least we ain't found his body. I'm takin' some comfort from that. If that youngster's still on the loose out there somewhere, he's liable to come through for us yet."

Smoke nodded and said, "We can't give up on him. Seeing as it's Cal, he might just pop up where we least expect him."

That day was a long one for Cal. The air inside the cabin grew warm and stifling. The pain in his side settled down to a dull throb. The ache in his head was persistent but not too bad.

The fat man called Charley showed up a couple more times during the day to check the dressing on Cal's wound and bring him food and coffee. Cal supposed he couldn't complain too much about the way he was being treated, especially since Charley made it plain the only reason he was still alive was because the boss had ordered it so.

But Cal hated being a prisoner and vowed that he would escape from the rustlers as soon as he got a chance.

If his luck didn't run out first . . .

As the light began to fade in the cabin, signaling that night was coming on, Charley reappeared with two other men following him into the crude shelter. The fat man carried two lengths of rope, so Cal had a pretty good idea what was about to happen.

The two other men drew Colts and aimed them in Cal's general direction as they stepped to the sides of the cabin. That way they could cover Cal as Charley approached him and the fat man wouldn't be in the line of fire.

"Turn around," Charley ordered. "It was one thing leavin' you loose in here durin' the day, but it's gonna be night soon and you ought to be gettin' some strength back by now. We can't take a chance on you tryin' anything funny."

"I don't suppose you'd take my word for it that I won't try to escape?"

Charley laughed. "Kid, you are just full of wild notions, aren't you? Now, turn around like I told you, and in case you're gettin' any loco idea about these fellas not shootin' you because I'm in the way, you ought to know they ain't that fond of me."

"That's the damn truth," one of the men growled.

Cal sighed and twisted around on the ground. The

movement made a twinge go through his side. It hurt enough to cause a grimace.

"Sorry," Charley said, "but it's still better than bein' dead."

Cal couldn't argue with that.

Charley tied his hands behind his back and then lashed his ankles together. The two guards didn't pouch their irons until that chore was finished. Charley helped Cal sit upright with his back propped against the log wall.

"You just stay right there," he said. "Me and these other two fellas have been stayin' in this cabin, so you won't be hurtin' for company."

"Turn me loose again and the four of us could play poker," Cal suggested.

A booming laugh came from the portly rustler. "Kid, you just never give up, do you? Don't make a pest o' yourself or I'll gag you, too."

Cal figured he might as well save his breath and shut up. He sat there and watched as the three outlaws lit a candle, rolled quirlies and smoked, talked for a while as night settled in, and then turned in. Charley took one of the bunks while the other two flipped a coin for who got the other bunk tonight and who got a bedroll on the ground.

It didn't take long after the candle was blown out and stygian darkness enfolded him for Cal to doze off, despite him thinking it might be a good idea for him to stay awake. His strength was just too depleted for that.

Another day passed in much the same fashion as the first, except that Charley no longer untied Cal's hands except when he was eating, and he never untied the young cowboy's feet. A third day came and went, and Cal felt himself getting stronger as he recovered from the deep bullet crease in his side. He was still a long way from normal, but he was getting there, he told himself. If he got an opportunity to make a break for freedom, he stood at least a small chance of escaping, and that was better than no chance at all.

He had been paying attention while he was a captive. There was nothing else for him to do. He could hear the rustlers talking outside and tried to identify as many different voices as he could so he would have some idea of how many were in the gang. There were upwards of a dozen, he decided, although he wasn't able to get an exact count. There wasn't any guarantee they were all here at the hideout, either—wherever "here" was.

He didn't overhear any conversation that would give him a clue where they were or who the mysterious boss was, nor did he hear the voice that had sounded familiar to him the night he was captured. Those were the things he wanted to know most of all, just in case he was able to get away from the rustlers. If he knew the location, he could lead Smoke and a posse back here and wipe out the wideloopers. And if he knew who the boss was, he could make sure the man didn't escape justice.

Several times, he heard cattle bellering not too far away. The stolen stock was being held here, wherever here was, just as Smoke had speculated. The thieves were putting together a good-sized herd before they drove it out of the valley.

After three days had passed, Cal believed it was

likely the outlaws probably were getting ready to strike again and raid another ranch. In order to do that, they would have to leave the hideout.

They wouldn't go off and leave him unguarded, which meant either a few men would have to stay behind—or they would get rid of him before they left, just to make things simpler. The boss might have wanted to question him, but the varmint hadn't shown up to do so.

He couldn't afford to leave his fate to chance, Cal decided. If he was going to make a break, it had to be soon.

The last few meals, only one guard had come into the cabin with Charley. As inevitably happened when some tedious job went on for too long, the men carrying it out got a little lax in their diligence. Charley wasn't being as careful to stay out of the line of fire when he loosened Cal's bonds and then gave him his food and coffee.

Knowing that, Cal began to make plans.

That evening, as the light faded inside the cabin, the door opened and Charley and another rustler came inside. Charley had the usual tin cup of coffee in one hand and a plate full of beans, salt pork, and a biscuit in the other.

"Here you go, kid, just like a fancy restaurant in Denver or San Francisco," he gibed. "Sorry we don't have no nice linen tablecloths."

"That's all right," Cal said. "Just give me my supper."

"Hold your horses." Charley set the cup and plate on one of the crates and bent to untie Cal's wrists.

While he was doing that, the other man drew his gun

and aimed it in Cal's general direction. His degree of alertness was purely perfunctory, though. After all this time, none of them expected Cal to try anything.

When Cal's hands were free, he flexed his fingers several times. Charley didn't tie the bonds so tightly that the circulation in Cal's hands and feet was completely cut off, but it always took several seconds to get a normal level of feeling back in those extremities.

Charley straightened and stepped back, but before he could turn to the crate to pick up the plate and cup, Cal pointed at his right foot and yelled a curse.

"Scorpion!" he went on. "I just saw it crawl in there! Damn it, he's gonna sting—*Owww!* Oh, hell! He's stinging me! Get it off, get it off!"

"Stop screechin'!" Charley said as he hastened forward. He bent over Cal again and reached for the young cowboy's right boot. "I'll see if I can find the blasted thing—"

Cal drew up his legs and unleashed a kick. Both boot heels crashed against Charley's chin and jaw. The fat man flew backward just as the other rustler lunged forward. Charley fell against his companion, their legs tangled, and both men went down hard, just as Cal hoped they would.

He used the momentum the kick gave him to lever himself up from the ground. He pitched forward and landed on the floundering Charley, driving a knee into the fat man's gut.

At the same time, he reached past Charley, clamped his left hand around the other man's gun wrist, and shoved the weapon aside. He smashed his right fist into the rustler's face.

The blow stunned the man long enough for Cal to wrench the Colt out of his grip. He slammed the gun butt against Charley's skull, then crushed the other man's nose with a second blow. Both of the outlaws shuddered and then lay still, knocked cold.

Cal didn't know if the shouts he had used to draw Charley into his trap had been heard outside. It all depended on how close the other rustlers were to the cabin and what they were doing. But it was certainly possible that some of them were on their way right now to see what the commotion was.

Cal shifted the gun to his right hand and reached down with his left to snag the butt of the Colt holstered at an angle on Charley's thick hip. Armed with both revolvers, he rolled off the two unconscious men and aimed the guns at the door in case more rustlers burst in. They might get him, but he would give them a hot lead welcome first.

Nobody showed up. The camp outside was quiet.

Cal shoved the right-hand gun into the waistband of his trousers and used that hand to pluck and tug at the rope around his ankles. He had watched the way Charley tied the knots and knew what he had to do to free himself. His fingers were still a little clumsy, but he quickly regained his usual deftness and loosened the bonds enough to kick free of them.

With that done, he stood up and moved quickly to the door, positioning himself just beside it. Shifting the gun to his right hand again, he grasped the latch string with his left and pulled it carefully. He let the door swing inward a few inches of its own accord.

That gave him a gap through which he could peer, but all he saw was what looked like a solid gray wall about twenty yards away. At the base of that wall, a narrow stream bubbled along a rocky bed.

Cal leaned forward and risked exposing his face to get a better look. That gray edifice looming above the stream was an almost sheer cliff that rose some seventy or eighty feet.

He had been here before, or at least in this same area, Cal realized with a shock, but several years had passed since his last visit.

He and Pearlie had been hunting in the foothills. They weren't on Sugarloaf range, but that didn't matter. None of the spreads in the valley claimed that wild country. It wasn't good for much of anything.

Pearlie had shot a deer, but the animal had spooked and taken a leap at the last second, ruining the foreman's normally flawless aim. The deer was only wounded, and Pearlie wasn't just about to leave any injured creature to suffer needlessly. He and Cal had tracked the deer up a creek and into a region of cliffs and canyons and ravines where nothing grew and the landscape was fit only for mountain goats. There they had found the animal and ended its suffering.

That was where he was now, Cal mused, deep in those canyons. He couldn't tell if he and Pearlie had penetrated this far on that previous visit or if the rustler hideout was even more isolated.

But the whole thing didn't make any sense, he thought

with a little shake of his head. Some of the canyons were wide enough that cattle could be driven up them, a few abreast, and water was available since several small creeks trickled through the region, but you couldn't graze a herd in this wasteland. Enough grass grew along the streams that horses wouldn't starve, as long as there weren't too many of them, but a few dozen cattle would graze it clean in a day or two.

Those thoughts went through Cal's mind in a flash. They were intriguing, but they didn't have anything to do with his immediate dilemma. The twilight gloom was thickening outside, but in spite of it, he hadn't spotted any rustlers as he studied the narrow angle of vision he had. He didn't hear any talking, either.

Was it possible the rest of the gang had pulled out already, heading for a raid on one of the other ranches? They could have left Charley and the other man behind to guard the prisoner. That seemed to be the most likely explanation, even though Cal knew it was a massive stroke of luck for him if it was true.

He glanced over his shoulder at Charley and the other man. Both were still out cold, as far as he could tell. And the only way to find out what was waiting for him outside the cabin was to go out and see.

He pulled the second gun from his waistband. With irons in both fists, he used his foot to pull the door open wider and stepped out into the gathering shadows.

CHAPTER 18

Smoke wasn't the sort of man to brood, but if he had been, he would have found plenty to worry about. Not only had the search party been unable to track the rustlers and the stolen cattle through the foothills, but Cal was still missing, as well, and three days had passed.

Pearlie was almost beside himself from fretting over the youngster. He had combed every foot of the Sugarloaf searching for any sign of Cal, and he had ridden over all of the Mirror 3, as well, since the rustlers had raided that spread on the night Cal disappeared.

"Cal can take care of himself," Smoke had assured Pearlie. "Chances are, he's still on the trail of those wideloopers and hasn't been able to get back yet to tell us where they're holed up."

"Or they caught him spyin' on 'em and are holdin' him prisoner," Pearlie responded darkly. "Or worse."

"If anything happens to Cal, we'll even the score."

"I know, but that won't bring the pestiferous young varmint back."

Despite Pearlie's distraction, the ranch work had to go on. Thankfully, the members of the Sugarloaf crew were seasoned veterans capable of doing what needed to be done without much supervision. Smoke didn't worry about leaving the spread long enough to ride into Big Rock. He wanted to check with Monte Carson and find out if the lawman had heard any news about the stolen cattle or anything else pertaining to the troubles in the valley.

He asked Sally if she wanted to go into town with him, but she refused. She'd been busy baking, and by now she had enough pies and bear sign to feed an army of hungry cowboys. That was her way of dealing with her own worries about Cal, Smoke figured, so he didn't press her on the issue. He just told her he'd be back before dark and rode out.

Monte wasn't in his office, but Smoke found him in Longmont's, sitting at Louis's private table and having coffee with the gambler. Louis waved at an empty chair and said, "Sit down and join us, Smoke."

"Don't mind if I do." Smoke signaled to the bartender to bring him a cup of the potent, chicory-flavored coffee, as well. "Monte, I don't suppose you've gotten any responses to those telegrams you sent to Wyoming a while back?"

"Nothing that helps us any," Monte replied as he shook his head. "I swear, judging by what those law officers up there tell me, Wyoming had broken out all over in peace and quiet. Normally, I'd say that's good, but all that tells us is that those rustlers didn't run that stolen stock up there."

"Maybe they went the other direction with it," Louis suggested.

"I thought of that," Monte said. "I sent wires to the law down in Pueblo, Walsenburg, and Trinidad, even over the New Mexico line to Raton and Taos. No sign of any suspicious cattle dealing in any of those places."

"Then they went west over the mountains to the gold camps," Louis said.

Smoke said, "I thought of that, and it seems like a possibility. It would be a hard drive and a lot of work, but they'd get a good price over there and there wouldn't be many questions asked about where the beef came from, if any. I still have a hunch they're holding the cattle somewhere in these parts, though, before they make the drive."

"From what I've heard," Monte said, "Stratten and the rest of those blasted regulators have searched the valley from one end to the other without turning up hide nor hair of that stolen stock."

"That's true," Smoke allowed.

Louis leaned back in his chair, steepled his fingers together in front of his face, and frowned in thought. After a moment, he said, "Then the question becomes . . . do you trust Deke Stratten and his men?"

"You mean, just on general principles?" Monte snorted. "I trust 'em about as far as I could throw a blamed ox!"

"Normally, yes, but they were hired to put a stop to the rustling, after all. What reason would they have to lie?"

"That's true. I don't have the answer, though. I just know that lying comes second nature to skunks like

Stratten, and the rest of that bunch is cut from the same cloth."

"Cloth we know well," Louis said with a smile.

"Stop remindin' me. Those days are over and done with, thank goodness."

The three old friends sat and talked and sipped their coffee for a while. Smoke didn't say anything about Cal being missing. The young cowboy's disappearance had caused enough worry already; there was no need to spread it to Big Rock, especially when Smoke's instincts told him Cal was still alive.

Smoke didn't have any other reason for being in town, so when he finished his coffee, he stood up and said his goodbyes. He stepped outside and headed along the boardwalk toward the hitch rack where he had left his horse.

He hadn't gotten there when he heard his name called from up ahead. He lifted his gaze and saw Emmaline Bolton coming toward him.

She wore a cream-colored suit and a small hat of the same shade sporting a feather set at a jaunty angle in the band. Tan gloves covered her hands. She carried a small bag.

A smile lit up her face as they met on the boardwalk. "Why, Smoke, I'm so glad I ran into you in town today," she greeted him. "It's been so long since we've seen each other."

"Only a little more than a week," he pointed out.

A pout briefly pursed her lips. "Well, that seems like a long time. How are you?"

"All right, I suppose." He wasn't going to tell her all the things he had on his mind right now.

Her face grew solemn. "I know, all the things that have been going on are terrible, aren't they? Those poor men who were killed, and all those cattle lost. I heard the young man who owns the last ranch that was raided is just a struggling rancher who has a family relying on him."

"Most folks have somebody relying on them, but yeah, Warren Dunlap has a wife and three little ones. He'll make it, though. His neighbors will see to that. We won't let a good neighbor go under if we can help it."

Emmaline nodded and said, "I'll have to speak to Thaddeus about the matter. There might be something he can do to help. A loan, perhaps, if the young man needs one."

"We'll have to see what happens," Smoke said. "I don't think any of us have given up on the idea of finding those rustlers and recovering the stock they stole."

"I certainly hope you do." She brightened again. "In the meantime, why don't you drop over to the Triangle B sometime? I'd love to visit more with you."

"Thanks for the invitation. I'll be sure to say something to Sally about it."

"Actually . . . I was thinking you might want to pay a visit by yourself. Thaddeus isn't really around that much—he's off somewhere on the range trying to learn how to be a cowboy, of all things—and I thought it might be nice for the two of us to sit and . . . talk."

Smoke kept his face carefully expressionless. The sultry look in Emmaline's eyes and the seductive smile on her lips made it perfectly clear that polite conversation wasn't what she had in mind.

At times in the past, even after he was married, various women had expressed a romantic interest in Smoke, but of course, he had never responded in kind to any of the hints they had dropped. Seldom had any of them been quite as blatant about what they wanted as Emmaline Bolton, though. Smoke had no intention of taking her up on it—

But then a thought burst in his mind, a veritable explosion of realization that made such perfect sense it was a wonder he had never thought of it before. A few glimmerings had been playing around in the back of his head, but until this moment, they had never come together to form a coherent picture.

Somehow, he managed to keep everything that was going on in his brain from showing on his face, or at least he hoped he did. Only a couple of heartbeats had gone by since Emmaline had issued her not-so-subtle invitation. That was long enough for a slight frown to put a few tiny creases on her forehead.

But before she could say anything else, Smoke smiled, dropped his voice a little, and said, "I think that's a mighty fine idea."

She responded with a bright smile of her own but sounded a little surprised as she said, "You do? Why, I think that's just wonderful." She rested the gloved fingertips of her right hand on his left arm. "I'm sure we'll have the most stimulating conversation."

"I reckon we will," Smoke said.

"When?"

The sharpness of the question caught him a little off-balance. "You mean, when will I be riding over to the Triangle B?"

"That's right. Today?"

Smoke pretended to think about it for a moment before shaking his head. "I can't today. I have to get back out to the Sugarloaf. What about tomorrow?"

"Tomorrow will be fine. Better than fine. I believe Thaddeus plans to be out with the crew all day. They're going to show him one of the pastures where they plan to move some of the stock." Emmaline rolled her eyes. "Thaddeus likes to be involved in all the decisions that have to be made in running the ranch. I think he believes he's going to be an actual cattleman."

"Sounds like he is, if he's working with the cowboys every day and calling the shots. How does Matt Coolidge feel about that?"

Emmaline laughed. "Matt is like the rest of us. We want to keep Thaddeus happy."

"But not necessarily involved with everything that goes on?"

"No," Emmaline said with a meaningful shake of her head. "Definitely not everything."

Other than that brief touch on his arm, there had been no contact between them, and Emmaline had kept a respectable distance. There was nothing improper about the two of them standing on the boardwalk in broad daylight and having a friendly conversation, but even so, Smoke felt a little twinge of unease. The plan that had sprung into his mind was for a good cause, he reminded himself, and it wasn't going to go exactly the way Emmaline thought it was.

He spotted movement from the corner of his eye that distracted him from the beautiful woman standing in front of him. When he cut his glance in that direction, he saw Susannah Bolton crossing the street toward them. The young woman wore a blue dress and hat and looked quite pretty in a wholesome, innocent way.

"I'm finished at the dress shop, Mother," she said as she stepped up onto the boardwalk beside them. She nodded to Smoke and added, "Hello, Mr. Jensen."

"Miss Bolton," Smoke said as he returned the nod and pinched the brim of his hat.

She looked past him as if searching for someone. "I don't suppose Cal came into town with you today?"

"No, I'm afraid not. He's busy with a chore that I gave him."

Smoke hoped that was true.

"Well, you'll tell him that I said hello, won't you?"

"I sure will," Smoke promised.

Emmaline said, "Don't pester Mr. Jensen about that young cowboy, dear. I'm sure you'll see him again sometime."

With a note of defiance in her voice, Susannah said, "Maybe I'll just ride over to the Sugarloaf and see him again."

"You don't need to be riding around all over the countryside by yourself," Emmaline told her daughter. "That's a good way to get in trouble. Isn't that so, Mr. Jensen?"

"The valley's a lot more settled than it used to be,"

Smoke allowed, "but you still might run into a mountain lion or a bear or something like that." He added dryly, "You never know when there might be some two-legged critters around that can cause trouble, too."

Emmaline nodded. "You see, Susannah? Mr. Jensen agrees with me, and he probably knows this valley better than anyone else around here."

The girl eyed Smoke speculatively. "What if I was to carry a gun when I'm riding?" she suggested. "Maybe one of those, what do you call them, a carbine?"

"That wouldn't be a bad idea," Smoke answered honestly. "If you're going to be out riding, that is. Have you ever used a rifle?"

"No, but I'd love to learn," Susannah said. "Maybe Cal could teach me."

Emmaline didn't look so pleased with him now.

"It would probably be best if you do like your mother says, though," Smoke went on. "Stick close to the Triangle B headquarters, at least until you've been around here for a while and are more familiar with the area."

"Fine," Susannah said. "But in that case, you tell Calvin Woods I expect him to pay me a visit from time to time."

"Susannah, don't be so bold. It's not ladylike."

Emmaline was a fine one to talk about being ladylike after the way she'd been acting with him, Smoke thought, but he knew very well it wouldn't be a wise idea to point that out. Instead, he nodded to Susannah and said, "I'll pass that request along, Miss Bolton."

He just hoped that Cal would be home soon and he would get a chance to deliver that message.

"I'm going back to the wagon, Mother," Susannah said.

"I'll be along in a moment," Emmaline said. "I just want to say goodbye to Mr. Jensen."

With another little eye-roll, the girl headed off along the boardwalk. Smoke wondered if she knew what her mother was actually like. It was possible—but none of his business.

He had other things on his mind at the moment.

"You'll be riding over to the ranch in the morning?" Emmaline asked quietly.

"That's what I intend."

"I'll prepare a light midday meal for us. We'll have a very nice visit." She smiled. "But you're not to bring your wife, remember?"

"I don't reckon I'm likely to forget," Smoke said.

She touched his arm again, just a fleeting brush of her fingertips, and then she turned and went along the street in the same direction Susannah had gone.

Smoke stepped over to the hitch rail, untied his horse, and swung up into the saddle. The conversation with Emmaline had been, if not exactly intimate, familiar enough that it might have been noticed by some of Big Rock's citizens who happened to be nearby on the street. He didn't believe it would cause much gossip, if any, but even if it did, he wasn't particularly worried about Sally finding out what had happened.

That was because he intended to tell her all about the rendezvous he was planning to have with Emmaline Bolton.

CHAPTER 19

"Wait . . . You're going to . . . with that woman . . . Smoke, I . . . I just don't—"

Sally was staring at him in complete and utter confusion, and she had the beginnings of a fierce, explosive anger sparking in her eyes, too.

Smoke held up both hands, palms out, and said, "Hold your horses. I don't think I'm explaining this right."

"Well, I certainly hope not!" Sally took a deep breath and went on, "Because it sounded to me like you said you're going over to the Triangle B tomorrow to have an . . . an illicit assignation with that woman!"

"That's what *she* thinks is going to happen, but she's wrong." Smoke shook his head. "I give you my word, Sally, I don't want to be part of any sort of improper carrying on with Emmaline Bolton. I just want to see if I can get any information out of her that'll confirm the theory I've got percolating in my head."

"And what theory is that?"

"That Thaddeus Bolton is responsible for all the rustling that's been going on in the valley."

Sally continued staring at him as they sat at the

kitchen table in the ranch house, but she didn't appear angry now, just baffled.

"How is that possible?" she asked. "His ranch was the first one the rustlers raided."

"And that would be a mighty effective way of convincing everybody else that he doesn't have anything to do with what's been going on. We don't have any proof of what happened except for what Bolton's men said, and I'm not sure that proves anything."

"But a man who worked for him was killed."

"If the fella wasn't in on the plan, he never would have seen it coming. One of the other punchers could have ridden up to him and gunned him down without warning."

Sally shook her head. "That would have been a terrible thing to do."

"It sure would have," Smoke agreed. "But men have betrayed their friends for money, and done worse than that, plenty of times before. And not everybody who rides for the Triangle B would have to be part of the gang, either. Some of them could be honest cowboys who don't know what's going on, like that hombre who was killed by the rustlers, supposedly."

He could tell from the look on his wife's face that she was considering the theory he had just proposed, turning it over in her mind and looking at it from every possible angle. Sally was smart; Smoke knew she would see what he was talking about, and he figured she would be as intrigued by it as he was.

"Whatever made you think Bolton could be the ringleader of the gang to start with?"

"Actually, he's not the first one I considered to be a suspect. Matt Coolidge was."

"Bolton's foreman?"

Smoke nodded. "When we were trailing that first bunch of stolen stock, Coolidge, Pearlie, and I were well out in front of the others. That was Coolidge's idea. When we were ambushed, the shots seemed to be aimed at Pearlie and me. None of them came near Coolidge."

"So you think he led you into a trap?"

Smoke shrugged. "Could be. He could have had men waiting, with orders to shoot whoever was with him."

"But it could have just as easily been coincidence."

"Maybe."

"And if you're right, it could also mean that Coolidge is the boss of the rustlers, not Bolton."

"That's true," Smoke said, "and like I said, that's the way I was leaning for a while. But then I thought about Deke Stratten and those other regulators Bolton got the association to hire."

"That's right! He couldn't be the leader of the gang. He was the driving force behind hiring those men to *stop* the rustling. Would he have done that if he wanted the rustlers caught?"

"Again, we've got only Bolton's word that's what they're really supposed to do."

Understanding dawned on Sally's face. "You mean they're not actually trying to put a stop to the gang's activities. It's all a sham, a distraction, a way for Bolton to cover up what's really going on."

"That's the idea that kept trying to kick in the doors in my brain," Smoke said, "until it finally broke through.

You understand, I don't have a lick of proof of any of this. It's just something that makes sense to me."

Sally leaned back in her chair and nodded slowly. "That's why you want to carry on with Emmaline Bolton. You're hoping you might find some evidence that would point to her husband as the mastermind behind all the trouble."

"That's what I'm hoping, all right, but I'm not actually going to carry on with her." Smoke smiled. "You can't believe I'd really do that, can you?"

"Well, you came in here and told me you're going to ride over there tomorrow for a private rendezvous with her, and she *is* a very attractive woman . . ."

Smoke stood up, stepped around the table, and bent over to slip his arms around her from behind as she sat in the chair.

"She's not half as attractive as you," he said as he nuzzled his lips against her ear. "Nowhere near."

Sally made a little noise of satisfaction. "But she is pretty, and obviously, she has the morals of an alley cat—" She stopped short and turned in the chair to look up over her shoulder at him. "She's going to expect to get something out of this meeting, Smoke, and if you're going to get what you're after, you can't disappoint her."

"I reckon I can sure try."

Sally shook her head and said, "That woman won't be satisfied with that. You're going to have to fight her off like she's some sort of mountain lion!"

"I've been in plenty of dangerous spots before," he reminded her. "Although I don't believe I've ever had to wrestle a mountain lion."

"You'd better figure out how," Sally warned him, "or you're going to be in even more danger when you get home!"

Cal stopped just outside the cabin where the rustlers had held him prisoner and looked around the canyon in the fading light.

A cliff almost identical to the one across the stream rose behind the cabin. The gorge formed by those cliffs was no more than fifty yards from one side to the other, and in some places, it was even narrower than that, Cal saw as he looked along it in both directions. He could see a couple hundred yards before bends in the canyon cut off his view.

The cabin where he'd been held wasn't the only structure in sight. Three more of the crude shelters were to his left, and beyond them a primitive corral fashioned from brush and peeled saplings. Approximately half a dozen horses milled around in that enclosure; in the poor light, Cal couldn't get an exact count of the animals, but there were at least that many.

Based on those horses, Charley and the other outlaw Cal had knocked out probably weren't the only ones left here in camp, although the whole gang wasn't on hand, that seemed sure. However, Cal didn't see any of the other men around at the moment. He didn't know where they might be, but his escape hadn't been discovered yet and that was all he cared about.

He listened intently, and once again he heard the familiar sounds of cattle not far away. Now that he was outside, he could tell the noises came from his right, up the canyon, or so it seemed, although he was a mite turned around and wasn't sure of directions. He took another moment to orient himself, studying the fading light in the sky to determine where the sun had set.

He was facing south, he decided. The cattle were to the west, the other cabins, the corral, and the horses to the east. That was the direction he needed to go. Heading east would take him toward the valley where the Sugarloaf and the other ranches were located. The smart thing to do would be to steal one of those horses and light a shuck out of here without any further delay.

Cal's curiosity got the best of him. Instead of getting out of here as quickly as he could, he turned and hurried toward the bend beyond which the cattle were being held. He wanted to find out what the situation was with them, how large the herd was, how many guards were posted to keep an eye on the stolen stock. All that was vital information he could take back to Smoke, along with the location of this hideout.

Cal moved over to catfoot along the base of the cliff. Scrub brush grew along the rocky wall near the bend. He used it for cover as he approached and finally reached a spot where he could risk a look around the corner.

The canyon widened out on the other side of the bend, the cliffs angling away from each other until they were more than a hundred yards apart. The stream continued to flow along the southern side. The park-like area between it and the northern wall was covered with grass and had numerous trees and bushes scattered here and there. The place was a stark contrast to the barren, rocky, rugged landscape surrounding it.

A name popped into Cal's brain: the Devil's Garden. He had heard rumors about this place, a tiny bit of paradise supposedly tucked away in a desolate, isolated location, but he had never been here. He thought he remembered Smoke mentioning it once. Smoke had laid eyes on it during his first exploration of the region, but it was too small to be of any practical value.

As a hideout for rustlers, though, it worked very well. The cattle—more than a hundred of them, by the looks of it—grazing here were proof of that. Cal spotted a couple of men on horseback riding slowly across the far end of the canyon, near the spot a quarter of a mile away where it narrowed back down and entered a wall of cliffs as little more than a ravine. The riders were there to keep the cattle from straying up in there.

Cal wondered where the ravine led. Like the canyon leading into this hidden grotto, it was wide enough to drive cattle through it, but only a few abreast. If it eventually ran up into the mountains and over a pass, it could serve as a backdoor to this place, a route for the rustlers to move the stolen stock when they were ready to dispose of it.

As those thoughts raced through Cal's brain, his confidence grew that he was right about what was going on here. Now he needed to get back to the Sugarloaf and tell Smoke everything he had learned. Once Smoke knew where to find the rustlers, he would clean out this rat's nest.

Cal eased back from the bend and pressed himself

against the rock wall for a moment as he caught his breath. His pulse hammered inside his head and his heart slugged in his chest. In his excitement over what he had discovered, he couldn't forget that he was still in great danger, as if he had fallen into a den of rattlesnakes. It was time to get out of here.

He moved quickly toward the row of primitive cabins and the makeshift corral beyond them. He wouldn't take the time to saddle one of the horses. He could ride bareback. Now he was kicking himself for not escaping as soon as he got loose.

He had just trotted past the cabin where he'd been held prisoner when somebody behind him yelled, "Hey!"

Cal whirled and saw Charley burst out of the cabin. The fat man lunged toward him. Cal brought the guns up and could have blasted holes in the outlaw, but Charley was unarmed. Cal didn't squeeze the triggers. But he did twist aside and slam the left-hand gun against Charley's head as he avoided the fat man's attack.

Charley stumbled and dropped to his knees as blood welled from a fresh gash on his head that the blow opened up. He was stunned, but only for a second.

Then he started bellowing for help at the top of his lungs.

Cal turned to run again. Charley threw himself forward, grabbed the young cowboy's right leg, and spilled him off his feet. Cal landed hard on the ground but managed to hang on to both revolvers. Charley still had hold of his leg and was trying to climb up him.

Cal writhed around and drove the heel of his other

boot into Charley's face. That knocked him loose. Cal rolled away and scrambled to his feet. He wished he was cold-blooded enough to put a bullet in Charley and make sure the outlaw wouldn't cause any more problems for him, but he couldn't do that.

The men watching the herd must have heard the shouts. Swift hoofbeats drummed from around the bend. Cal made a run for the corral as the two riders he had seen earlier swept into view.

He stopped just outside the corral gate, which was made of several peeled poles lashed together. Turning, he leveled both Colts at the onrushing riders and triggered two rounds from each gun. He didn't figure he would hit either of the rustlers, but the gunfire might slow them down. They veered apart but kept coming.

Cal shoved the guns in his waistband, jerked up the rope loop that kept the gate closed, and flung the barrier open. Spooked by the shooting, the horses inside charged out past him as he jumped aside. Cal timed his move and leaped up onto one of the animals as it pounded past him. His arms went around the horse's neck and he threw a leg over its back.

Cal clung to the horse for dear life as it followed the others out of the enclosure and turned east, the way he wanted to go. That was a lucky break. If the horse had bolted toward the rustlers, it was unlikely he would have been able to turn it. At least he was going the right direction.

He settled himself more securely on the horse's back. It was running free and easy, stretching out and generating all the speed it could. Cal pulled one of the guns, thrust it behind him, and triggered the rest of the rounds in the cylinder. Again, he was just trying to slow down the pursuit.

Because of that, when he glanced over his shoulder, he was surprised to see one of the rustlers' horses rearing up and dancing around. The rider slid loosely from the saddle and thudded solidly to the ground. The limp way the man fell told Cal he was either dead or badly wounded.

Luck could guide a bullet sometimes, and it was just as deadly that way as when it was meticulously aimed.

Clouds of powdersmoke erupted from the other rustler's gun and flowed backward behind him as he threw lead at Cal. Cal leaned forward over his horse's neck to make himself a smaller target. He didn't want to be the victim of bad luck, either. He kept his left hand wrapped in the horse's mane and his legs clamped around its straining body.

He reached the next bend in the canyon heading east, and it gave him a temporary respite as the bulge of rock cut him off from the view of his pursuer. No more bullets came his way for a few moments. Cal saw another bend up ahead. If he could reach it before the rustler rounded the turn behind him, he could stay out of the line of fire.

He didn't quite make it. He was still ten yards from the bend when the outlaw galloped around the one behind him, spotted him, and fired several shots as fast as he could squeeze the trigger.

Just before the horse carrying Cal darted around the bend, the young cowboy felt the hammer blow of a slug striking him in the right side. The impact rocked him and almost caused him to fall off the lunging mount. He dropped the gun he had emptied and used both hands to make a desperate grab at the horse's mane. He stayed on the animal's back and gradually steadied himself.

While he was doing that, he tried his best to ignore the pain flooding through him. He couldn't tell how badly he was hit or even where the bullet had caught him, because a cold numbness followed hard on the heels of the white-hot pain.

The last vestiges of light were gone from the sky now. Darkness closed in around Cal. Or maybe the sea of shadows that enveloped him meant that he was passing out; he didn't know one way or the other. But a voice clamored in the back of his head, warning him to hang on, to keep riding, to put as much distance as he could between himself and his pursuers. By now, probably more of the rustlers had heard the shooting and yelling and were after him.

But he knew that if he passed out and fell off the horse—or if he allowed them to catch him and wound up in the gang's hands again—this time he would never wake up.

CHAPTER 20

"Wish me luck?" Smoke said the next morning as he paused on the ranch house porch.

Sally had followed him out of the house. She crossed her arms as she stood there and frowned slightly.

"I'm not sure if I ought to or not," she said. "You're about to ride off to a rendezvous with another woman. A very beautiful woman, I might add."

"But like I said, not anywhere near as beautiful as you." Smoke rested his hands on Sally's shoulders as he looked down into her eyes. "As far as I recall, I've never lied to you, and I give you my word, you don't have a thing to worry about where Emmaline Bolton is concerned."

"I know that." Her tense attitude evaporated. She put her hands on Smoke's chest and went on, "But you're going to try to get evidence against a gang of vicious killers and thieves. You have to admit, that could turn out to be dangerous."

"I suppose it could, if Bolton or Coolidge happened to tumble to what I was doing. I don't intend to let that happen, though." He chuckled. "Anyway, I've ridden off into gun trouble countless times, and you never batted an eyelash about that."

"Ha! That just shows how little you know, Smoke Jensen. I always worry about you, especially when you're deliberately getting into trouble, and I always will. You just don't know about it."

"Well, ignorance is bliss, as they say." He bent and kissed her, a quick kiss but one that packed considerable passion in its brief meeting of lips. "I'll see you when I get back. If there's any problem, you know where I'll be."

"Yes," she said dryly, "I do. But I won't know what you're doing."

"Nothing out of line, I promise you that."

Sally just nodded and watched wistfully, her hands resting on the porch railing, as Smoke swung up into the saddle, turned his horse, and rode away from the ranch house.

She knew he wasn't riding away from her in anything except the physical sense. She knew as well that he would be back. Reminding herself of that calmed her nerves a little.

She asked herself if she would have preferred that he didn't tell her what he was doing. He could have ridden over to the Triangle B to see Emmaline without ever saying anything to her about it. She wouldn't have known any different.

Yes, Sally realized, that would have been worse. She and Smoke weren't in the habit of keeping secrets from each other, and it was best that way. She didn't want that to change.

She knew she'd be very glad when he was back home on the Sugarloaf where he belonged, though.

Smoke had tried to keep things light as he was taking his leave of Sally, but inside, he didn't feel that way.

For one thing, there was still no sign of Cal. The young cowboy had been gone for so long by now that Smoke couldn't keep telling himself Cal was just off trailing the rustlers somewhere. Something must have happened to him. All Smoke could do was hope that it hadn't been anything fatal.

He was more worried than he let on about this meeting with Emmaline, too. As Sally had pointed out, she would be expecting romance, and he wasn't prepared to deliver that, no matter what the cause.

That was something he'd just have to play by ear. Ultimately, the worst thing he could do was offend her by turning down her advances, leading her to order him off the Triangle B. That wasn't a killing matter.

Smoke had to grin as he mulled that over. He was thinking like some delicate flower of a heroine from a melodramatic novel. As he rode, he said aloud, "Shoot, the next thing you know, I'll be out in a field somewhere picking daisies!"

The likelihood of that was pretty dadgum small.

He cut across country from the Sugarloaf to the Triangle B. He wasn't sure which part of the ranch Thaddeus Bolton and his crew would be on today, so he kept his eyes open for any sign of them. If he spotted any other riders, he would find a place out of sight and lie low for a bit until the way was clear again.

He wasn't expecting to run into a lone man, but that was what happened when he rode past a tumbled heap of boulders and a rider emerged from behind them to come up on his right. Smoke's hand moved slightly toward the Colt holstered on that hip, but he relaxed when he recognized the man as Matt Coolidge. He didn't trust Coolidge, but he didn't have any proof that the man was mixed up with the rustlers, either.

The Triangle B foreman raised a hand in greeting and gave Smoke a friendly grin.

"Howdy, Mr. Jensen," he said as both men reined in their mounts. "What are you doin' over here on Mr. Bolton's range?"

"I thought I'd pay him a visit and talk over some association business," Smoke replied easily. "I'm curious if those regulators have come up with anything on the rustlers."

"If they have, I haven't heard about it." The two men began walking their horses side by side in the direction of the Triangle B headquarters. "Of course, that hombre Stratten reports to the boss, not to me."

Smoke hadn't forgotten that at one time he had considered the idea that Coolidge might be tied in with the rustlers. He hadn't ruled out that possibility, either. But the man seemed as affable and unsuspicious as ever.

Not only that, he didn't sound all that friendly to Deke Stratten, either.

"How do you get along with Stratten?" Smoke asked, apparently idly.

"I don't, in particular," Coolidge replied. "No real reason for him and me to spend much time together. My only concern is what happens here on the spread. It's the responsibility of Stratten and those fellas who work with him to chase down the rustlers."

"That makes it sound like you might've been told to steer clear of the regulators," Smoke commented.

Coolidge's shoulders rose and fell. "It's up to the boss how he splits up the work." He paused for a moment and then went on, "Speakin' of the boss, if you wanted to talk to him and were headin' for the ranch house, you're out of luck. He ain't there today."

"Oh?" Smoke tried to sound as if he weren't already fully aware of Bolton's absence from the ranch head-quarters.

"He rode with the rest of the crew up to the northern part of our range. We're gonna be shiftin' some stock up there pretty soon, and he wanted to take a look at the layout."

"I'm a little surprised you didn't go with them."

"Bart can handle that chore all right. Mr. Bolton's made him segundo."

"Bart Hudson?"

"I know he tangled with that rider of yours," Coolidge said, "but that was just a misunderstandin', and Bart's mighty sorry about it. And even though he don't really look like one, he's a top hand."

"So what are you doing today instead of showing Bolton that new range?" Smoke knew he might be pressing a little too hard with that question, but Coolidge was the talkative sort who didn't seem to hold much back.

"What I do most days—ride around the spread and sort of keep an eye on things."

"Like the regulators?"

"They cover the whole valley. All I care about is the Triangle B." Coolidge chuckled. "I reckon I'm, what do they call it in the army? A second line of defense?"

"That's not a bad idea," Smoke said, although he wished he hadn't run into Coolidge. It would be all right with him if Thaddeus Bolton didn't know he'd been on the Triangle B today. He especially would have preferred Bolton not knowing he'd been to the ranch house. It looked like the plan might have to be adjusted.

Smoke went on, "If Bolton's not at headquarters, I'll just talk to him some other day. Reckon I'll head back to the Sugarloaf."

"Well, shoot, we're not that far from the ranch house. Why don't you ride on in and say howdy to Miz Bolton? I'm sure she'd be grateful for the visit."

"I don't know. I wouldn't want to intrude."

"I don't think she'd consider it an intrusion. It's a shame, though, that you don't have your wife with you. Those two ladies seemed to hit it off pretty well."

Coolidge might think that because he didn't know about Smoke's encounter with Emmaline in Big Rock the previous day—and he certainly didn't know why Smoke had ridden over here today—the real reason *or* the one Emmaline believed.

Things had gotten muddled and awkward. Even though it was more dangerous, Smoke wasn't sure but what he preferred predicaments he could shoot his way out of. This is what he got, he told himself, for becoming a dang flower-picker!

"I guess it wouldn't hurt anything to stop by and say hello. We can ride the rest of the way together."

Emmaline couldn't very well try anything too familiar with Coolidge there, and she could blame the rendezvous being ruined on the foreman, not on Smoke. That was good.

But it would put Smoke right back where he had started, still lacking any proof that Bolton was involved with the rustlers.

However, Coolidge shot down that suggestion with a shake of his head.

"I need to get on about my rat-killin'," he said. "You know the way to the ranch headquarters from here, don't you?"

"Sure," Smoke said. He thought about lying, but he didn't figure Coolidge would believe it.

"I'll see you some other time, then." Coolidge lifted his hand again, this time in farewell, and turned his horse to lope away, heading south. Smoke paused to watch him ride off.

Then Smoke drew a deep breath, nudged his horse into motion, and rode on toward the Triangle B headquarters.

Coolidge had been right: It took him only a quarter of an hour to come in sight of the ranch house and all the outbuildings sprawled around it. Linus Hunsacker, the original owner, had kept the place in top-notch order, but after the old cattleman's death, it had deteriorated some before his widow sold the ranch to Thaddeus Bolton.

As Smoke approached, he saw that Bolton's men had been busy fixing up the place. The two-story frame house had a fresh coat of whitewash, some damage to the bunkhouse roof had been repaired, and the rails on the corral fences were tightened up. Smoke didn't like Bolton and was suspicious of him, but he had to admit, it was nice seeing this spread put back into good shape.

He saw an older cowboy carrying a handful of harnesses into the barn, probably intending to mend them. A big, shaggy, black and tan dog trotted into the cavernous building after him. A few horses milled around one of the corrals. Those were the only living things Smoke saw as he rode in.

Then the ranch house's front door opened and Emmaline Bolton walked out onto the porch. She wore a blue dress that plunged lower in front than polite society allowed, and her blond hair was loose around her head.

She smiled and raised a hand to wave at Smoke. "I'm glad to see you," she greeted him as he reined in at the porch. "I was hoping you wouldn't change your mind about coming over here today."

"Not likely," Smoke said, returning the smile. "Now that I see you, Emmaline, I'm glad that I didn't."

The lie and everything it implied put Smoke's teeth on edge. He wasn't cut out for this sort of subterfuge. It was highly likely he was going to wind up hurting this woman's feelings, and no matter what sort she was, he didn't like the idea of doing that.

"Just tie your horse to the post there and come on inside," she said.

Smoke cast a glance toward the barn and inclined his head in that direction. "I noticed one of your punchers going in there. Who else is around?"

"Oh, you don't have to worry about Clate. He's as deaf as that hitching post and half blind, to boot. Not only that, he minds his own business and is the least talkative man I've ever seen. Even if he notices that someone is here, he won't think anything about it and he certainly won't say anything to Thaddeus or anyone else."

She sounded confident. If he had ridden over here intent on having an actual affair with her, Smoke didn't figure he would be quite that nonchalant about the whole thing.

But since that wasn't what he was here for, he supposed it didn't really matter that much.

He swung down from the saddle and looped the reins around the hitching post as she'd told him to do. She waited on the porch as he came up the steps. When he was standing in front of her, she surprised him by coming up on her toes, leaning forward, and brushing a kiss across his lips. From the look in her eyes as she stepped back slightly, he thought she expected him to throw his arms around her and return that kiss with plenty of passion.

Instead, he said, "We're, um, sort of out in the wide open, aren't we?"

"I told you, you don't have to worry about Clate. The only other person anywhere around is the old man who cooks for the crew, and he's down at the cookshack, I think they call it."

"What about your daughter?"

"Susannah went out for a ride earlier, and I don't expect her back until sometime this afternoon."

"With rustlers on the prowl, I'm surprised you'd let her roam around like that. You were just getting on to her about that yesterday in town."

Annoyance flashed in her blue eyes. "You don't have any children, do you, Smoke?"

"I had one boy. He died when he was just a baby."

She looked a little taken aback by his response. "I'm sorry," she said. "I didn't know about that. Sally never said anything—"

"It was before I met Sally," Smoke explained. "I was married to another woman first. She died, too."

He didn't offer any more details. Even though the deaths of Nicole and Arthur had occurred a number of years earlier, the memories were still painful if he dwelled on them for too long.

"Smoke, I—"

He smiled and shook his head. "It's all right. Everybody has things in their past that hurt, and things in their future that won't be very good, either. That's why I like to live in the here and now and try to appreciate the good things in life."

She put a hand on his upper arm and squeezed. "That's a very wise attitude to take. What I was going to say when I asked you about having children is that there are times when, for the sake of both parent and child, there needs to be some separation. Especially when those children start to get older and think they know everything—"

She stopped and shook her head. "There's no need to go into that. Susannah promised me that she wouldn't go far, but she was annoyed enough with me when she left that I expect she'll be gone for quite a while. Now . . ." Emmaline moved closer and linked her arm with the one she'd just squeezed. "What do you say we go inside and get to know each other better?"

"That's why I'm here," Smoke said as he suppressed the urge to get back on his horse and ride hellbent-for-leather away from the Triangle B.

CHAPTER 21

Susannah Bolton was still angry as she reined her mount to a halt at the top of a tree-lined ridge. Her mother had gotten on her nerves quite badly this morning, harping at her and finding fault with everything she did. It had seemed almost as if her mother was trying to get under Susannah's skin and run her off from the ranch headquarters.

If that was what she wanted, she had accomplished her goal. Susannah didn't plan to return to the ranch house until late that afternoon. She had a full canteen hanging from her saddle, and she had stopped at the cook shack and begged some biscuits from old Cottontop, so-called because of the tuft of white hair sticking up on his head. The biscuits would be enough for Susannah's midday meal.

She had been riding for a while, pushing the horse she had saddled herself into a fast pace over the rolling landscape of the Triangle B. When she was mad at her mother like this, she felt the urge to move, and the wind in her face helped push away some of the bad feelings inside her.

She had realized that the horse must be getting tired, so she'd stopped when she came to this ridge crest. Despite still being in a bad mood, she was willing to sit here for a while and let the animal rest.

Gradually, the beauty of the scenery sprawled out in front of her began to penetrate the cloak of hurt feelings around her. The slope swept down to a broad pasture lush with grass that would almost reach a horse's belly. Beyond it lay a tree-lined creek, and on the other side of the creek was another ridge. Off to Susannah's left, several miles away, bulked the rugged foothills at the western end of the valley, and past them the mountains rose, looming majestically over the landscape.

Yes, it was a beautiful view, but there were views just as breathtaking back in Tennessee, she thought, and she could have appreciated them without having to uproot herself and leave everyone and everything she cared about, just so her father could come out here to Colorado and pretend to be a cattleman. She was angry with him, too, she realized, although it was her mother who caused her the most vexation, day in and day out.

She was just glad there hadn't been any special young man she'd had to leave behind.

That made her think of Calvin Woods. Cal was intriguing, no doubt about that, and so far, he was the one person in this valley who actually interested her. He was handsome, in a rough-hewn way, and he seemed to be good at cowboying, as the men called it. Susannah remembered how nice it had felt to have his arm around her, holding her safely after he'd saved her from that

runaway horse, and the memory made her pulse begin
to beat a little faster—

What was that?

Something had caught her eye in the trees along the
creek. A flash of movement of some sort. She recalled
what Mr. Jensen had said the day before about running
into a mountain lion or a bear while she was riding the
range.

Without thinking about what she was doing, she
rested her hand on the smooth wooden stock of the carbine nestled in a leather scabbard strapped to the saddle.
She had never fired a gun like that, but she knew how
to cock this one and was confident she could aim and
fire, especially at a target as big as a bear.

Please, she thought, *let it not be a bear.*

A moment later, as she saw the thing moving again,
she realized it wasn't a bear, or a mountain lion, either,
for that matter. She heaved a sigh of relief. It was just a
horse, drifting along slowly as it grazed on the grass
among the trees.

Susannah's first thought after that was that if there
was a horse down there, there had to be a rider, too. But
not necessarily, she told herself. As the horse moved a
little more out into the open, she saw that it wasn't
wearing a saddle. So maybe it was a wild horse, and she
ought to just leave it alone. If she tried to approach,
probably it would get scared and run off.

Or did wild horses attack humans? She didn't
know, but she didn't remember ever hearing of such a
thing happening.

While she was sitting there pondering about what she ought to do next, if anything, she noticed something else moving in the shadows underneath the trees. This thing was a lot smaller than the horse, whatever it was. Susannah leaned forward in the saddle and squinted, trying to make out the creature as it crawled slowly toward the creek.

She gasped in shock as it came out in the open and she realized it was a man.

He was too far away for her to recognize him or even make out any details, but the shape of a human being was unmistakable as he struggled slowly across the ground in what appeared to be great pain. Something about him struck Susannah as familiar, as if she had seen him before even though she couldn't tell who he was.

The longer she looked at him, the more convinced she was that he was hurt. He would push himself onto hands and knees and crawl a few feet, then sag to the ground and lie there as if gathering his strength again.

He repeated that process a couple of times while she watched, but after the last time, he couldn't make it back up. Instead, he inched along, pushing himself with his elbows and toes.

Susannah debated furiously what her best course of action was. She could gallop back to the Triangle B headquarters and fetch help, but as far as she knew, the only men there this morning were the cook Cottontop and an old cowboy named Clate Dawson, who was too "stove up," as he put it, to sit a saddle for very long at a time. She was sure both men would do what they could to help, but that might not amount to much.

Or she could ride down there herself, find out how badly the man was hurt, and see if there was anything she could do for him. She hadn't had any training as a nurse, but a lot of what they did was just common sense, wasn't it?

As that thought went through her brain, she made up her mind. The heels of her riding boots dug into her mount's flanks, and she headed the horse down the slope at a fast clip.

The horse had rested long enough that it responded eagerly. Susannah held the animal in a little, not wanting to take a tumble. She couldn't be of any help to that injured man if she fell and broke an arm or a leg.

As she reached the grassy pasture and started across it, another thought occurred to her. The man might be wounded, and in that case, it was entirely possible that whoever shot him could still be after him. Pursuers bent on finishing him off might be closing in on him right now, and if they were, that meant they would threaten Susannah, too. They wouldn't kill a man in front of her and then allow her to live.

She put her hand on the carbine's stock again before telling herself firmly that she was letting her imagination run away with her. The sort of thing she was thinking about was the stuff of dime novels, those ludicrously exaggerated, garishly illustrated, yellow-backed chronicles of frontier life she had seen young boys reading back in Nashville.

She wasn't going to be attacked by a gang of outlaws, right out here in broad daylight on her father's ranch. That idea was just loco, as Cottontop would call it.

Those thoughts went through her mind in the time it took for her to ride across the pasture. She reached the creek and saw that it was shallow enough to ford, no more than a foot deep as the clear water flowed briskly over a rocky bed. The horse didn't hesitate, its hooves throwing a spray of sparkling droplets high in the air as it splashed across the stream.

The injured man lay face down about thirty feet on the other side of the creek. He hadn't moved for the past several minutes. Susannah hoped he was just unconscious and not—dead.

She had seen a few dead people in her life, but never outside the solemn confines of a church during a funeral. She didn't relish the idea of having to deal with a corpse out here in the middle of nowhere.

Susannah reined in and studied the man for a few heartbeats before dismounting. He was good-sized and appeared to be young. He wore regular range clothes, the sort of garb any cowboy would wear. A gun belt was strapped around his hips, but the holster was empty. She didn't see a hat anywhere.

The butternut shirt he wore had a large, dark stain on the right side a few inches above the waist. That was an ominous sign, Susannah thought, an indication of a likely bullet wound.

The feeling that she had seen him before was stronger than ever. A gasp came from her as she realized why she felt that way. She couldn't see his face, but she recognized the set of his shoulders and the thick brown hair. She dismounted as quickly as she could and ran to his side.

"Cal!" she cried.

She dropped to her knees beside him and took hold of his shoulders. Being careful to roll him over on his left side and not his injured right, she maneuvered him onto his back. The face with its closed eyes was drawn and haggard, but it belonged unmistakably to Calvin Woods.

"Cal!" she said again, but there was no response. Fighting off the panic that threatened to overwhelm her, Susannah stared at his chest. After a tense moment, she was able to tell that he was breathing. His chest rose and fell fairly steadily. He was hurt, no doubt about that, and had lost a considerable amount of blood, but he was alive.

Susannah lifted her head and looked around wildly. No one was in sight. That was good in one way and bad in another. She needed help. She didn't know anything about taking care of bullet wounds, and she wasn't sure she was strong enough to lift Cal's senseless form onto her horse. She didn't even consider trying to catch the unsaddled horse he must have ridden here.

"What am I going to do with you?" she practically moaned.

To her surprise, his eyelids flickered, although his eyes didn't open, and he rasped something. She couldn't make out the words. She leaned closer and asked, "What is it, Cal? What are you trying to say?"

This time she understood as his lips formed the questions, "Who . . . where . . ."

"It's Susannah Bolton. Do you hear me? It's Susannah.

You're on my father's ranch. You're on the Triangle B. Cal, how . . . how badly are you hurt?"

"Smoke," he husked, his eyes still closed. "Got to . . . tell Smoke . . ."

She had no idea where Smoke Jensen was right now, and she couldn't have left Cal alone to go find him, anyway. Whatever Cal had to tell Smoke, it would just have to wait. The only chance she had of saving his life was to get him on her horse and back to the ranch head-quarters.

"Do you think that if I help you, you can stand up and walk?"

" . . . Rustlers . . . after me . . ."

That sent a painful jolt to her heart. He must have found the gang of thieves that had been stealing cattle from the ranchers in the valley. They had wounded him, but he had gotten away from them.

They would be tracking him, Susannah thought. They would be bent on finding him and killing him—and anyone else who happened to be with him.

A part of her—a tiny, shame-ridden part—wanted to leap back onto her horse and ride away from here as far and fast as she could. She couldn't help him, so it didn't make sense for her to lose her life, too.

Susannah's jaw tightened. She pushed that disgrace-ful thought away and leaned over Cal to slide her arm around his shoulders.

"Come on," she told him. "We have to get you out of here."

She gritted her teeth and let out an unladylike grunt

of effort as she struggled to lift him to his feet. He seemed to be trying to get his legs under him so he could help her, but his muscles wouldn't cooperate. He was as limp as a rag doll.

Susannah got behind him, stuck her arms under his, and said, "I'm sorry if this hurts."

She summoned up all the strength she could muster and straightened her back and legs. She had never lifted that much weight in her life, but somehow, she found the determination to do it. Cal was up and on his own feet, and that took some of the strain off of her.

He gasped in pain as she hoisted him. Holding him like that had to pull on his side where he was wounded. If his injury had stopped bleeding, it would probably start again. But once he was up, he stayed there. His eyes were open and he blinked blearily as he turned his head to look around.

"Who . . ." he said again.

"Susannah," she told him.

"Su . . . Susannah? Susannah Bolton?"

"That's right. Now, can you walk?"

"I . . . I'm fine."

That was so blatantly false that she wanted to laugh. Instead, she leaned forward and tried to urge him to take a step toward her horse, standing nearby and waiting patiently with its reins dangling to the ground.

Cal lurched ahead. She lurched with him. She kept her arms around his chest from behind, gripping her left wrist with her right hand and holding on for dear life. Cal took another unsteady step.

Then he said, "They'll be . . . coming for me . . . The rustlers . . ."

"I know," Susannah said. "We'll get you back to the ranch—"

"No time. They weren't . . . far behind . . . Surprised they're not . . . here by now." He shook his head. "Got to . . . hide."

"Where?" she asked with an edge of desperation and panic in her voice. She jerked her head from side to side as she searched for some place they could get out of sight.

Large boulders littered the top of the ridge that rose on this side of the creek, she saw. If they could get up there, they might be able to hide among the rocks. But the climb would be a hard one, and she didn't know if Cal could make it.

He could if he was on horseback, she reasoned. "Come on," she said again. "You have to get on my horse. Then we'll hide."

Cal didn't argue. His head sagged forward. He seemed to be barely conscious. Susannah forced him to walk again, and as she did, she whistled for the horse, hoping that would make the animal come closer so they wouldn't have as far to go.

Instead, the horse shied away at their approach, maybe spooked by the smell of blood coming from Cal's wound. Susannah bit back a frustrated sob. She braced Cal up as best she could, hung on to him with one arm, and extended the other hand toward the horse.

"Come here," she urged. "Come on, sweetie. Come on over here to me."

The horse just gave her a wall-eyed look.

Cal leaned hard against her, more unconscious than awake. Susannah planted her feet and ordered herself not to give in. She had never faced a challenge like this in her life. She wanted to throw her hands in the air and give up.

But Cal was depending on her, whether he was fully aware of that or not. She continued talking in a calm and cajoling voice to the horse, and gradually the animal seemed to relax. Curiosity finally impelled it to come closer. Forcing herself to move slowly and carefully instead of lunging for the reins, Susannah reached out and snagged them. She pulled the horse closer. It was cooperating now.

"Reach up and get hold of the horn," she told Cal. "I'll lift you, but you'll have to help pull yourself up."

He didn't respond.

"Cal!"

His head came up a little. He shook it, blinked his eyes open again.

"S-Susannah?"

"Get hold of the saddle horn. Do it now. We have to hurry."

The urgency of her tone must have gotten through to him. He lifted shaking hands and clasped them over the saddle horn. Once he had a good grip on it, Susannah risked letting go of him and bending to take hold of his left leg. She raised it and awkwardly worked his foot into the stirrup. Then she hugged him around the middle, took a deep breath, and said, "Up you go!"

CHAPTER 22

Everything whirled crazily around Cal as if the world had suddenly started spinning the wrong way. His stomach lurched. He fought down the sickness and kept his hands clamped on the saddle horn. His muscles felt as weak as those of a newborn kitten, but he forced them to work anyway as he tried to lift himself. His left foot was snugly in a stirrup, he realized.

The arms around his waist tightened and strained. He began to rise and put more weight on his foot in the stirrup. Long ingrained habit made him swing his right leg over the horse's back. He never had to think about mounting up; he just did it.

Then he was in the saddle, sitting there with his heart pounding so hard in his chest he worried it was going to bust right through. He leaned forward and groaned as the world tipped one way and then the other. Somehow, he stayed on the horse and didn't topple off.

"Hang on. I can't hold you in the saddle. You'll have to stay up there yourself. I need to lead the horse."

The clear, musical voice penetrated the fog of pain

and weakness surrounding him in a clammy grip. The voice belonged to a girl, Cal thought, and that brought memories of the past few minutes flooding back into his brain.

Susannah Bolton stood beside the horse, holding its reins in one hand while the other rested lightly for a moment on Cal's denim-clad thigh. She said, "We're going up this ridge to see if we can find a place to hide from the rustlers."

Rustlers . . .

Cal's eyes snapped open wide. A shock jolted along his nerves. The rustlers had been chasing him, he recalled. A wild shot—very good luck for them, nothing but bad luck for him—had wounded him as he fled the hideout canyon, far back in the foothills to the west.

Maybe the shot had held a tiny shred of good luck for him, too, because it hadn't killed him—not right away, at least. But he had lost a lot of blood and it might do him in yet.

He sure wouldn't make it if those blasted outlaws caught up to him, and neither would Susannah. Her life was in just as much danger as his.

"I'm all right," he rasped. "Let's get . . . out of here."

She squeezed his thigh. Gripping the reins tightly, she began leading the horse through the trees and away from the creek. They soon reached the base of the ridge and started up the slope.

It was rough, rocky going, but Susannah's horse, a sturdy little mare, was sure-footed. Susannah seemed to sense that. She allowed the horse to pick out its own path as she urged it to keep moving. They had left the trees along the creek and now ascended a rugged, brush-dotted incline.

That meant they were pretty much out in the open. The pursuers might come along and spot them at any moment. They could open fire with rifles from a distance. Some damned owlhoot might be drawing a bead on Susannah right now.

"You ought to . . . leave me here . . . and light a shuck," he told her.

"If that means what I think it does, I'm not going to do that," she said without looking around at him as she climbed just ahead of the horse. "We've come this far and I'm not going to abandon you."

"But if they find us . . . they'll kill you, too."

"They'll try to. But I'll fight. I have a carbine, you know."

Cal had seen the stock of the weapon in the saddle boot. Susannah was armed, all right, but he didn't have any faith in her ability to use the carbine. The shape he was in, he wasn't sure he was capable of it right now, either.

Not only that, he also heard the fear in her voice although she tried to mask it with bravado. From what he knew of her, she had lived a pampered, easy life until now. She'd never had to deal with some cowpoke wounded by rustlers.

She had gotten him on his feet and into this saddle, he reminded himself. She was doing pretty good for a girl with her background.

And since he was riding a saddled horse, it had to be

her mount, he reasoned. He had known that before, but now his brain was starting to work better. The horse he had used to escape from the wideloopers' hideout must have wandered away after he fell off it. It was probably still around the creek somewhere. The rustlers would find it, but not him, and they would know he was afoot.

They wouldn't stop looking until they found him.

And found Susannah at the same time.

He suppressed a groan. Fate had doomed her by letting her come along and stumble across him. He wasn't going to allow that to happen. He would figure out a way to save her, whether he survived or not.

"We need to split up," he told her.

"We just had this argument," she snapped. "Don't you remember?"

To tell the truth, he didn't, which was no big surprise since his brain, even though it was functioning better, was still full of cobwebs. He said, "When we get to the top of the ridge . . . leave me there. Take the horse and . . . get back to your pa's ranch . . . as fast as you can."

"We're already on the Triangle B."

He went on as if she hadn't spoken. "You can leave me this rifle. I'll hold those varmints off. You'll have plenty of time to . . . get away."

She blew out an exasperated breath. "You just don't listen at all, do you?" she said. "I'm not leaving you, Cal. Whatever happens, we'll face it together."

He didn't have the energy to argue with her. They could talk more about it when they got to the top of this ridge, which still seemed miles away, rather than the forty or fifty yards it actually was.

Cal held on to the saddle horn so tightly that Susannah might have to pry his fingers off it once they reached the top, assuming they made it that far. He felt a wet heat on his side and knew the wound there had started bleeding again. It had closed up sometime during the night while he was trying to stay ahead of the rustlers chasing him. That whole experience had been a nightmare, and like most dreams, he remembered only bits and pieces of it, none of them pleasant.

The pain was worse now. He felt it with every step the horse took. Every thudding impact of hoof against stony ground made fresh jolts of misery shoot through him. His jaw was clenched so tight he started to worry that his teeth might break.

After what seemed like a year or two, and with stunning abruptness, the angle went away. The horse walked over level ground once again. Cal hunched forward in the saddle and swayed.

Susannah was there beside him, reaching up to take hold of his arm and steady him.

"Almost there," she told him. "There's a nice cluster of boulders just up ahead. We'll get among them and anybody who's looking for us won't be able to see us, especially from down below."

But if the rustlers were decent trackers, they might be able to follow the horse's trail up here, Cal thought. The ridge was rocky enough that it wouldn't take prints well, but that might not be enough to throw off the pursuit.

They couldn't go much farther. Cal sensed that he was in danger of passing out again.

Susannah led the horse through a gap between two boulders that were larger than the log cabin in which Cal had been held prisoner. Beyond them was a roughly circular open space about thirty feet across. Some smaller rocks and thick clumps of brush surrounded the small clearing. A half-dozen men could have defended the place effectively from attackers.

How good a job a spoiled, inexperienced young woman and a badly wounded cowboy could do remained to be seen. Cal hoped fervently they wouldn't find out.

"Let's see if we can get you down," Susannah said as she let go of the horse's reins. She moved to Cal's side and reached up with both arms. He kicked his right foot out of the stirrup and started to swing that leg back and around as he normally would have, and with no warning, the world once again did that thing where it turned sideways.

He fell off the horse, right into her arms.

Susannah yelped in surprise and fear, but she didn't jump out of the way. She stood her ground and caught hold of Cal as he toppled against her. For a second, it appeared she was going to be able to stay upright, but his unexpected weight was too much for her.

Both of them lost their footing and went down. Cal landed on top. Susannah let out a sharp cry of pain.

The fall and the sudden worry he felt for her drove his brain back to full awareness. "I'm sorry," he exclaimed.

"Oh, Lord! I didn't mean to fall on you." He got a hand on the ground and tried to push himself up. "How . . . how bad are you hurt?"

"I'm all right," she told him, but he heard the strain in her voice that said otherwise. "Just . . . just get off me."

She put her hands on his shoulders and pushed while he tried to roll to the side at the same time. He wound up on his back. She lay beside him in the same position. Both of them breathed hard as they tried to recover.

Finally, Cal turned his head to look over at her. Her face was pale. He was afraid she had broken a bone or that he had crushed something inside her when he landed on her.

"I'm sorry," he said again. "The world just turned into a bucking bronco there, without any warning."

She drew in a deep breath and then winced. "I think I may have bruised a rib or something, but really, I'm all right, Cal. You didn't do any real damage when you landed on me."

"This is downright humiliating."

Susannah pushed up on an elbow in order to gaze over at him. She cocked an eyebrow and asked, "What is? Falling off a horse? Or being saved by a girl? I imagine a tough cowboy would be embarrassed about both of those things."

"I'm not embarrassed," he insisted. "Just worried about you, that's all."

"Yeah, sure. Let's get you sitting up. You think you can scoot over so that your back is propped against that boulder? Now that we're out of sight, I need to check on that wound of yours."

Slowly and clumsily, with the two of them both straining, they got him into a sitting position where he was able to lean against the rock. Susannah was about to pull up his shirt when he said, "Leave that alone for now. You need to . . . to get the horse tied so it can't . . . run off."

"Oh. Yes, that's a good idea." Susannah scrambled to her feet and went over to the horse. As Cal watched her, he had to admit she didn't move like she was badly hurt. Maybe bruised, like she'd said, but no broken bones.

In fact, even under these terrible circumstances, he realized that she looked pretty darned good. She wore a Stetson that had fallen off and hung behind her neck, caught there by the chin strap. Her blond hair was in disarray, but its tousled appearance didn't detract from her beauty.

She was dressed for riding in denim trousers, a white shirt, and a lightweight denim jacket. Expensive, bench-made boots were on her feet. The saddle on the horse was an expensive one, too, Cal noted as Susannah took hold of the reins. Nothing but the best for her.

Yet she had risked it all to help a forty-a-month-and-found cowpuncher, and she was still risking her life. She would be in mortal peril as long as she was with him.

Sometimes you found good solid quality underneath the frills and fripperies—if you were lucky.

She led the horse over to some brush and tied the

reins to a sturdy-looking branch. Then she came back across the clearing to kneel beside Cal. She reached for his blood-stained shirt, but once again, he stopped her.

"Listen," he said in a low, urgent voice.

They stayed there, silent and motionless, as they strained intently to hear the sounds around them. Once again, Cal picked up the distinctive thudding that had alarmed him.

"Horses," he breathed.

"I hear them," Susannah responded. "They're still a good distance away."

"But coming closer."

"Yes. I think you're right."

They continued listening. The hoofbeats got louder. Then Cal stiffened as he heard a man call out. It wasn't an urgent shout, more like how a searcher would sound reporting that he hadn't found any sign of what he was looking for. Another man answered and sounded the same way, although Cal couldn't make out those words, either.

"It's a search party," Susannah whispered. "The rustlers?"

Cal nodded. That explanation made the most sense. Since he had been missing for several days, it was possible Smoke and Pearlie and the other hands from the Sugarloaf crew were looking for him, but he couldn't risk calling out to whoever it was. There was too big a chance he would lead would-be killers right to them.

"Stay quiet," he whispered to Susannah as she leaned closer to him. "Go over and hold your hand over your horse's nose, or else she's liable to make a racket when the other horses go by."

"Hold her nose?" Susannah sounded like that was a disgusting idea, but when Cal nodded firmly, she stood up and moved across the clearing to do as she was told.

"Wait a minute. Bring me that carbine first," he called softly after her.

Susannah gave him another dubious look, but she pulled the carbine from the saddle boot and carried it across the clearing to him. As she handed it to him, she said, "You're in no shape to be fighting."

"I know, but at least I've used one of these before."

"After this is over, you'll have to teach me how to shoot."

Cal nodded curtly. He liked that idea more than he was willing to let on right now, but first they had to survive the next few minutes. He motioned for her to go back to her horse and keep the animal quiet.

Susannah did so, making a face as she closed her hand over the horse's nose. The horse didn't like it much, either, but it didn't put up a fight.

The tension grew worse inside Cal as the hoofbeats came closer. He felt like he was wound up so tightly that he might fly apart like a watch when somebody was foolish enough to pry the back off.

Susannah grimaced again when a man called, "I don't see anything!" He sounded like he was at the bottom of the ridge, no more than a hundred feet from them.

"I'll go on up the other bank a ways," another man

replied. He was farther away than the first one but still too close for Cal to feel good about it.

"Maybe I'll ride up on top of this ridge and see if I can get a good look around from there."

Cal's heart sank as he heard the first man say that. If the fella rode up here among the rocks, he couldn't help but see Cal and Susannah.

Cal checked the carbine. No round in the chamber, of course. That meant he'd have to work the lever before he could open fire. That would make some noise, and it was a sound most men out here on the frontier would recognize instantly.

Susannah's eyes were wide with impending panic as rocks and gravel clattered down at the bottom of the slope. The searcher had started up toward them. Cal motioned to her, trying to communicate his assurance that everything would be all right, but he couldn't tell if she understood or not. The man's horse made enough noise coming up the incline that Cal was able to cock the carbine without having to worry too much about the searcher hearing it.

Cal braced his back against the rock and lifted the carbine. As he nestled the stock against his shoulder, he leveled the barrel and aimed at the approximate spot where the rustler's head was likely to come into view when he reached the top of the slope.

The idea of shooting a man without any warning like that rubbed Cal the wrong way, but he didn't see any other option. The shot would attract the attention of the second man and any other rustlers in the area, but that couldn't be helped.

At least if he ventilated that varmint, the odds against him and Susannah would be whittled down a little, Cal told himself.

Without even thinking about it, he held his breath as he waited, and Susannah began to look more and more scared and horrified.

CHAPTER 23

Judging by the sound of the hoofbeats, the rider had almost reached the crest when another shout came from the other side of the creek.

"Hey, Dunnigan! Come here! I found the kid's horse!"

With a clatter of steel-shod hooves against rocks, the searcher turned and started back down the slope. Cal could tell what was happening from the sound as well as if he were able to see it.

As he listened to the hoofbeats fade, he realized he was holding his breath. He let it out with a sigh and lowered the carbine. The motion made a twinge go through his injured side.

He hoped the horse on which he had escaped had drifted a good way on down the creek. If it had, the rustlers might continue their search in that direction, rather than doubling back up here on the ridge.

Susannah looked at him and raised her eyebrows. He figured she was asking if she could let go of her horse's nose. He shook his head. They needed to wait a little longer before they assumed it was safe.

Cal sat there with the carbine across his legs until he

judged that enough time had passed. Then he nodded to Susannah and set the weapon aside.

She hurried across the clearing and knelt beside him again. Quietly, she said, "I thought we were, how would you say it out here? Done for?"

"That's as good a way as any," Cal told her. "And I thought the same thing. It was mighty close. We've got a guardian angel watching over us today, that's for sure."

"What would have happened if they'd found us?"

"We'd have had a fight on our hands," he said with a faint smile. "But they would have had a fight to deal with, too. I don't plan on crossing the divide easy-like when my time comes."

"Crossing the divide? You mean dying?"

"That's what it means."

"I would have fought, too, however I could." She leaned forward. "Now, I really need to take a look at this wound. You don't want to go to all the trouble of escaping from those rustlers and then die from a simple bullet wound festering."

He leaned his head back against the rock and told her, "Go ahead. And don't worry about trying to be easy."

"I won't."

Despite what she said, he could tell she was being as careful as she could while she lifted his shirt and tried to bare the wound. The recent bleeding had loosened the shirt from where it had been stuck, but a few places were still stubborn and didn't want to let go because of the dried blood. He caught his breath several times when she finally had to pull the fabric loose from his skin.

"Oh, no," she said in a hushed voice. "I've started it bleeding again."

Through clenched teeth, he asked, "You don't happen to have . . . any whiskey . . . in your saddlebags . . . do you?"

"You want a drink at a time like this?"

"As a matter of fact . . . that doesn't sound . . . half bad. But I was thinking more of . . . using it to clean the wound. What does it look like?"

"Let me get my canteen," she said. "We'll have to use water to get some of that blood off."

Hurriedly, she fetched the canteen and then tore some cloth from the tail of her shirt. When she pulled the garment loose from her trousers to do that, she revealed a strip of bare belly for a moment. Under the circumstances, Cal shouldn't have even noticed that, he told himself, but he did. He sure did, and he found the sight pretty intriguing, to boot.

Susannah soaked the cloth and then bent to the task of cleaning the bullet wound.

Cal gritted his teeth even more. A few shots of Who-hit-John would have come in mighty handy right about now.

Finally, Susannah sat back and said, "It really doesn't look too bad."

"That's good to hear, I reckon," Cal said, "because it sure hurts like blazes."

"I imagine it does. The bullet left a gash in your side about four inches long. It didn't penetrate deeply, though. It just plowed a furrow, I suppose you could say."

"A furrow in the flesh," Cal muttered. "Well, if I'm not shot through and through, I reckon I'll probably live."

"I think there's a good chance of it. You just need that wound cleaned properly and bandaged, then a couple of weeks rest. I'll take you back to the ranch and my father can send to Big Rock for the doctor."

"Not just yet. Not with those killers roaming around. I think we'd better stay right here for now. Maybe try to make it after night falls if they haven't come back around by then."

Susannah thought about it and nodded. "That will give you a chance to rest for a while, too," she said. "I think you need that as much as anything right now."

"You're probably right about that."

She sat down beside him and leaned back against the massive boulder. "Why don't you tell me about what happened?" she suggested.

That sounded like as good a way as any to pass the time. Well, almost as good a way as any, he corrected himself, but as stove up as he was, he wasn't in good enough shape for anything else. He sat there and told her about the events of the night the rustlers raided the Mirror 3. He explained how he had watched the running fight between the rustlers and the regulators, then trailed the cattle thieves after Deke Stratten's men turned back.

"I ran into some bad luck, though, and they caught me. I figured they'd kill me, but they decided they would keep me prisoner instead. They thought their boss might want to talk to me. I don't know why. Maybe they figured he'd have some questions for me. Not that I would have cooperated and answered."

He paused for a moment and then resumed. "After that fight, when I was listening to them talking, a funny thing happened. I thought one of the voices was familiar."

"How is that possible?" Susannah asked. "It was the rustlers who captured you, right?"

"Yeah."

"And you don't know any of them."

"You wouldn't think so," Cal said, "but I would have sworn I'd heard that voice before." A thought occurred to him. "You heard those two hombres yelling at each other earlier. Did you recognize either of their voices?"

"Not at all. Did you?"

"Nope," he admitted. "I'd say they were both strangers to me. But I'd sure like to know who that other fella was."

They were both quiet again for a minute, then Cal took up the story once more, telling her how he'd escaped from the cabin in the hideout canyon. He described the place for her, and she said, "It certainly sounds inhospitable."

He chuckled. "You could say that, all right."

She surprised him by leaning her right shoulder against his left one. "Go on," she urged. "What happened after you got away?"

"A lot of riding and hoping I wasn't going to pass out from losing all that blood. I don't know how I stayed ahead of that bunch and kept them from catching me, but somehow I dodged them. When I figured I'd given them the slip, I put as much ground between us as I could, because I knew they'd likely pick up the trail and come after me. That's how it turned out, all right."

"But now you have a chance to get away from them and be safe," she murmured. Her head rested against his shoulder now. "We are safe, aren't we?"

"For now," Cal told her. His voice was calm and strong, but that took an effort. Weariness kept welling up inside him, and his eyelids felt mighty heavy from time to time.

Susannah said something else, but he couldn't make out the words. Her head was close enough to his that he smelled the clean fragrance of her hair. That made him feel good, but it didn't do anything to ease the tiredness in him. If anything, the warmth and closeness of her just made an overpowering lassitude steal over him more and more.

When he could tell from her deep, regular breathing as she leaned against him that she had dozed off, he knew it was hopeless. An exhausted slumber was going to claim him, too. He couldn't afford to fall asleep, he told himself sternly. One of them had to remain awake and listen for the return of the rustlers. Smoke would expect him to stay alert under these circumstances.

But the weight of everything was just too much. It pulled Cal's eyes closed, and in moments, he had slipped off into a restful darkness.

* * *

Once they were inside the ranch house, Emmaline Bolton offered Smoke a drink.

"It's a mite early in the day for me, and to tell you the truth, I'm not that much of a drinker to start with," he told her. "Just a beer now and then will do for me when it comes to that sort of thing. I prefer coffee, to be honest."

She regarded him with interest and said, "You just used the words *truth* and *honest*, Smoke. Being truthful and trustworthy is important to you, isn't it?"

"I'd say that's mighty important."

"And yet here you are, a married man, in the home of another woman who's not your wife, about to make love to her."

Smoke's mouth tightened. "When you put it like that, it sounds pretty bad."

"It sounds pretty far-fetched, is what it sounds." Emmaline shook her head. "Smoke, now that you're actually here, I can't bring myself to believe that you'd go through with such a dalliance. And believe me, I've seen plenty of men who were more than capable of such a thing."

He was certain she had, but he didn't see any point in saying that.

"So tell me"—she smiled—"why you're really here?"

He couldn't very well tell her he'd hoped to find something confirming that her husband was the ringleader of the rustlers. He still believed that was possible, even likely, but the idea of finding evidence this way was a long shot, at best. Suddenly, he felt foolish, in over his head, and that was a very rare sensation for Smoke Jensen to experience.

"Maybe I'd better just go back to the Sugarloaf—" he began as he started to turn away.

"No." She moved sharply toward him. "Not yet."

Then she was right in front of him, close enough to reach up and twine her arms around his neck as she leaned against him, pressing her body to his with a hard urgency. Her arms tightened and drew his head down to hers. Her lips found his and clung to them with a heated persistence.

Purely out of instinct, his arms went around her waist. No man alive could have failed to embrace her in that situation.

But the reaction lasted only an instant. Smoke got control of himself, put his hands on her waist, and gently but firmly moved her back so that he no longer felt the soft, warm thrust of her bosom or the arching pressure of her hips. He lifted his head, which broke the kiss, although he still seemed to taste her on his lips.

For a moment, Emmaline looked like the kiss had affected her, too, even though she was the one who'd initiated it. She was breathing a little hard and had a slightly stunned expression on her face, as if she were surprised at the depth of feeling the brief contact had aroused in her.

Then she tipped her head back a little and let out a merry laugh. Smoke wasn't expecting that at all. He couldn't find a thing to say as he wondered why Emmaline was laughing.

She put her hands against his chest and gently pushed him away. "Oh, my," she said. "Sally really is a lucky woman. Does she know what a lucky woman she is, Smoke?"

"You'd have to ask her that," he said.

Emmaline shook her head and said, "No, I don't believe I will. She strikes me as the sort of woman who wouldn't take that very well. I imagine her response would be emphatic, to say the least."

Smoke shrugged and nodded. "More than likely."

Emmaline stepped back, putting even more distance between them. "I believe there's actually a pot of coffee on the stove in the kitchen. Why don't I get a cup of it for you?"

"That would be nice. Thank you."

"Come with me. You can have it in the kitchen."

It was amazing how quickly the atmosphere had changed, Smoke reflected as he sat at the kitchen table and sipped from the cup of coffee Emmaline poured for him. This was like a neighborly visit now instead of an illicit rendezvous.

Emmaline sat down across the table from him and said, "I'd still like to know why you rode over here today, Smoke, if you had no intention of going through with what I thought was going to happen."

"I never said I had no intention of it," he told her, and in a way, that was the truth. He hadn't said that to her, only to Sally. "Maybe I just wanted to find out . . . well . . ."

"Just how faithful you really are?" She laughed again.

"I suppose most men are curious about that at one time or another. And most fail the test, I suspect. But perhaps it's best things worked out this way. Now we can be friends in the future."

"I don't see why not," Smoke said.

They chatted for a few more minutes, then Smoke lifted his head as he heard something outside that caught his interest. He didn't have any trouble identifying the sound, having heard similar ones many times in the past.

"Rider coming," he said to Emmaline. "I'd say he's in a hurry, too."

"Is that bad?" she asked as he got to his feet.

"It can be. There's no way of knowing until he gets here. But since your husband isn't here, I reckon I'd better go see who it is and what they want."

Emmaline started to look worried. "You don't think those outlaws would come here in the middle of the day, do you?"

"Not likely. You just stay here, and I'll see what it's all about."

Smoke walked back through the luxuriously furnished house and stepped out onto the front porch. The rider who was galloping in was close now.

Smoke recognized him as one of Stratten's regulators. The man brought his mount to an abrupt halt in front of the ranch house and frowned in apparent surprise at Smoke, but he didn't demand to know what Smoke was doing here. Instead, he asked, "Where's Bolton?"

"Out on the range with his crew," Smoke replied. "Do you need to see him? Has something happened?"

"You could say that." A curt nod accompanied the gunman's answer. "We've caught those damned rustlers."

CHAPTER 24

Smoke managed to conceal his surprise as he said, "What?"

"I told you, we caught those damn rustlers." The regulator shrugged. "Some of them, anyway. Came on half a dozen of them cutting out a jag of cattle to drive off."

"In broad daylight?" Smoke didn't bother to hide his skepticism.

"We didn't ask 'em if they'd gone loco, if that's what you mean. It was plain as day what was going on. We rounded them up, and then Deke said he was gonna question them while he sent me to fetch Bolton. Reckon he figures on trying to make them tell where their hideout is." The man turned his head and spat. "So you say Bolton isn't here? Deke thought he might want to see what's gonna happen."

That comment had an ominous sound to it. Smoke said, "That's right, he's up on the north part of the spread with his crew, checking out some fresh range."

The gunman thought about it for a moment and then shook his head. "I don't reckon Deke'll want to wait long enough for me to fetch Bolton from all the way up yonder. He'll just have to go ahead without him."

The man started to turn his horse. Smoke said sharply, "Hold on. I'm coming with you."

"Nobody said anything about bringin' you back with me, Jensen."

So the hired gun knew who he was, Smoke thought. That might be a good thing. The man probably wouldn't be inclined to argue too much.

"Stratten didn't tell you not to bring me, did he?"

The gunman fingered his chin and frowned as he turned that over in his mind. Then he said, "No, I reckon he didn't, seeing as how he didn't even know you'd be here. Come on, I suppose, if that's what you want."

Smoke untied his horse and swung up into the saddle. Emmaline had followed him onto the porch. He nodded to her and pinched the brim of his hat as he said, "I'll give my wife your kind regards, Mrs. Bolton."

"You be sure to do that, Mr. Jensen," she said.

Smoke didn't know if that little exchange fooled the regulator, nor did he care. This whole thing had been a fiasco, a rare miscalculation on his part.

And if the regulators really had caught some of the rustlers, that might mean all his fancy theories about Thaddeus Bolton being the gang's ringleader were wrong, too.

The two men rode side by side, moving at a fast pace across the range. They headed west from the ranch headquarters. After covering several miles, the regulator said, "We're gettin' pretty close."

"How did you happen to find those rustlers?" Smoke asked.

"Just came across them on one of our regular patrols, that's all. You know we've been riding all over the valley. Today we happened to be in the right place at the right time."

"The wrong place and time for those rustlers, I suppose."

The gunman just grunted.

A few minutes later, they came in sight of a large number of horses standing near a scattered group of trees. Several men had been given the job of holding the horses; each man hung on to the reins of three or four mounts. The rest of the regulators were clustered near the trees.

Half a dozen horses were standing in the shadows underneath the trees, too, but these had riders, Smoke noted. Those men sat stiffly in their saddles, and as Smoke and his companion came closer, he saw why they seemed so tense.

Each man had a rope around his neck, leading up to a tree branch above his head. Those ropes were fashioned into traditional nooses with the hangman's knot snugged up under the left ear, ready for the fatal drop.

Smoke reined in sharply and said, "This is a lynching."

The man who'd brought him here spat and said, "Justice is more like it. You know how these things work out here on the frontier, Jensen. When you catch a horse thief or a cattle rustler in the act, you string him up. Quick and simple, over and done with."

That was true. That sort of rough justice was common

and always had been ever since settlers had started to move into the West. There were plenty of places where the official law was too far away to be of any practical use. Honest men took care of outlaws on the spot.

Smoke had delivered his own brand of justice from the flaming muzzle of a gun too many times to claim any moral high ground in a situation such as this. But that didn't mean he had to like seeing hombres with nooses around their necks.

Deke Stratten was one of the men who had dismounted to watch the hanging. He turned to look at the two newcomers and then strode toward Smoke.

"What are you doing here, Jensen?" Stratten demanded. "I sent Rusty to fetch Mr. Bolton, not you."

"I happened to be there at the Triangle B headquarters, and Bolton wasn't," Smoke said. He didn't offer any more explanation than that. "When I heard that you'd rounded up some of the rustlers, I wanted to see for myself."

"You didn't trust what Rusty said?" Stratten shrugged. "Well, it doesn't matter." He waved a hand at the horses underneath the trees. "Take a look for yourself. There they are."

The six horses fidgeted slightly under their grim burdens. In addition to the nooses around their necks, the prisoners' hands were tied behind their backs. Four were white, the other two Mexican. One of the white men was older, probably in his fifties to judge by his leathery, weathered face and thinning white hair. All the others were in their twenties. They were all dressed in well-worn range clothes.

They didn't look much like outlaws and cattle thieves to Smoke, but it was hard to tell about such things by appearances.

The old-timer lifted his head and called to Smoke, "Hey, mister, are you the boss o' these men?"

"Not really, but they work for the Cattlemen's Association, and I'm a member."

The man licked his lips in obvious nervousness and said, "Well, then, how 'bout tellin' 'em that they're makin' a mighty big mistake?"

"The hell we are," Stratten snapped before Smoke could say anything. "We caught you red-handed messing around with cattle that don't belong to you. That's rustling in my book, or anybody else's book."

One of the younger prisoners yelled, "That's a damn lie! We were just ridin' through. We weren't stealin' any of those cows!"

Smoke moved his horse forward. On horseback, he was on the same level as the prisoners and he wanted to stay there so he could get a better look at them. Several of the regulators frowned and stiffened like they wanted to stop him, but they moved aside when Stratten gave them a curt nod.

"What's your name?" Smoke asked the old man.

"Amos Porter. Those are my boys, Edsel, Vince, and Tim. The two down on the end are friends of ours, Diego and Manuel Sanchez." The old-timer swallowed and licked his lips again. Talking with a noose tight around his neck was awkward. "We're on our way over the mountains, headin' west to the gold fields. Figured we'd try our luck there."

One of the regulators laughed and said, "You're not on your way anywhere but hell, you old pelican."

"Please, mister, I'm tellin' the truth," Porter said to Smoke. "Yeah, we rode up on some cows without meanin' anything by it, and they spooked and took off, but we weren't drivin' 'em anywhere. I swear it on the memory o' my wife, these boys' ma. I sure wouldn't lie about nothin' like that."

The old man sounded sincere. Now that Smoke had gotten a better look at him and the younger men, he could see the resemblance. He didn't doubt that the old-timer was telling the truth about them being his sons.

But that didn't mean he was being honest about their intentions. Smoke had heard about plenty of families that had turned outlaw, and he'd run across some of them himself. From what had been said so far, he could understand why Stratten and the other regulators believed they'd corralled some of the rustlers. It was a logical conclusion after coming across strangers being around moving cattle.

It was just as possible the old man wasn't lying. Smoke felt just enough doubt to say, "I think you should take them into Big Rock and turn them over to Sheriff Carson, Stratten. Let the law sort this out."

"That'd be a waste of time and effort," Stratten said. "I tried to get them to tell us where the hideout is so we can round up the rest of the bunch, but they won't admit anything."

The young prisoner who had spoken up earlier said, "That's because there ain't anything to admit! Our pa's tellin' the truth. We're not rustlers."

Amos Porter looked at Smoke and said, "If you can, uh, see your way to clear to convincin' these fellas not to string us up, sir, we'll be outta this valley by nightfall and you won't never see hide nor hair of us around these parts again! I swear it, sir, by all that's holy."

"If we turn you over to Sheriff Carson and you're telling the truth, you won't have to worry—" Smoke began.

"There ain't no need to bring the law into this," Porter interrupted with a wheedling tone in his voice. "I'm tellin' the truth, as the Good Lord is my witness, and if you'll just let us go—"

A harsh laugh from Stratten cut off the old man's entreaty. "You see, Jensen? He doesn't want us to turn him over to the sheriff. Why do you reckon that is? You think maybe it's because him and these whelps of his are wanted?"

That actually seemed pretty likely, Smoke thought with a sigh. Otherwise, Porter would have jumped at the suggestion that the regulators take the prisoners to Big Rock.

The old man must have realized his misstep. Hastily, he said, "It's true, me and the boys might've got crosswise with the law a time or two in the past, but that don't mean we tried to rustle that stock or done anything else unlawful around here. We ain't wanted in Colorado, but, uh, there might be a little paper out on us in Kansas . . ."

His voice trailed off as a look of despair settled over his face. His shoulders slumped.

Smoke said to Stratten, "No matter what they're

guilty of in Kansas, that doesn't mean they're part of the gang that's been raising hell around here."

"I'm tired of this argument," Stratten replied. "You're just one member of the association, Jensen. You can't give me any orders. My job is to clean up the rustling around here, and when I took it, I was told I'd have a free hand. Now, I'm going to see to it these men get what's coming to them. If you don't like that, take it up at the next meeting."

Smoke glanced around. The regulators were all watching him now. Some of them had their hands on gun butts; others who held rifles had shifted the barrels so they were aimed in Smoke's general direction.

"You're about to be out of a job," he said in a low voice to Stratten, "and I'm not going to wait for the next meeting, either."

"You pull iron and you'll have a pound of lead in you two seconds later."

"You'll be just as dead, though, no matter what happens to me," Smoke pointed out.

He didn't know how the standoff was going to turn out, but he thought he saw a flicker of surrender in Stratten's ice-cold eyes. The regulator boss might be about to order his men not to hang the prisoners after all. Smoke would have been satisfied with that outcome—but it never came about.

Because at that moment, Amos Porter's nerve broke. The old man let out a strident yell and banged his feet against the flanks of the horse underneath him. The horse jumped ahead and Porter dropped. Everyone there heard the sharp crack as the noose broke his neck.

A couple of the regulators yelled and fired rifles into the air. The other prisoners shouted curses, screamed in fear, or prayed for deliverance, but all the racket was cut short as their horses leaped out from under them, too, and they plummeted to their deaths. One of the Mexicans didn't die instantly, but he kicked frantically only twice before his legs went still and he hung as limp and lifeless as the others, before Smoke could even think about trying to save him.

A bitter taste filled Smoke's mouth as he looked at the dead men. "You still could have gotten this wrong," he said to Stratten.

The cadaverous gunman shook his head and grinned. "Nobody around here is going to believe that, Jensen, and you know I'm right."

Smoke had to agree. When the story got around, a few folks might harbor some doubt about the guilt of this bunch, but they would give Stratten the benefit of those doubts. The regulators wouldn't be in any trouble over what had happened here today.

Smoke didn't say any of that out loud. Just knowing it was bad enough. His gaze was every bit as cold as Stratten's when he told the man, "At least have the common decency to bury these men."

"Sure," Stratten said, still grinning. "But we're not going to waste time digging six holes. One big one will be enough."

Disgusted, Smoke turned his horse away sharply before the tight rein he had on his temper slipped. He didn't look back as he rode off.

Looking back wasn't going to change anything, or do any good.

Sally must have heard his horse approaching, because she was waiting on the front porch when Smoke rode up to the ranch house. The anxious expression on her face became even more worried when she saw the bleak lines in which his features were set.

"Oh, Smoke," she said as he reined in. "You didn't . . ."

He swung down from the saddle, looped the reins around the hitching post, and started up the steps.

"Didn't what?" He asked the question, then stopped short and stared at her for a second before he went up the rest of the way to the porch. "With Emmaline Bolton? Not hardly!" He put his hands on her shoulders. "Not with her or anybody else."

"Thank goodness," Sally said with a sigh. Then her forehead creased in a frown again. "But something has happened. I can tell by looking at you."

"Let's sit down," Smoke said as he nodded toward the rocking chairs on the porch. "I'll tell you about it."

He proceeded to do so, and Sally's expression grew horrified as he told her how Stratten and the other regulators had strung up the six drifters.

When he was finished, she said, "I've never known you to be upset about outlaws getting what's coming to them, Smoke. Does that mean you believe those men weren't rustlers at all?"

"I don't know what to think, and that's the honest

truth," he said. "From the things the old man said, it's pretty clear they were on the run from the law in Kansas. But they might have been telling the truth about heading for the gold fields. The whole story about just happening onto the cattle and then being jumped by Stratten and his men right afterwards might well be true."

"I suppose we'll never know, now that they're dead."

"That's right," Smoke said, nodding slowly. "We'll never know. But even if they were part of the gang, this probably won't put an end to what's been going on. There are more rustlers than just the six men who were hanged today."

"Maybe what happened to them will scare the others and make them leave this part of the country once they hear about it."

"That's possible," Smoke allowed. "But if they do, we'll never recover the stock they already rustled."

"Better that than them continuing to raid the valley's ranches, stealing and killing, isn't it?"

"Sure. I just hate to see them get away with it, that's all."

Sally cocked her head and frowned in thought. "What does this do to your theory about Thaddeus Bolton being behind the rustling?"

Smoke laughed, but there wasn't any genuine humor in the sound. "It puts us right back where we started. I had my doubts that Stratten and the regulators were really trying to put a stop to the raids if Bolton was in back of them, but they seemed bound and determined to hang those men today. The whole thing doesn't put

Bolton in the clear, but it weakens the case against him, that's for sure."

"You didn't find anything incriminating at the Triangle B ranch house?"

This time Smoke's chuckle was more sincere. "All I found there was a feeling that I was being a big old fool. And Emmaline wasn't taken in by the act, either. When it came right down to it, she knew I wasn't going to betray you."

"Well, I can't say I'm disappointed by the way that part of it turned out. I always trusted you, Smoke, but you're really not cut out to play games like that. You're too fine and decent."

"I'm glad to hear you say that, but it still leaves us in the dark when it comes to rounding up that gang."

"What do we do now?"

"Wait for a ray of light to break through, I reckon," Smoke said, "and not give up hope."

And at the mention of hope, he thought about Cal.

He hadn't given up on the young cowboy, either.

CHAPTER 25

The sun had gone down by the time Cal woke up. Full dark surrounded him and Susannah, and at first, he was disoriented, with no idea how much time had passed or where he was, other than the fact she was there with him, warm and soft as she rested against his left side.

He had jerked a little when he woke up, and that must have partially roused her from slumber. She murmured something unintelligible and shifted a little.

His left arm was around her shoulders. Instinctively, he tightened the embrace. That must have reassured her and kept her from coming fully awake. He felt her relax against him. Within a minute or two, her deep, regular breathing told him she was asleep again.

No matter how good it felt just to sit here and hold her, Cal's heart slugged in his chest and a sense of alarm filled his brain as the cobwebs began to clear. He remembered escaping from the rustlers' hideout, falling off the horse, and passing out as he tried to reach the creek and drink so he could relieve his parched mouth and throat.

His recollection of Susannah finding him, helping him onto her horse, and hiding all three of them from the pursuers was a lot fuzzier, although he recalled enough for the whole thing to make sense. One of the rustlers had come close to discovering them in the rocks, but then, fate had intervened and saved them, at least for the moment.

Clearly, since they were still here among the boulders where they had dozed off after Susannah tended to his wound as best she could, the rustlers hadn't found them. By now, the outlaws must have given up the search and headed back to their hideout. That was what Cal hoped, anyway, because he still wasn't in any shape to handle a gunfight and he didn't want Susannah mixed up in anything so dangerous.

Cal sat there, not moving, just listening intently to the night sounds. They all seemed normal. He heard bird songs and small animals moving nearby, and they wouldn't be rustling around if they felt threatened by humans. His eyes adjusted to the darkness well enough for him to be able to make out the large, dark shape of Susannah's horse on the other side of the clearing as it nibbled on the brush to which it was tied.

Cal tilted his head back, studied the stars, and tried to figure out what time it was. The moon was nothing but an orange crescent hanging low in the sky off to his right, so it wasn't much help.

Susannah stirred again. This time, she was waking up naturally, rather than being disturbed by him. He had to admit, he was a mite relieved. As pleasant as it was to sit and hold her, he had stiffened up some and it would feel good to move around a bit.

She sat up straighter and shook her head. "Where . . . ?" she muttered. "Why am I—Oh! Where am I? What is this place? *Cal?*"

"You're all right," he told her, keeping his voice calm and steady. "You're fine, Susannah. Don't get upset."

"Upset? But you—Cal, you were wounded!"

"I'll be all right," he said, although to be honest, a throbbing ache had developed in his side that was a little worrisome. He felt somewhat lightheaded, too, and wondered if he might be running a fever.

"The rustlers . . . ?"

"I reckon we can assume they didn't come back. We wouldn't still be sitting here if they had."

He didn't speculate on what might have happened if their hiding place had been discovered. It wouldn't have been anything good, that was for sure, and he didn't want to think about it. He would rather look ahead and try to figure out their next move.

"Do you think they're still lurking around here somewhere?" she asked.

"I don't know, but it doesn't seem likely. I think there's a better chance they've gone back to their hideout." Something occurred to him. He went on, "If they did, they're liable to clear out because of the chance that I got away and can lead a posse back there. They probably won't try to drive those cows in the dark tonight, but it wouldn't surprise me if they made a move first thing in the morning."

"What should we do?"

"I need to get to the Sugarloaf and tell Smoke what's going on. There's still a chance he can round up the whole bunch, but he'll have to hurry."

"The Triangle B is closer," Susannah said, "and you still need medical attention. Why don't we try to make it there, and my father can send a rider to the Sugarloaf to fetch Mr. Jensen?"

At first, Cal wanted to insist that he had to ride directly to the Sugarloaf, but what Susannah suggested made sense. And in the long run, it might get word to Smoke sooner, because they couldn't move very fast with him wounded and riding double.

"All right," he said. "We'll go to your pa's ranch. First, though, I could sure use a drink if there's any water left in that canteen of yours."

"I'm sure there is." Susannah climbed hurriedly to her feet. "I'll get it."

The canteen was lying nearby where she had dropped it after using some of the water to wash away blood from his wound. She was going to hold it to his mouth for him, but he felt strong enough after sleeping to take it and tilt it up himself. The cool water felt wonderful sliding down his throat.

He could have drained the canteen but forced himself to stop. He didn't want to get sick from putting too much water into an empty stomach. And it was empty, for sure. In fact, he couldn't remember the last time he'd had anything to eat. The previous night, maybe? However long it had been, it was too long.

But creature comforts could wait. The most important thing right now was to let Smoke know where the hideout could be found. Cal had intended to lead a posse back there himself, but he knew he might not be able to, the shape he was in. He was confident, though, that Smoke would be able to find the place once Cal told him where to look.

He handed the canteen back to Susannah and said, "Let's see if I can get on that horse."

"I'll help you," she offered immediately.

"I think I can do it this time. But if I need a hand, I'll be mighty happy to have you lend it."

"First things first," she said. "You need to get on your feet."

Cal laughed and said, "Yeah, that may be harder than it sounds."

She stood beside him on his left, got her arms under his arm, and lifted as he tried to stand up. He came up pretty wobbly and swayed some once he was upright. He was able to lean on Susannah, though, and after a moment he felt stronger. She stayed beside him, supporting him as he shuffled across the clearing toward the horse.

Once they were there, he hung on to the saddle while she slid the carbine back in its scabbard and hung the canteen from the horn. He lifted his foot to the stirrup by himself, and then with Susannah behind him pushing, he pulled himself up onto the horse's back. He took his left foot out of the stirrup so she could use it. She was able to swing up behind him and settle down right behind the saddle.

"Put your arms around my waist and hang on," Cal told her.

"I don't want to hurt you," she protested.

"It'll be a lot bigger problem for both of us if you were to fall off and break a leg," he said.

"That's true." Her arms went around his waist. "Can you handle the reins, or would you like me to reach around you and take them?"

That sounded like an intriguing idea, but Cal figured he could manage. He said as much and took the reins from where Susannah had looped them around the saddle horn. He tugged gently on them and tapped the horse's flanks with his boot heels. The animal turned toward the slope.

The horse didn't want to go down the ridge in the dark, but Cal knew how to get balky mounts to cooperate. He had started to feel even more lightheaded, but he forced himself to ignore that and concentrate on what he was doing. He insisted that the horse descend the slope, but he let the animal pick its own path.

Just as on the previous ride, every step made Cal's side throb with pain. Maybe it wasn't quite as bad as before, but it was still enough to make the journey miserable as they reached the base of the ridge and started toward the Triangle B ranch house. Cal was glad Susannah seemed to know where they were going, because he was turned around and easily might have gotten lost, wandering around in the dark night. He might have even headed back in the direction of the rustlers' hideout without knowing it.

Cal could only hope that all the outlaws had left these parts. If they ran into any enemies now, it would be a disaster, and probably a fatal one, at that.

Time meant nothing to him. He had no idea how long they had been riding. It might be almost morning, for all he knew. He wouldn't be able to tell unless the sun rose right in front of his eyes.

"Where . . . where are we?" he asked Susannah. "How much . . . longer?"

"I think we're getting close," she said. "It's so dark I'm having a hard time making out any landmarks, but I'm pretty sure we're still going in the right direction."

"Pretty . . . sure?"

"I'm certain," she declared, but to Cal, she didn't sound as confident as she was obviously trying to be.

More time dragged past before Cal spotted a light in front of them. It wasn't the sun coming up, though, he realized. It was a small yellow glow, and as they came closer, he recognized it as the light coming through a window in a building.

Susannah saw it, too, and exclaimed excitedly, "That's it! That's the ranch headquarters! I—I think that's the cook shack. Cottontop must be up already, getting breakfast started for the hands."

Breakfast meant coffee, biscuits, bacon, maybe flapjacks. Cal's stomach rumbled in response to that thought. At the same time, he felt a little sick and wasn't sure he would have enough of an appetite to eat, no matter how good the food sounded.

Susannah banged her heels against the horse's sides and sent it loping forward. The light grew bigger, and then a door opened and spilled even more light into the darkness. A tall, lanky figure was silhouetted against the glow for a moment as someone stepped outside. The reedy voice of an older man called, "Who's that ridin' around out there at this time o' the mornin'?"

"Cottontop!" Susannah cried as she reached around Cal, grabbed the reins, and hauled the horse to a stop. "Cottontop, it's me. I need help!"

"Miss Susannah? Good Lord, girl, the whole place's been in an uproar over you. Nobody could find you, and your folks are fit to be tied!"

The old cook came up next to the horse and went on, "Who's that with you? He looks like he's hurt."

"It's Cal Woods from the Sugarloaf. He's been shot. Can you help me get him down and take him into the house? He needs a doctor, and we need to get word to Mr. Jensen."

Excitement bubbled over in Susannah's voice as she added, "Cal found the rustlers' hideout!"

"Lord have mercy!" Cottontop reached up to assist Cal from the saddle. "We can take him into my room here in the cook shack. Be easier gettin' him into the bunk there than takin' him up the porch steps and into the house."

Cal thought that was a good idea. The ride here had worn him out, and the prospect of stretching out on a bunk sounded wonderful.

"Thanks," he muttered as he dismounted shakily. "I'm liable to . . . get some blood on your bunk, though."

"I ain't gonna worry 'bout that, boy. Blood'll wash out most of the time."

Susannah slid down from the horse's back and landed beside Cal. She took his right arm while Cottontop supported the left. Together, they turned him toward the cook shack.

They hadn't taken a step when another figure came out of the night and moved into the slanted rectangle of light coming from the open doorway. A voice that was vaguely familiar to Cal said, "I heard somebody ridin' in. What's goin' on here? Is that that young fella from the Sugarloaf?"

"That's right, Matt," Susannah said. "He's been wounded."

Cal had stiffened as soon as the newcomer spoke. Because of the weariness that gripped him from the blood loss and the ordeal he had gone through, his head had sagged forward. It rose now as he peered at the man standing in the light. He recognized Matt Coolidge, the Triangle B foreman.

And he knew beyond a shadow of a doubt it had been Coolidge's voice he'd heard giving orders to the rustlers a few days earlier.

CHAPTER 26

Despite his condition, Cal's mind worked swiftly. He forced the tension from his muscles and let his head droop forward again. He could only hope that Coolidge hadn't noticed his initial reaction. If he knew that Cal was aware of his connection with the rustlers, there was no telling what he might do.

And as long as Susannah was right here with him, Cal wasn't going to place her in danger.

"Let me give you a hand there," Coolidge said with nothing in his tone but apparent friendliness and concern. "I'll take him, Miss Susannah. Your folks are gonna be mighty glad to see you, by the way. They've been worried as all get-out about you bein' missing."

"I should probably let them know I'm back," Susannah said. "I hate to wake them, though. And I want to make sure Cal's all right."

"I reckon you can wait a while to go and see them, Miss Susannah," Coolidge said as he and Cottontop steered Cal toward the cook shack door. "Anyway, I think your ma took something to help her sleep. You might have a hard time wakin' her up. It'll be mornin' in another hour, hour and a half. Lettin' your folks know you're safe can wait until then."

Those comments struck Cal as suspicious, but Susannah seemed to accept them wholeheartedly. He wanted to get her away from Coolidge. She would be safe in the house with her parents, so he said, "No, Susannah, you . . . you should go find them right now. Think about . . . how worried they must be—"

"Come on, Woods," Coolidge said, urging Cal toward the door. "The gal just wants what's best for you."

Cal tried to hold back as the Triangle B foreman and the old cook practically dragged him toward the cook shack. "Susannah, don't—" he began.

"Hush, son," Cottontop said. "Take it easy there! Nobody's gonna hurt you."

Cal wasn't so sure of that. If Matt Coolidge got a chance, he might try to put Cal out of the way—permanently.

Both men had firm grips on his arms. Cal was too weak to pull away. If he kept struggling, Coolidge might lose his patience and kill him. If Coolidge did that, he couldn't afford to let Susannah and the old-timer go. He would have to get rid of them, too.

Cal allowed his muscles to go limp. He sagged in the grasp of the two men flanking him. Cottontop said, "Poor varmint's done gone and passed out."

"Appears so," Coolidge agreed. "Let's get him inside."

Making Coolidge believe he posed no threat at the moment was the best chance he had, Cal told himself, and that chance extended to Susannah, too. He didn't offer any resistance as the two men half-dragged, half-carried him into the cook shack.

The smells of baking biscuits and boiling coffee stabbed at Cal's empty belly, but he had to act as if he wasn't aware of them. Coolidge and Cottontop maneuvered him through a doorway into the cook's living quarters. Cal's eyes were closed, but he heard Susannah following them.

They lowered him onto a bunk. He opened his eyes a slit and saw Susannah kneeling beside him.

"Do you have any whiskey, Cottontop?" she asked.

"Well, I, uh . . ." The cook hesitated.

"Oh, for goodness' sake! I don't care if you have a little nip now and then. I don't care if you guzzle down a bottle every night. But Cal said whiskey would be good to clean this wound, and I think we ought to go ahead and do that since it'll be a while before the doctor can get out here from town."

Coolidge said, "That's a mighty good idea, Miss Susannah. And while you're doin' that, I'll roust out one of the boys and tell him to saddle up for a fast ride to Big Rock. He can bring the sawbones back with him."

"Thank you, Matt. Now, about that whiskey—"

"Yeah, I got a bottle in the pantry," Cottontop admitted. "I just take a little in my coffee now and then. For flavorin', you know."

"Go and get it."

"Oh, yeah, sure! I'll be right back."

Cal heard Cottontop hurry out of the room. He opened his eyes the rest of the way, weakness causing the lids to flutter as he did so.

"Cal, you're awake again," Susannah said as she leaned over him.

"C-Coolidge . . . where . . ."

"He's gone to send someone to Big Rock for the doctor. You're going to be all right, Cal. I'm sure of it."

The two of them were alone in the room. Cal tried to speak again, ran his tongue over dry lips, and managed to say, "Coolidge is—"

"Don't worry about Matt," Susannah interrupted him. "I told you, he's going to send for help. We can trust him."

That was the very last thing they ought to do, Cal thought. He had to summon up the strength to explain that to her.

Before he could do that, Cottontop hurried back into the room. He had a whiskey bottle with a cork in the neck tucked under an arm, and each gnarled hand held a tin cup.

"I brung you both some coffee," he said. "Seems like what you both need after a long night. Drink up, and then I'll see about cleanin' up that bullet wound on the youngster."

"We ought to do that first," Susannah said.

"It's waited this long. It'll wait another few minutes while you get some o' this hot coffee in you."

That actually sounded reasonable to Cal. The coffee might perk him up and help him think straighter. He knew he would have a hard time convincing Susannah that her father's foreman was in league with the rustlers, so the clearer his mind was, the better. He lifted a trembling hand to take one of the cups from Cottontop.

The old man bent over him. "Don't worry, son, I'll help you," he said gently. He held the cup to Cal's lips.

The coffee was hot but not scalding. Cal gulped down a healthy swallow, paused, then drank some more. The heat and the bracing bite of the strong black liquid caused renewed strength to flow through him. He looked past Cottontop and saw that Susannah was drinking from the other cup.

Then, without warning, the cup slipped from her fingers and fell to the rough wooden floor, spilling the coffee that was left in it.

Cal's eyes widened when he saw that happen, and his shock grew even worse when Susannah's eyes rolled up in their sockets and her knees buckled. She crumpled to the floor next to the fallen cup.

A jolt of alarm sizzled from Cal's brain to his nerves and muscles. He raised his right hand to knock aside the cup Cottontop had been holding to his mouth. He tried to get up.

Whether or not he would have managed to do so, he would never know. The old cook planted a hand in the middle of Cal's chest and shoved him back down on the bunk.

Cottontop didn't weigh much, but the condition Cal was in, it was enough to keep him pinned to the thin mattress. The friendly eyes in the wrinkled, kindly old face had turned cold and merciless.

"Just take it easy, boy," Cottontop said.

"Susannah—"

"The gal's all right. You will be, too, as long as you cooperate."

The sound of a footstep made Cal glance past Cottontop. He saw Matt Coolidge appear at the cook's shoulder. The two men exchanged a meaningful look and nods of agreement. Cal knew then that the rot at the Triangle B went a lot deeper than just the foreman.

Whatever Cottontop had doped the coffee with, it took effect quickly. The room began to whirl around Cal—it had been doing too blasted much of that lately, he thought—and then it spun him right off into nothingness.

Smoke and Sally were having breakfast when Pearlie came into the dining room and said, "Thaddeus Bolton is about to ride up, Smoke."

Smoke looked up from his plate with a frown. "What's he doing over here, especially first thing in the morning like this?"

"Don't know," Pearlie replied, shaking his head. "As soon as I spotted him comin', I came in to tell you."

"Is he by himself?" Sally asked.

"Yes, ma'am."

Sally looked at Smoke and said, "I thought maybe Emmaline might be with him."

To be honest, she was just as glad that Emmaline Bolton hadn't accompanied her husband over here to the Sugarloaf. Emmaline had tried to seduce Smoke, and even though nothing had happened between them—

and never would—Sally still couldn't bring herself to feel kindly toward the woman.

Smoke sighed with regret as he looked at the flapjacks and bacon still on his plate, but he set his napkin aside and rose to his feet.

"I'd better go see what it's about," he said. "I don't think Bolton would be paying us a visit without a good reason."

Pearlie nodded and agreed. "He ain't the type to just drop by, neighborly like, that's for sure."

Sally stood up and followed the two men out of the dining room. As the three of them stepped onto the porch, she saw Thaddeus Bolton reining his horse to a stop in front of the house.

He was dressed in expensive range clothes, as usual, but the outfit was a bit disheveled. The clothes looked like he had slept in them, Sally realized.

Not only that, but Bolton's normally handsome face had a drawn and haggard look about it, as well. Clearly, something was bothering him and had been for a while.

Bolton didn't dismount, but he raised a hand in greeting and nodded to the three people on the porch.

"Jensen," he said curtly to Smoke. His tone softened a bit as he added, "Good morning, Mrs. Jensen."

He ignored Pearlie. In his eyes, an employee wasn't worthy of acknowledging, Sally supposed.

"Morning, Thaddeus," Smoke said. "What brings you over here?"

"Have you seen any sign of my daughter?"

The blunt question took the trio from the Sugarloaf

by surprise. Sally responded first, saying, "You mean Susannah? Has something happened to her?"

"That's what I'm trying to find out," Bolton said, his face and voice grim.

"I haven't seen her since the other day in Big Rock, when she was with her mother," Smoke said. He looked over at Pearlie. "How about you?"

"Ain't laid eyes on the gal since the day of that party," the foreman replied. "None of the hands have mentioned seein' her, either. Of course, I haven't asked them about her, but I think there's a good chance they would've said something if they'd run into her on Sugarloaf range."

"How long has she been missing?" Smoke asked.

"She rode away from the ranch headquarters yesterday morning," Bolton said, "and no one has seen her since."

Sally had known that Susannah wasn't at home during Smoke's visit to the Triangle B. That was one of the details he had mentioned when he told her what had happened—and more important, what hadn't happened. From the sound of it, after the squabble with her mother had sent Susannah out riding the range, she had never returned.

That was worrisome, indeed. Sally had no children, but she could imagine how it would feel for a mother to have a child missing and not know where she was or what was happening to her. It would be a terrible experience.

"Since the Sugarloaf is the closest spread, I decided to check here first," Bolton went on. "And I'd like to know where that cowboy of yours, Calvin Woods, is, as well."

Sharpness crept into Bolton's tone as he asked that question. Sally saw the suspicion on his face.

Smoke didn't miss that, either. He said, "Are you implying that Cal and your daughter may have run off together?"

"It seems like the sort of thing a couple of foolish, reckless young people might do."

"Cal is neither foolish nor reckless," Smoke said. "But as it happens, he's not here."

Bolton stiffened and leaned forward in the saddle. Smoke raised a hand to forestall the man's reaction and went on, "He's been gone on an errand for me for several days. I don't see how it's possible he and Susannah are together."

Bolton scowled. "You're sure?"

"I wouldn't have said it if I wasn't sure."

After a moment, Bolton nodded. "All right. I've no choice but to take your word for it."

Pearlie said, "You can take Smoke's word for anything, mister." He didn't bother trying to hide his annoyance, but then he added, "I'm sorry your gal's missin'. The hands haven't ridden out for the day's work yet. I'll tell all of them to keep their eyes open for any sign of Miss Susannah."

"Thanks, Fontaine. I appreciate that."

Sally said, "How's your wife holding up, Mr. Bolton?"

"As you might expect, she's extremely worried. She had to take a sleeping draught last night to get any rest at all. Even so, she's exhausted this morning."

"Tell her I'm sorry."

"I will when I see her again. That may not be for a while. I'm going to ride to the other ranches in the valley and let them know that Susannah is missing. I plan to stop in Big Rock and inform Sheriff Carson, as well."

"That's a good idea," Smoke told him. "The more you spread the word, the better. I'm sure somebody will find Susannah, or she'll turn up on her own."

Bolton lifted his horse's reins and nodded. "I certainly hope so," he said. He turned his mount around and rode off without looking back.

"I feel sorry for the fella," Pearlie said quietly, "but I still don't like him."

"That about sums it up," Smoke agreed with a nod.

Sally said, "I feel sorry for his wife. At least Mr. Bolton is out doing something to try to find Susannah, but poor Emmaline can't do anything except sit home and worry. She's there by herself, too."

Smoke cocked an eyebrow at her and seemed surprised by her comment. Sally didn't see why he would be. She didn't like Emmaline, that was true, but she didn't have to like the woman to sympathize with her when something like this happened.

"In fact," Sally went on, "I think I'll drive over there and pay her a visit. I'd like to see if there's anything I can do to make her feel better."

"I don't know if that's a good idea," Smoke said. "With everything that's been going on in the valley lately, I'm not sure if it's safe."

"You don't think I can take care of myself, Smoke?"

"I know you can, but I hate to see you running any unnecessary risks."

Pearlie had been practically a member of the family for so long that he didn't mind speaking up in situations such as this. He said, "How about if one of the boys rode along, Smoke?"

Smoke considered the suggestion and nodded. "Well, that would be better, I suppose."

Sally told herself not to take offense. Besides, she truly didn't mind having company.

She didn't want the men thinking that they could make decisions involving her without her having any say in it, though. She told them, "That's all right with me."

"I'll send Tom Gruber," Pearlie said. "He's a dependable hombre. I'll go tell him to get ready to ride, and then he and I will hitch up the buggy team, Miss Sally."

"Thank you, Pearlie."

The foreman hurried off to carry out those tasks. Smoke and Sally went back into the house, where Smoke said, "Are you sure this is something you want to do?"

"Of course. It's not like I consider Emmaline to be any sort of threat."

"There's no reason for you to feel that she is," Smoke conceded.

"We can't actually be sure that Cal and Susannah aren't together, though, can we, Smoke?"

"Not entirely," he admitted. "It seems like a pretty far-fetched idea, but since we don't know where either of them are right now, we can't rule it out, can we?"

"That was my thought." Sally headed for the stairs so she could go up to their room and put on a traveling outfit in place of the house dress she had worn to breakfast.

"Just be careful," Smoke called after her. "It's not likely you'll run into trouble going over there in broad daylight, but we can't be certain about that, either."

"How about if I pack a pistol in my bag? You know I can shoot."

"I'll feel a heap better if you do," Smoke answered with a nod.

CHAPTER 27

Tom Gruber was a tall, lanky man with dark blond hair. In his late twenties, he was one of the older members of the Sugarloaf crew and had been cowboying for more than a decade. He wore a red shirt, a buckskin vest, and a brown Stetson as he rode alongside the buggy with Sally at the reins.

Like a lot of cowboys when they were around anyone other than their best friends, he was also taciturn, so Sally had to carry most of the conversation as they headed for the Triangle B. She didn't know much about Gruber's background. Eventually, she pulled out of him that he was from somewhere in central Texas and had drifted over most of the southwest during his years of working with cattle.

"How well do you know Cal?" she asked him. "You don't think he'd run off with Miss Bolton and marry her, do you?"

Gruber shook his head. "No, ma'am, I don't. Cal can be a little rambunctious and hotheaded at times, but mostly he's a pretty serious young fella. Smoke gave him a job, and he wouldn't abandon it to go chasin' off after some gal."

"That's exactly what I think," Sally declared with an emphatic nod. "But where can he be?"

"Don't know." Gruber paused and then added, "Sure wish I did. He's a good youngster."

Sally knew that all the members of the crew were worried about Cal. So were she and Smoke.

"Maybe I'm talkin' out of turn," Gruber said, surprising Sally by volunteering anything, "but I reckon there's a good chance Cal will be the foreman of the Sugarloaf one of these days. Not now, mind you, but when he grows up a mite more. I figure he'd be a perfect fit for the job. I wouldn't mind ridin' for him, and I don't think the other boys would, either." The cowboy let out a brusque laugh. "Assumin' that Pearlie ever decides to hang up his spurs. I wouldn't bet a hat on that."

"Neither would I," Sally agreed with a smile.

A short time later, they came in sight of the headquarters buildings at the Triangle B. The place appeared somewhat deserted. Sally supposed that most, if not all, of the riders were out on the range, taking care of their daily work or searching for Susannah. Or both.

Sally brought the buggy to a stop in front of the house. Gruber reined in alongside the vehicle and swung down from the saddle.

"I'll tie up these animals and then mosey on over to the bunkhouse and see if anybody's around," he said after he helped Sally down from the buggy.

"Thank you, Tom."

He nodded and pinched the brim of his hat. "Happy to help, ma'am."

Sally went up the steps to the ranch house porch. The wooden door was closed behind the screen. She used the brass knocker mounted on the trim board next to the door.

There was no response. She doubted if Emmaline Bolton would have gone anywhere else. Emmaline would want to be home in case Susannah returned. It was possible she was sleeping, though; her husband had mentioned that she had taken a potion the previous night to help her with that.

Sally hadn't driven all the way over here just to turn around and go home. She tried the knob on the door.

It wasn't locked and turned easily.

Feeling a little like a trespasser—a lot like a trespasser, actually—she opened the door soundlessly and stepped inside. She was in a foyer with a parlor to her left and a staircase straight ahead. In the hallway beyond the stairs, several doors stood open.

The parlor was empty, so Sally walked quietly along that corridor. She thought it probably led eventually to the kitchen, and Emmaline might be in there, having some coffee or a late breakfast. If she'd had something to help her sleep, she probably hadn't risen early this morning.

She probably ought to call out, Sally thought. She didn't want to surprise anyone and cause an awkward situation.

It was too late for that, she realized as she came to the first open doorway and looked into what appeared to be a combination office, study, and library. A large desk dominated the center of the room. Bookshelves filled with heavy, leather-bound volumes covered three of the walls. The other wall had a pair of curtained windows on it. Between those windows stood a floor safe with its door open. The shelves inside the safe were empty, but no doubt they had held the bundles of cash and stacks of papers that were now sitting on the desk.

Two people stood beside the desk, their arms around each other and their mouths pressed together in a passionate kiss. Clearly, they had no thought for anything except each other, which might explain why Sally's knock had gone unheard.

They heard Sally's sharply indrawn breath of surprise, though, and jerked apart, turning to stare at her.

Instantly, she recognized Emmaline Bolton and Matt Coolidge, the Triangle B foreman.

Coolidge looked startled and upset, but Emmaline's eyes blazed with hatred and anger. "What are you doing here?" she demanded through clenched teeth as she took a step toward Sally.

Given the way Emmaline looked and sounded, Sally couldn't help but interpret that move as a threat. And threatening Sally Jensen was exactly the wrong way to proceed. Anger stiffened her spine. She didn't give any ground.

At the same time, part of her was embarrassed. She had already been well aware how Emmaline felt about being faithful to her husband; the woman's affairs were none of Sally's business. She was a little shocked to see Emmaline carrying on with another man while her daughter was missing, but again, that wasn't Sally's concern.

"I'm sorry," she said. "I was worried about you and about Susannah, and I came over to see if there was anything I could do to help. You seem to have things under control, though, so I should go."

"You're not going anywhere," Emmaline said.

Coolidge spoke up, saying, "Now, hold on. We don't want to get carried away here. This is a mite embarrassin', but I'm sure Mrs. Jensen doesn't want to stir up any trouble. If she can keep this to herself—"

"This is none of my business," Sally interrupted him. "I don't plan on saying anything to anyone."

"Don't believe her," Emmaline said. "She'll tell that husband of hers." She sneered at Sally. "They're not the type to keep any secrets from each other."

Sally smiled, but there was nothing friendly about the expression. "Thank you. I'll take that as a compliment."

Emmaline took another step toward her and said, "I didn't mean it that way, you—"

She didn't finish whatever insult she had in mind, because at that moment, gunfire crashed from somewhere outside the ranch house.

Cal didn't know how much time had passed when he woke up from the stupor caused by whatever had been in the coffee Cottontop had given him. All he knew was that his head pounded savagely and sickness made his stomach clench when he tried to open his eyes.

Instead of forcing that, he just lay there in the darkness and waited for his condition to improve.

Over the next few minutes, it did. Eventually, he was able to get his eyes open, but he still couldn't see much. That was because he was in some cramped space thick with shadows. No light penetrated the place except for a few faint glimmers that made it through cracks between the thick beams in the walls.

The dusty, sweetish smell of grain filled his nostrils. He figured out that he was inside some sort of storage shed. The vaguely seen, bulky shapes piled around him were bags of horse feed.

Not surprisingly, his hands and feet were tied—again.

Cal sighed. He pummeled his brain into working. Matt Coolidge was working with the rustlers. Cal had known that as soon as he recognized Coolidge's voice. Coolidge had been giving orders to the outlaws when Cal was captured the first time, so it was possible he was the leader of the gang. At the very least, he was someone in a position of authority.

Cal realized with a bit of a shock that he couldn't rule out Thaddeus Bolton himself being the rustlers' boss. The raid on the Triangle B could have been simply a way of diverting suspicion away from himself as Bolton opened up a campaign of cattle theft.

Cottontop was in on the scheme, too; that was obvious from the way he'd drugged Cal and Susannah.

The thought of Susannah made Cal's heart pound harder and caused fresh throbs of pain inside his skull.

Where was she? Was she all right? Surely, Coolidge wouldn't hurt the boss's daughter.

Cal wasn't gagged. He whispered hoarsely, "Susannah! Susannah, are you in here?"

The question didn't get any response. Over the past few minutes, Cal's eyesight had adjusted enough that he could see better than at first. He lifted his head and craned his neck to look around at his makeshift prison.

The shed was small, maybe ten feet by twelve feet. Most of the floor space was taken up by the piled sacks of grain. The door looked sturdy but not impregnable. There was a similar feed shed on the Sugarloaf, and it was designed to keep varmints out of the grain, not to keep anybody locked up. As battered and weak as he was, Cal was still confident that he could get out of here if he managed to free himself somehow.

He thought about yelling for help but discarded the idea quickly. If the foreman and cook on the Triangle B were part of the rustling gang, he wasn't likely to get help from anybody else here. He had no proof that the whole crew was in on the rustling, but for the time being, he would have to proceed on that assumption.

What had they done with Susannah? Taken her into the house? If they were going to do that, why knock her out with the same drug they'd given Cal? Something more was going on here, but he couldn't come up with any answers.

For now, he needed to concentrate on getting free. That was the most important thing.

Cal managed to sit up. Then, pushing with his feet, he scooted over against the nearest wall. He braced his back against it and planted his bound feet in front of him. Bit by bit, he wiggled and shoved until he was upright, leaning against the wall. He moved along it, feeling the beams with his fingers until he found a rough, splintery place on one of them. He was able to work the rope around his wrists against it and scrape back and forth, picking at the strands with the jagged edges of the rough spot.

Fraying the rope enough to get loose that way was going to take a long time, but he didn't see any other options.

As he worked, Cal heard men and horses moving around outside. The ranch was going about its business this morning. Again, he thought about yelling for help, but he didn't want to risk it. If the wrong person heard him, he might wind up with his throat cut. He continued his struggle in silence.

With his hands bound behind his back, he couldn't tell if he was doing any good with the rope. All he could do was hope that his efforts were weakening it.

No one came near the shed. He considered that a stroke of good luck. Thirst assailed him, weakness sapped much of his strength, and dizziness made it difficult for him to stand up. But he continued working at the rope. He might be giving in to false hope, he warned himself, but it felt to him as if the rope had begun to fray. Some of the strands had parted.

After a seeming eternity, he twisted his hands as much as he could and tried to feel the rope with his fingertips. It was definitely frayed; only a few strands were holding it together now, Cal discovered.

It was about time. In addition to damaging the rope, the jagged wood had scraped and scratched his wrists. He felt slick heat and knew it was blood—blood that he couldn't afford to lose after having spilled so much already in the past couple of days. He stopped rubbing the bonds on the splintery area and gathered his meager strength. With a grunt of effort, he pulled on the rope with both arms, willing it to break apart.

The strands resisted stubbornly. He tried twisting his wrists out of them but failed at that, too. Breathing hard, Cal leaned against the wall and told himself not to give up. He was getting ready to make another try when he heard what sounded like a buggy rattle up and stop somewhere outside, not too far away.

A moment later, the sound of a woman's voice drifted to Cal's ears. He couldn't make out the words, but a thrill of recognition jolted through him anyway. He knew that voice.

Sally Jensen was out there.

Cal's first impulse was to shout for help from her. He reined that in before any sound could emerge from his mouth. He didn't know whether Smoke was with Sally. If he was, she would be safe, but if he wasn't, revealing to her that he was a prisoner might put her in deadly danger. He had to try to find out what the situation was before he raised a commotion.

Knowing Sally was here gave him a fresh burst of strength. Once again he heaved on the rope around his wrists—and this time, with an audible snap, it parted. His arms, unbound at last, fell free at his sides.

Cal winced as renewed blood flow sent pins and

needles through his fingers. He kept flexing them until a semblance of normal feeling had returned. Then he bent over and began tugging at the knots in the rope lashed around his ankles.

Whoever had tied him up had done a decent job of it, but the knots couldn't withstand Cal's desperation. As soon as the rope began to loosen, he redoubled his efforts. When his feet were free, he straightened and stumbled toward the door.

His strength and balance deserted him. He pitched forward onto his knees and caught himself on his hands. The fall made pain stab into his side where the bullet had creased him. His head was spinning again.

He stayed there on his hands and knees only for a couple of heartbeats while he mustered up his determination once more. He got one foot underneath him and heaved himself upright again. Three more unsteady steps brought him to the door. He leaned against it, bracing himself with one hand while he fumbled at the latch with the other.

The door had no lock or bar on it, just a simple latch holding it closed. Cal lifted it and carefully eased the door open a few inches. He put his face to the gap and peered out.

He was at an angle from the Triangle B ranch house but could see the front of it from where he was. A buggy was parked there, its two-horse team tied to a hitching post. The reins of a saddle mount were looped around the post and knotted, as well. Cal recognized the buggy and the horses. They all came from the Sugarloaf.

Coming in the general direction of the shed was a

tall, lanky figure Cal also recognized. The man was Tom Gruber, one of the Sugarloaf hands. Cal's brain put everything he had seen together instantly.

That was the buggy Sally drove. She had come to the Triangle B for some reason, and Smoke had sent Tom Gruber with her as protection in case she ran into any trouble. Smoke didn't know where the hideout was or about Matt Coolidge's connection to the rustlers, but he would soon.

Cal jerked the shed door open all the way and called in a hoarse, croaking voice, "Tom! Over here, Tom!"

Gruber jerked to a stop and twisted his head toward the shed. His eyes widened in surprise as he saw Cal standing there, clutching the jamb for support and wearing a shirt with a large blood stain on the side.

The older cowboy's shock lasted only a moment before he exclaimed, "Good Lord, Cal!" and broke into a run toward the shed.

He had gone only a few feet when several booming blasts from a revolver crashed somewhere nearby. Tom Gruber stumbled as the bullets ripped through him. Momentum carried him another step.

Then he fell to the ground, shot to pieces.

CHAPTER 28

The sound of gunfire made Sally whirl toward the doorway. She didn't know what was going on, but she had left Tom Gruber out there and he rode for the Sugarloaf. She had to make sure he was all right.

"Stop her!" Emmaline cried.

Matt Coolidge's hand closed around Sally's arm and gripped it hard before she was able to take more than two steps.

"Hold on there, Mrs. Jensen," he said as he jerked her to a stop and turned her back toward them. "You don't want to go rushin' out there. You don't know what's goin' on."

"Don't mollycoddle her," Emmaline snapped. "She's not a fool. She's seen enough to figure out what this is about."

She waved a hand toward the open safe and the bundles of money on the desk.

"And she saw us together," Emmaline went on coldly.

"I don't care who you kiss," Sally said. "Why would

that matter to me?" She tried to pull away from Coolidge's grasp, but he was too strong. "I only came over here because I was worried about you. Your daughter's missing."

"That little fool is around somewhere. Her sense of self-preservation is too strong to let anything happen to her. I suppose that's one thing she inherited from me, anyway."

"We've got to figure out what to do here—" Coolidge began.

"What we do is simple," Emmaline said with a cool air of authority. "Put Mrs. Jensen out in the storage shed with that young cowboy, if he's still alive. He may have tried to escape. That would explain those shots. If he's dead, so much the better. It'll save us some trouble later. You should have killed him when you first had the chance several days ago, Matt."

Coolidge looked like he didn't care for her talking to him in such a domineering tone, but he didn't say anything.

"Once you have Sally taken care of, you can finish packing up the money and the bonds and put them in my buggy. Then you'll make sure those cattle are pushed out of that canyon and on across the mountains to the gold camps. Sell them for as much as you can, and then meet me in Denver, just like we planned all along."

Smoke had been on the right track, as he usually was, Sally thought.

He'd just been wrong about which of the Boltons was actually the mastermind behind the rustling ring.

"The boys ought to have those cows rounded up by

now and will be movin' 'em out," Coolidge said. "They don't need me around to boss things. Might be better if I stayed with you."

"I told you what to do," Emmaline said. Her tone made it clear she wasn't going to put up with any argument.

Tight-lipped, Coolidge said, "All right, fine. I just wish things hadn't fallen apart like this so soon. We could've cleaned up a lot more from this valley before pullin' out if that kid hadn't found the hideout and then gotten away. He didn't tell anybody about us bein' mixed up with it except for Susannah. If we get rid of Cal and convince Susannah not to say anything—"

"You're forgetting that someone else knows now." Emmaline nodded toward Sally.

"Oh, yeah." Coolidge made a face and shook his head regretfully. "I'm sorry, Mrs. Jensen. I don't reckon we could ever trust you not to tell your husband what's goin' on."

Sally said, "What I want to know is where Susannah is? Is she really missing?"

"Of course not," Emmaline said. "She's locked up in her room. Thaddeus doesn't know that, though." She laughed. "There are so many things Thaddeus doesn't know . . . I'm sure I can convince Susannah to be reasonable about the whole thing. After all, she's my daughter. My flesh and blood. She won't turn me over to the law. And she likes money, too. She'll have plenty of it if she cooperates. Everything we make from the stolen cattle and everything we cleaned out of Thaddeus's safe."

"What about Cal? Is he all right?"

Coolidge said, "He's got a bullet wound in his side, but he's alive. At least, he was the last time I saw him. I don't know what just happened outside. But that's enough stallin', Mrs. Jensen. Let's go—"

He started to pull her toward the door. Sally reached into her bag and came out with the Smith & Wesson pocket pistol she had put in there before leaving the Sugarloaf. It was a .38 caliber Baby Russian model, quite potent at close range. She deftly eared back the hammer as she shoved the muzzle into Coolidge's ribs, high on his left side.

"I'm not going anywhere with you," she said in a flat, hard voice. "Let go of me."

Coolidge gave her a warning look. "You don't want to do this, Mrs. Jensen."

"That's right, you don't," Emmaline said from behind the desk. She jerked the center drawer open and plucked a gun from inside it. Sally glanced in that direction and saw Emmaline aiming the weapon at her. It was larger than the Smith & Wesson, probably a Colt Lightning. Emmaline held it with two hands as if she were quite familiar with it, and the barrel was rock-steady.

Emmaline went on, "Put that gun down and step away from him."

"So you'll have a clear shot at me?" Sally asked. "I don't think so. And even if you do shoot me, you can't stop me from pulling the trigger. The bullet will go right through Mr. Coolidge's heart."

"That would be a shame." Emmaline's tone made it

clear she would consider the loss an acceptable one, however.

Coolidge picked up on that, too, and gave her a narrow-eyed glance. "Look, nobody has to die here," he said.

"She does," Emmaline stated. "It might as well be here and now."

Her finger tightened on the trigger.

When Cal saw his friend shot down like that, he charged out of the shed and rushed to Tom Gruber's side. Ignoring the pain from his own wound and the danger from whoever had shot the Sugarloaf rider, Cal dropped to his knees next to the fallen man.

As he leaned over Gruber, he saw there was nothing he could do for him. Gruber's eyes were still open, but they stared sightlessly ahead. He must have died within instants of being shot.

"Move away from him!"

The command came in a shaky old voice. Cal looked up to see the cook, Cottontop, advancing toward him. Cottontop held an old Remington revolver, the weapon he had just used to gun down Tom Gruber. Wisps of smoke still curled from the muzzle. The barrel wavered some, but not enough for Cal to take a chance on rushing the old man.

Cal glanced down at Gruber's body, thinking that maybe he could make a grab for the cowboy's iron. When Gruber had fallen, though, he had landed with the holstered Colt underneath him. Cal couldn't dig it out before Cottontop opened fire again.

Keeping both hands in sight so the cook wouldn't get trigger happy, Cal reined in the anger he felt at his friend's murder and said, "Take it easy, old-timer."

"Stand up and move away from him," Cottontop ordered again. "I don't know how you got loose, boy, but since you're awake, I don't reckon I can tie you up by myself without you jumpin' me. I don't like doin' this, but I figure the best thing is for you to die right here and now."

He took a deep breath and steadied the Remington as he aimed it at Cal.

Earlier, Susannah had heard hoofbeats and gone to the window in her room to look out. She had seen a buggy and rider approaching the ranch house. She didn't know the man on horseback, but when the woman at the reins brought the buggy to a halt and climbed out, she recognized Sally Jensen.

She wanted to open the window and call out a warning to Sally, but she hesitated. Everything that had happened was so confusing. She had believed she and Cal finally were safe when they reached the Triangle B early that morning before dawn, but then something she still couldn't explain had happened.

She had passed out, and when she came to, she was here in her own room. The door was locked. She had no idea how she had gotten here or why she was locked in.

Pounding on the door and shouting for help hadn't done any good. No one had come to let her out.

Since then, she had paced worriedly back and forth, but of course, that hadn't done any good, either. Then Sally Jensen had arrived.

Susannah stood at the window and watched as Sally went up onto the porch and disappeared from her line of sight. The man who rode in with her tied up his horse and the buggy team before starting to walk toward the bunkhouse.

He had taken only a few steps when the door of the feed shed next to the bunkhouse flew open. Cal stood there holding onto the door jamb for support, Susannah saw as she stiffened in surprise. He called to the stranger, who broke into a run.

Gunshots roared. The man stumbled and fell, obviously badly wounded. Cal rushed out and knelt beside him.

Watching from the second-story window, Susannah's mind whirled from the shocking suddenness of what she was witnessing. But she knew that Cal was down there, he was still hurt, and he might need help.

She reached for the bottom of the window sash and tried to lift it. The window didn't budge, and when Susannah looked closer at it, she saw that a couple of nails had been driven into the sash from the outside, making sure that it couldn't be opened.

Now there was no doubt in Susannah's mind—this was no longer her bedroom as much as it was her prison.

She was about to slap her hand on the window and try to shout through it to Cal when movement in the corner of her eye caught her attention. When she turned to look in that direction, she received another shock.

Cottontop, the kindly old white-haired cook, was stalking toward Cal with a long-barreled revolver in his hands. The gun's hammer was cocked, and from the threatening way in which Cottontop pointed the gun at Cal, Susannah thought that he must have been the one who shot the other man.

Now he appeared to be threatening to do the same to Cal.

Susannah struggled to take in everything she was seeing and make any sense of it. Cottontop had always been friendly to her, treating her like a kindly old uncle, but she reminded herself that, in truth, she had known him only for a couple of months. That wasn't long enough to form a lasting opinion of someone. She didn't want to think that he would shoot Cal, but honestly, she didn't know what he was capable of.

Those thoughts flashed through her mind in a heart-beat, followed instantly by an overpowering urge to *do something*.

She did the only thing she could, since she was locked in.

She turned, picked up the chair that sat in front of her dressing table, and smashed it through the window as hard as she could.

The crash of breaking glass made Cottontop twist toward the house in surprise.

Cal barely glanced up long enough to see Susannah standing at the window she had just broken out with a chair. Then he was up and lunging toward the old cook. That brief glimpse of Susannah had been enough to tell him that she appeared to be all right, so he needed to concentrate on dealing with Cottontop.

The old man realized Cal was charging toward him and tried to bring the Remington back around into line. Cal left his feet in a diving tackle. He hit Cottontop's legs and drove them out from under him. The old man went down with a yell, landing hard on his back.

Cal scrambled up on hands and knees. He hated to hurt anyone as old as the cook, but Cottontop hadn't given him much choice. He slammed a fist into the man's face and didn't hold back. Cottontop might be old, but he had gunned down Tom Gruber without even hesitating.

Cottontop was already stunned from being knocked down. Cal's punch put him out. Cal snatched the Remington from the old man's now limp hand and turned his head to look toward the house as he heard a clashing sound coming from that direction.

The racket came from the window where Susannah was using a leg of the chair she held to knock fragments of glass out of the window frame. When she had enough of it cleaned out to be safe, she climbed through onto the porch roof. Cal stood up and hurried toward the house as Susannah clambered down the roof's easy slope to the edge.

The fight with Cottontop, brief though it had been,

had taken most of the strength out of Cal. The revolver seemed incredibly heavy in his hand, but he knew he could use it if he had to. Susannah reached the roof's edge, sat down, and slid off it to drop to the ground just as Cal reached the house.

She fell awkwardly when she landed, but she was up instantly and met him, throwing her arms around him and holding tightly as he looped his left arm around her.

"Cal!" she cried. "Are you all right?"

"I will be, now," he told her. "What about you?"

"I'm fine, I'm not hurt at all, but I don't know what's going on. Where are my father and mother?"

"I don't have any idea, but we'd better get out of here while we've got the chance."

He hated to leave Tom Gruber behind, but the man was dead and Susannah was alive, and she was his main responsibility right now. He had to get her someplace safe as quickly as he could.

In order to do that, he would have to remain conscious and on his feet, which might be easier said than done. The weakness that had gripped him earlier had come roaring back, and his head wasn't any too steady.

Knowing that he might not be able to stay upright and moving for very long, Cal let go of Susannah and stepped back.

"Come on," he said. "We need to get out of here."

"But, Cal, Mrs. Jensen is inside. She'll help us."

She was right. Cal had seen Sally go into the house. In the violence and chaos of what had happened after that, it had slipped his mind for the moment. He bit back a groan. He couldn't leave Sally to the mercy of whatever was going on here. And if he could find her, she would indeed help them, he knew that.

He took Susannah's arm and started to lead her toward the steps.

Matt Coolidge struck faster than Sally expected, twisting away from the gun barrel she had thrust into his side. She pulled the trigger anyway, but he lashed out at her wrist at the same time, striking it with his elbow.

Combined with the desperate wrench of his body, that was enough to keep the Baby Russian's bullet from ripping through his heart. It plowed a bloody furrow along his back instead. He cried out in pain but managed to clamp his hand around Sally's wrist and shove her gun arm toward the ceiling.

Emmaline lowered her gun and rushed around the desk. "Kill her!" she spat. "Kill her!"

Sally fought back desperately. She clenched her other hand into a fist and drove it into Coolidge's face. She was strong and the blow rocked his head back, but it didn't stun him.

He struck a blow of his own, backhanding her across the face while at the same time wrenching her wrist hard enough to make her lose her grip on the Smith & Wesson. It flew out of her hand, thudded to the floor, and slid under the desk.

Coolidge hit her again with his open hand. Sally's knees began to buckle. She tried to stiffen them and stay on her feet, but then Emmaline hit her from behind, landing an awkward, glancing blow against her head with the Colt Lightning.

Sally went down but didn't pass out.

Vaguely, she was aware of shots going off somewhere else. Outside, maybe. She didn't know what was going on. Maybe Tom Gruber had run into trouble. Anything was possible on this ranch where it seemed that everything had gone mad.

Even in her battered state, Sally knew her life was hanging by a thread. Emmaline would kill her without a second's hesitation, and Matt Coolidge probably would, too. She had to do something—and Emmaline's feet were within reach from where she lay on the floor.

Sally's hands shot out and closed around Emmaline's ankles. A hard yank upset the woman, who fell over backward with a startled cry. The hard landing jolted the gun out of Emmaline's hand. Sally scrambled for it.

The toe of Coolidge's boot drove into her side in a vicious kick before she could grab the Colt. The savage attack rolled her onto her side and made her gasp. She couldn't force her muscles into action as Emmaline retrieved the gun and scooted backward on the floor to wind up sitting with her back against the desk.

"Damn it, don't kill her, Emmaline!" Coolidge said, his voice strained by anger and the pain of his wound. "We're liable to wind up needin' her as a bargainin' chip. I need to find out what's goin' on outside. Can I trust you?"

Emmaline glared up at him. "How dare you give me

orders?" she demanded. "I'm the one who came up with this whole scheme."

"Yeah, and the one who lured me into helpin' you. But I ain't complainin' now. No point. Will you not shoot this woman?"

"All right," Emmaline responded in surly tones. "We'll keep her alive in case we need her—for now."

Coolidge jerked his head in a nod and hurried out of the room. He had his gun in his hand. Whatever he found outside, he was going to be ready to kill.

That left Sally alone with Emmaline Bolton, and as she looked at the blonde gazing hatefully at her over the barrel of the Colt, Sally realized she had never been closer to death than this instant.

Cal felt as much as heard the wind-rip of the bullet passing close by his head. A man he recognized as Matt Coolidge rushed onto the porch and fired again. Cal had already twisted around to pull Susannah behind him and shield her body with his. As Coolidge's second shot whined past him, he brought up the Remington and triggered it.

Coolidge staggered but didn't go down. Cal thought he had scored a hit with his shot but couldn't be sure.

He went to the ground and dragged Susannah with him. Coolidge slammed another shot toward them, but it went high this time

Cal let the hammer fall again on the Remington.

Coolidge ducked behind the horse that Tom Gruber had tied up next to the buggy.

The next moment, Coolidge had jerked the animal's reins loose and was swinging up into the saddle. He just wanted to get away now, Cal realized. He didn't even try to throw another shot toward Cal and Susannah. Instead, he hauled the horse around, bent low in the saddle, and raked his spurs across the animal's flanks. The horse leaped into a gallop.

Cal was willing to let Coolidge go if it meant Susannah would be safe. Justice could catch up to the treacherous foreman later. Cal had no doubt that it would once Smoke knew what the situation actually was.

For now, Cal wanted to make sure Susannah was all right. As the fleeing Coolidge dwindled in the distance down the trail away from the ranch, Cal sat up and pulled Susannah into a sitting position, as well. Her head lolled loosely on her shoulders, and for a terrible moment, he thought she had been mortally wounded.

But then she groaned and shook her head, and relief flooded through Cal as he realized she was unharmed, just shaken up.

"Cal, what . . . what happened?" she asked.

"Matt Coolidge is working with the rustlers," Cal said. "The cook was part of it, too." He struggled to his feet and helped Susannah up, as well. They hung on to each other, but he couldn't tell which of them was holding up the other. Maybe both.

"My mother—" Susannah began.

The door of the ranch house banged open. "I'm right

here," Emmaline called as she forced Sally out onto the porch in front of her. She had her left arm clamped tightly around Sally's waist. Her right hand pressed the Colt's muzzle against the other woman's head. "Get away from that cowboy, Susannah! *Now!*"

CHAPTER 29

Sally wasn't surprised that Emmaline lacked the patience to sit there and wait while Coolidge went to see what was going on—especially when more gunfire erupted outside. Clearly, the traitorous foreman had run into trouble.

"Get up," Emmaline ordered. "And if you want to try anything, please go right ahead." A cold smile appeared on the woman's face. "Nothing would please me more than to put a bullet in you, you sanctimonious, prissy little—"

"At least I'm not a brazen, husband-stealing hussy," Sally broke in, unable to contain her anger.

"There was never any chance I was going to steal your husband. Smoke's as boring and pompous as you are. Which is a shame because he really is a very attractive man in a rugged way." Emmaline motioned curtly with the Colt. "Now, on your feet like I said."

Sally stood up, slightly unsteady because her head was spinning a bit from the rough treatment she had received at the hands of Coolidge and Emmaline. She had to brace herself with a hand against the wall. After she did that, she felt a little better.

Emmaline got to her feet, as well, leaning on the desk to do so. The gun barrel never wavered enough in its aim for Sally to even think about jumping her.

"Turn around," Emmaline ordered.

"What if I refuse?"

"I think you know the answer to that. I'll pull this trigger—and I'll enjoy it."

Again, Sally saw that she had no opportunity to make a move right now. She had to wait for her chance, maddening though that might be.

Emmaline was careful to keep some distance between them as they stepped out of the library and office. She told Sally to turn toward the front of the house. As Sally did so, she could look along the corridor to the front door. It was empty and the door stood open, allowing a bright rectangle of sunlight to fall into the foyer.

The gunshots had stopped, but from somewhere outside came the swift rataplan of hoofbeats. Somebody was lighting a shuck away from here and not wasting any time about it.

"Go ahead," Emmaline snapped.

Sally moved forward. Just inside the door, Emmaline told her to stop again. The next instant, the blonde moved up close behind her, and Sally stiffened in surprise as Emmaline grabbed her around the waist. She jammed the Lightning's muzzle against the side of Sally's head, just in front of her right ear.

She heard a young woman's voice say something as

Emmaline forced her through the doorway and onto the porch.

"I'm right here," Emmaline called. "Get away from that cowboy, Susannah. *Now!*"

Sally's heart pounded. With the gun pressed so hard to her head, she was afraid to move much, but she was able to cut her eyes to the left and see Cal standing there with Susannah Bolton. They had their arms around each other.

Sally spotted a large dark stain on the left side of Cal's shirt and recognized it as dried blood. He had lost quite a bit at some point while he was missing. His face was pale and drawn and certainly showed the strain of the ordeal he had endured.

But he stood straight and held a long-barreled Remington revolver. Sally knew he was both fast and accurate when it came to gun-handling, although far from being at the same level as Smoke or even Pearlie, for that matter.

She was a little surprised when she realized she didn't want Emmaline killed or even hurt, especially not right in front of the woman's daughter. But to a large extent, that might be up to Emmaline. This showdown was going to have to play out.

In a tense voice, Sally called, "Do as she says, Cal. You and Susannah move apart."

The two young people put a little distance between them, but not enough for Emmaline to risk a shot at Cal unless she was supremely sure of her gun skill. Sally doubted if she would chance it.

"Mother, what's going on here?" Susannah demanded.

"Everything's gone insane! Cottontop drugged us, and then I was locked up in my room, and then Father's foreman tried to kill us—"

"Oh, shut up," Emmaline interrupted her. "Don't be tiresome, Susannah. You're intelligent enough to know that things are seldom as they seem. I'm leaving your father." She paused. "You can come with me, if you want."

The offer didn't sound very sincere, Sally thought, and from the way Susannah's face flushed with anger, she realized the same thing.

"Let me guess," Susannah said coldly. "Mr. Coolidge is really your lover."

Emmaline didn't deny the charge.

Susannah went on, "Do you know he's been stealing from Father and the other ranchers? He's the leader of that gang of rustlers everyone's been trying to find!"

"No, dear," Emmaline said. "He's not."

Susannah's eyes widened with horror as understanding of what her mother meant sunk in on her stunned brain. She didn't want to accept it, though, prompting her to take a step toward the porch and exclaim, "No! That can't be true. You wouldn't—"

The drumming of rapid hoofbeats suddenly sounded in the morning air. Emmaline jerked Sally to the right so that both of them were facing toward the trail leading to the ranch headquarters. A lone man rode toward them, and Sally's heart slugged hard as she recognized him.

Smoke!

Emmaline spat a vile curse in Sally's ear and jerked the Colt away from her head. From the corner of her eye, Sally saw her thrust out the revolver and aim it toward Smoke. The range was still pretty far for a handgun, but Sally wasn't going to risk letting Emmaline blaze away at her husband.

She grabbed Emmaline's arm and twisted her body, throwing her hip against the older woman. Emmaline cried out in surprise as Sally hauled her around. Sally clung to Emmaline's arm for dear life and kept the gun pointed away from Smoke. Emmaline shrieked in rage and tried to pull away.

They were close enough to the edge of the porch that as they stumbled back and forth in the desperate struggle, both of them toppled off the edge and crashed onto the steps, rolling to the ground at the bottom.

Sally hadn't been able to put up a successful fight against Matt Coolidge, but she and Emmaline were more evenly matched. As they rolled around in the dirt, Sally got hold of Emmaline's wrist and wrenched hard on it as she slammed that arm against the ground. Emmaline lost her grip on the Colt. It slid several feet away.

Sally didn't try to retrieve the gun. This was a personal, hand-to-hand battle now. She let go of Emmaline's arm and grabbed her hair instead, intending to use it to bang Emmaline's head on the ground.

Emmaline threw a punch, shooting her fist up to smack into Sally's jaw. The impact threw Sally to the side. Emmaline rolled and went after her. She brought a knee up into Sally's belly. That vicious assault caused Sally to double over. Emmaline's hands flashed to her face. Fingers hooked like talons clawed at Sally's eyes.

Sally jerked her head to the side and batted Emmaline's raking fingers away. She slashed out with the side of her hand and caught Emmaline across the throat. It was a lucky but effective blow. Emmaline fell back, gagging. Sally pushed herself up on hands and knees and dived after the other woman.

Fury roared up inside Sally. Not only had Emmaline masterminded a plan that had resulted in several of Sally's friends losing their stock, but innocent men had lost their lives as well. To make Emmaline's crimes even worse as far as Sally was concerned, the woman had tried to seduce Smoke. It didn't matter that she never would have succeeded. She had tried to do something that would have ruined Sally's marriage, and Sally could never forgive her for that.

She straddled Emmaline with a knee on each side of the woman and hit her in the face three times, right, left, right, rocking Emmaline's head back and forth. She might have continued if strong arms hadn't looped around her from behind and lifted her away from Emmaline as if she were weightless.

She knew that embrace, and as soon as the man holding her set her feet on the ground, she turned in his arms, clutching at him desperately, pressing her face against his broad chest, and saying, "Smoke, Smoke, oh, Smoke!"

One of the things that had kept Smoke alive this long was the ability not to get thrown for a loop by unexpected developments.

Finding Sally on top of Emmaline Bolton walloping the bejabbers out of her was certainly unexpected.

And that didn't even take into account the other things he found at Triangle B headquarters—a bloody but apparently unbowed Cal Woods standing nearby with Susannah Bolton, the lifeless body of Tom Gruber, and the sprawled form of an old man Smoke didn't know. It was easy to see that Gruber was dead, shot up as he was. Smoke didn't know about the old-timer; he might be just unconscious.

Checking on that would have to wait. For now, Smoke was out of the saddle while his mount was still making a sliding stop. Momentum carried him forward as he ran the last few feet to where Sally was hammering punches into Emmaline's face.

He bent, got his hands under her arms, and pulled her away. Emmaline appeared to be unconscious. Her features were bloody and already swelling. If Sally kept hitting her, she might kill the woman. Smoke figured Sally didn't really want that.

"It's all right," he told her, although he wasn't sure she heard him. "It's over. She's done."

Sally turned, threw her arms around him, called his name a few times, and then started to sob.

Smoke held her, patted her back, and waited for her to calm down. While he was doing that, he looked over at Cal, who approached him slowly, shuffling like an old man because he appeared to have been knocked around quite a bit.

Susannah ran to her mother and dropped to her knees beside Emmaline. She put her arms around Emmaline's shoulders and helped her sit up. Emmaline wasn't out cold; she moved her head slowly from side to side. Her blond hair hung in front of her face in disarray. She appeared to be stunned, as if she had no idea what was going on.

"Cal, are you all right?" Smoke asked when the young cowboy came up to him.

"Reckon I will be," Cal said. "A bullet dug a ditch along my side and I lost some blood."

"Yeah, I can see that."

"It's not very comfortable, but I think I'll live. I'm hoping I'll feel a mite better once it's patched up."

"I'm sure you will," Smoke told him. "Where have you been?"

"That's what I need to tell you. Those rustlers captured me, but I got away from them after a while. I know where their hideout is, Smoke. There's a little canyon, 'way back up in the hills ten or fifteen miles west of here. Everything around it is as barren as can be, so it would never occur to you that anything might be hidden in there."

Smoke nodded and said, "The Devil's Garden."

Cal's eyes widened. "You know the place?"

"I've been up there a few times, hunting. Mountain goats come down to that little stream now and then. I don't think any of that area has ever been claimed by the ranchers around here. There's some good grass, but it's too far away and too much trouble getting there for anybody to run stock on it on a regular basis." Smoke nodded slowly. "But I can see how it would work for a bunch of rustlers to hold a stolen herd as they built it up."

"I think there's a trail leading west through the mountains toward the gold camps."

"That's right," Smoke said with a nod. "Again, it's too rugged for anybody to use it regular-like, but if you just want to get rid of a herd of stolen stock, it would be worthwhile." His voice sharpened. "That's where you were when you got away from them?"

"Yeah, night before last. They tried to track me down and stayed on my trail until last night, but I finally gave them the slip with Susannah's help."

He smiled as he nodded toward the girl.

"If they lost your trail last night, they'll be getting ready to move those cows today, if they're not on the trail already," Smoke said. "I'll round up some of the boys and head up there hellbent for leather to see if we can stop them. I ought to be able to find Bolton's foreman Matt Coolidge—"

He stopped short as Cal shook his head with a grim look on his face.

"Not Coolidge," he said. "He's one of the gang. For all I know, all of the Triangle B hands are."

"I knew it," Smoke declared with a curt nod. "Thaddeus Bolton's behind the whole thing."

Sally had stopped crying and gotten control of herself again. She stepped back, wiped her eyes with the back of her hand, and looked up at Smoke.

"I've never known anyone as almost infallible as you are, Smoke," she said, "but even you make a mistake now and then. Thaddeus Bolton isn't the ringleader of the rustlers."

"He's not?" Smoke frowned. "Well, then, who is? Is Coolidge the actual boss?"

Sally shook her head, half-turned, and looked toward the spot where Emmaline still sat on the ground with Susannah kneeling beside her and holding an arm around her shoulders. Emmaline appeared to have regained her senses after the beating Sally had given her. She glared at the others, her icy blue eyes filled with hate.

"No," Sally said in answer to Smoke's question as she pointed at Emmaline. "There's the boss, right there."

Once again, Smoke's ability to accept surprises without being thrown off his stride came in handy. Even so, he had to ask, "Are you sure?"

Cal said, "There's no doubt about it, Smoke. We all heard Mrs. Bolton confess." He lowered his voice, evidently so that Susannah wouldn't overhear, and added, "Although it wasn't so much confessing as it was bragging."

Sally nodded in confirmation of that statement.

A few yards off to the side, the old cook groaned and rolled over as consciousness returned to him. Smoke jerked his head toward Cottontop and asked, "What about the old-timer?"

"Yeah, he's part of it, too," Cal said. "When Susannah and I finally got back here and figured we were safe, he wound up slipping us something that knocked us out. That's how Coolidge and Mrs. Bolton were able to take us prisoner."

"She made her own daughter a prisoner?"

"I'm afraid so," Sally said.

Smoke pulled in a deep breath and took stock of everything he had just heard. "Is anybody else here?" he asked as he looked around.

"Not that I know of," Cal said.

"Well, if we can't trust Emmaline or the old man, I can't leave you here with them."

"I can take care of things, Smoke," Cal insisted. He hefted the Remington. "I'm armed now, and I'll be all right."

"Yeah, if you don't pass out." Smoke shook his head. "I'm sorry, Cal, but you look like you've been dragged behind a wild bronco for the last ten miles. You need to get in the buggy with Sally and the two of you head back to the Sugarloaf as fast as you can get there. Once you do, tell Pearlie where that rustlers' hideout is. He can take care of things from there."

"What are you going to do, Smoke?" Sally asked.

"I'll head on up into the hills."

"You mean you'll take on the entire gang of killers by yourself?" Sally shook her head. "Not even you can do that, Smoke."

Cal pointed out, "He's done things pretty close to that before," and drew a quick frown from Sally for saying so.

"I won't jump the whole bunch," Smoke said. "But I can find them and keep an eye on them, so we'll have a pretty good idea what to do once Pearlie gets there with reinforcements."

"I'd ask you to promise not to take any unnecessary

chances . . ." Sally sighed. "But I know by now it wouldn't do any good."

Cal said, "We need to do something about Mrs. Bolton and that old-timer."

Smoke nodded. "I'll tie them up before I leave. We can collect them later."

"What about Susannah?"

Smoke looked over at Sally, who said, "We can take her with us to the Sugarloaf, if you think she'll go."

They turned toward Susannah and Emmaline, who had gotten to their feet by now. Susannah still had her arm around her mother's shoulders. Emmaline looked like she would have enjoyed carving on Smoke, Sally, and Cal for a while with a dull knife.

Cal took a step toward them and said, "Susannah, you need to come with me and Mrs. Jensen. Everything will be all right now—"

"No, it won't," she said. "How can you think that, Cal? I—I can't even believe what's happened—"

"No, he's right, Susannah," Emmaline interrupted her. "For your own sake, you should abandon me. Everything is ruined for our family. These people will send me to prison. That is, if they aren't responsible for me being hanged."

"No! No, I won't let that happen." Susannah tightened her arm around Emmaline as she glared at Cal and the Jensens. "You know where to find the men you're after and those stolen cattle. Can't you just go after them? Do you have to—"

"Smoke," Sally said. "The old man."

Smoke looked around and saw that the cook had

gotten to his feet and broken into a shambling run. He didn't head for the barn or the corrals, where he might have grabbed a horse and tried to make a getaway. He stumbled along the trail leading to the ranch house as if he intended to just keep running until he was far, far away from the scene of his crimes.

Smoke sighed and said, "I guess I'd better go after him."

Before he could take a step, half a dozen horsemen moving at a steady lope swept around a bend in the trail about a hundred yards away. Smoke recognized the black-clad, cadaverous figure of Deke Stratten in the lead. One of the regulator patrols was coming in.

And as Smoke had been thinking for a while, if the center of the rustling operation actually was the Triangle B, the regulators might be part of it along with the regular ranch crew. He had believed that Thaddeus Bolton could be trying to divert attention from himself with the ruse of pretending to hunt for the owlhoots, even going so far as to hang those drifters while claiming they were part of the gang.

Emmaline could have come up with the same ruse.

Cottontop confirmed that a moment later. He continued running toward the regulators as he waved his gnarled hands over his head to get their attention. He yelled, "Deke, help! You gotta kill 'em! Kill 'em all!"

CHAPTER 30

"Stratten's one of them," Smoke snapped as he grabbed Sally's arm and urged her toward the steps. "Get inside!"

Cal turned toward Susannah, who was struggling with her mother. Emmaline had tried to break away as soon as Stratten and the other regulators rode into sight.

"Mother, come on!" Susannah cried. "We can't stay here—"

Emmaline jerked loose from her daughter's grip and dashed toward the newcomers. "Deke!" she screamed. "Deke, help!"

Stratten sent his mount charging toward the house. He leaned forward in the saddle and drew his gun. Cottontop scurried to get out of the way as Stratten pounded ahead, heedless of the fact that the old-timer was in his path.

The cook was too slow. He threw his arms up and screamed in terror just before the surging horse struck him and knocked him off his feet.

The other riders galloped after Stratten, pulling their irons as well. These hired guns might not know exactly what was going on, but they were always ready to kill without hesitation when the order came.

Susannah ran after her mother, but Cal shoved the revolver in his waistband and lunged after her to grab her.

"Bullets are fixing to fly out here," he said. "Come on!"

Desperation must have given him strength. Even in such bad shape as he was, he swung a struggling Susannah off her feet and half-dragged, half-carried her toward the ranch house steps. She fought him and yelled for him to let her go, but Cal didn't listen to her.

Flame spurted from the muzzles of the regulators' guns as they hurtled toward the house. Smoke palmed out his Colts and threw lead back at them as he hurried sideways after Sally, Cal, and Susannah. One of Stratten's men flung up his arms and pitched out of the saddle, drilled by a slug from Smoke's guns, but the others pounded on toward them, blazing away.

Once again, an unintended target was in the path of that savage assault. Emmaline Bolton cried out as one of the bullets struck her. She stumbled and fell as she pressed her hands to her chest.

Susannah probably hadn't seen her mother go down because Cal had reached the porch with her by now and was forcing her through the doorway, but she must have heard Emmaline's cry of pain. Susannah screamed and redoubled her efforts to get away from Cal.

She might have succeeded if Sally hadn't grabbed her and jerked her into the house. Cal disappeared into the house after them and Smoke was right behind him, Colts still booming in his hands. He only stopped shooting when he was inside and could kick the door closed behind him.

Cal dropped to a knee at the window in the parlor and used the Remington's barrel to knock out the glass. He thrust the barrel through the opening he'd made and triggered the long-barreled revolver.

"Got one of the varmints!" he said.

Smoke thumbed fresh rounds from the loops on his shell belt into one of the Colts. He had pouched the other iron while he reloaded this one. He had performed this task so many thousands of times over the years that he didn't have to pay any attention to what he was doing. His nerves and muscles carried out their job flawlessly without him thinking about it.

"Are you all right?" he asked Sally, who stood there with her arms around a weeping Susannah, holding the girl against her.

"Yes," Sally replied. "What about you?"

"So far, so good," Smoke said.

Susannah turned her head to glare at him. "Not for my mother! Is she dead?"

"Cal?" Smoke said to the young cowboy kneeling at the window.

"She's moving around some," Cal said. "She's still alive. I can't tell how bad she's hit."

The shooting outside had stopped. "Where are Stratten and the others?"

"They rode into the barn," Cal said in answer to Smoke's question. "Reckon once we got some cover, they decided not to ride straight into our guns. We've already whittled them down some."

"We're still outnumbered," Smoke said, "but not by much, unless more of the regulators are close by and heard that shooting. If they come to see what's going on, the odds against us could pile up in a hurry."

He was reloading the second Colt by now. When he finished, he went to the window and stood beside it with both guns in his hands.

"Can you see them?" he asked Cal.

"Nope. They haven't poked their noses out since they rode in there."

The words had no more than come from Cal's mouth when a barrage of rifle fire blasted from the barn's open double doors. Cal had to duck down as bullets chewed splinters from the window sill and broke out what was left of the glass, spraying shards of it down over his hunched shoulders.

Smoke hunkered next to the young cowboy and said, "I only hear two rifles. I've got a hunch the other two went out the back of the barn and are circling around to try to take us from behind." He held out one of the fully loaded Colts and a handful of cartridges. "That Remington's bound to run empty soon. Take this and use it to keep those two in the barn occupied."

"You'll deal with the ones coming in the back?"

"That's the plan," Smoke said with a nod.

Cal took the Colt and the cartridges from him and said, "Good luck, Smoke. I don't reckon you'll need it, but . . ."

"A man always needs luck," Smoke said. He gave Cal another nod, then stood up and moved over to Sally, who had retreated past the stairs into the hallway with Susannah.

The girl said, "I want to go out there and see about my mother. You have to let me go. They won't shoot when they see it's me."

"They had to be able to see it was your mother standing out there, and they didn't hesitate at all to start throwing lead around her." Smoke shook his head. "I'm sorry, Susannah. We'll check on her as soon as we can, but for now, you need to stay in here and keep your head down."

Sally said, "Emmaline wouldn't want you to get hurt, too, Susannah."

"It doesn't matter," Susannah said, her voice wretched with grief and misery. "Those men are going to kill all of us."

"Not if I have anything to say about it," Smoke said.

He left them and hurried to the back of the house. He reached the kitchen and plucked back the curtain at the window in time to see two regulators dashing toward the house, rifles clutched in their hands ready to fire.

Smoke kicked the back door open, figuring that would take them by surprise and maybe throw them off their stride, and stepped out with the Colt thundering in his hand.

He saw that the two men had veered apart, probably an instinctive action to make it harder for an enemy to target both of them. Smoke's first two rounds punched into the chest of the man on his right and drove the hombre backward off his feet as violently as if he'd run into a wall.

The Winchester in the hands of the man to Smoke's left cracked twice. Both bullets came close enough for Smoke to hear them scream through the air. He shifted his aim and fired before the man could get off a third shot. The regulator's head jerked as the slug drilled into his forehead just above his left eyebrow, leaving a black, red-rimmed hole. It blew out the back of his skull in a grisly pink spray. He stumbled ahead two more steps before he pitched forward onto his face, dead.

Hearing the gun he had left with Cal crashing in the front room, Smoke wheeled and plunged back through the house. He reached the parlor in time to see that the other two regulators had launched a frontal attack at the same time as the men behind the house.

Crouched at the window, Cal suddenly went over backward, sprawling on the floor. Sally and Susannah had retreated onto the stairs now, stopping several steps up. Sally called out Cal's name but didn't dare try to reach him with so much lead buzzing through the room like a swarm of maddened hornets.

Smoke dived forward onto his belly, avoiding the worst of the bullet storm, as the front door crashed open and a hired killer charged through it. The man must have emptied his rifle during the charge; he had tossed it aside and now held a revolver that spouted flame.

Smoke tipped up the barrel of his Colt and squeezed off a shot that caught the man under the chin and ripped on up through his brain at an angle to burst out the top of his head and send his hat flying.

The dead man fell back, blocking the door for a split second. The last of the regulators leaped over him and landed inside the foyer. He still had his rifle in his hands and trained it on Smoke, whose Colt boomed again just as the rifle cracked.

The rifle bullet ripped a long gash in the floor beside Smoke's head. Splinters stung his cheek but, thankfully, missed his eye. Squinting through the clouds of acrid powdersmoke that clogged the air in the house, Smoke kept his finger taut on the trigger in case another shot was necessary and watched as Deke Stratten dropped the rifle and reeled back against the wall just inside the door.

Stratten pawed at his chest where Smoke's bullet had struck him. Crimson threaded between his splayed fingers as blood welled from the wound. Stratten coughed and more blood spilled over his bottom lip. He struggled to say something but then slowly slid down the wall to end in a sitting position with his legs stretched out in front of him. His head sagged forward and then, gradually, he toppled over on his side.

Smoke leaped to his feet and went to the stairs. Sally came to the bottom of the steps and threw her arms around him.

"You're still all right?" he asked her.

"Fine. We . . . we stayed out of the line of fire as much as we could."

Susannah crowded past them and stopped in the foyer. Her head jerked back and forth as she looked at Cal and then outside, searching for her mother. Cal was struggling to sit up.

After a moment of hesitation that must have seemed much longer to Susannah, she let out a little cry and rushed into the parlor to kneel at Cal's side, heedless of the broken glass on the floor.

"Be careful," he told her. "You'll hurt yourself."

"But you . . . you . . ."

"I'm all right," he assured her. "At least, as good as I was before this ruckus started. One of those bullets hit the windowsill right in front of me and made me jerk back. I lost my balance, that's all. I wasn't hit again."

She flung her arms around his neck and clasped him tightly. He returned the embrace for a few seconds and then looked over her shoulder at Smoke and Sally.

"Those other regulators . . .?"

"All done for," Smoke told him.

"You'd better go see about your ma," Cal said to Susannah. "It'll be safe now."

She sniffled, got hurriedly to her feet, and ran out of the house.

Smoke let go of Sally and reloaded his Colt. Then he gripped Cal's arm and helped him to his feet, and the three of them followed Susannah outside, stepping over bodies and avoiding pools of blood along the way.

Once again, Susannah had helped Emmaline sit up. A large blood stain had spread darkly and ominously on the front of the older woman's dress, but she was still alive. Susannah was crying as her mother reached up shakily to cup a bloody hand against the girl's cheek.

"D-Don't cry, d-dear," Emmaline said in a husky voice as Smoke, Sally, and Cal approached. "Who knows, maybe it's b-better this way . . . although I do wish . . . the two of us could have . . . g-gotten away from your father."

"You're going to be all right, Mother," Susannah choked out.

"N-No, I don't think so. I . . . I might have been . . . if I'd left a long time ago . . ."

Hoofbeats—a lot of them—made Smoke and Cal look around quickly. A large group of riders came around the same bend in the trail where the regulators had appeared earlier. This bunch was three or four times as large, though. More than twenty men, and they bore down on the small group of figures in front of the ranch house as if they intended to trample them into the dust.

CHAPTER 31

Thaddeus Bolton was in the lead, and as he came close enough to recognize his wife and daughter, shock and rage darkened his features. He kicked his mount into a hard gallop.

Smoke stepped away from Sally, putting himself between Bolton and the others. He would stop the man if he had to.

Cal moved up alongside him, haggard and obviously staving off collapse, but ready to summon up the determination for one more fight.

Smoke recognized the men with Bolton as members of the Triangle B crew. Maybe they were part of the rustling scheme, but maybe they weren't. Smoke saw that the man right behind Bolton was Bart Hudson, the cowboy who had roughed up Cal and tried to whip him viciously when Cal first encountered Susannah.

Bolton yanked his horse to an abrupt halt and swung down from the saddle. He wore a gun on his hip, but his hands were empty as he said, "Get the hell out of my way, Jensen."

The man's wife was badly wounded, Smoke reminded

himself. Bolton hadn't made any threatening moves and seemed to be at least partially in control of himself, so Smoke stepped aside. Bolton rushed past him to drop to his knees beside Emmaline and Susannah.

Bart Hudson reined in, too, and motioned for the men behind him to do likewise. He had been appointed the ranch's *segundo*, Smoke recalled, second in command among the crew to Matt Coolidge, the foreman.

Without dismounting, Hudson glared at Smoke and Cal from the saddle and demanded, "What in blazes is going on here?" He looked shocked as he glanced over and spotted the cook's crumpled form lying on the ground. "Cottontop!" His hand moved toward his gun. "If you've hurt that old man, I'll—"

"Deke Stratten is the one who rode him down," Smoke said. "I'd advise you to take it up with him, but you can't." Smoke leaned his head toward the house. "He's in there, dead."

Cal said, "We know you're part of the gang, Hudson. Don't waste your breath denying it."

"Gang?" A baffled expression appeared on the young man's face. "I don't know what the hell you're talking about, Woods."

Hudson's confusion looked and sounded genuine, Smoke realized. Since it had turned out that Emmaline had come up with the rustling scheme and recruited Coolidge to carry it out, it was possible he was the only member of the crew who'd betrayed Thaddeus Bolton.

Before the confrontation with Hudson could continue, Emmaline cried, "Get away from me!" and that caused the men to turn and look toward her.

She was still sitting on the ground with Susannah holding her. Bolton knelt beside them and had one hand lifted, as if he'd reached out to Emmaline. But she shrank back against Susannah and continued, "Leave me alone! I hate you, I hate you! You . . . you ruined everything! I never should have . . . never . . ."

A spasm went through her as her eyes opened wide. Smoke had seen death claim too many people not to recognize it wrapping its bony fingers around Emmaline. Susannah cried, "Mother!" as a long sigh escaped from Emmaline's lips and she sagged back against her.

"Emmaline!" Bolton shouted. "No!"

Bart Hudson dismounted, took a step forward as he clutched his horse's reins.

"Who did this?" he asked, a tortured expression on his face now. "Who hurt the boss's wife?" His furious gaze cut over to Smoke and Cal. "You, Jensen? Woods?"

"Again, it was Stratten," Smoke said in a flat voice. "He and some of his regulators charged in here shooting and Mrs. Bolton was in the way, just like the old man was."

"Why in hell would they do that?"

"Because they've been working with the rustlers all along. Matt Coolidge was the gang's ramrod, but Mrs. Bolton is the one who came up with the idea."

Hudson shook his head, slow at first then faster. "No," he said. "That's loco. Matt never would have done such a thing—"

"He did, Bart." The dull voice came from Susannah. She was walking toward the group of men now. Behind her, her father had taken Emmaline's body in his arms and held her cradled against him as he sobbed. Now that she was dead, she couldn't pull away from him.

Susannah went on, "It's all true. I heard my mother admit it. Matt and Cottontop were part of it, and so were Mr. Stratten and the men who rode with him." She looked at the mounted cowboys, and her words lashed out at them. "What about the rest of you? Are you rustlers, too? Outlaws?"

Hudson looked horrified. "Rustlers? Me and these other boys? No, Miss Susannah, no. I swear it. We've been searching everywhere for you, worrying out of our minds about what might've happened to you. We . . . we would never—"

"You were mighty quick to jump me that day," Cal broke in, scowling. "Maybe you had something to hide."

"No! Ever since that happened, I—I've regretted it. I've always been too hotheaded at times. I wish I wasn't, but I can be a real jackass. If there was anything I could do to make up for it—"

"Maybe there is," Smoke said. "Thanks to Cal, we know where to find that gang and all those stolen cattle. If you want to ride with me, we can go get them back."

"You just show us where to go, Mr. Jensen," Hudson declared with eagerness in his voice. Several of the ranch hands nodded emphatically to show their agreement. "We'll get those cattle, and we'll hand those rustlers what they've got coming to them! But . . . you're sure Matt's one of them?"

"We're certain."

Hudson took a deep breath and then nodded. "Then

he'll get what's coming to him, too. That's the way life works, isn't it?"

Smoke glanced over his shoulder, saw that Cal was holding Susannah and trying to comfort her, and beyond them was the tragic tableau of Thaddeus Bolton clinging to the dead wife who had hated him.

"That's true," he said in response to Hudson's comment, "and sometimes it's a mighty big shame."

Sally took responsibility for getting Cal and Susannah back to the Sugarloaf. Susannah didn't want to leave her mother, but Bolton insisted. Hudson picked a couple of men from the crew to remain behind and hitch up the ranch wagon. Bolton personally wrapped Emmaline's body in a fine bedspread from the house, and the men loaded her in the back of the wagon to take her into Big Rock to the undertaker. Bolton rode in the back of the wagon, as well, his face like stone as he sat beside his wife's body.

By the time they rolled out, Smoke and the rest of the Triangle B crew, led now by Bart Hudson, were mounted on fresh horses and riding hard toward the hills where the rustler stronghold was located.

Cal had offered to come along, but Smoke had assured him it wasn't necessary; he knew how to find the place from Cal's description. Cal needed medical attention that had already been delayed for far too long.

Also, when they reached the Sugarloaf, Cal could tell Pearlie where to find Smoke and the Triangle B riders.

It wouldn't take long for Pearlie to gather the Sugarloaf crew and set out to provide reinforcements.

Smoke set a fast pace. It was already past noon, and it would be mid-afternoon before he and his companions reached the narrow canyon where the Devil's Garden was located. It was called that, Smoke had been told, because it was a pocket-sized Garden of Eden, but a fella would have the Devil's own time getting to it, especially driving cows! But it could be done, and clearly, Coolidge and the other rustlers had found the arrangement to be a good one.

At one point, Smoke glanced over at Bart Hudson, riding beside him, and said with a smile, "I sure hope you're not double-crossing me, Hudson."

"Not a bit, Mr. Jensen. I want to settle up with those varmints as much as you do. Joe Archibald was a friend of mine."

Smoke recalled that was the name of the Triangle B hand who had been killed during the first raid. He said, "Are any of the men who were on duty with Archibald that night here in this bunch?"

"No, not a one. I don't know where they are. Or rather, I've got a pretty good idea." Bitterness tinged Hudson's voice as he went on, "They must be with the rest of their widelooping pards. The way I see it, they probably rode up to Joe and blasted him out of the saddle without him ever having any idea what was coming. You can't get much more lowdown than betraying a friend for money."

Smoke considered those comments for a moment and then said, "You know, Hudson, if you get that temper of yours under control, I think you might make a pretty good hand."

"I'm sure going to try, sir. And I appreciate you showing some faith in me today."

"Just don't let me down," Smoke said.

Hudson nodded curtly, determination etched on his face.

With Smoke in the lead, the group of riders reached the hills and penetrated deeper into the increasingly rugged terrain. Some of the Triangle B hands had been part of search parties that had explored this region, looking for the rustlers, but it wasn't long before they reached areas that were new to them. Smoke, however, knew exactly where he was going and led them straight to the narrow canyon that had served as the gang's hideout.

As Smoke had expected, the place was deserted. The rustlers were gone, and so was the herd of stolen cattle. They would have waited until today to move the stolen stock, in the hope that Cal could be found and eliminated before he revealed the secret hideout, but once it was clear he had gotten away, they had to cut and run. Coolidge's arrival would have guaranteed that.

"They're gone," Hudson said in disappointment. "Now what do we do?"

"There's only one trail through the mountains," Smoke explained. "Since we didn't run into them on the way here, that's the only way they could have gone."

"Then we can follow them," Hudson said with excitement back in his voice.

"We'll let the horses rest for a little spell first, but that's exactly what we're going to do."

Half an hour later, they moved out. The canyon narrowed even more, enough that only three or four cows could have moved through it abreast. The herd would have been strung out for a long way in the twisting passage. The droppings the searchers found provided plenty of proof that the cattle had come this way.

Although the steep walls on the sides remained the same height, the trail began to climb. As the sun dropped steadily toward the peaks in the west, Smoke studied the sign left by the herd and said, "We've already made up quite a bit of ground. They can't do any better than move at a crawl."

He tilted his head back and frowned in thought as he gazed up at the rocky terrain rising ahead of them.

"As soon as they go through that pass up there, the trail widens out enough they can pick up some speed, especially since those cows will be going downhill. What we need to do is be on the other side waiting for them."

"How is that possible when they're between us and the pass?" Hudson asked.

Smoke chuckled. "I said this was the only trail they could use to take the cattle out of there. There's a path horsebackers can use. That is, if they're not prone to getting dizzy."

"High and narrow, is it?"

"That's right." Smoke looked around at the men. "We're going to split up, a dozen in each group. One bunch will follow this trail to block any retreat by the gang. The other will take the shortcut and get ahead of the rustlers on the other side of the pass. We'll jump them as soon as the cattle are through. When the men bringing up the rear hear the shooting start, they can hit the gang from behind."

"You're not going to give them a chance to surrender?" Hudson wanted to know.

"I suppose we ought to—but I reckon we can be pretty sure they won't take it."

"I hope not," Hudson said fervently. "I want to get those skunks in my gunsights."

Mutters of agreement came from the other punchers.

"You know these men, Bart," Smoke said. "You pick the groups."

"Fine, but I'm going with the bunch that'll be waiting on the other side of the pass. I want first crack at those no-good rustlers."

Smoke nodded. "That's where I intend to be, too."

Quickly, Hudson sorted the men into two groups. A few complained, but since it was likely that all of them would get in on the action before it was over, there wasn't much protesting.

A short time later, they reached the spot where the smaller trail, the one that cattle couldn't use, branched off. Smoke, Hudson, and ten more men followed that trail as it bent and climbed to dizzying heights. It was a nerve-wracking passage that had the men pale and clutching their saddles as empty air fell away for a hundred feet or more, seemingly no more than a handspan away from where their horses set down their hooves.

"You didn't say this way would give a damn mountain goat the fantods!" Hudson said from his second spot in line, behind Smoke.

"Cow ponies are sure-footed," Smoke said over his shoulder, "and we'll be at the pass before you know it."

"Can't be soon enough to suit me," Hudson muttered.

Eventually the trail stopped hugging the edge of the harrowing drop-off and entered a narrow cleft. Still riding single file, the men followed it for what seemed like miles and finally emerged from it into the pass where the other trail crossed over the mountains. Shadows had begun to gather there.

In the fading light, Smoke studied the ground and declared, "No cattle have come through here. We're ahead of them."

Hudson nodded. "If you listen, I think you can hear them coming up. They're not far away."

"Come on," Smoke urged. "We'll get in position."

The men hurried through the pass, which was about twenty yards wide and maybe a hundred yards long. At the far end, it opened out into a broad, sloping bench covered with bands of pine trees. Smoke led the men into the closest bunch of trees, where they dismounted and tied their horses in the thick shadows under the branches.

Then they pulled Winchesters from saddle boots and ran to the edge of the trees, stopping where the cover ended.

Smoke heard the rumble of hooves and the clattering clash of horns. "They're in the pass," he called softly to the Triangle B riders. "Wait until the cattle are through and start to spread out. The rustlers will be right behind them. When enough of them are in the open, we'll make our move. Follow my lead."

"Do what Mr. Jensen says, boys," Hudson added, "and be glad it's the Triangle B that gets to put an end to this bunch of killers and thieves."

To Smoke, he went, "Thanks again for giving me this chance, Mr. Jensen. After that business with Cal, I don't reckon I deserve it."

"Deserve it from here on out," Smoke told him with a nod.

"Yes, sir. I'll sure do my best."

A couple of minutes later, the first rank of cattle emerged from the pass, a dark mass in the twilight. More and more of them poured from the opening, spreading over the slope as Smoke had said they would. At last, riders followed them, also veering to right and left as the rustlers positioned themselves to contain the herd and move it downhill.

The time had come, Smoke knew. Motioning for Hudson and the other men to remain where they were, he stepped into the open at the edge of the trees, lifted his rifle to his shoulders, and bellowed at the top of his lungs, "Throw down your guns and lift your hands! You're finished!"

Instantly, the rustlers reacted exactly as he anticipated they would. They yanked their horses to a stop, and the crimson flowers of muzzle flashes bloomed in the dim light as gun-thunder rolled over the mountainside.

CHAPTER 32

Flame lashed again and again from the muzzle of Smoke's Winchester as he fired, swiftly working the rifle's loading lever between shots. Along the line of trees, more shots cracked wickedly. The volley of lead scythed through the rustlers, knocking several of them out of their saddles. Others were unhorsed when their mounts went down. Those men came up shooting, but slugs from the Triangle B guns ripped through them and rapidly put them back down.

The gunfire spooked the tired cattle and they began charging back and forth, adding to the chaos. More shots rattled from the mouth of the pass as the other bunch of Triangle B punchers charged through and fell on the rustlers from behind. The muzzle flashes were like a swarm of a thousand fireflies had descended from the darkening sky.

Smoke's Winchester ran dry. He tossed it aside and drew his Colts as one of the rustlers charged him. Smoke triggered, left and right, and the attacker's horse went down violently, its front legs folding up and throwing the rider over its head. The man hit the ground hard but rolled and lithely came back up on his feet. He had closed the distance between himself and Smoke until Smoke was able to recognize him.

"Coolidge!" Smoke shouted.

"Jensen! Damn you!" the treacherous foreman blazed back. The gun in his hand blazed, too, as he triggered again and again.

Both of Smoke's Colts boomed at the same time. Coolidge went backward as if slapped down by a giant hand instead of the pair of .45 slugs crashing into his chest. His arms flung out to the sides. He landed on his back and kicked one leg while the other drew up in a death spasm.

Smoke reached him in time to hear Coolidge gasp, "Jensen, how—"

He died without knowing the answer to his question.

The gunfire had died down already to a few scattered shots, and then even those ended. Silence fell except for the racket generated by the cattle.

More hoofbeats pounded from the pass. Smoke called Hudson and the other men around him, asked Hudson, "How many did we lose?"

"Two men dead, as far as I know," Hudson answered grimly. "Another couple wounded. But I reckon those rustlers are wiped out, unless this is more of them coming now."

It wasn't. Smoke heard a familiar voice shouting his name and lifted his own voice to call out, "Over here, Pearlie!"

Pearlie and more than a dozen men from the Sugarloaf galloped up and came to sliding stops that raised clouds of dust. Looking around, Pearlie said disgustedly, "Dadgum it, it's all over, ain't it, Smoke? We didn't get here in time."

"Oh, I don't know about that," Smoke said with a grin. "You got here in time to help round up all those cattle and hold them here until we can push them back over the mountains in the morning."

Two days later, Smoke and Sally were waiting on the platform at the train station in Big Rock when Thaddeus Bolton and Susannah emerged from the depot. Father and daughter were both soberly dressed, Susannah in a black traveling outfit with a veil over her face. Both of them were in mourning.

Emmaline Bolton's coffin had already been loaded on the eastbound train that sat beside the platform, steam and smoke puffing from the locomotive.

Bolton nodded as he and Susannah came up to Smoke and Sally. He shook hands with Smoke, who said, "We wanted to say goodbye and tell you again how sorry we are things worked out this way."

"Thank you," Bolton murmured. "You're not going to try to talk me into coming back out here once Emmaline's been laid to rest in Tennessee, are you?"

Smoke shook his head. "No, that's your decision to make." He smiled. "I'm glad you're going to keep the Triangle B, though. Maybe you'll come visit from time to time."

"Perhaps," Bolton said, but he sounded like that wasn't much of a possibility. He went on, "I do have one more favor to ask of you, Jensen. Keep an eye on the spread until I can locate and hire a suitable manager, will you? Bart Hudson seems to have the makings of a good man, but he's too young to leave in charge permanently."

"That's probably true. I already told him he can call on me if he needs any advice, and the other ranchers in the valley feel the same way."

Sally and Susannah were talking quietly while the men spoke. Sally hugged the girl and patted her shoulder. Both of them smiled.

Then Bolton took his daughter's arm and they boarded the train. A few minutes later, with a clash of steel drivers on rails, the locomotive pulled out and the long line of cars followed. Smoke and Sally watched it go.

"What were you and Susannah talking about, there at the last?" Smoke asked.

"Oh, she was just asking me to pass along a message to Cal," Sally replied. "She wanted me to let him know that she'll be visiting the Triangle B from time to time, whether her father ever does or not."

Smoke laughed. "He was recovering by leaps and bounds already," he said. "That news will have Cal back on his feet before you know it!"

Western legend Luke "Tomahawk" Callahan
agrees to lead one last wagon train across the
Mexican border—where revolution is brewing,
bullets are flying, and all roads lead to death . . .

With just a single journey under his belt,
first-time wagoneer Tomahawk Callahan
became a national hero.
It started as a challenge waged by a railroad
mogul—a race between an old-time wagon train
and a brand-new rail line—with the whole world
watching. Against all odds, Tomahawk led
his family business to victory.
At the time, he thought it would be his first—
and last—wagon train.
But at his sister's urging, he's agreed to take on
one final job, a never-before-attempted trip
across the Mexican border . . .

But Mexico is undergoing bloody changes. After a brutal coup, General Porfirio Diaz is determined to bring "order and progress" to the country—while revolutionaries plot against him. Tomahawk's wagon train could help modernize Mexico, bringing railroad workers, miners, and supplies—across a desert full of rattlesnakes, Apache, and other threats. The deadliest of all is a former priest known as Generalissimo "Padre" Rodriguez, who has his bloodthirsty sights set on the wagon train. Tomahawk's got to drive his wagons out of this frying pan and into the fire— or they'll all end up on a wagon trail to Hell . . .

NATIONAL BESTSELLING AUTHORS
WILLIAM W. JOHNSTONE
and J.A. Johnstone

A COFFIN FOR TOMAHAWK

THE THRILLING
SECOND INSTALLMENT OF
THE LAST WAGON TRAIN SERIES!

Live Free. Read Hard.

williamjohnstone.net

Visit us at kensingtonbooks.com

On sale now, wherever Pinnacle Books are sold.

PROLOGUE

The American clipper ship *Pride of New Orleans* spotted Veracruz late in the afternoon. It eased into the harbor, docked, and spilled its passengers onto the wharf.

Kent Arbuckle, green with seasickness, was first off the ship, wanting nothing more than to feel dry land under his feet again. Roy Benson followed closely behind with the luggage. Benson wasn't Arbuckle's valet—the bruiser served a more important function—but Arbuckle was in no condition to lug baggage. His gut threatened revolt, and his legs felt like noodles. An acrid belch escaped his lips, and he thought he might heave again although he couldn't imagine what was left in his belly to throw up.

The hucksters and beggars descended upon them almost immediately. Arbuckle was in no mood to have gaudy trinkets and poorly woven baskets shoved in his face, and he shot Benson a look. *Will you do something?*

A growl from Benson was enough to send the pests

scurrying, and again Arbuckle decided the money he paid Benson was well worth it.

"It's González's new nickel currency," Benson said. "It's kicked the economy right in the crotch. And they always seem to know when an American ship is coming in."

Arbuckle had heard the Mexican lower classes were in a bad way, and he wondered if they were in any danger. Desperate, hungry men had been known to do all sorts of dreadful things. He'd traded in his six-shooter for a more concealable Smith & Wesson top-break .32 revolver. It hung in a shoulder holster under his jacket. They were on a business trip after all, and it wouldn't do to be seen swaggering around Veracruz with heavy iron on their hips. Benson had also switched to a shoulder holster, although his Schofield made a more noticeable lump under his jacket.

"Let's just get to the hotel," Arbuckle said, maneuvering through the mass of humanity. "Is there such a thing as a hansom cab in this town?"

"They'll charge you an arm and a leg," Benson told him. "The hotel's only a couple blocks."

Might as well be a hundred miles the way Arbuckle felt, but he trudged on and kept his mouth shut.

Once past the waterfront, the crowds thinned to a tolerable level. The pits and collar of Arbuckle's shirt were soaked with sweat by the time they reached The Grand Emporio Hotel, an impressive structure with columns and a wide stairway and broad arches. The lobby was an open, airy place with colorful tiles. Arbuckle's footfalls echoed as he crossed the space to the long front desk.

The clerk wore a perfectly pressed green jacket, trimmed in gold, the same color scheme worn by the bellhops. His moustache was well oiled, black, and curled. The part down the center of his slicked hair was the straightest thing Arbuckle had ever seen.

"Good afternoon, sir, and welcome to the Grand Emporio." The clerk's English was quite good with only the hint of an accent. "How may I serve you today?"

"A reservation for Arbuckle."

"One moment." He turned to the endless rows of cubby holes lining the wall behind the desk and seemed to know just the right one to reach into, turning back to Arbuckle with a folded piece of paper in his well-manicured hand. "Here we are, sir. A suite of rooms. I can have your bags taken up."

"Don't bother," Arbuckle said. "My man has things well in hand."

Benson cleared his throat unhappily but made no further objection.

Arbuckle signed the register, and the clerk handed him the key.

"I do hope you enjoy your stay, sir."

Arbuckle smiled weakly. "I'm sure I will."

A wide stairway made a gentle curve up to the second floor. Arbuckle climbed slowly, feeling better now that he was off the ship but still weak in the legs. Benson huffed up the stairs behind him with the luggage.

The suite was at the end of the hall. Arbuckle turned the key, pushed open the heavy, wooden door, and they entered. Benson dropped the bags with a grunt. The rooms were clean and possessed an old-world luxury, with thick rugs, tapestries on the walls, furniture of rich, polished wood and plush, velvet upholstery. A sitting room in the center had a bedroom on either side.

Arbuckle pushed open the French doors to the balcony and stepped outside. The city of Veracruz stretched out before him, brown stucco and muted red roof tiles and the spire of a large cathedral in the middle distance. Shaggy palm trees lined the wide boulevards. Not a bad view really, but he was disappointed not to see the Gulf of Mexico. Funny how he liked the water so much better when seeing it from the land.

He went inside to a sideboard and looked into a ceramic pitcher. Water. He poured some into a glass.

"I wouldn't drink that if I were you," Benson said. "Trust me."

Arbuckle made an impatient noise in his throat and set the glass down. "It's hot."

"Stay here and don't drink that," Benson insisted. "I'll be back as soon as I can."

He left the suite.

Arbuckle took off his jacket and draped it over the back of a chair. He peeled off his shirt and tossed it into the seat, then went back out to a balcony, hoping for a breeze. There was none. Still, he took the air and felt better. Eventually, he'd need to get back on a ship and return home, and then he'd be ill all over again.

A problem for another day.

He heard Benson return and went back inside.

Benson held a small crate of bottles with ceramic tops.

"Beer," Benson said. "Safer than water."

"What kind?"

"Cerveza Victoria."

Arbuckle held out a hand. "Let's try it."

Benson handed him a bottle and took one for himself. They thumbed off the tops and drank. Not quite cold but cool enough. Arbuckle got through half the bottle and felt better.

"What now?" Benson asked.

"We wait to be summoned," Arbuckle said.

"Who's doing the summoning?"

"One of Gonzalez's lapdogs," Arbuckle said.

Benson swallowed a mouthful of beer. "One of Porfirio Diaz's lapdogs then."

Arbuckle shrugged. "That's a way of looking at it."

José de la Cruz Porfirio Diaz Mori had been president of Mexico until about a year ago. His handpicked puppet Manuel González had taken over, but in the halls of power, everyone knew it was still Porfirio Diaz pulling the strings. Arbuckle was indifferent to the entire situation. Mexican politics didn't interest him. He was here to conduct a business transaction.

"This lapdog got a name?" Benson asked.

"Juan Carlos Esteban."

Benson raised an eyebrow. "Minister Esteban? Secretary Esteban?"

Arbuckle shook his head. "Just Esteban."

"Definitely one of Diaz's thugs." Benson drained the beer bottle, then reached for another.

"You seem to know a lot about this place," Arbuckle said.

"Fella in my line of work needs a place to lay low on occasion." Benson thumbed the ceramic top off the bottle. "I like it here."

"You speak the language then."

Benson snorted. "You'd think so, but no. Enough to order beer and beans and say rude things to shady ladies."

Roy Benson had been a professional outlaw, trying his hand at rustling, bank robbery, strong-arming, stage-coach holdups, and multiple other illegal ways to turn a buck. Arbuckle had hired the man to help undermine a wagon train going to Oregon. Arbuckle's efforts had ultimately failed, but Benson had *mostly* proved to be a competent and tough right-hand man. Steady work seemed to agree with Benson, and in his light brown suit and bowler hat, he almost looked like a civilized human being instead of an outlaw, although the Schofield's bulge slightly spoiled the effect.

Never mind, Arbuckle thought. *Even the civilized need protection from the unexpected.*

They each finished another beer, and then there was a knock at the door.

Arbuckle opened it, and a short, fastidious man stood there, smiling ingratiatingly, hands clasped formally in front of them. He wore the green jacket of the hotel's staff.

"*Señor* Arbuckle?"

"That's right."

"I am Enrique, one of the assistant managers here at the Grand Emporio. Juan Carlos Esteban sends his compliments and asks that you join him upstairs. At your convenience, of course."

"I'll need to put on a fresh shirt," Arbuckle told him.

"I shall wait in the hallway, *señor*, and escort you when you are ready," Enrique said.

Arbuckle closed the door, dressed, and took a last swig of beer. "Let's go," he told Benson.

Enrique escorted them up three flights of stairs. Four dour-looking men in tan suits waited for them on the landing, hard eyes and grim expressions. They looked cut from the same cloth as Roy Benson.

One of them took a step toward Arbuckle—a brooding, bulky man, muscles bulging under his jacket, with a thick black beard, and dark eyes. "Are you armed, *señor*?"

"I am, in fact."

Black Beard held out his hand. "It shall be returned to you."

Arbuckle reached inside his jacket, took out the .32, and handed it to the bruiser.

"I reckon you'll want mine, too," Benson said.

"*Lo siento mucho, señor*," Black Beard said. "But only *Señor* Arbuckle is expected."

Benson sighed and sat on a narrow bench against the wall. "Okay if I wait?"

The bruiser briefly conferred with the other three in Spanish before turning back to Benson. "You may wait."

Benson offered a weak smile. "Glad to hear it."

Arbuckle offered Benson an apologetic look. "If this goes on too long, feel free to go find some dinner."

Benson leaned back against the wall, pulled the brim of his bowler hat over his eyes as if he was ready for a nap, and crossed his arms. "I got nowhere to be."

Black Beard opened the door, and gestured Arbuckle should enter.

Arbuckle went inside, the door clicking closed again behind him.

The suite was massive and airy. Arched windows, all open, circled almost the entire room, a warm breeze stirring the wispy curtains. The furnishings were of the same make as in Arbuckle's suite, but more—lounges and plush chairs, a table of gleamingly polished wood. To the left, the suite transitioned to a wide, tiled veranda, a view of the sea beyond.

Another prim hotel servant in a green jacket presented himself, a starched white towel over one forearm, a silver tray in the other hand, a long-stemmed crystal glass atop it filled with red wine.

"*Señor* Esteban will be with you shortly," the servant said. "In the meantime, he's asked me to open a bottle of wine. It's an excellent vintage if you'd care to partake."

Arbuckle took the glass from the tray. "Thank you."

The servant bowed, then scurried away.

Arbuckle sipped the wine. It was, indeed, excellent, light but not too sweet.

He wandered out on the veranda and took in the view, the setting sun behind him illuminating the light chop, the sky a picturesque orange red. It gave him a hint of why Benson liked it here. Not the worst place to hide after a bank robbery or some other such skulduggery.

A slight movement in the corner of his eye caught his attention, and he turned his head with a start.

A women stretched across a wicker divan with red velvet cushions. She was lithe, one long leg exposed, the slit in her gossamer black dress going almost to the hip. Barefoot. Her sandals sat side-by-side on the tiled floor next to the divan. Hair the color of deep midnight spilled over her shoulders, skin a very light brown, lips stained ruby red. One mischievous eye, deep and dark and implacable, the other covered in a black patch, the tail end of a thin white scar leaking from underneath. The patch took away from her looks—slightly—but added an additional air of mystery, and on the whole, Arbuckle estimated she'd come out ahead. She held a glass like Arbuckle's, half empty of red wine.

An amused smile quirked to her lips at Arbuckle's start.

"Sorry," he said. "I didn't know anyone else was out here."

"Don't trouble yourself about me," she said. "I'm just part of the furniture."

Arbuckle recovered, smiled in a way he hoped seemed nonchalant, and took a step toward her. "You're rather more well-upholstered than most furniture I've seen."

Her laugh was a light and absent-minded titter as if she were amused by a little boy's attempt to seem grown up.

Arbuckle gulped wine and tried to think of something clever to say.

"Sorry to keep you waiting, *Señor* Arbuckle," said a voice behind him.

Arbuckle turned to see the man walking toward him, hand outstretched.

They shook.

"I am Juan Carlos Esteban," he said. "Pleased to make your acquaintance."

"Likewise."

Esteban was a lean, handsome man, black hair slicked back with a dashing touch of gray at the temples. A thin black moustache, but clean-shaven otherwise, skin clear and brown. He wore a spotless white suit and a pinky ring on his left hand with a glittering ruby.

"My schedule is such that I was forced to skip lunch. Will you join me for an early supper?" Esteban gestured to a table across the veranda.

No sooner had the words left his mouth than a gaggle of green-jacketed servants descended upon the veranda, draping a white cloth over the table, covering it with dishes of steaming food.

"I've just come off of a ship, and I must admit sea travel don't agree with me." Arbuckle put a hand on his stomach. "But don't let me stop you."

In fact, Arbuckle was feeling much better now that he was on dry land, but he didn't want to risk any of the local cuisine just yet. Anyway, he was here to talk business and didn't want that sluggish feeling that came with a heavy meal.

"Some more wine at least," Esteban suggested.

"Yes, thank you," Arbuckle said. "It's quite good."

They sat at the table as the servants heaped roasted pork and stuffed poblano peppers onto Esteban's plate. Arbuckle's wine glass was refilled. Arbuckle waited for

Esteban to introduce the woman lounging on the divan, but he never did. Instead, the Mexican made small talk as he ate. *The ship from America was comfortable? The weather was good for your passage? The weather has been mild in Veracruz. There is a café a block from here you should try. There is good music most nights in the* zocalo. *Are you sure you will not have a bite to eat? The chef here at the Grand Emporio is one of the city's best.*

And so on.

At last, Esteban sat back in his chair, wiping his mouth with a napkin, the ruby of his pinky ring glittering in the lanternlight. Arbuckle only just noticed that night had fallen as they sat chatting amiably, the lights of Veracruz twinkling below them.

"Well, you've come a long way, my friend, and not to hear about all of the local points of interest here in Veracruz, I'm sure," Estaban said. "Now we must come to the business at hand."

The servants instantly understood they'd been dismissed. One of them set a freshly opened bottle of the red wine on the table, and they all filed out without so much as a backward glance.

Esteban's eyes shifted to the woman on the divan. It was the first time he'd acknowledged her existence.

She smiled and rose languidly, scooping her sandals by the heel straps with two fingers, letting them dangle as she padded quietly back inside.

Arbuckle wanted to ask about her but didn't.

Esteban reached across the table for the wine bottle, filled each of their glasses, and set it down again. "It was good of you to make such a trip on the limited information I gave you."

"You made it easy enough for me," Arbuckle said. "You paid for my passage as well as my man's. You said I was uniquely experienced to head a large project, and you said I would be well compensated. Since I happen to be . . . let's say *between* opportunities . . . yes, I'm intrigued. Although details were in short supply in our correspondence."

"You are a clever man," Esteban said. "I'm sure you understand there are delicate things one should not commit to writing."

"I gathered."

"Silver," Esteban said. "A very rich find. *Very* rich. In Sonora. We intend to open a mine. It will be a large operation."

Arbuckle had no idea where Sonora was.

Esteban must have seen it in his face. "In the north. Near the border of Arizona."

Arbuckle sipped wine. "I'm happy for you. Sadly, I know little of mining. I'm not sure what good I'd be to you."

"You might be surprised. We have use for a man with your railroad know-how," Esteban said. "The mine is in a remote location, the nearest town more than a hundred miles away. We need a branch railway to take supplies to the mine and to bring back ore. This railroad is essential to the mine's success."

"I suppose that's where I come in."

"Just so."

"But surely you have men in your own country who can build a railroad," Arbuckle said.

"Indeed." Esteban took a cigar from inside his jacket pocket. "Would you like to smoke?"

"No, thank you."

Esteban cut a small piece from one end, stuck the cigar in his mouth, then went back into his jacket pocket for matches, found them, then took his time lighting the cigar and puffing it to life. To Arbuckle, it seemed clear Esteban was mulling his answer, weighing what to say or at least how to say it.

He sat back again and blew a long stream of blue-gray smoke into the air. "It is important that this enterprise is approached with . . . discretion. For this reason, we believe an outsider is perhaps best to carry out this task."

Arbuckle drained his wine glass. "Just so we're all on the same page, who exactly is *we*?"

A mischievous smile from Esteban. "I answer directly to *El Presidente* Manuel González, and you would answer directly to me. No one else needs to know."

"But others *would* know," insisted Arbuckle. "You can't lay miles of track without a lot of men swinging hammers and pickaxes. Then they've got to be fed, so that's a cook and cleanup outfit, and latrines and housing and . . . it's a lot of ears to hear things and a lot of mouths to repeat whatever those ears have heard."

"There will be challenges, yes."

Arbuckle snorted a laugh, which he immediately hoped didn't come off as rude.

"Something that will help keep our secret is that these men will be Americans," Esteban continued unperturbed. "There is much revolutionary activity in the area leading to the mine. Instead, we plan to use American investment and American workers brought down through Arizona. These Americans will be isolated, and in this way, we can maintain our secrecy. As you may have read in the newspapers, Presidente Gonzalez has taken steps to encourage trade between our two nations. Our mining enterprise will encourage this further."

It struck Arbuckle that the potential for graft in such a situation was enormous. Keeping the mine secret from the overwhelming majority of the Mexican government meant González could do literally anything he wanted with the profits, including lining his own pockets.

Not that it would matter to Arbuckle. If he was hired to build a railroad, then that's what he'd do. The corruption of the Mexican government was none of his business.

"There is, of course, another reason Presidente González has selected you for this job," Esteban said.

Arbuckle raised an eyebrow. "Oh?"

"Even in Mexico, the great race between your railroad and the wagon train made quite a splash in the newspapers."

With great effort, Arbuckle stopped himself from sighing and rolling his eyes.

"You built your railroad line with great speed," Esteban said. "You showed much drive and determination."

"And lost the race anyway," Arbuckle reminded him.

"But it was a very close thing," Esteban insisted. "Some slight twist of luck one way or another could have changed the entire outcome. Presidente González followed the story with great fascination and very much admired both participants. You and the other gentleman . . . uh . . . forgive me, I am actually quite proud of my English, but this word escapes me." He made a chopping motion with his hand. "Like an Indian hatchet."

"Tomahawk." Arbuckle's eyes narrowed. "Tomahawk Callahan is the man you're talking about."

"Yes, that is the name!" Esteban said with enthusiasm. "Of course, we must hire him also."

Arbuckle blinked. "What?"

"As I implied earlier, most of the men and supplies will come from America," Esteban said. "We currently have buyers and recruiters in Kansas City. The materials for the new railroad line will come by wagon train, so naturally, we must have the famous Tomahawk Callahan to lead it."

"But . . . but . . ." Arbuckle's head was spinning. "There are plenty of men who can captain a wagon train. It doesn't have to be Callahan."

Esteban shook his head. "No, *Señor* Arbuckle, I must insist. *El Presidente* was quite adamant. The story of your great race captured his imagination. We must have Arbuckle for the new rail line, just as we must have Callahan for the wagon train. González will accept nothing else."

Arbuckle couldn't believe his ears. He was being offered a very lucrative deal to build the silver mine's new railroad. The offer of a lifetime!

But he could only collect if he partnered with his old foe, Tomahawk Callahan.

PART ONE

CHAPTER 1

"He's a big one, all right. You sure you want to be doing this on your wedding day?"

Luke "Tomahawk" Callahan knelt in the mud next to the grizzly bear track. It was as big as a dinner plate. They'd tracked the bear two miles already, and Callahan wasn't about to call it quits now. Anyway, the wedding wasn't until later in the afternoon.

Callahan squinted up at George Berringer. "Don't worry, George. Becky won't get stood up. But this grizzly's made off with two of Ida's goats, one of old man Morrison's sheep, and Fred Lumen's prize hog. And don't forget he tore into Barney Kroeger's smokehouse last week. The bear knows it can eat good around here for little effort, so he's not going away on his own. Goats today. Maybe somebody's toddler next time. We're going to kill this animal while we've got the chance."

Berringer scratched behind one ear, thinking hard making all the lines on his weathered face scrunch together like a cranky old prune. A light frosting of white stubble down each jaw and across his chin. He was spry for a man in his late sixties and had insisted on coming along as going into the woods alone after a killer bear was nobody's idea of smart thinking. He rested a Sharps carbine on his shoulder, his relaxed posture in direct contradiction to the nervousness both men felt.

"A big mean bear might take a few rifle shots and not think it's very funny," Berringer said. "Might just get him mad."

Callahan's grip tightened on his Henry rifle. "Then we'd better make sure we shoot straight. Come on."

They stalked deeper into the woods, listening, eyes open, Callahan stopping periodically to examine a broken branch or another track. No more banter between the two men; they could feel it, like the whole forest was holding its breath—the animal was close. Callahan suddenly found he was second guessing himself. Maybe Berringer was right about this being a bad idea. It wouldn't have delayed them too long to round up a few more of the fellas.

Forget all that, he scolded himself. *You made your call, now stand by it. The rest is distraction.*

They slowed their pace further still and froze when a rustling noise off to their left drew their attention. Callahan raised the Henry and held his breath. A heavy silence had fallen over the world, Callahan's heartbeat in his ears the only sound.

An explosion of shrubbery.

Callahan swung his rifle to the right.

A pair of flapping, fat doves winged past him then spiraled upward, vanishing into the canopy.

Callahan and Berringer grinned nervously at each other.

Easy, mister. Don't get spooked by every little thing. He tried to will his thumping heart to calm. *Nervous Nellies don't shoot straight.*

They moved deeper into the woods, stepping even more cautiously than before. The entire area seemed impossibly silent, and by contrast, each of Callahan's footfalls—no matter how gingerly he stepped—seemed like a crackling racket of dry leaves and twigs. A minute later, he knelt next to another huge bear track, clearly outlined in the mud. Something had smeared the bottom half of the track. Callahan's eyes narrowed as he wondered what he was looking at. He stood and moved a few feet to the left, glancing ahead.

He knelt again, examining a new set of tracks. They angled in, crossing the first set of tracks. He squinted closer. Bear tracks. And they looked to be the same size as the first set. It only took Callahan a split second to realize it was the same animal making a circle.

But why would he double back . . .

Oh no!

Callahan spun, bringing the rifle up just as the gigantic animal came barreling through the brush, snarling, and then letting out a terrific bellowing roar. The grizzly was massive, the biggest bear Callahan had ever seen.

Callahan fired the Henry, and a laughably small chunk of lead disappeared into the wide, fur-covered chest of the grizzly. As Berringer had predicted, the shot only served to enrage the animal, and it reared up on its hind legs with another earsplitting roar, towering over Callahan at least nine feet tall.

Berringer pumped lead into the beast with his carbine, but the shots might as well have been horsefly bites.

Callahan levered another shell into the Henry's chamber but never got the chance to fire. The bear swept forward with a big paw, claws raking across Callahan's chest, ripping through his buckskin jacket and the shirt and flesh underneath, knocking the Henry away in the same motion.

Callahan took half a step back and drew his Peacemaker as the bear leapt for him. He fanned the hammer, emptying the six-shooter into the animal, just as it pounced.

The bear's entire weight slammed into Callahan, driving him to the ground. He landed hard on his back, and the wind was knocked out of him, fur shoved into his face, the animal's weight making it impossible to catch his breath.

He lay beneath the grizzly, trying to squirm out from under and realized the animal lying on top of him wasn't moving.

With grunts and groans, George Berringer managed to shift the bear just enough for Callahan to crawl out from under. Callahan crawled a few feet away, panting for breath. He sat against the trunk of a big-leaf maple and opened his shirt.

Three red lines about four inches long. Lots of blood. He prodded at the wounds, investigating the damage.

"Not too deep," Callahan said. "But it hurts like the devil."

Berringer bent over to squint at the claw wounds. "Could have been worse. Animal like that? Could have been *a lot* worse."

Callahan stumbled to his feet and retrieved his rifle.

Berringer gestured to the dead bear. "Lot of good meat there. Good pelt, too."

"We'll send somebody back," Callahan said. "I've got a wedding to get to."

They hiked at a brisk pace back to the place where they'd left the horses tied. Callahan was covered in sweat, the wounds in his chest throbbing. They mounted up and rode for Salem, the farms and fields passing by.

Salem wasn't a bad town, but Callahan had grown accustomed to the wilderness. He'd built a small log cabin overlooking a shallow stream, and liked his solitude, but in the past year, he'd gotten to know the folks who lived and worked on the outskirts. He liked them and had wanted to help them when the bear had started causing a problem.

And, truth be told, he wasn't always perfectly comfortable walking down the streets of Salem. Not because the people weren't friendly, quite the opposite. Callahan was something of a local celebrity, and people were still clapping him on the shoulder or buying him drinks whenever the opportunity presented itself. He appreciated the sentiment but found the attention uncomfortable. He considered himself a normal, simple man just going about his business.

Tomahawk Callahan had led a wagon train from Kansas City to Oregon. That in and of itself, while an accomplishment, was not newsworthy. Hundreds of other wagon trains had made the same journey over the years. But Callahan hadn't just led settlers west.

He'd been in a race.

A boastful rogue named Kent Arbuckle had been building a branch line to Salem and had wagered he could finish building the new rail line and that his train would pull into Salem long before Callahan and his meandering wagon train even crossed the state line. By luck or skill or the good Lord's intervention, Callahan had won the bet in dramatic fashion, and the historic event was still a popular topic of conversation nearly a year later.

They galloped into Salem, reining in the horses in front of Winchell's Butcher Shoppe, not because they were looking for a good cut of meat but because Delbert Cole lived in a room upstairs. Callahan might have asked one of the boys from the wagon train to stand up for him, but they'd gone back to Kansas City to work for Aunt Clara. Cole had become an occasional drinking buddy, had been instrumental at the last minute in helping Callahan win his bet with Arbuckle, and was a good-natured sort in general. Callahan could do a lot worse for a best man.

Callahan leaned against his horse, breathing hard, his chest throbbing. Sweat matted his hair.

"You don't look so good," Berringer told him. "You might want to have Doc Parker look at your chest."

Callahan groaned. "I've got to get up to Delbert's place. He's got my good suit. I've got to change."

Berringer took his pocket watch out and looked at it. "You've got time. You don't want an infection."

"Okay, but let's hurry," Callahan said. "But if he's not in, it'll have to wait for later."

Doc Parker's office was two doors down, and he did happen to be in.

Parker *tsked* and fussed and grumbled about the wisdom of chasing giant bears into the woods as he peeled off Callahan's bloody and ruined shirt. Callahan winced and hissed when Parker hit the slashes with disinfectant.

"I've seen deeper cuts," Parker said. "But you should still have stitches."

"No time, Doc," Callahan said. "I've got an appointment with a bride."

Parker shrugged. "Don't say I didn't warn you. I can at least wrap it up tight."

"Thanks, Doc."

Callahan winced and grunted when the doctor cinched the bandages tight.

"Hurts?" Parker asked.

Callahan nodded. "It hurts."

"Hold on," Parker said. "I have something for that."

Doc Parker mixed two liquids and a white powder into a glass and stirred it vigorously before handing the glass to Callahan. "A little mixture of my own I've perfected over the years. That'll make you feel good. Numb the pain."

Parker turned away from Callahan to wash his hands in a ceramic basin.

Callahan titled his head back and drained the liquid in one go. The bitter taste almost made him spit it out again, but he managed to get it all down.

Parker dried his hands on a towel. "Have a small swallow now, and I'll give you a flask to take the rest as you need it." He turned, blinked at the empty glass in Callahan's hand. "Where'd it go?"

"I drank it."

The doctor blinked again. "*All* of it?"

"You gave it to me," Callahan said defensively.

"Oh." Parker *tsked*. "Well, you'll need to be someplace comfortable in about twenty minutes. "That's strong stuff."

Callahan grabbed his buckskin coat and shrugged into it. "Gotta go, Doc. I can't pass out before I get married."

Parker shouted, "Good luck!" as Callahan raced from the room.

He ran down to the butcher's shop and climbed the back stairs two at a time. He knocked on the door.

The door swung open, and Delbert Cole stood there. He was a tall man and wide, and his muscles fit awkwardly into a brown suit, but his hair was slicked back, and he was clean-shaven, ready to be Callahan's best man.

"Where you been?" Delbert asked. "You better get a move on or—what happened to you?"

"I ain't got time for long stories, Delbert," Callahan said. "Where are my clothes?"

By the time Callahan had changed into his blue suit, he could feel it, a vague lightheadedness, a warm numb feeling to the tips of his extremities. The pain from the wounds on his chest had faded to a dull and distant ache.

"Come on!" Callahan's own voice echoed strangely in his ears. "We're late!"

They ran to the end of the street and a block over to the side door of the Methodist Church. Callahan's legs felt strangely heavy even as the rest of him felt oddly light, like his head might detach and float away. They entered, and the pastor glowered at them.

"Sorry to be late, Parson," Callahan said.

"Never mind. You're here now."

Becky's daughter Lizzy stood on the other side of the pastor, giggling at Callahan. She wore a pink bridesmaid's dress, a ring of white flowers perched atop her head like a crown. Callahan winked at her and grinned. It had been easy this past year to start thinking of the little girl as his own.

The pastor signaled to an old woman at an upright piano along the far wall, and she began to play a popular wedding tune. The notes sounded hollow and tinny in Callahan's ears, and the world was starting to blur at the edges. He felt no pain now, but there was a wetness on his chest. Blood was coming through the bandages. He hoped it wouldn't come through the shirt, too.

Callahan looked out across the interior of the church. Maybe two dozen people sat in the pews on both sides of the aisle, friends and acquaintances he and Becky had made in the last year.

He felt Delbert grab him under one arm.

"You're swaying," Delbert whispered. "You gonna be okay?"

"Just don't let me fall," Callahan whispered back.

He spotted an old woman in the back pew, and it

struck Callahan she was familiar. He couldn't recall where he'd seen her around town. Maybe she was a friend of Becky's or—

Aunt Clara!

Maybe it was Doc Parker's odd brew that had rattled Callahan's brain, or maybe it was the fact he couldn't remember the last time he'd seen his aunt in a dress, but she was almost unrecognizable at first glance. She still ran the wagon train outfit that had belonged to his uncle before he'd been murdered, and usually she wore the same sort of clothing as the wagon train crew: patched, threadbare trousers, a heavy man's shirt, and a floppy, sweat-stained hat. Now her hair was pulled back in a neat bun, and she wore a new dress with a pink and blue floral pattern.

Callahan had sent a letter weeks ago to tell her he was getting married. And while she was, of course, invited, he really didn't expect his aunt to make the long trip all the way from Kansas City.

She gave him a wave, fingers wriggling. He smiled and nodded in reply.

Then the double doors at the end of the aisle opened and Becky came through, a bouquet of white flowers in her hands. She looked radiant. Indeed, there seemed to be a hazy glow around her, and Callahan again realized it was the doc's brew still doing a number on him.

She held on to the arm of the mayor of Salem of all people who'd agreed to give her away. The man had given Callahan the key to the city when he'd won the bet with the railroad man. It was stuffed in a chest or something. Callahan hadn't seen it in months.

Becky's dress was one of the prettiest things Callahan had ever seen, and, of course, she'd made it herself. It drew in at the waist to show off her figure. Her red hair flowed down over her shoulders, which added to the golden glow about her. She beamed, and he felt love swell in his heart.

Halfway down the aisle, Becky looked at him, and her smile fell into little pieces. The mayor handed the bride off to Callahan, and she continued to look at him with a mixture of concern and disapproval.

"You look terrible," she whispered from the side of her mouth. "There's blood coming through your shirt."

"Long story," Callahan whispered back.

"Dearly beloved," the pastor began. "We are gathered here today . . ."

"I got hurt," Callahan whispered. "Doc Parker gave me something for the pain. I hate to say this, but I might pass out." Callahan felt even more dizzy now, the room threatening to spin.

"Oh, no, you will *not*," Becky hissed at him.

The pastor cleared his throat. "Is something the matter?"

"He's hurt," Becky said. "We might need to hurry this along."

"Hurt?" The pastor looked from Becky to Callahan. "Perhaps we should postpone . . ."

"No!" Becky said quickly. "Nobody's postponing nothing."

"How'd you get hurt?" the pastor asked Callahan.

"Got tangled up with a grizzly bear."

The pastor rolled his eyes. "Look, if you don't want to tell me . . ."

"Pastor," Becky urged.

"Oh. Right." The pastor flipped through the book he was holding. "Uh . . . if anyone can see any reason these two should not be joined . . ."

"Nobody sees any reason like that," Becky insisted.

Callahan felt his legs go. Becky held him up on one side, Delbert the other.

"Pastor!" Becky said with a grunt, struggled to hold up the groom. "Cut to the chase?"

"Do you take him?" the pastor asked.

"Yes!" Becky said.

"And you take her?"

"I do," Callahan said.

"Then I pronounce you man and wife," the pastor said proudly. "Go on and kiss."

Becky grabbed the back of Callahan's head and pulled him close. Their lips met, and a jolt of lightning sizzled the length of Callahan's body.

And then he fell over.